Maggie and Elliot Defy Gravity

K. R. Vanderport

IngramSpark

Contents

To Brian

Chapter 1

Drive it Like You Stole It

"We shouldn't be doing this." Agent Moira Winters glanced over her shoulder at the security camera.

Her partner, Agent Danny Markov, sighed heavily and continued walking out of the building. "We've been over this, Moira. They're probably just running late. It's not like it's never happened before."

She glared at him. "Protocol states that there should be two agents guarding—"

"—guarding the building at all times, yeah, yeah, yeah." Danny interrupted. "Look. We've been here – what? Five years?"

"About that, yes." Moira answered through her teeth.

"And how many times have we had an incident?"

"...Never."

"Exactly!" Danny spread his hands. "This isn't going to be the *one night* something happens."

"I don't know, Dan. I have a bad feeling about this." Moira pushed the door open and walked into the parking lot. She squinted at the fence surrounding the facility.

"Look, Moi, it's just a bunch of papers that haven't been touched since the 90's. Nobody wants this stuff anymore." He punched her shoulder gently. "Just go home and read one of those romances you like so much."

She batted his hand away. "Whatever. See you tomorrow."

"I don't know about that. I might be getting sick."

"Suck it up! You are not leaving me alone with Saul."

Danny laughed as the two split up, heading for their respective cars. He was stuck outside the driver's door, trying not to shiver as he hunted through his pockets when he saw it.

Movement.

Danny spun to his right, towards whatever he'd seen in his peripheral vision. In the twilight, all that was visible beyond the standard-issue government fencing was the normal mid-western underbrush which led up to a forest. A breeze shuffled the bushes around, reminding Danny of his own "innocent" whistling whenever one of Moira's emergency snacks went missing.

Danny turned slowly back to his car, taking a bit longer than normal to unlock his door and open it. Nothing happened, and he was too tired to walk around the forest in the dark chasing a shadow, so he slid into his seat, started the engine, and drove away.

In the bushes, dark eyes narrowed as they tracked Danny's truck until it disappeared. A soft breath rustled the leaves in front of the shadow's face.

"Sorry, guys." He said.

"No harm, no foul, Wendell." The voice was distorted over his earpiece.

A third voice joined the conversation. "I'm half convinced that guy had some sort of sixth sense, to be honest."

"Should we wait a couple minutes or go now?" A fourth person asked.

"The longer we wait, the more likely it is someone will show up." The fifth and final member of the team said. "We move now. Carly, are we clear?"

"As a bell, boss." The third voice said.

A van was parked on the side of a highway which stretched around a hill overlooking the facility. Carly Muñoz Ryan had one foot propped up against the dashboard and a set of binoculars glued to her face.

Carly was a tall, 28-year-old Latina with a toned body hidden beneath a black sweatshirt and army pants. From her vantage point, she could see everything within about a half mile radius of the building her team was getting ready to enter.

"Cool. On my mark, guys." The fifth voice belonged to Elliot Adiche, who was positioned directly behind the main generator at the back of the compound.

Elliot had hit his growth spurt early, so he was a seasoned veteran at maneuvering the long limbs of his 6'2" body. He was currently completely folded behind a bush. Not even the top of his fluffy blond hair was visible from the building.

He rubbed his hands together. "Three..." Sparks jumped between his palms. "...two..." He let the sparks gather and spread up his arms, crackling in the night air.

He sucked in a deep breath. When he let it out, he spread his hands towards the building and let the electric charge he'd built up surge into it, frying the generator and the rest of the facility. The machines groaned and sizzled with the force of it.

As the machines quieted down, a shocked silence seemed to stretch over the night life of the forest. Elliot closed his eyes, feeling around with his mind for any man-made electric charge (cleaner, sharper, more unnaturally defined than anything he could sense in nature). When he felt nothing, he let himself smile.

"Hero's Guild: move out."

As the Guild's designated spotter for this job, Carly watched as four shadows leapt from the darkness and converged on the building.

Wendell Green got to the door first, bouncing on his toes as he waited for the others. He was 26 years old, white, and average height though his long limbs made him look like a middle schooler.

Adanna Adiche, the second voice, crouched down as soon as she reached the door, pulling a bobby pin out of her thick black hair. She was almost as tall as Elliot, her slender but muscular black body reaching six feet easily.

Still, she looked short next to the fourth voice, Nehemiah Salinger. He was almost half a foot taller and built like a quarterback. He was white with brown hair and chocolate eyes. He turned and squinted up in the direction of Carly's van.

In case of emergency, she would flash a signal with her headlights just in case the team couldn't hear her for some reason. Judging by the fact it looked like a cement box, there was a good chance they wouldn't be able to hear Carly from inside the building.

Elliot was death-glaring the rest of the yard and the parking lot, daring it to let anyone in who would endanger his team. He knew that what they were doing was technically illegal, but that wouldn't stop him from keeping his friends out of harm's way. Besides, they were doing this for him.

"We're in." Adanna let the door swing open, and all four of them piled inside.

"Where to?" Wendell asked.

"Forward, first left, second right, third door." Nehemiah said.

Elliot ran point, fingers sparking in the darkness.

"Can you hear me, Carls?" Adanna let herself fall to the back of the pack.

Only static answered her.

"Fantastic." Wendell said.

"Don't let it get to you, Wen. We planned for this, remember?" Elliot pressed himself to the wall and peeked around the first corner. Not many people get killed by being too careful.

The short sprint to the file room felt like it took months. By the time they ducked inside the door, Wendell's legs felt like jelly and Nehemiah was breathing hard.

"Spread out. Find File #941996." Adanna said.

They each started at a different corner of the room and started leafing through the file cabinets as fast as they could. It took an uncomfortably long time. Long enough that cold sweat dripped down Elliot's back as he *felt* for any incoming energy.

"I've got it!" Nehemiah almost shouted.

"Really?!" Wendell said.

"Let me see!" Adanna beat Wendell to Nehemiah's side by two steps, snatching the file out of his hands. She flipped through its contents, mouth stretching into an almost manic grin. "This is it! We actually found it!"

"Great! Let's get out of here." Elliot had to force himself to put as much effort into getting out as he did into getting in. He opened the door a crack and peeked out into the hall.

He immediately jumped back and shut the door quickly.

"El?" Adanna frowned.

Elliot's mouth felt dry.

"What's going on? Is there someone out there?" Wendell was bouncing again.

Elliot cleared his throat with difficulty. "Hide." He said. "When I give the signal, start running and don't stop until you're in the van."

"You're not going to do something stupid and self-sacrificial, are you?" Adanna narrowed her eyes.

Elliot flashed her a quick smile. "I hope not."

The boots were now close enough to the room that the other three could hear them coming. They spread out, hiding behind the first row of file cabinets.

The door opened.

Elliot hadn't gotten a good look at the man before he'd backed up to warn the others, but there didn't seem to be much more to see now, even as the man flicked on the lights with a gloved finger.

He was dressed head to toe in loose-fitting, non-descript black clothes and a black trench coat. His head was covered by a black ski mask. Even the pistols hanging at his hips blended into his black gloves. He looked like a shadow; without any defining characteristics.

He looked around before heading in a familiar direction: directly towards where Nehemiah had found the file.

Elliot's curiosity was piqued, but he didn't let that stop him from lunging out of hiding and slamming his fist into the man's abdomen. Lightning followed the path of least resistance straight into his center of gravity.

He fell and Elliot sprinted after his teammates. They were already rounding the first corner. Elliot skidded behind them, stretching his mind to find Carly. She must have seen what was happening, because a van-sized ball of energy was waiting outside.

Wendell was the first to reach the exit and he didn't slow down; just rammed into the door at full speed. It swung wildly, smacking against the wall and bouncing back only to get shoved by Nehemiah. Adanna held out her hand to catch it, glancing back over her shoulder.

"Keep going!" Elliot shouted.

Adanna's eyes widened. "Elliot—!"

It felt like all the strength left his body at the same time, and he collapsed to the floor. It was like sleep paralysis or the time he got a concussion in high school and developed major depression. There was an invisible force pinning his body to the ground and he could barely find the strength to resist.

Elliot strained all the muscles he hadn't known he had in his neck to turn his head to the side. The man he'd stunned was stumbling towards him like a zombie in a horror movie. The man's clenched fist was the only part of him that wasn't shaking with the aftermath of electrocution.

"Hey!" Adanna's sneakers squealed as she spun on her toes and sprinted back towards Elliot.

The man glanced up at her, eyes narrowing at her intrusion. He raised his other hand and made a shooing motion at her.

Adanna shrieked as her body shot up to the ceiling, then dropped far faster than it would have if she'd just fallen. When she hit the ground, she laid still.

"NO!" Elliot slammed his eyes shut, *feeling* for the electrons in the man's body. All he had to do was excite enough of the valence electrons, and the man would shut down as his body panicked to get itself under control. It was something he'd always known that, physically, he was capable of. But he'd never done it before.

The man dropped without so much as a scream and the pressure on Elliot's body immediately disappeared. Still, he was shaking as he scrambled over to Adanna, lifted her gently into his arms, and dashed out to the waiting van.

"What happened?!" Wendell's eyes widened when Elliot climbed in, Adanna cradled to his chest.

"Just drive." Elliot said.

"Elliot, is that guy—"

"DRIVE!"

The man wasn't dead. Elliot was pretty sure he wasn't dead. After all, he should have been taken down by the first attack. Someone with enough power to do what the guy had done wouldn't have died that easily.

Elliot wasn't completely sure how he felt about that.

Wendell looked Adanna over as well as he could while riding in a van at eighty miles an hour in the dark. As far as he and his cellphone flashlight could tell, a few ribs were bruised at best – broken at worst.

The first thing she asked when she opened her eyes was, "What's in the file?"

Nehemiah, who had been flipping through it in order to feel somewhat useful, crawled over the seat and held a photograph so she could see it. "Baby pictures." He grinned.

The picture was of two little red wrinkles, each swaddled in white blankets with big black numbers printed across them.

Adanna reached one shaky hand for the picture while the other swiped at her eyes. "Oh, Elliot," she said. "You were so cute!"

"Which one is he?" Wendell asked. "And who's the other one?"

"According to this," Nehemiah looked back down at the file. "Her name is Margaret. If her adoption was processed by the same agency yours was, El, I should be able to find her."

"You better hurry." Carly said over her shoulder. "We might not be the only ones looking."

Chapter 2

Unhappy Homecoming

"Maggie, look out!"

She dove backwards, barely avoiding the beam that smashed into the ground where she'd just been standing.

"Sorry!" Someone yelled from higher up.

The skeleton structure the construction crew had erected could have been intended for anything. That was one of the things Maggie Posey loved about her job; every building had the same bones in the end. Like they were family.

Maggie rolled her eyes and dusted herself off. "No blood, no foul!"

"You are something else, kid."

She raised an eyebrow at her foreman. "How so?"

"Well, if it were me," he shrugged. "I'd probably be a little more upset about almost being impaled."

Maggie laughed, because it wasn't like she could tell him she'd *felt* the metal coming as soon as her clumsy crewmate dropped it. If she did, he'd probably assume his eyes had tricked him and the beam had really come down on her head. Besides, she hadn't gotten this job for attention.

"Work smarter, not harder." It was something her adoptive dad liked to say. Maggie bent down to grab the metal beam, letting out a semi-dramatic grunt as she straightened up, hands barely touching the metal her magnetic field was lifting.nm

The workers on the third floor were working on securing the support beams for the roof. She handed the beam off to two of her crewmates.

"I think you dropped this." She said.

"Girl, you need to tell me what gym you go to." The crewmate who hadn't almost flattened her was impressed.

Maggie laughed.

At the end of the day, Maggie wiped sweat from her forehead. While she hadn't actually done any heavy-lifting, she had gotten in quite a bit of cardio climbing all over the place like a monkey. She loved her job. It was like getting paid to do an obstacle course.

All around her, crew members were waving goodbye, shouting at each other, making plans to meet up at diners or bars.

She wove her way around all the human interaction and jumped up into her truck. It was a black Toyota Tundra with green undertones. It had been her loyal companion for six years. She tossed her safety vest and hard hat onto the passenger seat and thumbed the radio button.

"Are you feeling lonely?" The radio woman sounded like a public service announcer. *"Does it feel like everyone has their own group, their own friends, and you have no one? Like the people in your life would rather spend time with anyone else but you?"*

Maggie rolled her eyes and flipped the channel.

"The guards come along to find the place trashed, and their whole electrical system is burnt out. But here's the crazy part – there isn't any sign of whatever caused the blackout."

"So, Phil, what you're saying is that we're either dealing with some sort of extranormal event or our home-grown terrorist problem is going to the next level."

"Absolutely, Nels, and to be honest I'm not sure which one I'm more afraid of. Stay tuned for our in-depth analysis of the event, where we'll answer the question on everyone's mind: was the criminal truly human? Right here on Everyday Unidentified.*"*

"Ah, well." Maggie said aloud to no one. "I don't need the radio anyway."

She pulled out onto the street, which was almost empty even during rush hour. That was probably part of the reason the city wanted to put the new mall there. She herself was ambivalent about it. On one hand, she lived a few blocks away and she did not like the idea of more traffic in the neighborhood. On the other hand, she was getting paid for this.

Maggie eyed her gas gauge. She could have walked to work, but she wasn't used to being that close and had taken the truck based on pre-coffee muscle memory. Of course, that also meant she didn't use up a lot of gas to get there and back. Still, to her broke self it felt like a waste.

Outside her apartment building, Maggie put the truck in park and pulled out the keys. Instead of getting out, she let her neck fall back onto the headrest as her eyelids slid shut. *Do I really have to move again?*

She breathed in, breathed out, and started counting backwards from ten. When she was done, she hesitated for another half second before finally dragging herself up and out of the truck.

Despite the fact that it had been built in the 80's, the building had no elevator. The walk to the seventh floor left her calves whining like toddlers. She attempted to get her breathing under control as she stood outside her apartment door, hunting through her pockets for her keys.

Her phone went off and she rolled her eyes. Her adoptive mom had gotten her this motion detector that sent updates to her phone, and every time she walked in or out – or stepped foot in her kitchen – it went off.

Later, she'd blame her reaction time on the fact that she'd had a long day. It wasn't until she had her door key in her hand and had started reaching for the handle that she remembered two things:

1. The motion detector only recorded motion inside the apartment.

2. She was not inside the apartment yet.

Maggie blinked slowly. She felt something seize in her stomach and backed away as quietly as she could.

She made it back to the stairs before the door crumpled to the floor. Maggie's brain helpfully coughed up the image of an invisible anvil landing on it like in a cartoon. It also told her that the guy who stepped out of her apartment looked a little like Spider-Man Noir.

She turned and ran down the stairs.

The guy coming after her was extraordinarily fast – Maggie *felt* his magnetic field zipping towards her and threw a hand towards the metal support beams buried in the walls. She flipped her magnetic field to repel the ones from the beams and launched herself over the railing onto the next set of stairs.

The guy followed without hesitation, and that's how they got down the rest of the staircases; literally bouncing off the walls. Maggie reached out with her mind and *pulled* the heavy metal door that opened into the ground floor. It flung towards her and she dove through it, then pivoted and pushed the door at her pursuer with all her strength.

It seemed to take him by surprise, because he lost a foot of ground before somehow getting his footing and launching the door into the air.

Maggie had never seen anyone else with powers in all her twenty-five years of existence. She swallowed her words and the fantasies that resurfaced from her childhood of finding others like her and forming some sort of *X-Men*-esque club. Friendly people generally don't break into others' apartments and lie in wait for them.

The guy thrust both hands behind him and launched himself through the air, directly at Maggie. He didn't slow down until he had her pinned to the next wall, which was all the way across the lobby. Maggie grunted as her spine connected with the wall and kicked at the guy's groin. He dodged, but it offset his position enough that Maggie could shove him away and roll into a crouch facing him.

Maggie opened her mind and *felt* around the room for any weapons she could use.

"If anyone ever attacks you," her adoptive mother's words echoed in her mind, *"don't hold back. And don't play nice. I know it's hard, but if anyone tries to hurt you, you need to go for the kill."*

Maggie wrapped her mind around the screws that held the mailboxes to the wall and ripped them from their places, shooting them towards the man as fast as she could. She didn't want to see herself tear someone apart, but there was no way she was going to wait around for him to do it to her first.

The screws got within five feet of the man's body and slammed into the ground.

"What...?" Maggie felt like she'd been punched in the stomach.

The evil Spider-Man Noir tilted his head and laughed. Maggie couldn't see his expression through his mask, but she had the feeling she wouldn't like it. "You really are Lizzie's daughter, aren't you?"

And here she was thinking nothing else this guy did would surprise her.

"Of course, you don't have any of her skill, but that's to be expected." The guy waved his hand at her and Maggie felt herself lift off the ground and slam into the ceiling. She didn't fall so much as be dragged down by the same force to smash into the ground. Something cracked, and she was pretty sure it wasn't the concrete.

"Ahhhh!" It was half pain, half anger. She'd been able to take anyone who had threatened her without breaking a sweat until today.

Her vision was all messed up – whether from head trauma or the force that was still crushing her was anyone's guess – so she closed her eyes and tried to *feel* for the guy's magnetic field. Whatever power he was using gave her magnetic sense a numb-tongue feeling, but eventually she caught a hint of it. She latched onto his field, then flipped it to repel hers.

She was lucky there was a window behind her, because the force sent her through it and across the front yard. She rolled to a stop six inches from the road and gasped for breath. Now that the force wasn't attempting to press her into a pancake, oxygen flooded into her brain. That actually made her more dizzy than she already was, which was unfortunate because she knew for a fact that the guy was still coming.

With excruciating effort, she turned her head to face the building. Her mom once told her she was warped with morbid curiosity. Noir toppled over the windowsill, then pushed himself to his feet and lurched towards her.

The weakness that turned Maggie's muscles into silly putty wasn't like anything she'd ever experienced before. Not even her worst day of work could compete. She just wanted to rest, but had a feeling she'd be resting in peace if she took more than half a second to breathe.

What was this guy even made of?! Their minds hadn't knocked together, so he obviously wasn't using magnetic fields to do whatever he was doing. But what else could act like that? Throwing people around rooms and crushing them beneath some invisible force—

That's it! Maggie's eyes widened. Looking up at Noir, who was only about a foot away from her at this point, she struggled for breath. "Gravity."

He paused.

"Your powers." Maggie was having trouble translating her thoughts into words. "You use. Gravity."

"You look proud of yourself." Noir said. "If you would've asked, I would have told you. It's not a secret."

"Feels like. I was – *dying* – to know...."

"Cute." Noir raised a hand. "Just close your eyes, kiddo. It'll be over in a second."

Chapter 3

Murder, Interrupted

Before he could manipulate the gravity around Maggie, a bolt of lightning ripped through Noir's torso. He dropped to the ground in a heap.

Maggie turned to see who had done that, before remembering how much pain she was in, and collapsed with only the blurry image of a tall-ish person to show for it.

Someone swore, their voice jiggling around Maggie's head like the sound waves were bouncing off the sides of her skull.

"Is she okay?"

Maggie felt a static shock as yet another someone grabbed her wrist. "She's alive."

"That's about as okay as she's going to get right now."

"Is *he* okay?"

"Let's not stick around to find out."

"Margaret?" This voice was closer. "Can you hear me?"

Maggie wanted to reply, but the process of speech was suddenly very confusing. She felt like her brain had randomly developed the ability to phase through her skull and was currently on its way to join lost balloons in the clouds. But hey; at least she wasn't in pain anymore.

Voices were happening, but it was debatable whether they were accompanied by words. They pitched and wove like the ocean, and Maggie was being tossed and driven by them. She knew something was wrong, something was still very much a problem, but she was too tired to do anything but let herself float.

~

They drove in silence. Nehemiah was driving, knuckles white against the steering wheel and eyes focused on the road. With his floppy hair, he looked like a giant kid about to take his driver's test.

In the passenger seat, Adanna looked less like the type to be teaching a kid how to drive and more like the type who had gotten into a bar fight the night before. Her arm was in a sling and bandages bulged under her t-shirt.

Where Adanna had been lying a few days ago, Maggie was now spread out. Noticeably more comfortably, because this time the gang had come prepared with a sleeping bag and pillow. Elliot was wedged between her and the side of the van, sitting cross-legged and staring. The tension in the van seemed to wash over him like the Angel of Death over a bloody door.

Wendell and Carly were in the middle seats, arms crossed and eyes on their guest.

"We should have killed him."

Wendell and Carly's eyes snapped to Adanna. Even Nehemiah glanced in her direction for a beat longer than was technically safe. She pressed her lips together and twisted around in her seat to glare at Elliot.

"You know it's true." She continued.

Elliot's eyes moved, but the rest of him was still as a statue. "We don't kill."

"I'm sure he'll be just as considerate when he's the one standing over our bodies."

"Do you really think we could have killed him?" Elliot whirled around, clenching his fists. "You saw what he did to Margaret – what he did to *you* back when we first met him – and he took my most powerful attack like it was a minor inconvenience. If we would've taken the time to try and kill him, how do you know he wouldn't have just gotten right back up?"

"We could have done *something*—"

"Shut up, Adanna!" Wendell interrupted. "You have a gun, and I didn't see you shooting him in the face."

"Can we stop talking like this?" Nehemiah was trembling. "How can you talk about murdering someone so casually?! He's a bad guy, but he's a *person*--"

"He's a person who waited around to murder someone when she got home from work. It's not murder if he's trying to kill you." Adanna said.

"There has to be another option."

"Like what? Should we bring the police into this? You saw what he's capable of: there's no way a jail cell would hold him."

"What about the government?" Nehemiah paused. "They have to know something about containing people like that."

"People like Elliot?" Carly said. "I mean, on the off chance we could even get in touch with someone who specializes in superhuman containment, how could we be sure they wouldn't just take Elliot, too?"

"We might have to take that chance." Elliot's voice was quiet.

Adanna smacked a fist into the side of her seat. "You shut up!"

"You guys are getting way ahead of us; we don't even know if the government has any idea how to fight someone with powers." Wendell said.

"Why would they create something they couldn't control?" Carly asked.

"It's the United States government, Carly; they once blew up an atomic bomb to see if it would destroy the universe." Wendell said.

Nehemiah pointed at his friend. "The man makes a good point."

"Even if they didn't know how to control him at the beginning, he's older than Elliot, and Elliot was born with his powers as far as we know." Adanna said. "That's a lot of time to spend not knowing what to do about a potential threat."

"There's only one way to find out." Elliot's voice silenced the others. "We have to look through the file again; see if there's anyone we can find who was connected to the project. Maybe they'll be able to help."

"And what if all they want to do is help themselves to the assets they lost track of twenty-five years ago?" Adanna asked.

Elliot brushed a strand of Maggie's hair off her face, then dropped his hand with a sigh. "I don't know. We'll cross that bridge when we get to it, I guess."

"In the meantime, there's no way we can go home." Carly said. "I think it's time to finally use the Contingency Plan."

"You're enjoying this, aren't you?"

"Enjoying what? Being right about needing a Contingency Plan when all you guys thought it was a dumb idea?" Carly grinned. "No."

~

Maggie was underwater, but she didn't seem to need air. That was good, because the entire Pacific Ocean felt like it was pressing down on her chest. She couldn't even move her pinky finger. That was a minimal problem compared to the other one, though.

She was on one of those tectonic plates that slid under the next one, and she was being slowly pulled towards the place where they met. She may have inexplicably developed the ability to not need air, but given how painful the water pressure was, she was pretty sure she could still be crushed to death. Besides, the plate seemed to melt as it got sucked under, like it was transitioning into magma. Maggie did not want to be magma.

She wanted to scream, wanted to get up and run, but she was paralyzed by the weight on top of her. She felt around wildly, trying to find something she could push off or pull herself towards. There was nothing.

She was alone.

She was powerless.

She was going to die.

Maggie opened her eyes. She wasn't in the ocean anymore, but she wasn't in her apartment, either. She also wasn't a corpse on the lawn in front of her apartment, which was kind of a surprise.

Sitting up *hurt*. That meant she hadn't dreamed the fight, unfortunately. She was in a dark room with no windows, lying on an air mattress in the corner. There were no sheets on the mattress, but there was a pillow and a blanket. Light crept through from under the door on the far side of the room, and by it Maggie could just make out a folded piece of paper on the floor that literally had her name on it.

Maggie grabbed it and opened it up, discovering new pain with every movement.

I hope you slept well. The inside read. *You're safe; don't worry. We saved you from that guy at your apartment building and took you to a Safe House. It's not kidnapping, though. We're family! (I do realize that family members can sometimes kidnap other family members, but that's not what happened here.) I'll explain everything when we finally meet, officially. If you're still tired, feel free to go back to sleep for a while. You were beaten up pretty badly. When you're ready, come on out and say hi! We have food.*

~ Elliot.

Maggie seriously considered going back to sleep for a while, but she had a feeling she was never going to be awake enough to comfortably deal with this situation. Might as well get it over with. Maggie flopped onto the floor and pushed herself up, staggering over to the light source. She was groaning, half in pain, half with exasperation, the whole time.

She took a deep breath and opened the door. Four twenty-somethings were lounging on couches. They all looked up when she entered the room.

"Alright," Maggie said. "Which one of you is Elliot?"

"I am." The voice came from a doorway just out of Maggie's range of sight.

"Hi." Maggie didn't know what else to say. What was the polite way to handle this conversation?

"Hi." Elliot seemed as nervous as she was, at least. "I'm Elliot. But you knew that already."

"I'm Maggie." She said. "But you knew that already."

"Maggie." He hadn't known her nickname. "It's so nice to meet you. I'm..." He swallowed hard. There was no easy way to say this. "I'm your brother."

File: 9041996

Project: Kobold

Subcategory: Gemini

Status: Sealed

Reporter: Dr. Warren Xavier

Week 2 of post-birth observation period. Gemini subjects show no visible signs of possessing extraordinary abilities. However, scans confirm Gemini Alpha (designation: Margaret) has an uncommonly strong magnetic field while Gemini Beta (designation: Elliot) radiates low-level electrical currents. Teams have designated these fields "Auras." Intensity of Auras has shown growth. Further observation is required to determine whether the increase will continue over time.

Furthermore, tests have determined that the levels of the Auras spike when subjects appear distressed. When subjects are calm or asleep, Aura strength is greatly diminished. Possible link between emotional state and intensity of Aura. Further study required.

In all other categories, subject health is consistent with health of average infants of their age.

Note: Health and ability strength of subject Kobold Gamma (maternal predecessor of Gemini subjects) have returned to pre-gestational levels.

Chapter 4

A Family Matter

Maggie figured she had more important things to care about than how badly she was shaking, but when the paper was moving around too much for her to focus on, she forced herself to take a few deep breaths.

"Are you okay?" Elliot was hovering just within her personal bubble. He had one hand clenched on his opposite bicep like he was physically stopping himself from reaching out to her.

Maggie laughed. "They're talking about us like we're...like we're lab rats or something. They experimented on *babies.*"

"I know." Elliot said. "I always thought I was born with my powers, like one of the *X-Men* or something, but..."

"...turns out we were mutated before we were even born." Maggie nodded. "Yeah." She clenched her fist, half-crushing the report in her hand. "Can you believe...? What kind of sick mind thinks it's okay to...?"

Elliot did reach out then, but his hand stopped short like it had been repelled by Maggie's "Aura." He let it fall.

For a moment, there was silence.

"If you think that's bad," Wendell said finally, "you're really going to hate what we're planning to do next."

"Dude, you made it sound like we're going to experiment on babies." Carly said.

"It's kind of accessory after the fact."

"Can you be an accessory to a crime that you are also the victim of?" Nehemiah tapped his forehead. "Food for thought."

"Stop bantering and tell me what your terrible plan is." Maggie was tired.

"*They*," Adanna paused to make sure everyone caught her emphasis, "want to hunt down this chick who worked on the project to see if she knows how to defeat your crazy cousin."

"The guy with the gravity powers." Nehemiah clarified.

"Yeah, I got that. Why?"

"Because she's our best bet." Elliot said.

"No, I mean..." Maggie pressed the heel of her hand into her forehead. "I mean '*why* do we need to stop that guy?'"

"Besides the fact that he wants to kill us?" Elliot leaned up against the wall.

Maggie groaned. "Right. That."

"Also, we're the Hero's Guild." Nehemiah said.

"That's what we call ourselves." Elliot's face reddened. "We're actually just bounty hunters."

"Okay." Maggie said, stuffing that particular bit of information in a corner of her brain to digest later. "And we're *sure* there are no other options?"

"Trust me, if there were, I'd never agree to this." Adanna's eyes looked like lasers trying to bore into the wall behind Maggie's head.

"Maggie narrowed her eyes at her brother. "And what's the plan if Gravity Guy has the same idea?"

"Well, lucky for you, you don't have to worry about that." Elliot said. "You're staying here."

"Uhm. What?!" Maggie crossed her arms over her chest. "I am not staying behind like a little kid!"

"We prefer the term 'B Team,' but 'little kids' is fine, I guess."

The guy who had opened the back door without making a sound wasn't a little kid, but his grin belonged on one. A girl with a curly nest of red hair poked her head out from behind him.

"Sorry, boss!" Her cheeks were attempting to match her hair. "We were looking for the training room."

"It's cool, Lydia. This is actually perfect timing." Elliot said. He pointed grandly. "This is my sister, Maggie. She's going to be your new teammate."

~

The sandy-haired guy who'd crashed the meeting was Sean Bradbury. His cousin, Lydia Fitzgerald, was the youngest person in the "organization" at nineteen. According to Nehemiah, she made better decisions than most of the others combined.

Personally, Maggie didn't think the road to stealing government files was paved with good decisions. Better is always relative.

The other two members of the "B-Team" were a twenty-nine-year-old white guy named Kyle Applegate, who looked like he hadn't showered in a week, and a twenty-four-year-old bottle blue East Asian named Hailey Murakami. Maggie's first impression was that their hairstyles suited them.

"Remind me again why you're ditching me with the noobs."

Elliot sighed. "They're not noobs – they have a lot of training and experience. It's just that my team works together very well and has a lot of experience doing that. If there's even a chance we can run into that gravity dude again, we need to be able to fight together. There's no way we can beat him one-on-one."

Maggie wanted to protest, say something about how two super-powered people could take one, but he had a point. She couldn't just muscle her way onto a team she didn't belong on in the name of revenge.

Speaking of which. "What's with all this 'team' stuff, anyway? What is this, S.H.E.I.L.D.?"

Elliot smirked. "We're a little bit less official than that."

"A little less legal than that, you mean."

"Semantics." Elliot waved a hand. "We uphold the spirit of the law."

"Stealing from the rich and giving to the poor?"

"Stopping crimes when the cops aren't around, hunting down people who do things to get their faces on the news."

"Stealing from the criminals and giving to the poor?"

Elliot rolled his eyes. "No stealing. Sorry to disappoint."

"I'll live."

His smile slipped. "Yeah, you will. I'm going to make sure of it."

Maggie frowned. "I don't need you to protect me. I can take care of myself."

"Not against this guy."

Maggie opened her mouth to protest, but Elliot cut her off.

"I don't think either of us can." He said. "That's why I need to find out what this lady knows about him."

He crossed his arms over his chest and looked away. "My team started this. It's small, but...soon, we'll be able to make a real difference in the world." He shook the daydreams out of his head. "Anyway, right now, my team has the most experience working and fighting together, so we're going to handle this one on our own."

Maggie crossed her own arms and pouted, looking away. "I still think it would be better for me to go with you."

"I appreciate that, but you've never really used your powers like this before." Elliot glanced around and lowered his voice. "And, to be honest, I think it's safer for everyone to have at least one...superhuman...on each team."

"Hm." Maggie tapped her arm. "You're not wrong."

Elliot grinned. "I also need you here to protect our parents."

"What?!"

Elliot led Maggie into a side room that was probably some sort of makeshift kitchen if the microwave, coffee pot, and mini-fridge were to be believed. Three card tables were grouped together awkwardly, folding chairs of various kinds circling them. Four of the seats were occupied by people who were talking animatedly.

"Hi Mom, Dad." Elliot said. "Hello, Mr. and Mrs. Posey."

"Hi, honey." His adoptive mother, Taylor, answered. She was just a tad below average height, with cocoa brown skin and hair pinned tightly against her skull.

"Oh, Maggie, sweetheart!" Genevieve, or "Viv," Maggie's adoptive mother, almost flipped her chair over in her rush to get up and run over to her daughter. She was a little taller than Taylor, with olive skin and almond eyes. "Honey, are you okay?"

Her husband, Oliver, was right behind her. He was a tanned white with deep brown eyes and hair that was almost black.

"I'm fine, Mom." Maggie attempted to brush off the inspection. "What are you doing here?"

"You look terrible! Did you get into a fight? Who did this to you?"

"Viv," Oliver put a hand on his wife's arm. "Let her answer." He looked at Maggie and smiled. "How are you doing, kid?"

Maggie rolled a shoulder. "You should see the other guy."

"I hope we do." Viv's eyes flashed, her fingernails biting into her palms. "The nerve of that man to attack *my* baby girl...!"

"Mom." Maggie looked around. "Elliot. What are my parents doing here? How did you even find them?"

Elliot ran a hand through his hair. "Technically, we found them first. They were the ones whose names were in your adoption file, after all. And after what happened at the apartment..."

His father, Hugh, took a step closer. "He was afraid the mutant would try to use us to get to one or both of you, so he sent the B-Team to pick us up." Of all the parents, Hugh was the biggest. He was tall and broad, with skin black as night.

"The B-Team." Maggie said. "Great."

"It's just a chronological denotation..."

"Forget it, Elliot." Maggie took a deep breath. "Okay. So, today I've discovered that I'm not only a genetic experiment, but I also have a twin and another experiment who wants to kill me for some inexplicable reason. And the sun's not even down yet."

"And here I was thinking having your own apartment was going to be the most stressful thing you'd have to deal with until your marriage." Oliver sighed.

Elliot blinked. "You're getting married? Nothing showed up in our search. We should bring him here, too, though – just to be safe. I can—"

"He's joking." Maggie said. "It's fine. You did good."

Elliot's shoulders loosened just a tiny bit. He smiled softly. "Thanks, sis."

~

After a very awkward dinner, most of the organization – as well as Maggie and her parents – performed simultaneous and very convincing Houdini impressions and vanished. Elliot and Adanna ended up helping Taylor and Hugh unpack their suitcases.

"I can't believe you guys had go-bags ready." Adanna slipped her sling off and rolled her shoulder experimentally.

"Honey, you should leave that on." Taylor said.

"I'm fine, Mom." Adanna tossed the sling to the ground and grabbed the toiletry bag, heading for the small bedside table. "Exactly how long have you been prepping for this?"

Taylor put a hand on her hip. "How long have you and your brother been cosplaying Batman and Robin?"

"Batman didn't have any powers." Elliot reminded her as he shook out the two pairs of clothes his parents had packed before refolding them.

"Oh, you think *you're* Batman, huh?" Adanna said.

"If I still didn't think of you two as being five, this conversation would seem a little immature." Hugh said on his way through the door. "I found those blankets your friends mentioned before conveniently disappearing."

"Hall closet?" Elliot asked.

"They were actually still in boxes in the front room." Hugh dropped his armful on the mattress. "I'm sure someone was intending to move them to the closet at some point."

"Mom, what is this?!" Adanna had a handgun dangling from her fingers.

"Don't you recognize the gun you learned to shoot with, sweetie?" Taylor took it from her. "Don't hold it like that; if you drop it, it could get scratched."

"Do you always keep weapons in your toiletry bags?"

Hugh rested his chin on his wife's shoulder to get a better look at the gun in question. "You should have seen what she packed for our honeymoon."

Taylor rolled her eyes. "Girl scouts are always prepared."

"So..." Elliot fidgeted with his father's backup wallet, which contained a fake ID and an assortment of paper money. "What did you guys think of Maggie?"

Hugh and Taylor looked at each other. Adanna turned back to unpacking the toiletry bag.

"She seems nice." Taylor said. "She's taking this all very well. To be honest, if it were me, I don't think I would be handling all this craziness the same way."

"Says the woman who keeps Glocks with her Maybelline." Adanna said.

"Necessities are necessities, love."

"As far as sisters go, yours seems to have potential." Hugh tried to steer the conversation back on track.

Adanna tightened her grip on a bottle of moisturizer. "He knows." She said. "He was asking about *Maggie*."

"Don't be so sensitive, Ada, your father didn't mean anything by it." Taylor said.

"I'm not being *sensitive*, it was a *joke*." Adanna slammed the moisturizer down on the shelf. "What else do you need unpacked?"

~

"How are you guys doing?" Maggie asked. She and her parents were lying side-by-side on the bed in the room Viv and Oliver would be using.

"As long as you're safe, we're doing fine." Viv reached over and gave her daughter's hand a quick squeeze.

"So, you're not fine, then?" Maggie said.

Viv sighed. "I wish I could just make the world safe for you."

"That would be nice." Maggie huffed. "But Elliot and the others won't even let me come with them, so I should be fairly safe for now."

After a minute, Viv spoke again. "I had no idea you were – I mean you had been..."

"I know."

"...as a *baby*...!"

"I know."

Viv scooted over to rest her head on Maggie's shoulder. "It's not right. Someone should be held accountable for this."

"They won't be." Maggie said. "If Elliot gets the lady from the government to work with us, it won't be because he's planning on making her take responsibility for her actions."

"You think he's the kind of person who would let someone off scot free just because he gets something out of it?" Oliver asked.

"No, I think he's smart enough to know no one is going to cooperate if all they have to look forward to is confronting their mistakes." Maggie brushed the back of her hand against the back of her dad's hand. "And they hurt him, too, remember?"

"Do you remember?" Viv asked. "I mean, do you remember Elliot? Does he seem...familiar to you?"

"We haven't developed twin telepathy, if that's what you're talking about." Maggie shook her head. "I don't know. I feel like I *should*. That's what's supposed to happen in these situations, isn't it? Two mutant twins are reunited after being separated at birth, and they suddenly remember all this stuff about each other and their past? But, to be honest, I don't feel any different. I mean, I'm a little freaked out about the whole experimentation thing, but it's just information in my head. It's not even really...real to me. Like it happened to someone else."

Viv sighed. "I'm glad. I know it would be nice for you to feel connected to him, but I'd hate for you to remember anything that they did to you as a child. I hope...I honestly hope you never remember any of that."

"Yeah." Maggie rested her head on her mom's shoulder. "Yeah."

On her other side, Oliver laced his fingers through hers and gripped her hand tightly. His hands were twice as big, enveloping hers like a cocoon. "It's going to be okay, baby girl." He said.

Chapter 5

Wheels Up

Carly leaned against the van and sipped coffee from a thermos that proclaimed "The driver picks the music." She had a paper map in her other hand and was squinting at the colored squiggles that seemed to run around the page with no particular logic tying them together.

Footsteps stole her attention and she glanced up to see Wendell and Nehemiah coming towards her. Nehemiah had a thermos of his own while Wendell carried a worn Duluth Pack messenger bag which was slung across his body.

Wendell rubbed his eyes and yawned. "Good morning, Carl."

She frowned and shook the map. "Maybe it's a good morning in medieval terms; I hate using such boring, old-school tools."

"I'm guessing you weren't a fan of *Oregon Trail* as a kid."

"I preferred Samus."

"I have no idea who either of those people are." Nehemiah said. "But I can read a map like a CEO."

"Like a boss." Wendell corrected.

"That's what I said."

"Here," Carly tossed Nehemiah the map. "Thanks for volunteering to be the navigator."

"You're welcome." He smiled back.

"Where's Adanna and our fearless leader?" Wendell glanced around the rest of the garage.

Carly rolled her eyes. "We agreed to meet at the van right about now, so I'm guessing they'll be here in five to ten minutes."

"Score one for nurture." He glanced between his unsmiling team-mates. "You know, as in 'nature vs.?'"

"Is that supposed to be a joke, Wendy?" Carly asked.

"You're grumpy today."

"We're going to meet an evil scientist, possibly be attacked by a psychopath, and we can only bring these *stupid* burner phones with *no data*." She gritted her teeth. "So I'm going to need a lot more coffee to get my sense of humor back."

"Does it ever bother you how much your society is oriented around mild addictions?" Nehemiah asked.

"I think you mean 'our' culture. You're one of us, now, remember?" Wendell tapped his arm with a fist.

Nehemiah almost smiled, almost frowned, and looked away.

"Here." Carly dug a granola bar out of her purse and tossed it to Wendell.

"What's this for?"

"Just thought you might want something to put in your mouth that isn't your foot."

"Hilarious."

"Hey guys!" Elliot's voice echoed through the room.

Glancing at her watch, Carly raised an eyebrow. "Wow, only three and a half minutes. Someone's excited."

"Did you bring drinks?" Wendell shouted back.

"Of course!" Adanna pointed to a small cooler Elliot held up. "What would a road trip be without refreshments?"

"Right! I packed the food snacks, and we can hit drive-thru's for meals." Carly said.

"I've got the map." Nehemiah didn't know if it was necessary to point that out, but figured he might as well. "Also a burner phone."

"And I have all the medical supplies, because we can't seem to hang out these days without having someone come home injured." Wendell patted his messenger bag and rolled his eyes.

Carly frowned.

"Alright!" Adanna said. "Let's get on the road. The sadistic mad scientist isn't going to interrogate herself."

~

Elliot had made it clear that the room she'd woken up in was at her disposal. Maggie dragged her mattress into her parents' room, anyway.

"Should we let her sleep?" Viv whispered. "She's been through so much."

Oliver pulled his daughter's blanket up to her shoulders. He turned and maneuvered himself so he was sitting side-by-side with his wife, back resting on the wall.

"Did you ever think it would be like this?" Viv tried to hold in her laugh, so it came out high and strangled. "I mean, it was one thing when we discovered our daughter had inhuman abilities, but now there's an assassin after her – maybe even some evil government scientists. This wasn't supposed to happen."

Oliver hummed and reached down to take her hand.

Viv took a shaky breath. "I know. I know, I wouldn't trade her for the world, either."

Chapter 6

The Breakfast Incident

Hailey sat on the counter stirring cream and sugar into her coffee. Her blue hair was perched on her crown in a messy bun, escaped strands fluffing around her face like a Renaissance art corona.

"Hails. Shoes off the furniture. We've talked about this."

To Hailey, it seemed like Kyle had appeared out of nowhere. Her entire body flinched, sending a wave of coffee over the rim of her mug and onto her hand and thigh. Spasming in pain only flung more coffee on her, so she forced herself to stop moving.

"Kyyyyyyyyle!" She slid off the counter carefully, putting her coffee down and grabbing napkins. "Now I look like I peed!" She froze. "Are there two e's in that or three?"

"Do I look like Spell Check to you?"

"You look like *spill* check!" She grinned, then laughed at her own joke.

Kyle sighed heavily and grabbed for some caffeine. "It's too early for this. I don't even know why we have to stay here – the crazy dude's after Elliot and his freaky sister, not us."

"Yeah, but if he found out we work with Elliot, he could just wait outside our homes and follow us here."

Kyle scoffed. "If you can't lose a tail at this stage of the game, what are you even doing with this team?"

Hailey narrowed her eyes at Kyle as Sean and Lydia filed into the room behind him. "Hey, there's no 'jerk' in 'team.'"

"Aw, come on, Hailey!" Sean slung an arm around Kyle's shoulder. "Every team needs a Vegeta."

Lydia smirked. "Stone cold with a squishy center."

Kyle shrugged off Sean. "The Prince of all Saiyans will not be mocked by you peasants."

Hailey rolled her eyes, then turned to Lydia. "Are there two e's in 'peed' or three?"

"Two, I think." The younger girl said.

"Are you sure?" Sean frowned. "Because 'pee' has two e's, and if you add an 'ed'..."

"I think it's one of those weird rules, like how 'it's' with an apostrophe means 'it is,' but when you're talking about the possessive form there isn't an apostrophe, even though possessive s's are all supposed to have apostrophes in front of them."

"Don't you guys have your phones?" Kyle asked from a table. "Just look it up."

"Elliot said we're not supposed to have our phones, because they can be used to track us." Lydia said.

"Did you *bring your phone*?!" Sean turned on him.

Kyle waved it in the air and rolled his eyes. "Chill out! It's untrace-able."

"How can you be sure?" Hailey asked.

"Magic." Kyle sighed. "I'm a computer programmer, how do you think?"

"She didn't ask *how* you made it untraceable, your highness, she asked how you're *sure* it's untraceable." Lydia said.

"I'm bouncing signals across four continents. Trust me; it's untraceable."

"Four continents, huh?" Sean crossed his arms. "How's the battery life?"

Kyle grinned. "Sometimes it lasts a whole two hours."

"That sounds annoying." Lydia turned back to the coffee. "What kind of creamer do we have?"

"Well, your cousin was in charge of picking it up." Hailey made a face at the stain on her jeans and tossed the napkins into the trash.

"Irish Cream, then?" Lydia smirked. "For someone who's never actually lived there, you're pretty patriotic, Sean."

"Thank you."

"Uhm."

The four of them looked up at the sound of someone clearing her throat in the entryway. Maggie swung her arms back and forth before folding them across her chest.

"Well. Good morning." She said.

"Ah, if it isn't our new teammate with no experience or qualifications!" Kyle raised his mug to her. "Gotta love nepotism, right?"

Sean ground his knuckles into Kyle's hair. "Ignore him." He smiled at Maggie. "Welcome to the team."

"Yeah, welcome!" Lydia grinned. "We kind of met yesterday, but I'm Lydia if you forgot. You also met my cousin, Sean. The guy with the endearing personality is Kyle, and this over here is Hailey."

"I didn't pee my pants, I just spilled coffee on them." Hailey said.

"Yeah, Elliot told me about you guys. Nice to officially meet you." Maggie forced a smile.

For a minute, the only sound in the room was Kyle's obnoxiously loud slurping.

"Do you want some coffee?" Hailey asked. "It's not an attack coffee machine or anything, I'm just clumsy when people sneak up on me."

"That's understandable." Maggie said. "Yeah, I'd love some, actually. Thank you."

"Sean and I just got up, too." Lydia told her, pouring two mugs and handing one to Maggie. "After this, we're going to go to the pantry and hope someone actually bought breakfast food when they were stocking up for the apocalypse."

"It'll have to be ready-made, though." Kyle mentioned over his shoulder. "I tried to make pizza last night, but the oven isn't hooked up."

"You can bounce a cellphone signal across four continents but you can't hook up an oven?" Sean smirked.

"Those are two completely different fields, St. Patrick." Kyle said. "Why don't you teach boxing after your dance classes?"

"That's fair."

"You teach dance?" Maggie asked.

Sean smiled, puffing out his chest a little. "Yeah! Mostly jazz and modern, but I teach a few ballet classes, too. When I graduated from high school, I realized there weren't many dance studios for adults around here. The ones we have are just fitness clubs. Nothing competitive. So I double-majored in dance education and business management, and I fixed that problem."

He glanced away. "I'm trying, anyway. We still have to travel pretty far for competitions, which is a big sacrifice for a lot of the team because they all have jobs. I'm hoping more studios will open up in the area and we'll be able to have night competitions instead of traveling halfway across the state for the weekend."

"That's really cool." Maggie smiled. "I wish I had something I was passionate about like that."

"You don't like your job?" Lydia asked.

"No! I love it. It's like playing on giant playsets all day, and I get to use my powers without anyone noticing – I'm in construction, by the way – but sometimes I feel like I'm not really doing anything important." She stirred her coffee faster. "Sorry. I don't know why I'm telling you guys this."

"Because you already feel like part of the team!" Hailey grinned. "You do. Trust me, I know these things. I'm a psychologist."

"Yeah, for kids." Kyle interjected.

Hailey stuck her tongue out at him. "Oh *right*, I forgot that children are a *completely different species* than adults."

"Anyway!" Lydia said a little louder than necessary. "Your job is super important, Maggie! Without construction workers, we'd all be living in caves or we'd have to construct our own homes and trust me, you do not want to see what mine would look like."

"Yeah, you literally lay the foundation for our whole society!" Sean agreed.

Maggie smiled and shook her head. "You guys make it sound a lot more glamorous than it is."

"Or maybe you don't give yourself enough credit." Hailey said.

"I'd go with that one," Kyle nodded. "You seem like someone who might have a hard time giving credit where credit's due."

"And that is probably the nicest thing he's said all day." Sean smirked.

"On that note," Hailey raised her mug. "Cheers to finding breakfast food!"

"Cheers!" Lydia raised her mug, too, but she couldn't reach high enough to knock it against Hailey's.

"Scholl!" Sean tapped his cousin's mug on his way up to Hailey's.

Kyle gestured vaguely in their direction with his mug. "Here, here."

Maggie smiled at them until they started looking at her.

"Well?" Lydia said.

"Hurry up, my arm's getting tired!" Hailey bounced on her toes.

"Oh, uh..." Maggie lifted her mug and bumped it against Lydia's. "Scholl."

Kyle smirked. "You can't reach either, can you?"

Maggie frowned, then stretched her mind to feel the magnetic forces beneath her. Never breaking eye contact with Kyle, she lifted herself six inches off the floor and pressed her mug against Hailey and Sean's.

Kyle's mouth probably wasn't the only one that dropped open a little, but Maggie didn't look around to check. To his credit, he recovered pretty quickly. "Doesn't count."

"Oh what*ever*, Kyle!" Hailey crowed. "Maggie, that is *so cool*!"

"How are you even doing that?" Sean asked.

Maggie lowered herself to the floor, careful not to spill her coffee. She took a sip to buy herself time. "It's like Elliot's electricity, I think, but with magnetism."

"Elliot can't *fly*, though!" Lydia said.

"Really?" Maggie frowned. "I wonder why."

Hailey's stomach growled and she giggled. "I guess my tummy's wondering why we haven't raided the pantry yet."

Lydia rolled her eyes and Sean smirked.

"Your appetite is a super power." Sean said.

"No, her super power is where she *puts* all of it." Lydia argued, leading the way out of the room.

"What are you talking about? Have you seen my belly?" Hailey poked herself. "See? Squishy!"

"Hails, whatever fluff you have is not proportional to how much you eat. It's unnatural."

Maggie trailed after them. Everything had gone so well up to this point, which made her insides squeeze with desperation to leave and find her own breakfast. *I can't keep this up forever.* But there was no way to excuse herself without making it look like she didn't want to be around them.

Of course, she *didn't* want to be around them, but not because she didn't *want* to be around them. She took a sip of coffee and hoped the buzzing in her head would go away. It was getting stronger and louder, burning towards a fever pitch. Maggie had no idea what would happen once it peaked, but she was sure it would ruin her relationship with her "team" forever.

She shouldn't even be here. She should be somewhere else. She should be at *work* for crying out loud! She hadn't even called in, she had another team who needed her...but if she called in, Noir would probably find her. And the others. And her parents. And then Elliot would come back and find everyone dead because of her. And then Noir would kill him, too.

"What's with the face?" Kyle asked.

"Um." Maggie said. "I'm just feeling a little guilty about not calling my boss. I mean, I can't, obviously, but I still feel bad."

Kyle slid his phone out of his pocket and spun it, pointer finger brushing the sensor to unlock it. "Here. It's untraceable. It's also seven in the morning, by the way."

Maggie grimaced. "That's an hour after my shift starts."

His eyes widened. "That's inhumane."

Maggie laughed. "You get used to it. Besides, we usually get laid off in the winter, so there's plenty of time to sleep in then." She frowned. "Unless you're me, in which case you get a job as a barista and work the morning shift because you're an over-achieving masochist."

Kyle rolled his eyes. "Well, you've certainly come to the right place."

"Alright, let's have a look at our breakfast options." Hailey rubbed her palms together, looking around the pantry. "We have…soup, soup, canned chicken, canned tuna, canned vegetables, more soup, peanut butter, and is that – nope, sorry, it's just more soup."

"The peanut butter is the only thing here that's even close to a breakfast food." Lydia said.

"There are at least three sides of the food pyramid that are missing from this picture." Kyle sniffed.

"Four." Sean frowned. "There's no extra coffee. What do we do if we have to stay here for more than…" he divided the 21.6 oz container of coffee grounds by the fourteen people staying in the safe house. "…one week?"

Maggie smirked, leaning against the doorframe and watching the four of them bounce off each other. *This is actually okay.* She thought. If she had to be yanked cruelly out of the adult life she'd managed to build for herself and stuffed into a bunker full of strangers in order to stay out of the way of a homicidal maniac, she was glad these were the strangers she was with.

"Well," Lydia put her hands on her hips and turned to face Maggie. "What's the plan, boss?"

If she got many more of these gut punches, she'd probably die like Houdini. "Huh?"

Kyle's head tilted up instinctively so he was looking down at Maggie past the bridge of his nose. "Why is *she* the leader?"

"Because Elliot left her in charge." Hailey said. "Remember? Didn't I tell you that?"

Kyle crossed his arms and pivoted to face her head on. "No. No you did not."

"Oh. Well, I was awake when Elliot and the others left—"

"Wait, didn't they leave at, like, four in the morning?" Lydia asked. "Why did you wake up so early? You usually don't get up until noon."

"Oh, I didn't wake up then; I hadn't gone to bed yet." Hailey waved a hand. "What was I saying? Oh, yeah. I smelled coffee so I walked into the kitchen and Elliot was there. I was like, 'You about ready to go?' and he was like, 'Yup. You kids be good and listen to Maggie.' And I was like, 'Okay, have a nice time kidnapping evil scientists.' And he was like, 'We're not kidnapping her, we just want to talk to her.' And I was like, 'I bet you five bucks you end up dragging her back here.' And he was like--"

"Enough!" Kyle threw his hands up. "We get it! Elliot made Maggie the leader of our group even though she has no experience and has only been on the team maybe twelve hours."

Maggie winced.

"Come on, man." Sean said. "You know how excited El was to meet his sister. It probably just slipped out."

"Yeah, he probably didn't mean anything by it." Maggie latched onto that idea and did not let go. "I don't even want to be the leader, anyway."

Kyle smiled. "Cool. I'm in charge, then."

"Says who?!" Lydia asked.

"Well," Kyle said. "I'm the smartest. I can hack into things, which is obviously important in this cyborg society, and I'm the most mature."

"Oh please!" Hailey laughed. "We all know Lydia is the most mature."

Lydia inflated with the praise. "*I* should be in charge, then."

"No way am I taking orders from a teenager." Kyle scoffed.

She crossed her arms. "I'm almost twenty, I'm not a kid!"

"Pfft, try that on any bartender in America, I dare you."

"Lydia is a little young to be in charge." Hailey pointed out. "What if something terrible happens? The leader will feel like it's their fault, and I don't want Lydia to have to feel like that yet. People aren't fully matured until they're 25, therefore she must be protected at all costs."

"So, any of the rest of us, then?" Maggie wanted to grab her tongue and tear it out of her head as soon as she said it.

"That's a fair point." Sean said.

"Since it doesn't narrow it down at all, I still nominate myself." Lydia grinned up at Kyle.

"I'm not sure I want to take orders from my baby cousin, though." Sean continued.

"What?! Where is the family loyalty?"

"Sorry." Sean hesitated. "Maybe Elliot was onto something when he made that comment about Maggie. She's new, so nobody would feel like they didn't measure up if she was in charge. And it won't change the group dynamics at all; we're basically just a headless conglomerate as it is."

"That sounds like a business-themed horror movie." Hailey made her hands into claws. "*Beware the Headless Conglomerate!*"

"You say that, but if one of *us* is in charge at least we know we were passed up for someone who has actually put in the effort to earn their spot." Kyle narrowed his eyes at Maggie. "Isn't naming some new amateur leader the same as saying *none* of us measure up?"

"He has a point there." Hailey said. "But Maggie is the one who has powers."

"That has nothing to do with leadership ability!" Kyle shouted.

"Calm down! I was just contributing to the conversation!" Hailey shouted back, rising up on her tip-toes.

"Guys!" Maggie used her Being Heard Over Loud Machinery voice to get their attention. "Let's just drop it, okay? We were all fine with having no leader up until we started talking about having a leader."

"She has a point there." Hailey settled back onto her heels. "So, what do *you* think we should do, Maggie?"

Maggie crossed her arms and glanced at a wall no one was standing in front of. "I think we should just make all our decisions as a group. No one has to be the leader. When Elliot comes back, he'll be the leader again and this will all be for nothing."

"Hm." Lydia smiled. "I guess that's fine by me."

"I still think I would make the best leader." Kyle said, relaxing his posture.

"You just like to be difficult." Hailey rolled her eyes. "Sean?"

Sean shrugged. "I'm pretty comfortable with whatever. As long as I'm not taking orders from the kid who threw up on me the first time we met."

Lydia groaned. "I was *three weeks old*, Sean: *let it go.*"

"Alright." Maggie put her fist in the air, feeling ridiculous the whole time. "The Headless Conglomerate rides again!"

Hailey, Lydia, and Sean cheered. Kyle smirked and rolled his eyes.

Hailey's stomach interrupted them and she patted it. "There, there." She looked up. "We still haven't decided what to do for breakfast, have we?"

"No, we haven't." Kyle linked his fingers together and stretched his arms over his head. "I'm going into town for pancake mix and cereal, because I am not going to eat handfuls of peanut butter for breakfast until the end of the world."

"Elliot said we can't leave." Lydia crossed her arms over her chest. "We don't have another safe house, if someone follows you back here, we have nowhere to go."

Kyle scoffed. "No one's going to follow me. Besides, Elliot left, too! And he even said that whoever that crazy dude is, he's probably also going after that evil scientist who lives halfway across the state. There is literally no better time to go for a grocery run."

"I still don't like it." Lydia said.

Sean shrugged. "I'm with Lydia, but pick up some coffee while you're out, okay?"

"Sure thing." Kyle glanced at Hailey. "You coming?"

She laughed.

Kyle shrugged and headed for the door.

Maggie moved to the center of the doorway and forced herself to hold Kyle's gaze. "Whoever 'that crazy dude' is, he's way too dangerous for us to be taking risks right now. You should stay here until Elliot gets back."

Kyle stared her down. "I thought you didn't want to be the leader."

Maggie inhaled through her nose and stayed quiet for two full seconds. "I don't." She said, and moved out of his way.

~

Kyle had a lot of confidence in his own intelligence, so he was sure he was right about the gravity person being nowhere near the convenience store. He also had a lot of confidence in his ability to read people and knew he was on thin ice with the rest of the B Team, so he took the long way through the forest until he got to the highway and walked to town from there.

There, he thought at his team. *Now all the villains who aren't here won't know where to look for the safe house. You're welcome.*

Kyle had never really been one for teamwork or other people in general, so he enjoyed the solitude of his walk. It wasn't that he didn't *like* people, necessarily. After all, he wouldn't be wasting time walking to the convenience store *on foot* at, like, *point two miles per hour* if he didn't like people. He just didn't like them up close.

He'd gotten used to Hailey, Lydia, Sean, Elliot, and the rest of the "guild." They were quirky and interesting and, though he'd never admit it out loud, very good at what they did. Not only that, but they had the audacity and the drive to do what they did even though most people thought playing hero was "stupid," "childish," and "irresponsible." It wasn't unpleasant to spend his time with them.

Maggie was different. She wasn't there because she wanted to save the world. She was there because she needed saving. Staying at the safe house was one thing, but what was Elliot thinking putting her on the team, not to mention putting her *in charge*?! It was ridiculous!

Kyle had always known he took the Guild more seriously than the others, but did they just think this was a social club? He was trying to enact real change and they were playing Mutant Recruiter. When Elliot got back, they would need to talk.

Kyle fumed all six miles into town, seethed as he loaded up on pancake mix, cereal, coffee grounds, and creamer, and glowered at the cashier as he swiped his card.

He stepped out into the infuriatingly bright sunshine and cursed at the weight he was already struggling with. Of course he'd forgotten that he had a six mile hike back to the safe house. He decided the public could loan him a cart in return for all the times he'd helped keep the peace.

He was almost off Main Street when a small blue hatchback pulled into a parking space ten feet ahead of him. A woman stepped out and moved to the front of her car only to shove her hands in her pockets and raise an eyebrow at him.

"You're not supposed to take carts from grocery stores." She said.

Kyle frowned. He didn't think a town of six hundred people would have a plainclothes detective, and he knew for a fact that plainclothes detectives didn't bother with cart thieves. "Why do you care?"

The woman waltzed over to him. "Maybe I don't like to be seen in the company of known criminals."

"Well, lucky for you I'm not looking for company." He tried to ignore her and keep walking. "And I'm just borrowing it."

"No need to get upset, it was a just a joke between friends." She fell into step beside him.

"We're not friends." Kyle sized her up. If she was working with that crazy mutant, there was no way the others were going to find out about this. He'd take her down fast and keep his mouth shut. Nobody ever needed to know – especially *Maggie.* Kyle dropped his hand to his jeans pocket casually and wrapped his fingers around the small taser he carried for self-defense.

The woman wrapped herself around that arm and pressed something cold into his side, just under his ribs. Kyle stopped walking and glanced down. The sleeve of the woman's oversized coat completely hid her hand and the weapon it held.

"We are friends, Kyle." She said, smiling. "Because friends tell each other secrets, and you're going to tell me all of yours."

Kyle swore internally. She was much too close – if he even tried to move, she'd shoot him. *Then again,* he grimaced. *Dead men tell no tales.* He launched himself to the side, tearing his arm from her grasp. He managed to get the taser out of his pocket, but felt something enter his chest before he could use it.

He collapsed to the sidewalk, suddenly boneless. As his vision swirled and fogged up, he watched the woman bend down and pry the taser from his limp hand. *Oh, well.* He thought. *You win this round, Maggie.*

Chapter 7

Good Samaritans

The A Team was barely halfway there and Adanna was already contemplating homicide.

"I spy with my little eye—"

"Elliot, if you don't shut up, I will pop your *little eye* out of your head."

"Don't interrupt, Adanna, I'm trying to teach Nehemiah about an important part of our culture."

"I thought we were only teaching him about the parts of our culture that are worth talking about."

"Guys, it's okay." Nehemiah smirked. "I already know how to waste time on long trips. Although 'long' doesn't necessarily mean the same thing when you're in a horse-drawn buggy and not a miniature space shuttle hurtling across the country at one hundred miles per hour."

"I'm only going *five miles* above the speed limit, okay?" Carly said over her shoulder. "And that's only to compensate for the variances in other cars' speedometers."

"At least he doesn't throw up when you drive." Wendell said.

Nehemiah flushed. "That was *one time*."

"You don't have to justify yourself, 'Miah." Adanna patted his shoulder. "We've all driven with Wendell before."

Wendell crossed his arms and turned his head dramatically towards the window. Carly laughed.

"Hey, Nehemiah?" Elliot said. "Is it still weird for you?"

Nehemiah looked over at him, forgetting for a minute to avoid windows. "The driving, or...?"

Elliot shrugged. "Whatever."

Nehemiah dropped his eyes to his hands. They were still calloused, but the cracks had disappeared for the most part. He had an ironic longing for them in the same way he missed the scrapes and bruises he used to get from working all day in the fields.

"When I was a kid," he said, "I heard about the people who left the Amish way of life after Rumspringa. I always thought they'd been ensnared by the Devil or something. I couldn't believe they would leave their families for some shiny new toys the English offered them. But now..." He lifted his hands and dropped them, smiling bitterly. "Yeah, it's still weird."

"That's not what you did, though." Adanna said. "You didn't want to abandon your family or your lifestyle, that's not why you're here."

"Sometimes I wonder."

"Sometimes you doubt." Wendell said.

Nehemiah's eyes snapped to him, hard and burning. "What?"

Wendell didn't look away. "Say it like it is; sometimes you doubt you made the right decision to stay in this world. Whether you doubt your motives or you doubt that this is really where God wants you, it doesn't matter. Doubt is doubt. Don't fall for that 'wondering' shit."

"Language." Nehemiah interrupted automatically.

"Whatever! Just say it like it is, and then treat it the way you treat it."

"That's kinda harsh." Elliot said. "It's not like it's some cardinal sin to have doubts. That's why you have fellows to fellowship with, right? So you can take the battles out of your head and have people help you make sense of them."

"We're your fellows, by the way." Adanna said. "In case you were wondering."

"You mean 'doubting.'" Carly quipped.

"Shut up and drive, Carly." Wendell said.

Nehemiah smirked, then crossed his arms and squeezed his eyes shut. "It's just...I don't understand how this could be right, you know? It doesn't make sense. How can I honestly say it was God's will that I leave my family, leave everything I've ever known, and come to a place where I'm barely qualified for the lowest position?"

"Doesn't it say somewhere that the lowest position is the highest or something?" Adanna asked. "Maybe around the Jesus-washing-the-disciples'-feet part?"

"Pretty sure that describes four different parts."

"Shut up and drive, Carly."

"Stop asking questions you already know the answers to." Wendell ran his hand through his hair. "If you're going to repeat the questions, repeat the answers, too."

Nehemiah took a deep breath. "I wasn't really interested in Rumspringa; I always told myself I was going to stay regardless, so it didn't matter. My parents kept telling me it was important to make an informed decision, so I went to a party just to make them stop bugging me about it."

"And then you met us."

"Carly," Wendell said softly. "I have duct tape and I am not afraid to use it."

"Then what happened?" Elliot shot a quick glare at the front of the van.

"Then." Nehemiah said. "This guy started shooting the place up. And you guys stopped him.

"And I suddenly thought about the Good Samaritan. How the people who were supposed to be righteous walked right by the man who was dying on the road, but the one person everyone thought was a godless heathen saved him and made sure he had a good place to stay.

"I realized that when something had gone wrong I had hidden but you English ran right over to help and I just got this overwhelming sense that I should be helping people like that."

"And then you saw that there was a guy suspiciously strolling around behind us and you *flattened* him with your big strong farmer fists."

"Shut your heathen mouth, Carly." Wendell snapped.

Carly gasped. "Excuse me, I did not go through two years of confirmation to be called a heathen! What did they do at your church, huh? Pinky swear?"

"What have we said about interdenominational bickering in the car?" Elliot sighed.

Carly huffed and fixed her eyes resolutely on the road.

Wendell twisted around in his seat. "Do you still believe that you've been called to help people?"

Nehemiah blinked. "Yes."

"Then what are you so worked up about?"

Smiling slowly, Nehemiah shrugged. "It's more complicated than that."

"Yes, well, do you remember the more complicated parts now?"

"Yeah, I think so."

"Do you want to talk about them?" Adanna asked, putting a hand on his shoulder.

"No. I think I'm good." He said.

"Glad to hear it." Elliot smiled.

"Alright!" Wendell punched Carly gently in the arm. "Turn off on the next exit. I think I deserve a donut for basically single-handedly saving the future of this team."

Carly rolled her eyes. "Drama queen."

"He has a point, though." Elliot was just talking to Nehemiah now, voice too quiet to carry easily through the whole van. "This team wouldn't be the same without you."

"This *family* wouldn't be the same without you." Adanna corrected.

Chapter 8

Assimilation

After Kyle left, the four remaining "B-Team" members mean-dered back into the kitchen and slowly emptied the coffee pot.

"So, what made you guys want to be vigilantes?" Maggie ended up asking.

Lydia laughed. "Honestly, I have no idea what I want to be. I know I want to make a difference in the world, but I'm not really passionate about anything. I thought it was cool when Sean told me about it, so I asked if I could meet everyone and somehow ended up being one of them."

"Resistance is futile." Hailey grinned.

"I was friends with Wendell in college." Sean said. "That's how I met Elliot, Adanna, and Carly. I thought it was awesome that they were going out and changing the world like that, but I never really thought about joining them until, uh." He cleared his throat and looked away.

Maggie felt something solidify in her stomach. "You don't have to tell me."

"No, it's okay. I want to – you're part of the team now, so you should know." Sean gave her a quick smile.

Maggie forced a smile back and said nothing.

"I stayed late at my studio one night. I was prepping lessons and ordering costumes and time just got away from me. When I finally left, it was completely dark out.

"Then, while I was walking to my car, a couple punks jumped me. They hit me in the back of the head; stunned me. I fell over and they just...kicked me until I lost consciousness, I guess. Didn't even give me a chance to react or get a good look at them...they were pretty smart criminals." The corner of his mouth twisted up.

Lydia scooted closer to him and rested her head on his shoulder.

"My studio isn't in a bad part of town." Sean said. "They always warn you that those kinds of things happen in the 'bad' part of town. Like, 'nothing's ever going to happen here, in the "good" part of town.' But what I realized when I woke up was that things like that happen everywhere. Not only that, but things like that *happen*.

"It was suddenly real to me, you know? Before that, crimes only affected other people in this weird limbo of 'the rest of the world,' but nothing had ever happened to me or people I knew in 'real life.'

"When I got out of the hospital, I was hanging out with Wen and he was ranting about a room they were trying to search for information on a wanted criminal, and he was saying it would take a ninja to get in there and..." Sean smirked. "I'm not exactly a ninja, but I asked him to show me what he was talking about. And it was something I could do. So I did."

"Wow." Maggie said. "That's..." She wondered if there was a word to describe it. "...really cool." She finished lamely.

Sean looked directly at her again and smiled. Then he kicked at the shins across the table from him. "Your turn, Hails."

"My turn. Right." She took a long sip of coffee. "You wanna know my tragic backstory, huh?"

"You don't have to tell me if—"

"No! I want to, it's just – we've been talking about this for a while, you know? Like, don't get me wrong, I like campfire chats as much as the next girl, but I was hungry when Kyle left and he's been gone for, like, *two hours*."

"Oh." Maggie worked to keep her tone light. "Yeah, let's definitely eat something."

"Yes!" Hailey threw a fist in the air and scrambled up from her seat. "Handfuls of peanut butter, here I come!"

"Let's at least try to find something to put them on!" Lydia ran after her, grinning.

Maggie stood up, swallowing and crossing her arms over her chest. She didn't care. It wasn't like people were obligated to spill their whole life stories to strangers. She said it was fine if Hailey didn't want to tell her, and it was.

"She's not trying to shut you out."

Maggie just about jumped out of her skin. "Oh, man. I forgot you were there." She smiled at Sean. "Sorry."

"It's cool." Sean shoved his hands in his pockets and glanced in the direction his cousin and teammate had gone. "Hailey gets distracted a lot. It doesn't mean she isn't enjoying whatever she's doing or who she's doing it with. She just kind of...processes life faster than the rest of us."

"Oh." Maggie looked down, guilt arching through her chest. *Way to jump to conclusions, genius.*

"She told me once it's kind of like being set on a timer – like, the timer goes off and it's time to switch to something else." Sean smiled. "She tries really hard to be present when she's around people because she thinks it's what we 'deserve.'"

"What about what she deserves?" The words slipped out before she could stop them.

Sean sighed and ran a hand through his hair. "People haven't treated her the way she deserves, so she doesn't recognize it when we do. She thinks we're just being overly kind or something." He smirked at Maggie. "We'll convince her one of these days."

"Yeah." Maggie said, catching herself too late.

She followed Sean towards the pantry, lost in thought. When this was all over and Maggie went back to her real life, would Hailey think it was her fault? Would she feel abandoned?

Maggie could probably keep in touch; after all, Hailey was friends with the brother Maggie hadn't known she had. As long as she kept in contact with Elliot, she'd keep in contact with Hailey, too. Probably. Maybe.

And what about Sean and Lydia? They thought of her as part of the team. If they had voted, Sean might have helped Hailey elect Maggie *leader* of the team.

And Elliot…what was he thinking, telling these people she was their new teammate?! She was only here to hide from that man who attacked her! Not to put down new roots and change her whole life! In fact, she hadn't even chosen to come here! Elliot and the rest of his "A-Team" squad basically kidnapped her. She shouldn't feel bad about leaving at all!

She was so caught up in her head that she actually ran into Sean before realizing he'd stopped. She jumped back. "I'm so sorry!"

"No worries!" Sean laughed.

"A little tired there, sweetie?" Viv giggled. She, Oliver, Taylor, and Hugh seemed to be the reason Sean had stopped.

"Hi, Mom, Dad….Hi, Mr. and Mrs. Adiche." Maggie said. "Have you guys had breakfast yet?"

"I don't know if you could call it breakfast," Taylor said, "but we microwaved some soup."

"There's nothing that resembles a proper breakfast in that pantry." Hugh said.

"Yeah, we know." Sean told him. "Have you seen Hailey and Lydia?"

"I think I heard their voices in there." Hugh pointed in the direction they'd come from with his thumb.

"Are those two girls part of this club, too? We haven't officially met them yet." Viv said.

Taylor smiled at her. "You'll love them, Viv, they're the sweetest things."

Sean smirked. "Well, we better go check on those sweeties before they eat all the peanut butter."

"Have fun!" Viv said.

Oliver waved.

"And Maggie, dear?" Taylor called after her. "Call us 'Taylor' and 'Hugh.' We're practically family, after all!"

She should have just gone with her parents; distanced herself from the others right then. At least implied that she wasn't with them, wasn't part of their team, wasn't *staying*. But Maggie followed Sean to the pantry to steal peanut butter from Lydia and Hailey.

Chapter 9

Eliminate the Possible

Delilah Turner was buried so deep in classified upon classified upon classified files she was surprised she even got paid sometimes. Not that she was doing much to earn whatever income she made from the government at this point. Most of what she lived on was from her side gig.

Sure, she was still assigned to research projects, but she was too smart to be blissfully ignorant of the fact that none of her assignments had any future. Sometimes she considered applying to have her title changed to Official Goose Chaser. Being too important to let go but not important enough to risk associating with was unbelievably dull.

So when she pulled into her driveway and noticed her drapes pull themselves shut from inside the house, she was almost pleased.

Delilah flicked the lights on, scanning the entryway. No one was there. She rolled her eyes. "If you're in the kitchen," she announced, "you'd better be making me a snack. I'm famished, and it's the least you can do for showing up uninvited."

She walked purposefully into the kitchen. He didn't have a snack prepared for her, but he also didn't have a gun pointed at her so she was willing to let it slide. She set her grocery bag down on the counter and started unloading it.

"And you are?" She asked over her shoulder.

He was in his twenties with fluffy blond hair and green eyes. He was searching her, looking for something.

"You speak English, right?" She said, just to goad him into doing something other than stare at her like he was trying to read her mind.

"I need to know about Project Kobold." He said.

A smile stretched over her face. "You were the one who broke into that storage facility."

"I wasn't the only one." He said. "Another man was right behind me; he could control gravity."

Delilah nodded. "Grady. One of my greatest successes." She sighed. "Unfortunately, we ended things on a bad note."

"I need to know how to stop him."

She laughed. "You think pretty highly of yourself, don't you?"

He narrowed his eyes. "No. That's why I'm here. I need your help."

Delilah shut the refrigerator and turned to face the boy, one hand on her hip. "Don't you think that if I knew how to take Grady down that I would've done it by now?"

"Not necessarily."

She smirked. "Hm. What's he to you, anyway?"

The boy hesitated. "He tried to hurt someone I care about."

"Oh?" She studied the boy's face. "Grady's not the kind of man who does things without a reason." Would he respond better if she threw him a bone? "That's one of the reason's he's stayed under the radar for so long."

The boy's eyes flickered. He'd caught it. "There's a reason." He said. "It has to do with Project Kobold."

"Not the type to lose focus. I can appreciate that." Delilah pulled out a chair and sat down across from him. "Neither am I. So, let's settle this like adults; you answer a question, then I'll answer a question."

"How do I know you'll answer my question after I answer yours?"

"Fair enough." She nodded. "You can go first. Fire away, kid."

The boy glanced down as if he was listening to something. "What was the objective of Project Kobold?"

"That's a pretty big question. Maybe you should answer two after this."

"Don't try to change the terms after we've already started."

"I like you, kid." Delilah smirked. "We named it 'Project Kobold' after the German mythical creature. Arthur C. Clarke once said 'Magic is just science we don't understand yet.' We were trying to prove that we could create 'magical' beings using science."

"Why?"

She tsked, waving a finger. "My turn. Who are you?"

He swallowed. "My name is Elliot."

"Oh," she let out the word in a long exhale. "Gemini Beta. My how you've grown. How's Gemini Alpha? And your genetic donors?"

Something in his expression flickered. "My turn."

"Fair enough."

"Why was the project shut down?"

"Hm. It was a little hard to continue our research without our test subjects."

"They ran away?"

"My turn."

"Fine."

"How is Gemini Alpha?"

"Fine."

"Not good enough."

"Well it'll have to be."

"Protective, aren't you? That's sweet."

Elliot pressed his lips together. "My turn." Suddenly, his head snapped up, eyes losing focus. He nodded, then stood quickly, grabbing Delilah's wrist. "We have to go. Now."

"That's not a question." She shrugged him off and opened a drawer, grabbing a set of keys. "We'll take the back way."

"He's coming from the back way."

"Then we'll take the front way." Delilah glanced at him out of the corner of her eye. "How's that electric field of yours?"

Elliot held her gaze, not bothering to hide the sparks dancing along his fingers. "It's not your turn."

"Fry the house's system. It'll set off the silent alarm. We'll have five minutes to get out of town before they close the exits."

"We're at least ten minutes from the highway."

"Not if you disregard traffic laws." She slid one of the keys off the ring in her hand and tossed it to him. "Blue bike, far side of the garage. Get out of the city. We'll meet up later."

"What? No way. You're coming with me."

"That's a cute cop act you've got there, kiddo, but the best way to stay out of Grady's reach is to take the bikes. You can go on sidewalks and everything."

"Then we'll take the same bike."

Delilah laughed. "I've lived here for ten years and haven't had so much as a cat burglar in here. I don't think Grady's after me."

"We are wasting time—"

"No." She said, opening the door to the attached garage. "You're wasting time. Later." She sprinted over to a red motorcycle, shoved her key in the ignition, started the motor, and sped away.

Elliot's earphone buzzed with Carly's voice. *"Please tell me you got her."*

"Never mind that! Get out of there, now! We're right across the street!" Adanna's voice was unnaturally high-pitched and fast.

A shockwave ripped through the house. Elliot scrambled to his knees, shot an unrestrained blast of energy through the walls, and stumbled out of the house.

The absolute normality of the suburban scene juxtaposed with what was going on made his head spin – or maybe he'd hit his head during the explosion. What even *was* that?! Was the guy – *Grady* – so opposed to doors that he had to blow holes in every wall he walked through?

Some of the neighbors who had heard the noise were coming out of their houses to see what was going on – because obviously when you hear something explode, you should go *towards* it.

"Get back inside!" Elliot shouted.

Some people frowned and edged away from him, but not nearly enough and not anywhere close to before Grady took out his anger on the front wall.

There wasn't anything between Elliot and the explosion this time, so he hit the dirt and curled into an earthquake position. Debris and chunks of wall flew across the front lawn. One piece rocketed through a window across the street. More pieces attacked the cars parked on the road.

Elliot wondered, with the kind of thought that felt like breathing helium, whether Delilah's neighbors' insurance covered Supervillain Attacks.

Grady emerged from the epicenter of the destruction, dust parting around him. His outfit didn't have a speck of dirt on it.

Standing, Elliot wiped the dirt from his eyes and coughed. "You," he pointed to Grady, "are kind of a drama queen."

Grady anticipated the lightning bolt that shot out from the tip of Elliot's finger, dodging to the side. He clenched his fist and the earth between himself and Elliot sunk half a foot with the strain of his gravitational pull.

Through blurry eyes, Elliot saw Grady stroll towards him, mouth stretching grotesquely.

"Any last words?" Grady asked.

Elliot coughed. "Now...would be...good..."

In the attic of the house across the street, Carly grit her teeth.

Grady stepped forward.

Carly braced her shoulder for the Remington 700's recoil and pulled the trigger.

Chapter 10

Amateur Landscaping

Carly was in the attic of the house across the street from Delilah Turner's place. The muzzle of her Remington 700 was poking out the window, the barrel propped up on the sill. She switched from watching the events to peering through her scope and back. She was sweating.

As they'd gotten closer to their "target," Adanna and Elliot had launched back into their To Kill or Not to Kill debate. Elliot was still against taking a life on principle, but Adanna was of the opinion that turnabout is fair play and the guy *was* trying to kill him.

Nehemiah, who'd grown up with the Amish belief in strict pacifism, felt conflicted enough when he had to punch and kick people and was very hesitant to throw his vote behind Adanna. Wendell was all for 'eliminating the threat' before it could eliminate them. Carly had won many awards for her target shooting accuracy. Eventually, they'd compromised.

Incapacitating someone without killing them is hard with guns. It's even harder to do it on purpose. The only place you can really hit someone which will not kill them but *will* make sure they're down for the count is the pelvis. Shooting them in the leg might make it so they can't run, but the pain isn't bad enough that they can't shoot back. Also, there's always the possibility of hitting an artery.

Carly bit her lip as Grady emerged from the cloud of dust and confronted Elliot.

Contrary to popular belief, bullets do not go in a straight line. Even they are subject to the constraints of projectile motion; gravity pulls them down the longer they're in the air. This means anyone shooting at a target from a distance has to learn to compensate for the gravitational pull.

Grady knocked Elliot across the front lawn. Carly put her target in the crosshairs, then slowly raised the muzzle towards the sky.

Based on Maggie's quick retelling of her confrontation with Grady at the building, he seemed to have some sort of gravitational field surrounding him that protected him from projectiles. Pretty ingenious, really.

If Carly was going to make this work, she was going to need to compensate for an amount of gravity that could immediately stop a "bullet" fired from point-blank range. And hit him in the pelvis.

Adanna was still downstairs, assuring the owners of the house that the "FBI" had the situation under control. Her "partner" (Carly) had gone upstairs for better service to call for backup – the government had specially encrypted phones, but they needed altitude to get service. (It wasn't the most logical lie, but maybe that's why it worked so well.)

Elliot's voice was strained in her ear. *"Now...would be...good..."*

Carly grit her teeth and said a prayer.

Grady took one more step forward.

Carly braced for recoil and pulled the trigger.

When the bullet hit, Grady's immediate roar was mostly rage. It takes a few seconds for the pain to set in – more than that if shock gets there first. He dropped to the ground, clutching his thigh.

Carly cursed and ejected the casing and slammed the bolt back into place faster than she ever had, but she was still trying to line up her sight again when Grady turned murderous eyes on the house.

Carly's breath caught in her throat and she desperately fired again.

The bullet went wild.

Grady raised his hand.

Elliot lunged for him, lightning bursting from his fingertips.

With one hand, Grady sent Elliot flying into the air. With the other, he crushed the house across the street beneath the weight of his rage.

Chapter 11

Villainous Interlude

In the gutted remains of a failed donut shop, a woman dragged a body to a chair in a dark corner.

She swore under her breath as she maneuvered Kyle's deadweight until he wouldn't slide off onto the floor. After that, she worked his shirt off over his head, holding him to the chair with a foot braced on his stomach. Then it was simply a matter of tying his wrists and ankles.

Her phone rang and she dug through her deep pockets to find it. "I hope this kid watches movies or the effect will be totally lost on him." She told the person on the other end.

She listened for a minute, then barked out a laugh. "They *shot* you? A bunch of *Scooby Doo* cosplayers got past your 'impenetrable' force field?"

The voice on the other end became loud enough to echo into the building.

The woman held the phone away from her face and rolled her eyes. "Well, find something to stop the bleeding with. It didn't hit an artery, or you'd be dead already. If it's a through-and-through you can either cauterize it or sew it up, otherwise you'll have to get someone to take the bullet out."

She observed Kyle casually as she listened.

"Uh-huh. Well, you botched that operation real good. Lucky for us, I found one of the kids who hangs around the Gemini boy." She touched her heel to the floor and rocked her foot back and forth. "Yeah. I gave him enough juice to put out a horse, but he should be coming around in an hour or so. That, or the dose will be too much for him and stop his heart. Then we'll be back at square one."

The voice got louder again.

The woman's eyes narrowed. "Hey, don't be yelling at me! You're the one who got schooled by the Electric Company; I'm the one who found this lovely organic data drive. If he dies, we still win because we took out one of the pests. What did you do?"

Her eyes darkened at his response. "Okay, fine, you took out a sniper. Big whoop. We can't get anything from them either now, genius. Why don't you go find something to stop yourself from bleeding out? If you die, I don't get paid."

She hung up without saying goodbye and crossed her arms, staring at Kyle's unresponsive body. "I hope you don't die, kid." She murmured. "I really want to be able to gloat to that self-righteous lab rat."

Chapter 12

Fishing for Clues

In the kitchen at the safehouse, Sean grinned maliciously at his cousin.

"Go fish."

Lydia groaned. "I have the *worst* luck with cards."

"Don't ever go to Vegas, kiddo." Sean grinned.

"Maggie." Hailey said. "Hey, Maggie? Maggie!"

"Huh?" Maggie's hand stilled and she looked over at the blue-haired girl.

"No offense, but your finger-tapping is throwing off my game." Hailey said.

Lydia scoffed. "Hails, you're winning. By, like, half the deck."

"He's been gone too long." Maggie said.

"Who, Kyle?" Sean frowned. "He's probably just taking an obnoxiously long route so he can complain about how hard he has to work to make us happy."

"It's been almost four hours. What if Elliot was right to tell us to stay here? What if the gravity man didn't go after the scientist after all?" Maggie asked.

"Well, then." Hailey stood up and stretched. "I guess we'll be able to tell him we told him so after we rescue him."

"Wait, what?" Maggie said.

"You're worried about him, don't you want to go find him?" Lydia said.

"Well...I mean..." Maggie took a deep breath. "That guy is really powerful. He almost killed me before."

"Don't stress it, Maggie." Sean smiled. "We may not have powers, but we can defend ourselves with the best of them. We'll have your back."

"Yeah." Lydia nodded. "I mean, if the gravity guy really does have Kyle, we can't just let him die."

They were all looking at her. They were all staring and this was not her responsibility. She was not the leader; she wasn't even on the team. She had no experience being some sort of vigilante. She'd warned Kyle; they'd *all* warned Kyle.

And then she'd stepped out of the way and let him leave.

Maggie closed her eyes and breathed deeply. "Is there a way we can drive without being spotted easily?" She asked. "It's been too long already; we can't waste any more time."

Cars were big and noted for their ability to drive almost exclusively on roads, but ATV's were small enough to fit through the trees in the forest. And the Hero's Guild happened to have five of them. By the time they hit the highway, they could have come from anywhere.

They slowed down once they got into town, searching the sides of the roads for any sign of their teammate. Just before they turned onto Main Street, they saw a cart stocked full of food sitting abandoned at a bus stop. It could have belonged to anyone, but Hailey pulled over to check it out anyway.

"What is it?" Maggie asked.

"Lots of pancake mix, coffee grounds, cereal..." She announced things as she rooted through the bags.

"Breakfast food and coffee." Lydia said. Her hands twitched on the handlebars.

"I found a receipt!" Hailey waved it triumphantly.

"Does it have a time stamp?" Sean asked.

Hailey scanned it. "Yeah – three *hours* ago." She frowned, looking further.

"We should have come sooner." Maggie's leg bounced violently.

"We couldn't have known." Lydia told her.

"I should've gone with him." Sean clenched a fist. "We should always have someone to watch our backs."

"If you'd have gone, you'd probably both be missing." Lydia frowned at him.

"That *stupid idiot!*" Hailey shouted.

"What?" Maggie said.

Hailey pointed at print too small for her teammates to read from their seats. "He used his freakin' credit card! And he says *I'm* absent-minded."

"Ah, man..." Lydia face-palmed. "What was he thinking?"

"He *wasn't.*" Sean crossed his arms and sighed. "Whoever took him has a three hour head start. I'm assuming he's still alive because if he isn't it'll be a lot harder for me to *strangle him* when we find him. Should we start asking around, see if anyone saw anything?"

"You and I can take the left side of the street; Lydia and Maggie can take the right." Hailey said.

"No." Maggie said.

Hailey raised an eyebrow. "You want the left side? I'm not picky."

"No, we're not going to canvas the area or whatever it's called." Maggie straightened her back and looked up. "I have a better idea."

Chapter 13

In the Wake of Disaster

Delilah was pretty sure Grady would be enough to keep Gemini Beta busy and visa versa, but she still wanted to put some distance between herself and whatever that mess was going to look like in a few minutes.

Behind her, she heard another explosion. It sounded very distracting.

She smirked.

She stopped smirking when it felt like her arms and lower rib cage smacked into a metal pole. A metal pole whose fingers gripped the arm on the far side of her body and swung her through the air to press against its chest. The motorcycle kept going for a minute before faltering and careening into a parked car as if suddenly realizing it had no rider.

Delilah blinked as she was turned around and set down. Nehemiah didn't let go of her arm, though. He frowned, looking her over.

"Are you alright?" He asked. "I'm sorry if I hurt you, but I couldn't let you get away. We need your help."

"I'm fine." She wouldn't be surprised if she'd cracked a rib on that bicep of his, but she wasn't paid the big bucks to show weakness to glorified teenagers. "I'm guessing you're working with Gemini Beta?"

Nehemiah hadn't grown up in the same science-fiction saturated culture as the others, which meant he had a very different take on genetic experimentation: he wasn't desensitized. "His *name* is *Elliot*."

"We got her." Wendell said, sidling up to the two of them. "How are you guys doing?"

Frowning when he got no response, he met Nehemiah's gaze. "Hello? Guys?"

"Elliot?" Nehemiah joined in. "Adanna? Carly?"

"What's going on?" Wendell asked.

"Is everything okay?" Wendell's voice came through Elliot's earpiece just fine, but Elliot was having trouble processing...everything.

His head hurt from being thrown backwards into a tree. He wasn't sure if he had lost consciousness or not. His vision was foggy and he felt like his brain was spinning.

The house across the street looked like a giant fist had smashed it from above. That was bad. Why was that bad? Elliot closed his eyes. Sleep sounded really nice. But why was he sleeping on the grass? He didn't recognize this place, where was he? He'd come here with Adanna and the others; they probably remembered where it was and why they were there.

Adanna.

Carly.

The house across the street.

Elliot's mind snapped into focus and he felt something burning in his gut. The burning intensified and raced up into his chest and he couldn't breathe.

Grady was levitating, clutching his wound in pain as he struggled to stay airborne.

Elliot flung lightning bolts at him, but they were wild and uncontrolled and the man deflected them easily. Elliot was screaming and crying and Grady just turned and flew away.

Elliot collapsed to the ground. Everything hurt. Everything hurt. Every kind of pain was inside of him and he didn't know what to do.

He closed his eyes. The voices in his ears were louder now.

"Elliot! What's going on?"

"Are you alright?"

"We're almost there, just hang on!"

Elliot squeezed his eyes shut tighter. He didn't want to deal with this. He couldn't deal with this. This was too big, too much, how could anyone expect him to deal with this? Maybe he could just sleep and Wendell and Nehemiah would clean it up. Maybe he could sleep and when he woke up everything would be okay again.

He took a deep breath, let it out, and rose to his feet.

His whole body ached and trembled, but he forced himself to walk towards the wreckage. "I'm here." He said. "I'm fine. Grady – the gravity man – collapsed the house Adanna and Carly were in. I'm heading over to check it out now."

They could still be alive. People survived earthquakes and bombings all the time. *Please let them still be alive.*

"Don't try to dig them out by yourself!" He hadn't known Nehemiah could sound like that. *"You might end up collapsing it even more by accident!"*

Elliot backed away from the rubble, then fell into a sitting position and wrapped his arms around himself. What could he do? What was he supposed to do?

Someone had called the cops. He could feel the loud pulsating of the electricity in the lights as they flashed like annoying heartbeats.

Elliot gave a little squeak and scrambled closer to the wreckage. Shutting his eyes tightly, he stretched his mind into the rubble. He was careful and thorough. He checked and double-checked every signal, whether it felt man-made at first or not. It felt like he was on a different plane of reality where the only things that existed were electric fields and pulses.

The fire fighters were the first to arrive on the scene. Chief Wells looked around at the collapsed house, the house across from it with a hole in the front, several destroyed cars, and a front lawn which looked like the owner had hired a three year old landscaper who only used dynamite.

"What happened here?" He wondered.

His team shrugged.

"Hey, chief." Lindsey, one of the newer members, pointed towards the collapsed house. "Looks like someone's home."

Wells frowned, walking towards the young man who was crouched in front of the wreck. His hand felt heavy as he put it on the boy's shoulder.

When the kid looked up, there were tears falling almost unnoticed from his eyes.

Wells steeled himself. "Was your family home? At the time of the incident?"

The boy nodded. "They're going to be okay." He said. "They're alive."

Wells sighed. "I hope so, kid."

The boy smiled. "I know so – I can *feel* it."

Chapter 14

Introductions

Kyle was surprised to wake up alive. His upper body was freezing, hands and feet going numb from being tied up for so long. He didn't recognize the building, but it looked a little like the haunted house his neighbors had set up every year when he was a kid.

An aggravated sigh drew his attention to the woman sitting in a chair across from him. "Finally!" She threw her hands in the air. "I was beginning to think you'd never wake up." She stood and pinched her thumb and pointer finger together. "I was *this close* to just shooting you and calling it a day."

Kyle was becoming more awake by the second and he was not liking it one bit. He wanted to pull at his bindings, but he knew it was useless. Someone who went through the trouble of drugging him and dragging him to a building probably hadn't cut corners with her knots.

He met her gaze and glared, pressing his lips together. He would have preferred dying on the road, but if he had to withstand torture he would do it. He might not be as strong as Sean, but that didn't mean he was going to break.

"First things first." The woman said. "Introductions. I already know who you are, of course, but we may as well go through the formality. My name is Gertrude, but at work I go by 'Siren.' The criminal underworld goes crazy for allusion." She looked at Kyle expectantly.

He glared back.

"Really?" Siren said. "You already know I know your name. Why not save the defiance for information I don't know?"

"I'm not playing this game with you." He said.

"Why not?" She asked. "After all, this 'game' is all that's stopping me from cutting to the chase, if you'll excuse the pun." She frowned. "Of course, I haven't brought out my knives yet, so that would have gone over your head anyway."

He clenched his muscles to suppress a shudder. A shirt suddenly felt like a layer of armor he was missing. "My name is Kyle."

"Nice to meet you, Kyle." Siren took his bound hand in hers and pretended to shake it. "Do you mind if I make myself more comfortable?"

"Please do." Kyle said through his teeth.

"Thank you." Siren slithered out of her oversized jacket. "So, Kyle, tell me..." she slipped a switchblade out of her pocket and slid the blade out. "...what is it that you do?"

Kyle felt like his heart was blocking his airway. "I'm a computer programmer." He said. "I work at the computer repair shop a couple towns away."

Siren smirked. "Clever." She leaned forward and touched the blade to his bare chest. "Now tell me what you really do."

Kyle closed his eyes and tried to breathe normally. *Just don't say anything. It'll all be over soon.*

"Kyle...?" Siren asked sweetly.

Suddenly, a cheerful electronic jingle split the tension. Siren stood back up and grabbed her phone from her jacket. She opened the phone as the same jingle played again. She raised an eyebrow. The jingle played again. And again. And again. Every minute or so, the alert would sound.

"Well, well." Siren said around the fifth time it happened. "It seems you've been missed."

"What do you mean?" Kyle asked.

Siren turned the phone towards him to show him the alert. "Margaret Posey. She's the other Gemini, isn't she? She's used her credit card six—" the alert sounded again. "—*seven* times in the past ten minutes. All at a that little grocery store you went to this morning."

He'd used his *credit card?!* If Kyle's hands had been free, he would've slapped himself.

Siren sighed and started to put her coat on. "You'll have to excuse me for a minute."

"What are you doing?" Kyle asked. "Maggie doesn't know anything! She's just staying with Elliot to hide from your guy."

"Grady." Siren supplied. "And I'd think a smart kid like you could do better than that. Why would she be calling me out if she was just hiding?"

"I don't know, I only met her this morning." Kyle couldn't help but struggle when Siren started walking away. "Hey! I'm serious; she doesn't know anything!" He wracked his brain. Maggie wasn't one of them – she had no idea what she was doing! "It's rude to leave in the middle of a conversation!"

Siren stopped and turned around slowly, head tilted with curiosity.

Kyle felt like he was going to be sick. "I have...so much more to tell you." *Why am I doing this? Why is it so important to be the hero?* "Don't you want to finish talking to me first?" *I don't want to die.* "You don't need her to get your answers, anyway."

"I know." Siren smiled. "I'm not going to get her for a chat; she's much too powerful for me to risk any sort of extended interaction with." She shook her head. "Mutants have terrible manners."

"Wh-what are you going to do then?"

Siren laughed. "You're not that naïve. What do people usually do to monsters?" She turned on her heel and wiggled her fingers behind her. "I'll be back soon! Amuse yourself while I'm gone."

She vanished into the darkness of the hall, and soon enough a door opened and closed on creaking hinges. Kyle dropped his head on the back of the chair and groaned. This was a mess.

What did Maggie think she was doing?! Just because she had powers did not make her a hero! Look at him; he was tied up in an abandoned building because he forgot to avoid using his credit card. This stuff was way harder than it looked.

He rocked back and forth on the chair, trying to get free. No dice. He was stuck. He heaved a sigh and stared up at the ceiling.

So this is how it ends; tied to a chair while my friend's sister gets murdered because of me, then eventually tortured to death. He squeezed his eyes shut. He hoped the others didn't find him before he died. He didn't think he could look Elliot in the eyes and tell him he'd indirectly killed the person he was supposed to protect.

Chapter 15

Know Your Enemy

Nehemiah sat across from Delilah Turner. He rested his hands in his lap the same way someone else might position a gun; just a reminder that he could use them if he needed to.

Delilah had been too surprised when she was plucked from the back of her motorcycle to put up much resistance, and the way the boys had acted when they found out their friends were hurt had been...unsettling, so she'd cooperated when they told her to *get in the van, sit down and shut up.*

Now, in the parking lot of the local hospital, she sat with crossed legs and arms, analyzing the boy across from her. It had been a few hours since the other two had gone inside, and the time alone with Nehemiah had rebuilt her sense of security.

Despite the strength with which he had lifted her as if she were a child, he seemed vulnerable. His face was open and honest, eyes avoiding looking directly at her. Long, shaggy bangs threatened to spill over into them. He reminded her of the puppies she helped train for K-9 units during her internship.

"Where did they find you?" She wondered out loud.

The side of his mouth quirked up and he glanced quickly at her face. "I found them, actually."

Delilah was a brilliant geneticist, but that wasn't what had made her invaluable to the Project back in the day. She had a memory like a steel trap and was a genius at linking memories to traits and details dropped by others during interactions.

She automatically assembled psychological profiles on anyone she spent any time with. It made her unpopular with her coworkers, but the level of sophistication her research operated at was unparalleled.

The accent clicked into place in the profile she was currently assembling for Nehemiah. "I thought the Amish were pacifists." She said.

His emotions may as well have been printed in neon across his face. "How did you know I was Amish?"

She shrugged. "Why are you with these people if you don't fight?"

His cheeks flushed. "I fight when I need to." He said. "I'm not Amish anymore. Not really."

"Because you fight when you need to?"

"Kind of."

"Why did you come here?"

He smirked again. "So *we* could ask *you* questions."

She smiled, opening up her posture and letting her head tilt just a bit towards him. "Do you know what a *quid pro quo* is?"

His forehead pulled together. "I didn't take Spanish."

Of course not; Amish children usually leave school after eighth grade. Delilah leaned forward as if explaining things excited her. "It's Latin, actually. Latin is a romance language, too, though, just like

Spanish. That means they're part of the same language family and they share similar word parts."

"Uh-huh." He said, understandably confused.

"*Quid pro quo* is a Latin term that means 'if you do something for me, I'll do something for you.'"

"It's longer in English." Nehemiah observed.

Delilah pointed at him excitedly. "Yes! Exactly. Other languages can have words that translate to whole sentences in English."

His eyes widened. "Whoa."

"So," Delilah smiled shyly. "How after I answer one of your questions, you answer one of mine?"

Nehemiah glanced at the hospital. "We should really wait until Elliot gets back…"

"I'm sure he won't mind!" Delilah said. "We can just catch him up when he gets here."

Nehemiah frowned, conflicted.

Time to go for the kill. "Besides," she said softly. "You don't want anyone else getting hurt like your friends, do you?"

His eyes widened and snapped to her face. He studied it for a minute. "Of course not."

"Well, then—"

The van door swung open just far enough to reveal seventy-five percent of Wendell and two sandwiches in plastic wrap.

"Hey guys," he said, overly casual gaze never leaving Delilah. "I brought you some dinner."

"Thank you." Nehemiah said.

Delilah thanked him as well.

"How have things been going?" Wendell asked.

"Pretty good." Nehemiah said, unwrapping his sandwich. "Dr. Turner tried confusing me with Latin so I would let my guard down and answer her questions."

Delilah's jaw dropped.

"Oh, really?" Wendell leaned up against the side of the van. "How did that go?"

"It was pretty interesting," Nehemiah said between bites. "I think she wasn't just a scientist. Based on her confidence in her wordcraft, I'd say she was probably in charge of talking circles around the victims in order to get them to cooperate."

"They weren't victims." Delilah seethed. "They were there of their own free will!"

Nehemiah laughed shortly. "Free will isn't always what people tell you it is."

Wendell smirked. "Oh, I also came to tell you that Elliot wants us you to come in and take a nap or something."

"Okay." Nehemiah hopped out of the van and waved his sandwich. "Thanks again."

"Yeah, have fun, buddy!" Wendell said. He slammed the door shut and his face lost all friendliness. "Pretty smart for a dumb farm boy, isn't he?"

Delilah crossed her arms and leaned back. "I know what he said, but I was honestly just trying to have a conversation. I've been here for hours and I'm bored."

"Cut the crap." Wendell said. "You saw someone who looked and acted a little differently than a 'normal' person would and you targeted him as the weak link. It backfired. Let's not pretend there was anything else to it."

"Hm." Delilah eyed him. "You're very protective of your friends. Tell me, how did it feel to see them broken like that?"

His eyes flashed, but she didn't give him a chance to answer.

"Your little club is a joke. This has never happened before, has it? You play at being heroes, but you have no idea how to deal with anyone who could be classified as a villain. You slipped up for one second, and two of your teammates almost died. Next time it will be worse."

"How dare you—"

"You want information about Grady? Let me give it to you. The project wasn't shut down because the subjects escaped – it was shut down because the three original subjects murdered every scientist and staff member at the facility before burning the place down.

"Your little friends? The Gemini subjects? Their genetic donors were two of the original three subjects. Grady was the third. After the Gemini subjects were born, the three of them started having second thoughts about the morality of the project. That *morality* was what drove them to kill everyone in the building in the span of forty-five minutes. I only survived because I had a briefing at the Pentagon.

"You think the Gemini are some kind of heroes? They're vigilantes who take the law into their own hands no matter who is hurt in the process. Just like their parents. It's in their blood."

"You're wrong." Wendell said. "Elliot is nothing like that."

"Really?" Delilah leaned forward. "Let me ask you something; is this little group of yours legal? Are you being paid to protect the peace? Or are you bounty hunters and thrill seekers taking what you want and picking fights when you're bored? Do you know what type of project it was classified as? It was Weapons Development. Your buddies are weapons, and they always will be. That's what they're programmed for."

"Keep talking, Doc, we both know you're just trying to scare me." Wendell smirked, leaning back and digging a cookie out of his pocket.

"Am I?" She leaned back herself. When she spoke again, she was much calmer. "That's good news for you. I don't know how Kobold Beta and Gamma managed to keep the Gemini safe all this time, but now that Kobold Alpha knows where they are he won't stop until he finishes what he started. And the Gemini? When they feel threatened, their programming will kick in and they'll do what all weapons do." Delilah smirked. "Either way, the rest of you are just collateral damage in the making."

"That's a good story." Wendell said. "*Terminator* meets *300*; very ambitious. You forgot one thing, though."

"And what's that?"

Wendell grinned. "We're not letting you go until you give us the information we need, which means unless you cooperate Grady is going to finish what he started in more ways than one."

Chapter 16

Making a Scene

Maggie leaned up against the outside wall of the convenience store, arms crossed and hands shoved into her pits to hide the trembling. She tried to breathe evenly, tried not to focus on the fact that she was using herself as bait.

Instead, she catalogued the potential weapons in the area and held the ball of exasperation and anger tightly in her chest, feeding it like it was the only thing between her and the darkness.

Parking lots were gold mines of weapons. Even though the bodies of most cars weren't made out of metal anymore, engines and frames still generally had metal in them.

When Maggie rescued Kyle, she was going to make him wish she hadn't. They had all warned him not to leave, Elliot had told him it wasn't safe, but he just *had* to have his Lucky Charms.

Or was he just trying to prove he could come up with a better solution to their breakfast problem than she could? What a jerk. Maybe being kidnapped for a few hours would deflate his ego to a normal size.

She especially enjoyed the cart collecting stations. The bars fencing the carts in were built to last, which meant metal. And the carts themselves were woven metal baskets, which meant all she had to do was unweave a few strands and she'd have a treasure trove of skewers.

Whoever had grabbed Kyle had some nerve. How much evidence did they even have that he knew Elliot? People don't just hang out with the people they're in business or partners in crime with. So this person or those people just saw Kyle shopping for breakfast food and decided to grab him off the street on the off chance he might know something? Maggie realized that they were assassins or mercenaries or whatever, but attacking everyone in their target's life was just ridiculous.

Of course, everything has a magnetic field so Maggie wasn't limited to only using metal, but metals were ferromagnetic, or substances with magnetic fields which responded better than other materials. They were most convenient during emergencies. That being said, trace amounts of metal in human beings also made throwing them around an option.

Maggie remembered Elliot saying the gravity man had thrown Adanna around like a rag doll and a nasty smile formed on her lips. *I hope he's the one who took Kyle. We'll see how he likes it.*

She'd taken a page from said gravity man's book and flipped her magnetic field to repel metallic objects, so she didn't realize she'd been shot at until a glinting object rebounded away from her and smashed through the window of a car.

Maggie pushed off from the building and dropped her arms to her sides, tensing her muscles as she looked around for whoever had done that. She wasn't too surprised not to see anyone; if it was easy to get the drop on whoever this was, Kyle would've done it.

Someone had screamed when the car window seemed to spontaneously explode, but after that the humans in the area did what humans tend to do and ignored what they didn't have an explanation for.

Maggie clenched and unclenched her fists, looking around just to do something. She wanted to take cover, but she couldn't risk the shooter giving up and leaving before she could make them tell her where Kyle was. Still, standing in the open waiting to be shot at was sounding stupider with every moment that passed.

Maggie concentrated, opening her mind to *feel all* the magnetic fields around her. She was pretty sure assassins didn't take one shot and give up, and she didn't want to be caught off guard if whoever this was planned to use a wooden arrow and a crossbow next.

She was still surprised when a shower of bullets attacked the concrete overhang above her, sending it crashing down. She flipped her field to repel it but still dove out of the way.

She realized her mistake a split second before the bullet cut across her ribcage. The shooter had distracted her on purpose, but hadn't predicted that she'd move.

Maggie threw up a field to repel metal and grabbed at her side, hissing in pain. She scooted towards a nearby car for shelter, only to stop as it bent away from her. Tears pricked at her eyes and she let her head rest on the pavement, digging her phone out of her back pocket. She turned the volume back on halfway through a demand to know if she was okay.

"I'm fine, I'm fine!" Maggie struggled to keep her voice steady. "Please tell me you got him."

"It's a her, actually." Lydia said. *"She's pretty good! Sean threw a rock at her head, and she still almost fought the three of us off!"*

"I'm glad you're having fun." Maggie pushed herself into a sitting position. "Is she alone?"

"Looks like it." Sean said. *"I'd keep the field up, anyway. Just to be safe."*

"I'm coming down." Hailey said. *"Try not to move; you look like someone spilled paint on you."*

"Okay, cool." Her other hand was still holding her side, so Maggie pressed the back of her phone hand to her forehead, trying to fight off the dizziness. "People are screaming. We should go before someone calls the cops."

"Don't worry about that, boss." Lydia said. *"Just stay put. We're all over this."*

Maggie wanted to say something along the lines of "I'm not your boss," but she didn't. She just set her phone down and stared at the curious people who were peeking out from behind cars. She felt like she'd been sitting on the pavement for an eternity, then she blinked and Hailey was there.

Hailey said something, but the words sounded like a jumble of consonants and syllables with no real meaning. She frowned, then moved Maggie's hand away from the wound, gathering the bottom of her shirt and stuffing it in the sticky red palm.

Maggie got the sense she was supposed to hold onto the part of her shirt that had been handed to her, so she did. Hailey was nice, so Maggie would do this strange thing if it made her happy.

Hailey's mouth moved again, eyebrows creased. The only words that meant anything to Maggie's fuzzy brain were "hurt" and "sorry." Why was Hailey apologizing? She wasn't the one who hurt Maggie.

Hailey dumped something on the wound and the world snapped back into focus. Painful, burning focus.

"Ahhhh!" Maggie's fist flailed into Hailey's shoulder. "What the actual—"

"Sorry." Hailey wiped at Maggie's side with the jacket she'd taken off earlier. "I need to make sure it doesn't get infected."

"I think that hurt worse than getting shot." Maggie hissed. But at least she was fully awake now.

"Yeah, it'll do that." Hailey stuck one of those huge eight-inch bandages over the wound and grabbed Maggie's forearms, half-pulling her to her feet. "Come on, we have to go."

Maggie was suddenly aware of Sean, Lydia, and an empty ATV parked a few feet away. Sean had a woman in front of him, bound hand and foot with duct tape and looking bemused. Lydia had a sniper rifle pointed lazily in the direction of their captive.

"Come on." Hailey pushed Maggie gently towards the empty ATV, then climbed on in front of her.

"What about mine?" Maggie asked.

"We're leaving it. You're in no condition to drive on your own." Hailey said. She started the engine and hunted behind her until she found Maggie's wrist. She pulled it around her waist. "Hang on so I know I didn't drop you."

Maggie wrapped her arms around Hailey obediently, leaning forward out of pure exhaustion. Who knew being shot could take so much out of you?

Maggie realized very quickly that Hailey had been wise not to let her drive herself. She barely registered the scenery around them, and it took absolutely all of her concentration – and, occasionally, Hailey gripping her hand in warning -- not to let go.

At some point, they stopped. Maggie hadn't noticed them veering off the road, but they were in the middle of the woods now. Sean was suddenly in front of her, helping Hailey unlatch Maggie's arms, then lifting Maggie gently from the seat.

Maggie had been aware of her size for years – it was hard not to be when she'd stopped growing at age eleven – but Sean's strong embrace made her feel like a child. Or maybe that was the delirium talking.

He set her down gently, leaning her head back to rest on a tree. Smiling, he handed her an open bottle of Gatorade. "Here. Replenish your electrolytes."

Maggie nodded, lifting the bottle to her lips. She'd thought Hailey was being overdramatic, making her buy all those medical supplies with her credit card when she was trying to draw the kidnapper out. Now she felt naïve for believing they could go up against a professional and end up unscathed.

And the kidnapper hadn't even been the gravity man. Maggie wondered where he was, then thought of Elliot and the others. Something cold crept up her spine and she hunted for her cellphone. When they'd figured out Kyle had gone missing, she'd been glad Elliot hadn't called to check on them. Now she was worried about why he hadn't.

"What's up?" Hailey asked, sitting down next to her.

"Nothing, I'm...nothing." Maggie put her phone away. Even if something was wrong, Elliot could handle it. Kyle had been right before – Maggie had no experience with this sort of thing. She wasn't one of them. Elliot was their leader. And besides, he was miles away. Even if he needed help, there was nothing she could do.

Anyway, she had her own crisis to worry about.

Maggie looked around until she saw the cousins casually interrogating their captive. "Do they need help, do you think?"

"Nah." Hailey waved a hand. "They've been interrogating their other cousins since they were kids; they have this Good Cop/Bad Cop routine down to a science. That's why I came over here; I'd just be in the way."

Maggie's eyes drifted to the bloody smears of handprints she'd left on Hailey's shirt. "Sorry." She said.

Hailey glared. "Don't you dare apologize! You were amazing back there! I've never seen anything like it."

Maggie scoffed and looked away. "I just have powers. I'm not like you guys."

"That's what makes it so incredible!" Hailey pinched Maggie's chin and forcibly turned her head. "You didn't sign up for this; you're just here because of what people did before you were born. But you still put your life on the line to help a guy you just met yesterday. You know what that tells me?"

"Hm."

"It tells me you're more like us than you realize. In fact, you might be right where you're supposed to be." She grinned.

Maggie's mouth opened and closed. Finally, she took a long drink of her Gatorade. "Are you a nurse or something?"

"Psychologist, remember? Why?"

"Oh, right. How did you know all that first aid stuff, then?"

Hailey half-smiled and looked away, picking at her jeans. "I have a hard time concentrating on one thing for a large amount of time. So I try to concentrate on lots of things for short amounts of time." She looked at Maggie and wiggled her fingers. "Jack of all trades, master of none."

Maggie smiled back. "But better than a master of one."

Hailey's eyes widened. "Hey, I like that! I'm going to start saying that now."

Maggie giggled. "That's just the rest of the saying."

"Wait, really?" Hailey looked mystified. "Huh."

"Okay, we have a problem." Lydia said.

The two looked up at her.

"What?" Maggie asked.

Lydia rolled her eyes. "The lady – calls herself Siren – says she won't tell us where to find Kyle, but that she'll tell us how to call Grady – that's the gravity man's name – and we can do a 'hostage exchange.'"

Maggie narrowed her eyes. "She wants us to call the guy who wants to kill me and tell him exactly where to find us? Yeah, that's not happening."

"She says if she doesn't call Grady in half an hour, he'll kill Kyle."

"Half an hour from now?" Hailey asked. "Or half an hour from when she left?"

Lydia frowned. "Hang on a second." She walked back over to where Sean and Siren were.

"Good question." Maggie said.

Hailey shrugged, smiling.

Lydia came back over. "Half an hour from when she left."

"Which was?" Hailey prompted.

"About fifteen minutes ago."

Maggie's mouth felt dry.

"Hang on a second." Hailey pulled out her phone and opened a maps app. "I started a timer when Maggie used her credit card for the first time, and Siren started shooting about seventeen minutes later, which was five minutes after the last purchase. That means she has to be holding Kyle somewhere that's between five and seventeen minutes away. She was shooting at Maggie for four minutes, it took us three minutes to take her down, and we drove for about ten minutes before we got here. That makes twenty-three or thirty-four minutes."

Maggie's stomach dropped.

"Hey, hey, hey! What's with the face?!" Hailey said. "I'm not saying we're too late, I'm saying she has to be bluffing!"

"W-what?" Maggie struggled to focus on Hailey's voice and re-member how to breathe.

"Think about it!" Hailey looked between her friends. "If Grady was actually here, why would he send a human to take out a mutant when he basically wiped the floor with Maggie before? No offense."

"None taken."

"That's a good point." Lydia said, eyes widening. "He's probably not even here!"

"Which means we don't have to call him." Hailey said. She went back to looking at the map on her phone. "It's going to make a huge difference whether she walked or drove, though."

"Okay. Okay." Maggie felt like Grady had just stepped off her chest and her brain was shorting out from the sudden influx of oxygen. "Um. Why don't you two go check around the building you found her at and see if there's a car?"

"Sounds like a plan." Hailey smiled and stood up.

"Uh..." Maggie frowned. "Maybe you and I should stay here, actually."

Hailey raised an eyebrow. "Why's that?"

"We...kind of look like we murdered someone."

Hailey looked down at her t-shirt, stained with Maggie's handprints, and her own arms, which were covered in brown drying blood from her field dressing in the parking lot. "You have a point there."

"Are you sure you'll be okay by yourselves?" Lydia's forehead creased.

Maggie took a resolute swig of her Gatorade and nodded. "We'll be fine. Hailey can guard her, and I'll drink electrolytes until I can back her up."

"Call when you figure out if she drove," Hailey said. "I'll check the map and find possible hiding places."

"Thanks, Hails." Lydia nodded, then bounced over to tell Sean.

Siren looked annoyed that her plan had been foiled, which made Maggie grin. She was still worried about Grady, though. If he wasn't here, where was he? Should she call Elliot and warn him?

But if she called him, she'd have to tell him about Kyle being kidnapped. She knew she'd have to eventually, but she'd much rather do it after she'd already fixed the problem. Things tended to go over much better then.

She flexed her fingers over her phone and watched Sean hand Siren's rifle to Hailey, saluting the two of them before taking off with Lydia. They had this situation under control with one team member missing and no leader. And if they could do that, Elliot's A-Team could handle Grady without Maggie's help. There was no reason to call them. Not yet.

Chapter 17

Living on a Prayer

She'd only been in the hospital for an hour, but Adanna was already feeling the overpowering urge to move her arm. Every time she gave in and twitched, pain cut through the meds the doctors had given her and made her want to puke. The padding inside the cast was nice and soft, though.

She looked over at Elliot. The two of them were in the waiting room, sitting side by side in the pseudo-comfortable chairs. He was staring at the floor, arms crossed, and hadn't moved a muscle since she'd gotten her cast on.

Adanna frowned. It was so hard to read him sometimes. She'd known him almost his whole life; he'd only been a few months old when their parents had adopted him. She'd been three.

Her earliest memory was of his tiny eyes looking up at her from a face so strange in its creamy paleness. At three, she had been surrounded mostly by warm, dark skin like her own. After meeting Elliot, she'd thought babies were born peachy-white and grew darker as they got older until she'd met her Scandinavian kindergarten teacher.

From the time Elliot could move around on his own, the two of them were inseparable. They knew each other better than anyone else.

But still, sometimes, Adanna felt herself floundering. She knew her baby brother needed to be comforted, but she didn't know how to get past the anger on his face.

"Hey," She started by taking his hand in her unbroken one. "It's going to be alright."

His eyes looked up at her, unfamiliar in their brokenness. "You could have *died*."

Adanna squeezed his hand. "That's why we have to stop that guy, though." She narrowed her eyes at him, holding his gaze. "He's the one who did this. You know that, right?"

Elliot looked away. "I shouldn't have put you guys in danger."

"You didn't put us anywhere." She said. "We came of our own free will. We *knew* what we were going up against—"

"Don't give me that." Elliot scoffed, leaning away. "You didn't know he was that powerful, none of us did."

"We knew he had powers..."

"Yeah, but we thought his powers were like mine." Elliot looked down at his hands. "I've never done anything on that kind of scale...he *leveled* a whole *house*!"

"I was there." Adanna held up her cast. "Have you considered that you have never *tried* to level a house before? How do you know you're not capable of something you've never attempted?"

He looked at her like she was the crazy one.

"Don't give me that face." She pointed at him menacingly. "And don't sell yourself short! You have no idea what you're capable of, but I do. And I know that you can take this guy." She gave into her affection and bopped his nose.

Elliot smiled despite himself.

Adanna smiled back. "Of course, he's had decades more practice using his powers for evil, so you'll have to rely on me and the rest of your team to back you up."

Elliot's face fell. "Carly's been in surgery a long time."

Adanna sighed and wrapped her arm around her brother, pulling him close. "She's going to be okay."

"How do you know that?"

Adanna did not know that. She did know that their ability to pretend that they were immortal and that everything would always end well depended on Carly being okay. She knew that if Carly was okay, this manifestation of guilt and fear and despair that had them in a chokehold would fade over time. The wounds caused by the day would heal.

And if Carly wasn't okay...Adanna knew none of them would be either, especially her precious brother.

She stroked his hair like their mom had done when they had nightmares as kids. "I just know."

She noticed Nehemiah standing halfway across the room. He watched them, visibly conflicted about interrupting. Adanna rolled her eyes and gently pulled away from Elliot. "Hey, Nehemiah!" She called, waving her good arm.

Elliot looked over and forced a smile, waving.

Nehemiah joined them, sitting on Elliot's other side. "Are you okay, Adanna?"

"Just fine." She showed him her cast. "I busted my arm a little, because those people who let us use their living room are the kind who freeze in a crisis so I had to push them under the table."

"Wow." His eyes widened, because he'd seen the two towering over Adanna through the window when she and Carly had talked themselves inside. "You're pretty strong."

Adanna winked. "Was there ever any doubt?"

He smiled, posture relaxing. "Of course not." His expression slipped and he cleared his throat. "How's Carly?"

Elliot winced.

"She's going to be okay." Adanna tried to keep herself from sounding too forceful. "She's smart – as soon as she saw Grady move, she must have lunged under the desk. That gave her an air pocket, like the table did for us downstairs, and she was on the top floor so there wasn't much to collapse on her."

She glanced down. "She was right at the point of impact, though, so she was pretty bruised up. I think something came at her from the side and, uh," her mouth felt dry, "it stuck in her stomach. That's why she's in surgery right now."

Nehemiah's forehead creased.

"I wish there was something I could do." Elliot said, almost to himself.

Nehemiah bit his lip and brushed his bangs back. "I know you want to protect us all the time, Elliot, but you can't shield us from everything. Sometimes there are things that happen which you can't change. And then all you can do is pray."

Elliot sighed. "Okay." He said. "Will you?"

"Will I what?"

"Pray for Carly."

"Oh." Nehemiah nodded, then reached for his friends' hands.

Adanna bowed her head and tried not to think about how many things she had no control over.

Chapter 18

Vampire Assassins and Crimes Canceled Out

Sean pulled off the road near the town sign, Lydia right behind him. They hid their ATV's in the bushes and walked into town. If the police had talked to anyone at the grocery store, they'd be on the lookout for people on ATV's.

"How can we tell if the car is hers?" Lydia asked.

Sean shrugged. "Maybe it'll have a 'My Kid Has Killed More People than Your Honor Student' bumper sticker."

She laughed.

"How are you doing with all of this?" He glanced at his cousin out of the corner of his eye.

She lifted one shoulder and let it drop. "I don't think it's really sunk in yet. I mean, I feel fine, but that makes me nervous because people shouldn't feel fine in these kinds of situations."

"Sometimes it takes a while." Sean said. "When I woke up in the hospital after getting mugged, it took me probably two days to feel like it had actually happened."

"Really?"

"Yeah. I mean, I was in pain, but mentally it felt like a nightmare and not a memory."

"So I probably won't feel traumatized for a couple days?"

"Ask Hailey. I've never really been a psychology person." Sean smirked. "Let's hope it at least holds off until we're all back at the safe house."

"Yeah." Lydia forced a smile. "Uh, Sean?"

"Yeah?"

"Do you think Hailey was right about Siren bluffing us?"

Sean looked straight ahead. He felt like he'd rolled up in a toe-stand only to fall back down, landing too hard on his knees. If he kept his eyes on the road and just thought about the facts, he didn't have to be talking to his baby cousin about whether or not their friend was still alive.

"Probably." He said. *Anyway, if she's wrong, it's too late now.*

The grocery store where everything had happened was about halfway down Main Street, a five minute walk from the town line. Even before they could see it, the cousins could hear the sirens.

Squad cars had taken over the parking lot. Little flags and neon ribbon made the scene of the crime look like a dig site squared off by a drunken archeologist. The few civilians who were still in the parking lot were gesticulating wildly to policemen who nodded thoughtfully at their descriptions of a foiled creature slaying or the thwarted assassination of a telekinetic.

Sean and Lydia looked at the scene wearing their best confused expressions and crossed the street.

The building across from the grocery store was a comic book store/gaming center with windowsills which protruded out far enough and were spaced well enough that a very athletic someone could use them to climb onto the roof. That was how Siren probably gotten up there. It was definitely how Sean had gotten up. (Lydia and Hailey had taken the stairs.)

Fortunately, the building seemed to have shut down for the day after the shooting and the police hadn't traced the shots to their source yet. There was only one car parked off the alley in the back.

"Could it be this easy?" Lydia asked.

Sean bopped her on the head. "Don't jinx it."

They sauntered over to the hatchback and peered in the windows with all the casualness of people who have never broken into a car in their lives.

Despite being the only two people in the alley, Lydia felt the need to whisper. "What should we be looking for?"

"I don't know...handcuffs? Extra ammo? A copy of *Assassins Daily*?" Sean shook his head. "She outsmarted Maggie's force field; she probably didn't leave things laying around in plain sight."

"Although she did respond pretty quickly to our summons." Lydia frowned. "We're probably going to have to break in to find anything incriminating."

"But what if it's not her car?"

Lydia shrugged. "Then all our years of playing Cops and Robbers will hopefully pay off. Have you ever broken into a car before?"

Sean bit his lip. "Uhm, I've *watched* someone break into a car before."

His cousin raised her eyebrow.

Sean scratched the back of his head. "The guys I shared an apartment with in college went to a different university, and one day mine was cancelled but they still had to go, so we thought it would be smart if I rode along with them and then drove the car back afterwards."

Lydia, a college student, nodded sagely. "To avoid paying for parking. Smart."

"Yeah, but I locked the passenger side door out of habit when we got there and didn't realize my buddy had left the keys in the car for me until all the doors were shut."

Lydia grinned. "Oh no! Who broke in?"

"The guy whose car it was. He had a suit on a hanger that he'd borrowed from the school closet for a mock debate. It was one of those retro wire hangers, so he unwound it while we held his clothes and did this thing..." Sean looked around. "We need something to wedge the top of the door open."

"Like what?"

"Uh. Something really thin, like a knife or a paint scraper."

"The one time I leave my paint scraper at home!"

"Hilarious. Do you have a knife?"

"Hm." Lydia rolled up the right leg of her boot cut jeans to reveal a sheath strapped to her calf. She pulled the knife out with a flourish, grinning.

Sean blinked. "Why...?"

She rolled her eyes. "Dude, I'm like, barely five feet tall."

"You know you're more likely to get attacked by someone you know than a stranger, right?"

"Yeah, and who do I hang out with all day, cousin?"

"Touché."

Lydia crossed her arms and raised an eyebrow. "So? Do you have a retro hanger strapped to your leg or something?"

"Don't need one." Sean grinned. "We can just unscrew the antennae."

"Fascinating."

Sean held out one hand. "Okay, this is the part where you keep a lookout for the cops and let me do my thing."

"You saw it done once and now it's your thing?"

"Yeah, well, all this technology has me hardwired for instant gratification."

Lydia scoffed and moved to lean back against the building on the opposite side of the alley. This way, she'd be able to see anyone coming from either direction. Probably not before they'd see Sean doing something suspicious, but as long as he had enough of a head start he could probably parkour away.

Lydia wasn't quite sure what she would do in that scenario. Probably hang back, tell the cops she thought he was trying to break into his own car. She could play dumb with the best of them. And if she did get arrested, it wasn't like they could hold her on anything or like the team wouldn't be able to survive without her.

No. Bad brain. Don't go there.

"Ha! Got it." Sean grinned.

"Congratulations. Hurry up and get done with the criminal activity before the cops come over here to investigate where the shooter was."

Sean rolled his eyes. "So bossy." He crawled into the car anyway.

He looked around, talking softly to himself to keep his nerves under control. "If I were an assassin, where would I put evidence which might incriminate me?"

He went for the obvious; the glovebox. There was a map with several buildings circled in blue ink, the owner's manual, and a tube of lipstick. Sean shook the tube, remembering a documentary he'd watched on Cold War espionage. It didn't sound like there was anything hidden inside.

He pocketed the map and flipped the visors down. A paper fluttered down into his lap. "Huh." He looked it over, then pulled out his phone and dialed Hailey.

"*Hello?*"

"Hey Hails. Does Siren have an ID on her?" He asked.

"*Let me check. Talk to Maggie.*"

"Wha—who's this?"

"It's Sean."

"*Oh, hi. Did you find the car?*"

"I hope so. Otherwise I just committed a crime."

"*Pretty sure breaking and entering is always a crime.*"

"No way; if you do crime things to a criminal, the two cancel each other out."

"*I don't think that's how it works.*"

"Well, you're pretty new to the game. Trust me; that's how it works."

"*Okay then – Are you okay?*"

The phone barely picked up Hailey's voice in the background. "*Fine. She freaking bit me, though.*"

"Whoa, no way!"

"*Yeah, I think she's a vampire. Tell Sean to pick up some garlic on his way back.*"

"*You tell him.*" There were sounds of passing the phone.

"*Hey, Sean.*"

"So, she's a vampire, huh?"

"*Unfortunately.*"

"Did she have her ID on her?"

"*Yeah. It says her name is Mary Jones, but it's probably an alias. What did you need it for, anyway?*"

"I wanted to compare it to the proof of insurance I found in the car." Sean slid the paper in his pocket and got out of the car. "It matches. The car is hers."

"Ok, cool. Is the hood warm?"

"Lemme check." He walked around to the front of the car and felt the hood. "Yeah, a little. It's been over half an hour, though."

"So she drove there, then." Hailey said. *"Which makes sense. She'd have to be her own getaway driver, after all."*

Sean dug the map out of his pocket. "I also found this map in the glovebox. It has a bunch of buildings circled."

"That's incredibly convenient. Check those out first and call back if you find Kyle or if we need to go to Plan B."

"Will do." Sean hung up and grinned at Lydia. "Alright! Let's go on a scavenger hunt."

Chapter 19

The Night Watch

*C*arly cursed and ejected the casing and slammed the bolt back into place faster than she ever had, but she was still trying to line up her sight again when Grady turned murderous eyes on the house.

Carly's breath caught in her throat and she desperately fired again.

The bullet went wild.

Grady raised his hand.

Carly dropped back on her butt, looking around wildly. She dove under the nearby desk just as the ceiling started to cave in. The whole world shook and crumbled around her, and she curled up into a ball.

She was going to die and she wanted to pray but the only thing that came to mind was a scream so she screamed and hoped God understood until something cut through her side and the pain drove the air from her lungs.

Then there was just the pain and the darkness and she lost touch with everything else. Time froze, that one moment stretching towards infinity.

Carly opened her eyes. She was still in that moment of pain, but the darkness was gone and there was a different ceiling in its place. The rest of her body materialized around the agony in her side. She felt like she was being sketched back into existence bit by bit.

Something touched her shoulder and she turned, muscles moaning in complaint.

Wendell smiled softly at her. "Hey, sleepy head."

Carly blinked and time started up again. "Hey."

"You had us worried for a minute." He said. "Almost gave Elliot a heart attack, poor guy. I hope you're sorry."

She laughed and immediately groaned when her abdominal muscles protested the motion. "Ahhh. Trust me, I'm very sorry." She rolled her shoulders and pulled her arms back, trying to move herself to a sitting position.

"Whoa, whoa, what do you think you're doing?" Wendell pushed down on her forehead until she flopped back on the bed. "Haven't you ever been in a hospital before? There is a strict No Moving Without Permission rule."

Carly pouted. "Hospitals are the GDR now?"

"Yes, they are all embassies and therefore everything on the premises is subject to the laws of the country they represent. Try to keep up." But his smile was kind and he ruffled her hair. "You look sleepy."

"I feel like I pulled every muscle in my body at once." She lifted a hand to poke at the stabbing pain that had been strong enough to remain while the rest of the world disappeared. That was a mistake, and she threw her head back, hissing until the fire burned itself out.

Wendell was holding her hand when she came to. "Idiot." He said softly. "You took a piece of wall to the tummy. Missed all your internal organs, though, not quite sure how you managed that. Try a little harder next time and you might have a story to brag about later."

"I'll do my best." Carly huffed. "Where are the others?"

"Well," He glanced at his watch. "Elliot's on guard duty while Nehemiah and Adanna sleep."

"Guard duty...?" Her eyes widened. "You got her?"

Wendell grinned. "Oh yeah! You should've seen it – she was on her motorcycle and Nehemiah just grabbed her off it while she was riding past!"

Carly laughed and winced again. "Please tell me you got video!"

"Unfortunately, no." Wendell sighed.

"You had one job."

"I know." His eyes fell to the blanket and his smile slipped.

Carly let her own expression relax and turned back to the ceiling. "So, how bad is it?"

"Would you like to be less cryptic?"

She smirked. "How far over our heads are we?"

Wendell laughed shortly. "We're up against a mutant who has not only been hiding from the government for years, but can also crush a house without breaking a sweat. And he's beaten both of our mutants."

"Hm." Carly licked her lips. "I'm not sure this is something we can handle."

"Me neither, but what choice do we have?"

"I don't know." Carly rubbed her eyes with the back of one hand. "This was fun when we were up against petty criminals or even dangerous humans, because Elliot could always take them down if things got out of hand. But this..."

"...This isn't an easy fix." Wendell said.

"Yeah." She closed her eyes. "I think Adanna is right."

"About what?"

"You know 'about what.'"

He looked away. "I don't know if Elliot will agree. And I don't think it's fair for us to make him decide."

"You're right." Carly let her hand hover above her stomach. "I have a pretty good idea of how much I need to adjust the elevation of the shot now. And it's always easier to aim for the center of mass."

"Gravity might be greater at the center of mass."

"Gravity works the same way on everything regardless of mass, what were you doing in physics class, sleeping?"

"Maybe."

Carly let her fingers touch the sheet on top of her, feather-light and shaking. "It's not murder if it's self-defense, right?"

Wendell was quiet for a long time. Finally, he pulled her hand away from her stomach and held it tightly. "If you have an opening," he said, "do it. Kill Grady."

In the van outside, Adanna and Nehemiah were curled up in the middle and back seats. Adanna had an arm slung over her eyes to block the afternoon sun. If they were going to be able to keep an eye on Delilah all night, they needed to sleep now.

"Why don't you get some sleep?" Elliot suggested, keeping his voice down so he wouldn't wake the others.

"Do *you* sleep, Gemini Beta?"

Elliot breathed through his nose. His mom had told him time and time again to watch himself when he was tired and stressed, because things would upset him more than they might otherwise.

"Of course I sleep." He said. "I'm human."

"Close enough, anyway." She conceded. She tilted her head. "What are you feeling right now?"

He blinked. "Why do you care?"

"It's not so much care as professional curiosity." She said. "I haven't been able to observe you for years. You and Gemini Alpha are my greatest achievements. I was so looking forward to watching you grow."

Elliot couldn't decide if that was sweet or creepy.

No; no, it was definitely creepy.

"Tell me about Grady."

"Tell me about yourself."

"This is serious."

"I'm being serious." Delilah brushed a strand of hair behind her ear. "This is how things work in the real world, Gemini Beta. If you want something from someone, you have to give something in return. It's basic economics."

Elliot narrowed his eyes. "Grady didn't come to your house to reminisce about the old days," he said, "you have as much to gain from stopping him as I do."

"Hm." She smiled. "If you want to succeed – really succeed – you have to be willing to give up a lot of things. You have to be so motivated that nothing distracts you. Not a family, not friends, not hobbies. If you really want something, you don't have a life outside it." She leaned forward. "What I'm saying is that the Kobold and Gemini projects *were* my life. So, if I have to die to see the outcomes of my research, I'm willing to do that."

Elliot clenched his fists. He tried not to look at Adanna, tried not to think about Carly. Delilah was trying to play him. She might even be bluffing. He should talk to his team before making any huge decisions. Also, nobody should make big decisions so soon after a traumatic event. He should tell her he'd think about it and get back to her later.

"What do you want to know?" He asked.

Chapter 20

Turnabout is Fair Play

When the call disconnected, Hailey hit the power button to turn her screen off and put her phone back in her pocket. She tried not to move, because Maggie was cleaning the bite wound on her arm with a serious look on her face.

"It's not that bad." Hailey felt the need to protest, especially since the person so gently handling her wound was the same person who'd taken a shot across the ribs.

"Mm." Maggie was concentrating too hard for words. She finished wiping off the alcohol she'd used and grabbed one of the leftover bandages. "Don't minimize your pain."

Hailey blinked.

Maggie pressed the bandage gently over the wound.

Hailey opened her mouth to respond.

Siren shot through the air in a blur, leaping to kick Maggie in the head. Her skull slammed into the ATV she was leaning on, and she collapsed in a heap.

Hailey immediately moved to make sure Maggie was okay. It was sheer willpower that made her lunge backwards to avoid Siren's next strike.

Don't worry about Maggie. Focus on the fight.

Hailey kicked at Siren's knees, but the mercenary dodged, twisting and channeling the lost balance into a fist that Hailey blocked with her forearm. White pain blinded her for a second when the hit landed directly on her bite mark. She grunted and ducked under a second strike.

Hailey snapped a fist into Siren's stomach, then followed up with a knee to the face when she doubled over.

Siren laughed, dodging a follow-up punch. "You're good for a cosplayer."

"And you're not bad for an arrogant – uh – narcissist." She grimaced at the redundancy and took a left hook for her efforts.

Siren kicked Hailey in the chest when she reacted to the hook, knocking her to the ground. "It's not arrogance if you can back it up."

"Pretty sure you stole that from someone." Hailey said, rolling to stand.

Siren kicked her back down and dropped to land hard with a knee on her chest. "Possession is nine tenths of the law, sweetie."

Hailey gasped, air knocked from her lungs, and pushed at the knee.

"You'll learn that someday." Siren twirled a small knife between her fingers. "You'll also learn to always keep at least one trick up your sleeve."

Hailey threw a fist at Siren's stomach, but it was caught before it could land.

Siren squeezed the captive wrist. "These knives are great for cutting through ropes or tape," she continued, "but it takes *forever* to kill someone with them." She let her eyes drift towards the rifle that laid next to Maggie and the ATV. "*That* on the other hand, kills people very quickly. I like you, so I'm going to make you a deal."

"Don't even bother." Hailey glared.

"Hear me out." Siren said.

"As if I have a choice."

"I'm going to deprive your body of air until you pass out. Then, I'm going to take my rifle and head back to the abandoned donut shop where I'm holding your little friend. I'll probably get there at the same time those other two do, which means *I'll* be surprising *them* this time around. They won't stand a chance.

"When you and your pet freak wake up, you're going to come to the donut shop and we'll do a little prisoner exchange. You four humans will then leave and go about your business. My employer really has no interest in you, anyway." Siren grinned widely. "Got it?"

Hailey glowered. "You aren't going to get away with it."

"You may be right." Siren nodded slowly. "I'll probably kill *it* once you leave and get away with just myself."

Hailey tried to throw Siren off so she could pound her face in, but the woman just laughed and pressed her knee down harder on Hailey's sternum.

She patted Hailey's face. "Don't worry; I'll be quick. It won't feel a thing." Then she put her hand over Hailey's mouth and nose. "Neither will you."

~

About eight miles away, Sean and Lydia had already checked out three of the four buildings circled on the map. The last one they came to was an abandoned donut shop. The windows were boarded over, the sign faded, and a FOR SALE sticker was starting to peel off the door.

"It looks like this place has been for sale since the recession." Sean said.

"But look at this." Lydia pointed to a trail of bent grass that led around the side of the building.

The cousins followed it to a back door, which was unlocked. The inside of the building was dark, the smell of dust and decay wafting out to them like cologne from Aeropostle. Sean wrinkled his nose.

"Ladies first."

"Age before beauty." Lydia countered.

Sean laughed and stepped inside. "Hello? Kyle?"

"Wait, what if Siren left someone behind to guard him?" Lydia whispered.

Sean looked over his shoulder at her. "You probably should have said that before I started yelling." He whispered back.

"You probably shouldn't have started yelling before I said that."

Sean stuck his tongue out at her.

Lydia returned the gesture.

Sean tilted his head as if listening for noises from inside. "Well," he said, "we're not dead yet, so I think it's safe."

"Oh goody." Lydia said.

"Kyle!" Sean led the way into the darkness.

"Over here!"

The cousins exchanged glances, then ran towards their teammate's voice. He was tied up to a chair that had fallen on its side. Half his face was dirty from laying on the floor, and he was shivering. Goosebumps covered his exposed upper body. He struggled when he saw them.

"Guys! You have to listen to me. Maggie—"

"Came up with an awesome plan that resulted in the capture of your kidnapper? Yeah. We know." Sean grinned.

Lydia unsheathed her knife again. "Hold still." She said as she started sawing at the tape, careful not to nick Kyle's skin.

"Wait, really?" His eyes widened. "How did *that* happen?"

"I'll let her tell the story. Now," Sean's smile disappeared and his eyes darkened as he took off his jacket. "Did that bitch hurt you?"

Kyle blinked. "I don't think I've ever heard you swear before."

"She deserves it. Did she?"

"No, I'm good. I..." he couldn't help a shudder when he remembered Siren playing with her knife. "I'm just cold. You guys had great timing with that credit card stunt, actually."

Sean nodded and moved out of the way so Lydia could free Kyle's other wrist. Kyle sat up as soon as he could, rolling his wrists and hissing as they woke up. Sean handed over his jacket.

"So, where is she?"

Sean wasn't sure if Kyle meant Maggie or Siren, but the answer was the same anyway. "In the woods. We caused a bit of a scene in the grocery store parking lot, so we had to regroup off the highway before Lydia and I came back to get you."

"Okay." Kyle tried to stand, but hissed when he put weight on his sleeping ankles and feet.

"Hey, hey, don't worry about it." Lydia put a hand on his shoulder, which offered the dual benefit of comfort and holding him on the ground. "We can wait. We're not in a hurry."

It took a few minutes for Kyle to feel ready to stand. Sean offered to carry him, but was shot down with a venomous glare. That just made him smile bigger; he hadn't been sure he'd ever see that hate-filled expression again.

But now they'd found Kyle and Siren was in their custody. They could ask her questions about the gravity man. Not to mention Elliot would be so excited that his sister was starting to fit in.

This time, Lydia led the way out. They made their way through the dark like a human version of the bars that measured cell signals. Kyle could see over Lydia, and Sean could see over Kyle, which meant they could all see Siren blocking the exit, leaning casually up against her stolen ATV.

Her posture was lazy, but her finger was on the trigger of her rifle and her eyes were sharp. "You know," she said, "it's rude to come over without calling first. I'm expecting guests at any minute."

Chapter 21

Some Things Happen for a Reason

When the nurse came in to check on Carly, Wendell hid behind the bathroom door. Technically, Carly was supposed to only have visitors for fifteen minutes, but Elliot wanted to make sure someone was with her at all times just in case Grady found out she survived and attacked the hospital.

Carly pretended to be asleep, but by the time the nurse left she wasn't pretending anymore. Wendell smiled at her and took a seat under the window. Anyone walking by the room wouldn't be able to see him unless they ducked to see under Carly's bed.

He yawned and pulled out his phone, hoping that the whole blue-light-keeps-you-awake thing was true. He couldn't play a game and risk being too caught up to notice a nurse coming in, so he opened his Messages and started a new conversation.

[Wendell]: Hey, Elliot

[Elliot]: How'd you know I was up?

[Wendell]: Cuz I'm magic, duh

[Elliot]: lol

[Elliot]: How's Carly??

[Wendell]: She's ok! □ She woke up about half an hour ago, but she's sleeping again now.

[Elliot]: Oh good

[Wendell]: How are you?

[Elliot]: I'm fine.

[Wendell]: Try again.

[Elliot]: I'm not the one who got crushed by a house

[Wendell]: Nah, you're the one who finds some sort of masochistic pleasure in taking responsibility for all the world's problems.

[Elliot]: Just the ones I'm responsible for

[Wendell]: Well you're not responsible for this one

[Elliot]: Lying is wrong

[Wendell]: It's true

[Wendell]: TBH if anyone's responsible for this, it's Carly

[Elliot]: ????

[Wendell]: She didn't take him out like she was supposed to.

[Wendell]: I see that you're typing a lot.

[Wendell]: How long is this paragraph going to be?

[Wendell]: Can I at least explain myself before you kill me?

[Elliot]: That's completely ridiculous! We weren't even sure it was possible to account for the gravitational field's effects and she did! So what if it wasn't in the right place? She still did her job. My job was to keep Grady busy and protect Adanna and Carly. I failed. Not to mention it was my plan that put Carly at risk in the first place. If we would've just grabbed Delilah and left instead of trying to be clever, that never would have happened. I shouldn't have put them in that situation and I should have protected them regardless and I didn't. So don't tell me it's not my fault or try and convince me with some stupid blame game because I don't want to hear it. You weren't even there.

[Elliot]: Go ahead. Explain yourself.

[Wendell]: First of all, you need to back the flip up because you are way too close to the picture. Yeah it was your plan, but it was a CONTINGENCY plan in case Grady DID show up. And it's a good thing we had one, because otherwise a lot of people would probably have died. Also, Carly was the one who said she'd try to shoot him and she's a big girl. Taking responsibility for her choices is just insulting. With your logic, you could say that it's Maggie's fault for telling us about the field in the first place or it's Delilah's fault for starting the project. The only one who is responsible for hurting our friends is THE GUY WHO HURT OUR FRIENDS. Besides without Carly shooting him he definitely would have killed you and probably the rest of us. So shut up and accept that this isn't your fault or I will come down there and kick your superhuman butt all the way back to the safe house.

[Elliot]: ...

[Elliot]: I still feel like I should've done something.

[Wendell]: Just because you feel it doesn't make it true. Some people felt like Hitler was right. Doesn't mean he wasn't actually a genocidal maniac.

[Elliot]: □ That's kind of an extreme example

[Wendell]: Deal with it.

[Wendell]: Hang on, I think someone's coming.

In the parking lot, Elliot smiled softly at his phone before powering off the screen and turning back to Delilah.

She raised an eyebrow. "You seem conflicted."

"I just..." Elliot pressed his lips together and frowned at the floor. Maybe Wendell was right. Maybe this wasn't his fault. *But if I have the chance to get information on how to stop Grady and I don't take it, it will be my fault. This changes nothing.* "Nothing. Never mind. What was your next question?"

Delilah smiled softly. "How about we take a break?"

Elliot glared at her. "How about you stop pretending you care? I'm already giving you what you want."

"You know, if we're going to work together to stop Grady, you're going to need to trust me at some point."

"I trust you to act in your own best interest." Elliot said. "That's all I need to do."

"Alright." She shrugged. "Tell me more about how you sense energy. Is it just electrical impulses?"

Elliot nodded. "As far as I can tell, yes. I mean, I can sense man-made electricity and the electric charges that happen naturally. They feel different – man-made electricity feels more structured and uniform. Comparing it to natural electricity is like comparing a brick house to a tree. Did your mind games work on Grady?"

Delilah rolled her eyes. "You act like I'm a con artist – I have a background in psychology, I didn't get my PhD in manipulation. Yes, I can be persuasive, but I can't hypnotize you."

"So, did your mind games work on Grady?"

She sighed. "Any degree of persuasion is based on a foundation of trust. How much does the person trust you? How much do they trust your information? At first, Grady trusted me because we both worked for the government and he had a sort of naïve belief that the checks and balances meant the government was somewhere between lawful and chaotic good."

"And you think it's not?"

She raised an eyebrow. "Who am I to say if it is or isn't? Life is 90% interpretation. Whatever Grady experienced, he interpreted to mean that the government was bad and must be destroyed."

"So what did he experience?" Elliot frowned. "You keep saying that Grady started out loyal, then ended up killing a bunch of people. I feel like you're skipping a few steps."

"You certainly are your father's son." Delilah scoffed. "He was always looking for the reasons behind everything. Always thought people were justified in their own minds. He never understood random acts of violence, everyone had to have a backstory."

She leaned forward. "Sometimes people just decide to kill other people, and there's no reason for it. Not even to them."

Elliot looked away. "That might happen sometimes, but most of the time people have reasons for what they do. And I'm pretty sure Grady's one of them."

"Why's that?"

"Because this violence isn't random." He looked back to her. "He's not just lashing out at people, he's specifically targeting Project Kobold and anyone connected to it. There has to be some sort of motive."

She shrugged. "He could just be holding a petty grudge."

Elliot's eyes crackled with electricity. "You agreed to answer my questions if I answered yours. No BS. *Tell me what is going on.*"

She looked at him for a long time. Then, sighing, she uncrossed her arms. "When I tell you that I don't know for sure why Grady and your parents turned on the Project, I'm telling the truth. They were the best of the best before the procedure, and afterwards they became such a tight-knit group that we wouldn't have been surprised if they'd developed telepathy as a side-effect.

"What I do know is that it had something to do with you and your sister." Her upper lip curled as she said it. "It wasn't until Kobold Gamma became pregnant that things started going downhill. She and your paternal donor, Kobold Beta, were suddenly irritable and opposed to the testing. Words like 'objectification' and 'heartless' were thrown around, but I was sure they weren't the type to turn on us." She grimaced. "We should have tested their psychological states more thoroughly."

Elliot literally bit his tongue. "What did Grady have to do with anything?"

She scoffed. "Kobold Alpha was always an odd mix of follower and leader. He'd latch onto a cause, then serve it like a bull in a china shop. The best thing that could happen in a formal debate would be for him to disagree with you. If I had to guess, it was your parents who came up with the idea of sinking the project and Alpha who came up with the strategy."

Elliot nodded slowly. "He's still trying to sink the project, isn't he?"

Delilah inclined her head. "Probably just tying up a few loose ends."

Elliot shuddered. "Okay," he said, "so how do we stop him?"

Chapter 22

So Far Over Our Heads We Can't See the Surface

In the forest, Maggie attempted to listen as Hailey explained the situation. She felt like the entire left side of her face was one giant bruise.

"That doesn't make sense." She said. "Why wouldn't she just kill us now? Is this some sort of game to her?"

"Who knows?" Hailey paced back and forth in front of her. "Maybe? She seems crazy enough for that."

Maggie prodded her face gently and winced. "She must have some sort of plan. Why else would she tell us exactly where to find her?"

"I don't know. I don't *know!*" Hailey grabbed a fistful of her own hair, then seemed to come back to herself. She forced her fist to open, her fingers to let go. "We need to outsmart her. Somehow."

Maggie shook her head. "This lady is confusing. Is she trying to psyche us out? Her bullets aren't going to be much of a game changer when I stop them in midair."

"Maybe she's going to hold Kyle and the others at gunpoint or something. I mean, how quickly can you stop bullets?" Hailey asked.

"I'd probably just focus on stopping the gun." Maggie ran her fingers through her hair. "Not sure how accurate I'd be with this headache, though. Um...do you have weapons and stuff at the safe house?"

Hailey scoffed. "What kind of safe house doesn't have weapons?"

"Right. What was I thinking? Okay, let's head back there and grab some of those first."

"How do you know Siren won't just kill the others if we don't show up?"

Maggie opened her mouth. She closed her mouth. She shrugged. "They're not the ones she really wants."

Chapter 23

No Pain No Gain

When Carly opened her eyes – apparently she'd fallen asleep, when had that happened? – the first thing she thought was, *I really need to pee.* She remembered before sitting up that she'd been impaled, which didn't dissuade her from sitting up but did ensure that she did so much slower and more carefully than she would have otherwise.

The pain seemed to have manifested in the shape of the rod that had skewered her. Even pushing herself up with her arms made her abdominal muscles whine like toddlers deprived of ice cream.

"Whoa, whoa, whoa," Hands gripped her elbows, trying to take the weight off her abs.

"'m fine, Elliot." Carly located his face and smiled. "It's just some torn muscle. Like a really intense workout."

"What kind of workouts are you doing?" His voice was strained, but it was good to hear him make a joke. "Why are you trying to stand, anyway?"

She looked him dead in the eyes. "I have to use the little sniper's room."

He winced. Carly wasn't sure whether it was from the awkwardness or the fact that she'd mentioned her sniper status. "Uh. Do you...need...help...?"

"I would literally rather get stabbed again."

His expression was doused with relief. "Me too. I mean, *I'd* rather get stabbed! I don't want you to get stabbed again. Ever. Uh, I could probably get a nurse, though."

Carly waved a hand in his face. "I'm not the kind of girl who gets naked with strangers."

"Did they stop giving you drugs in the middle of the night or something? I heard irritability is a symptom of withdrawal."

"*Caffeine* withdrawal, maybe. Why don't you make yourself useful and raid the nurse's lounge or something? Meanwhile, I'll relieve myself of some of this discomfort."

"Oh! Right." Elliot gently removed his hands and stepped away.

Despite herself, Carly wavered a bit without his help. But she was not an invalid, she was not mortally wounded, and her friends would never listen to her if she told them they had to leave when she couldn't even walk to the bathroom on her own.

Elliot waited, watching her until she shut the door to the adjoining room. She leaned back against it, giving her aching side a break, until she heard footsteps moving out to the hallway.

Belatedly, she wondered whether visiting hours had officially started yet. Before she'd fallen asleep, she remembered it being yesterday. Was it still yesterday? She checked the clock next to the door. It was almost midnight. So...yes. It was still yesterday. And visiting hours hadn't started yet.

After taking care of business, she washed her hands slowly and thoroughly, leaning against the basin. She heard footsteps coming back into the room and gritted her teeth before pushing away. She looked at her reflection in the mirror, trying to move her face into a less agonized expression.

Elliot wasn't back yet, but a nurse was staring at her like she'd just said she didn't want pain medicine during labor.

"You're up."

Biting back a sarcastic reply was very difficult after spending a lot of time exclusively with people she was comfortable with. Like; surprisingly difficult. But she managed. "I had to pee."

"Of course, I'm just...surprised to see you walking on your own."

I've actually been doing that since I was one and a half. Carly swallowed. *Let the easy ones go.* "Yup. Guess I heal quickly."

The nurse's professionalism enveloped her surprise and she straightened. "Maybe so, but I'd like to take a look at you anyway."

"Sure." Carly attempted to keep her expression casual. "Mind if I take a seat?" The entire bottom half of her torso felt like it was on fire.

The nurse gestured to the bed, unknowingly mimicking Elliot's Hawk Eyes™. Carly felt triumphant when she sat down without gasping, grunting, groaning, or making any other verbal indication that she was in pain.

"So." The nurse said. "How are you feeling?"

"I have this weird pain in my stomach." *Dang it!* She really was polite to strangers, she was sure of it. It was that stupid house's fault.

The nurse smirked. "Is it a stabbing pain, a throbbing pain, or an aching pain?"

"Um. Stabbing, I think. It feels like the rod is still there, but the rod is just made of pain. Is that what stabbing pain feels like?"

The nurse smiled as if they were discussing how they liked their coffee. "Something like that. I'm going to check your wound now. I want to make sure your little quest didn't reopen it."

Carly paled. She hadn't even thought about that. "I don't – I didn't feel anything snap or whatever."

"Your body may not have made a distinction between it and the general pain of the wound." The nurse said. "Lie down."

Carly started to lower herself slowly, but that required ab muscles so she let herself drop. Which jarred her wound. *I can't catch a break.* She glanced at the doorway and saw Elliot start to come in with two cups, notice the nurse, and pivot mid-step to keep walking.

The nurse lifted the edge of Carly's hospital gown and prodded at her side. Carly hissed.

"I believe that was a stabbing pain." She said through her teeth.

"Hm." The nurse kept prodding, moving her fingers around to different parts of Carly's side like she was testing for wiggly blocks to pull out of a Jenga tower; cautious, but firm.

Now that the nurse's fingers had moved away from ground zero, the poking hurt less and Carly was able to keep her mouth shut. She stared at the ceiling. It was just plain white, which was boring.

Hospital ceilings should be decorated if people have to stare at them all day. Maybe with optical illusions or glow-in-the-dark stars. They could even mount the TV into the ceiling above the bed! Of course, falling TV's are apparently a major cause of annual deaths. Then again, if someone had to get hit by a falling TV, this would be the place to do it.

"There isn't any blood coming through," the nurse said, "but as long as I'm here I'm going to redress it."

"Cool." Carly didn't know the polite response to that statement. "Thanks."

The nurse explained what she was doing as she did it, and Carly did her best to remember. A few steps were particularly painful and she didn't hear them over the white-hot agony that demanded her brain's full attention.

"How are you feeling?" The nurse asked again.

"Fine." Carly lied. "Hungry."

"Your heartrate is elevated, so you're not 'fine.'"

Traitor. "I'm fine enough for waffles." Carly looked at her. "Do you have waffles here? And coffee. Oh! And bacon." She frowned. "You'd think I'd be less hungry with a hole in my side. Less of me to feed and all that."

The nurse smirked. "Healing takes a lot out of you. I'll get you a midnight snack, but it's going to have to be something a little easier on your stomach than all that."

"Hmph." Carly stuck out her lower lip.

The nurse was amused and left to get the promised food. She was barely gone a minute before Elliot sauntered in. He set the coffees down on a side table and helped Carly sit up.

"I'm fine." She insisted the whole time. "Really, I'm fine. I'm *fine.*"

"I'd be a lot less worried if you weren't a self-sacrificing liar." Elliot told her. He grabbed the little Styrofoam cups and handed her one. "Try to finish it before the nurse comes back, I'm pretty sure you're not supposed to have this."

"I appreciate you going against your better judgement for my sake."

Elliot shrugged. "Well, you took a house for me, so..."

Carly rested her cup on her thigh so she could focus on glaring. "Don't you dare blame yourself for that. I'm a big girl, and I don't appreciate you taking credit for my actions. It's very rude. And insulting."

Elliot frowned. "You and Wendell talked, didn't you?"

"Maybe." Carly took another sip of her coffee. "So, after the nurse serves me this 'good for your tummy' breakfast, how about we bust out of here?"

"What? No way." He crossed his arms. "You're staying in here until the doctor lets you out."

"You know, normally I'd agree—"

"Would you now?"

Carly leveled a glare at him. "Ok, normally I'd protest because being in a hospital is boring, but this time I have a legitimate excuse. We have to think about what might happen if the gravity guy—"

"Grady."

"—yeah, him -- tracks us here. There are, like, a million sick people in this building who aren't going to be able to run away if he decides to do some renovations." Carly's eyes widened when she saw Elliot's reaction. "Oh no...no, don't do that. Don't do that with the face."

"I'm not doing anything!"

"Yeah, you are. You're doing the face."

"This is my normal face!"

"It's your normal face with an ASPCA puppy expression on it."

"Are you serious?" Suddenly, Elliot's eyes widened and he dove under the bed.

The nurse walked in with a tray. "Breakfast is served." She put the plate down on the side table, then frowned at the Styrofoam cup sitting on it. "Where did this come from?"

"It's not mine." Carly said. "I'm holding it for someone else."

The nurse rolled her eyes and picked up the cup. "You shouldn't be having caffeine yet."

"I absolutely agree. That would be irresponsible. And unhealthy. I assume."

"You assume correctly." The nurse started out the door. "Now eat up. Your body needs to replenish its energy."

As soon as she was gone, Elliot crawled out the other side of the bed, peeking over Carly's legs to make sure no one else was coming.

Carly shoved a forkful of egg into her mouth. "Yeah, there's that disgusting hospital taste I know and love."

Elliot crossed his arms and pouted, but he couldn't argue with her keep-the-innocent-people-safe logic. His face scrunched together in a final grimace before he stood up and set his burner down next to her plate. "Call Adanna if anything happens. Her number is the first one on the Recent Calls list."

"Whe' you goi'g?" She asked around her food.

"If we're taking you out of the hospital, fine, but we're not leaving without pain medicine."

Carly swallowed. She hadn't thought about the fact that she was on pain medicine. She really did not want to find out what her side felt like without it. "Good plan. Wait, why can't I call Nehemiah or Wendell?"

"They're across town with Delilah. Adanna's across the street."

"What are they doing across town?"

Chapter 24

Playing Games

"**W**ell, this is embarrassing." Sean said, tugging at his bound wrists.

"Yeah. You guys suck at rescuing people." Kyle huffed.

Lydia rolled her eyes.

They were sitting against the donut shop's wall in a row, leaning against their wrists which were tied behind their backs. Their ankles were bound in front of them. A few feet away, Siren sat cross-legged on a chair, scrolling through her phone with her rifle resting on her lap.

Kyle hadn't taken his eyes off her since she'd surprised them at the doorway. His shoulders were hunched inside Sean's jacket. He felt like a kid trying to hide under their blanket from the monsters. But Siren hadn't touched any of them outside of tying them up.

In fact, she seemed to almost be ignoring them. Blue light from her phone's screen flickered on her face and her mouth twitched occasionally. Kyle wasn't entirely convinced she was the same person who'd left to kill Maggie three hours ago. Maybe she was the real Siren's twin. Stranger things had happened.

"So..." Sean said.

Kyle wanted to tell him to shut up, but held back on the off chance that Siren could smell fear.

Lydia glanced at her cousin, tapping her toes against the floor. "I Spy With My Little Eye something that is shadowy."

Siren's eyes flicked over to them. Kyle felt like he couldn't breathe.

"Is it...the wall?"

"No."

"Is it...Siren's chair?"

"Nope."

"Is it...that pile of wrappers in the corner?"

"Yes!"

"Ha! Third time's the charm." Sean looked around the room. "Okay, I Spy With My Little Eye something that is...shadowy."

Siren's lips twitched.

"Is it the wall?"

"How did you know?!" Sean gasped dramatically.

"I'm psychic." Lydia puffed her chest out. "Alright, Kyle, your turn."

Siren's casual interest was pressing into him, filling his lungs with cotton.

"I'm not playing your stupid game." He told her.

"Killjoy." Lydia said. "Hey, lady. Do you want to play?"

Siren's eyebrow quirked up. "Sure." She put her phone down and crossed her arms, looking around the room. "I Spy With My Little Eye something that is clear."

"The window!" Lydia shouted.

Siren grinned. "No."

"The other window." Sean guessed.

"Nope." She popped the end of the word.

"The doorway." Lydia said.

"No."

Sean's forehead creased. "The lightbulb?"

Siren aimed her pointer finger at him. "Eureka."

"That was a good one." Lydia laughed.

"That was *ridiculous*." Kyle glared at her. "What do you think this is, a sleepover? Siren's going to kill Maggie and then us. And you're playing *games* with her?!"

"Hey, everyone has different coping mechanisms." Sean leaned around his cousin. "I know you're stressed, Kyle, but that doesn't mean you have to take it out on everyone else."

"Stressed?" Kyle lifted his ankles. "I'm a prisoner! We're *all* prisoners! Worse than that; we're bait. As soon as Maggie comes for us, she'll die and her blood will be on our hands!"

"You really have no faith in her." Lydia observed.

Kyle felt like his brain was spinning. His muscles shuddered. "Faith in...? Are you insane?! This has nothing to do with faith or trust or pixie dust or whatever else you think she has up her sleeve! This isn't a Saturday morning cartoon, people can get hurt and *die* in this world. Nobody gets to live happily ever after!"

Siren giggled. "Looks like someone's in the wrong line of work."

Kyle slammed his head back against the wall behind him, relishing the pain that blinded him for a few seconds.

Lydia sighed. "Kyle. Dude. It's going to be okay."

"Yeah." Sean smiled. "'Until such time as the world ends, we shall act as though it intends to spin on', right?"

Kyle's chest heaved. He was on the edge of hyperventilating and the cousins were not helping with their stupid babbling. But...they were staring at him, amused, oblivious to the threat, showing no signs of being convinced by him that this was something to be worried about.

Kyle heaved a sigh and dropped his chin to his chest. "Whatever." He said. "I'm too tired to deal with your crap right now."

"That's the spirit!" Sean cheered.

Kyle could tell Lydia was grinning by the way she enthusiastically side-checked him with her tiny shoulder. He rolled his eyes and wondered why he hung out with these morons.

Siren took in the whole thing with a blank expression. *Very interesting*, she thought. She glanced down at her phone again. According to the tracking app she'd downloaded onto the girls' phones while they were unconscious, they were both heading further into the woods than they'd already been when she'd left them.

She hoped they hadn't discovered her ruse and strapped the phones to woodland animals. If they had, she might have to kill them with prejudice instead of just killing them.

Meanwhile, her new captives were almost as fun to play with as Kyle. Of course, she couldn't play her favorite game without getting distracted, and she couldn't get distracted without risking another blindside. So word games would have to do.

"Okay," she said. "A man is walking outside when it starts to rain. He doesn't have a hat, a jacket, an umbrella, or anything else to keep himself dry, but not a hair on his head gets wet. How is that possible?"

Lydia's eyes lit up. "Do hoodies count as jackets?"

"Yes."

"Does he have a backpack over his head or something?" Sean asked.

"No. He doesn't have anything to keep himself dry."

"Maybe he can manipulate water." Kyle said. He shrugged when they looked at him. "Stranger things have happened."

"Not stranger than you actually participating in a game." Sean said.

Kyle rolled his eyes.

"If you keep doing that," Lydia told him, "your eyeballs might fall out of your head."

"Yes, because that's how biology works."

"Do you guys give up?" Siren interrupted.

Apparently those were the magic words, because three sets of eyes snapped to her at once.

Sean grinned. "We never give up."

~

Across town from the hospital, Wendell had his hands shoved in his pockets, rocking back and forth from his toes to his heels and glancing out of the corner of his eye at Delilah. "They say criminals always return to the scene of the crime." He said.

The scientist shot him an icy glare. "What are you implying?"

"Maybe we should have this conversation later." Nehemiah was looking at them both, arms crossed over his chest. He tilted his head towards the house across the street. "Not sure how much longer that's going to be structurally stable."

Delilah just nodded and headed towards the house. The lawn was still a mess, and there was a giant hole in the wall right next to the front door. Wendell and Nehemiah fell into step behind her.

"So we're just going to walk in?" Wendell spoke under his breath to Nehemiah.

"How else are we supposed to get to the secret basement?"

"I know, but...don't you think it'll be suspicious? That someone will call the cops or something?"

"You'd be surprised what people ignore." Delilah said over her shoulder.

Wendell scowled. It hadn't been hard to hear them, but it was still rude that she hadn't pretended not to.

The inside of the house was dark and littered with debris from both of Grady's entrances. The wreckage also let plenty of moonlight in, so the three of them didn't have to worry about stumbling on anything.

Delilah led them into the kitchen only to grab a bottled smoothie from the refrigerator and leave the room. Wendell jerked open the refrigerator door, grabbed two smoothies, and headed after her without closing it. He tossed a smoothie behind him.

Nehemiah caught it and put it back in the fridge. He kicked the door shut on his way out.

There was a closet at the end of the hallway. Delilah handed her smoothie to Wendell. "Hold this for a second." She pulled up the carpet from the bottom of the closet to reveal a trap door. She took her smoothie back as she straightened and looked at Nehemiah. "If you'll do the honors."

Nehemiah exchanged looks with Wendell, then cleared his throat. "You have arms." He said.

Delilah glowered.

Wendell grinned.

This time, she set her smoothie down before lifting the hatch. Reaching into the passageway, she felt along the wall for a light switch. Wendell handed her his smoothie and started down the ladder.

"Thank you." Nehemiah brushed past Delilah and climbed after his friend.

It was like climbing down a chimney; a cramped space enclosed by dirty brick walls. The light switch controlled strands of twinkle lights stapled to them. Nehemiah's shoulders barely fit through the passage, and he closed his eyes for a minute as he choked down the claustrophobia.

The ladder only extended twenty feet down, and Wendell felt around until he found a way to turn on the lights in the room itself. Bare bulbs flickered on overhead.

The furniture in the room was crude and basic, as if it had been collected from a dozen different yard sales. On tables and shelves sat state-of-the-art materials, sophisticated computers, and what looked like props for sci-fi movies.

It reminded Nehemiah of cliff sides with different layers of sediment; shiny metal on top of rough wood. Wendell sauntered over to poke at the unholy offspring of a lava lamp and a toaster.

"The juxtaposition is strong with this room." He said.

"Will all these things work on Grady?" Nehemiah asked.

"This technology is light years beyond even what the government has access to." Delilah said. "I made it all myself. But when it comes to our mutant friend," she pressed her hand to a sensor in the wall and a safe popped open, "there are very few which will be effective."

What she pulled out of the safe was extraordinarily underwhelming considering the strangeness of the half-finished devices scattered around the room. It looked like a pair of handcuffs and a Taser. Granted, the handcuffs looked like they might light up, but that was seriously Original-*Star Trek*-level special effects stuff. The Taser looked even more boring than normal Tasers did.

"You're kidding, right?" Wendell scoffed. "We want to take Grady out, not invite him to play Cops and Robbers."

Delilah looked at him with the patented Misunderstood Genius expression of disgust. "And I suppose you think running around with weapons that look like they were delivered by a flying saucer is a better way to take him by surprise?"

"I'd rather have powerful obvious weapons than stealthy pea-shooters." Wendell told her. He grabbed what appeared to be a blaster off a work bench. "What about this? What does this do?"

"*That* is powered by an incredibly unstable ion, and it's not finished." Delilah said. "Perfect for making sure your enemy will never lay a finger on you – because you'll have blown yourself up before they get the chance."

Wendell made a show of putting the device down. "Okay, so how is your stun gun better?"

She scoffed. "It's not a stun gun; it fires an electrostatic charge that spreads over a wide area. The charge is specifically calibrated to target and reverse the charges of neurons in the brain."

"So..." Wendell said over his crossed arms. "...it's a stun gun."

She glared. "This is much more powerful than a stun gun. It can take out an entire group of people in one hit. But, if you're going up against someone like Grady," she pointed to a dial on the side, "you can use the electrostatic energy to charge up a dart, then fire it directly into him. It'll break apart inside his body and deliver the shock from multiple locations. Should at least put someone like Grady in a coma for a few days." She frowned. "You'd have to remember to charge it first, though. Otherwise it's just grapeshot, and I engineered Grady to withstand things like that."

"Don't worry about it. We have the best sniper in the business." Wendell snatched the gun from her hands. "Amaze me with your disco cuff science."

He handed the gun to Nehemiah. The ex-farmer looked at it, frowning.

Delilah glowered. "The handcuffs are specifically designed to detect and reverse any sort of energy field that someone wearing them creates.

If someone is wearing these and tries to make some sort of...gravitational field, let's say – the field would reflect back at them."

"Hm." Wendell said. "Okay, so we hit Grady with the stun gun and then cuff him so he can't kill us when he wakes up."

"That sounds like an excellent plan." Delilah said. She handed the cuffs to Nehemiah. "Now help me pack up some of these projects. If we're going to be hiding out for a while, I want to have some way of amusing myself."

Chapter 25

All I got was This Stupid T-Shirt

E lliot glanced at his phone. "Ready to go?" He asked. He still did not look happy.

Carly nodded, bracing herself as she swung her legs over the side of the bed and slowly stood up. "What's the plan?"

"The plan is simple." Adanna was suddenly at the door, a shopping bag hanging from her cast. "You change into these clothes, and we walk out and hope we don't run into the one or two people who would recognize you."

"You better not have gotten me something weird." Carly said.

Adanna's eyes widened with innocence. "Please. We're trying to be sneaky here, Carly; do you really think I would mess around in this kind of situation?"

"Kind of." Carly took the shopping back from her friend. "Okay, I'll go change."

Adanna nodded. "Try to work on that walk while you do. You look like a granny. Or, you know, someone who just got shish-kabob'd."

"I appreciate the sympathy." Carly said over her shoulder.

Adanna snorted. "You only had the ceiling fall on you, drama queen. I was on the ground floor under two thirds of the building."

"Yeah, yeah, yeah." Carly shut the bathroom door and pulled the clothes out of the bag. The jeans were nice – deep blue boot cuts; her favorite – but that didn't make up for the shirt.

It was sunflower-yellow, which *was* her favorite color, but fabric marker had been applied in Adanna's blocky handwriting. *I survived gravity and all I got was this stupid t-shirt.*

Carly made sure she was glaring when she opened the door, fully dressed in her new outfit. As expected, Adanna was ready to snap a picture as soon as she emerged.

"I hate you so much." Carly looked around. "Where's Elliot?"

"Pulling up to the doors so we can make a quick getaway." Adanna said, pocketing the disposable camera. "You look lovely."

"Shut up. Just you wait until you're in the hospital."

Adana laughed. "Come on; let's get away from the scene of the crime."

Carly did her best not to walk like a human shish-kabob, but it was difficult. Adanna took one of Carly's arms and wrapped it around her own shoulders.

"Just watching you is painful."

"I'll bet you any money that it's still not as bad as *being* me." Carly let out a breath and transferred some of her weight onto her friend. "Thanks."

Adanna shrugged. She was leading them towards the elevator, but she seemed to be looking through it into whatever was beyond the shaft.

They were the only ones in it, so Carly let go of Adanna and leaned back against the wall, hands braced on the support rail. She was trembling all over. "I never knew that walking could be so difficult."

"You've obviously never been to Times Square on New Year's Eve."

Carly squinted at her friend. "Are you okay?"

Adanna shook her head as if something she didn't like had landed there. She forced a smile. "Yeah. I'm fine."

Carly sighed and let her head fall back against the wall. Adanna and Elliot were annoying for many reasons, one of which was their reluctance to "burden" their friends and family with their problems. They'd both rather bottle up their pain until it exploded. She'd think it was in their blood if they were biologically related. Another point to nurture.

"*I'm* not fine." Carly said. "I'm not sure we can take another attack by Grady and that's terrifying. I feel like I blew our only shot."

"That's ridiculous!" Adanna said. "You did amazing! You actually hit him. It's just..."

"It's just that he's in a completely different league from the people we normally deal with." Carly nodded. "It was fun when we were sure we could win, but now..."

Adanna made a face. "It sounds terrible when you put it that way."

"I know, but..." The doors opened and Carly paused as they exited onto the ground floor. "Elliot was always our trump card, but we could handle normal, non-mutant humans without him."

Adanna nodded. Her pain became visible, manifesting as rage which twisted her features. "I...can't...protect...him." She spoke through gritted teeth. It sounded like she was struggling to say the words, like every syllable was painful.

Carly felt a stabbing in her chest that had nothing to do with stray support beams. "Adanna..."

Adanna turned to look her straight in the eyes. "If you don't want to kill Grady, that's fine. I just need you to distract him so I can get a shot in."

Her voice was low, steady, and sent chills up Carly's spine with the dangerous earnestness in it. *What are we becoming?* Carly thought. *One challenge and we're ready to commit homocide?*

What kind of people are we?

"Carly." Adanna said in a softer tone.

Carly realized her mouth was open, but she had no idea what to say.

"Please." Adanna whispered. "He's my baby brother."

They were twenty feet from the glass doors, and Carly could see the van outside. She took a deep breath. "Wendell and I talked." She said. "We agreed; we do anything to keep Elliot safe. Anything."

Adanna blinked rapidly, her mouth curving up. "Thank you."

Chapter 26

You Can't Hide Anything From the Parents

If Maggie hadn't been so caught up in trying to figure out Siren's thinking, she would have put more effort into trying to avoid her parents at the safe house. Or at least into making herself look less like an extra from *The Walking Dead*. But she was completely absorbed with trying to come up with a foolproof counterplan, so she didn't think about any of that until her mother came into the room and screamed.

Maggie jumped about a foot in the air. "Mom! What the heck?!"

Viv's normal complexion was suddenly Scandinavian-white.

Maggie's overly stressed brain found that interesting, because she'd never actually seen someone "go pale" in real life. Apparently, it's something that does happen.

"What happened to you?"

Oh. OH. "I'm fine!" Maggie held up her hands in a surrender pose, but undermined her words by grazing her wound with her bicep and wincing.

"You are NOT FINE!" Viv's vocal range was expanding by the minute, venturing into a terrifying tone of tenor. *"You're BLEED-ING!"*

A blur shot from the hallway to Viv's side and materialized into Oliver, who was holding a steak knife and looking for threats.

"It's just a graze!" Maggie said. "Really! Hailey already looked at it and we have everything under control."

"Is Hailey a *nurse*?" Viv seemed to be exuding a visible field of righteous anger. At least her voice was quieter.

"She's a psychologist..." Maggie said. "That's a type of doctor..."

Taylor and Hugh emerged from the hallway, both with guns drawn.

"I took a summer course in first aid." Hailey added.

"What's going on?" Taylor asked. "Is there someone here?"

"No; we're all good." Maggie held up her hands. "Look, Mom, I know you're worried, but Hailey and I just came back to grab some stuff and we're in a hurry."

"You are not going *anywhere* but to the hospital to have that looked at by a professional! What happened out there, anyway?"

Luckily, Taylor chose that moment to holster her weapon and join the conversation. "The others got captured, didn't they?"

"Yeah." Hailey nodded. "Not by the gravity dude, though; some psycho assassin lady took them."

"They get caught rescuing Kyle?"

Hailey raised one shoulder. "In a way."

Taylor rolled her eyes. "If I've told you kids once, I've told you a thousand times; you cannot just walk around without someone to watch your six. How hard is it to stick to the Buddy System?"

Hailey put a hand on her hip. "Uh, have you met Kyle?"

"Fair point." Taylor shrugged.

"Excuse me." Viv was still seething. "Did you just say 'assassin?'"

Maggie wished she had the power of teleportation.

"Just a human one." Hailey said, eyes widening as they took in Viv's molten aura. "Not even very sneaky. Just annoying, really. Nothing Mags can't handle with her powers, right?" She glanced out of the corner of her eyes at Maggie.

Who was covered in blood. From the dark patch on her shirt to the matted hair where she'd hit the four-wheeler. "Yeah." Maggie dead-panned. "I've got this covered."

Hugh laughed. "Even the best poker face isn't enough when you're showing everyone your cards."

"We don't have time for this!" Maggie said. "We need to change, grab some weapons, and go get our team back."

"Your *team*?" Viv held up her hands. "Did I miss something? Didn't you just meet these people ten hours ago?"

Oliver put a hand on his wife's arm before Maggie could reply. "Regardless, those kids do need to be rescued." He looked at his daughter. "But we're not about to let you walk into danger without—" his eyes darted to Taylor "—someone to 'watch your six.' Your mother and I are coming too."

Maggie was shaking her head even before he finished. "No. No way."

"Yes way." Viv said. "You either take us with or you don't go at all."

"Mom, you can't...I don't...do you even know how to fight?" Maggie asked.

Viv laughed, but it wasn't a comforting laugh. "Sweetie, remember when I told you there are things in my past I'm not proud of?"

Maggie nodded slowly. "It's a very vague statement."

"Yes, well." Viv shrugged. "I know how to fight because of some of those things."

Oliver smiled at her for a second, then turned back to Maggie. "And you know I'm a champion knife thrower."

"Really?" Taylor put a hand on her hip. "Are there championships for that?"

Oliver shrugged, looking at the ground. "I was in the circus."

"What? No way!" Hugh peered around his wife. "That's awesome!"

Taylor gestured to herself and her husband. "I don't know if our kids told you, but we're pretty good with guns."

"Yeah, that's not suspicious at all." Maggie would later claim it only slipped out because of her blood loss, but Hugh laughed.

"Then it's settled." Taylor clapped her hands. "Margaret, darling, go get cleaned up. Hailey; help her. We adults will go see that the practical concerns are taken care of."

Viv looked like she wanted to protest, but Oliver squeezed her hand and she deflated.

"Okay." Maggie nodded, too relieved that her mother's face was returning to its natural shade to insist on going alone.

Hailey looped an arm around her and steered her towards the exit on the opposite side of the room. "I know you don't have any of your own clothes here, but I've always wanted to steal clothes from another girl's closet, haven't you? I didn't have any sisters growing up and stealing from my friends seemed more criminal than mischievous, you know? But now we have a *totally legitimate* excuse...!"

Her voice faded as they got further down the hallway. Viv still hadn't moved. Oliver wrapped an arm around her waist and leaned his head on her shoulder.

"Love," He said, and it was a pet name, a declaration, a reassurance, and a promise in one low, gravelly sound.

Viv wrapped her arms around him and squeezed as tightly as she could. As tightly as she wanted to hold onto her baby girl and keep her safe. And Oliver let her squeeze the air out of him because he'd give up his breath for her in a millisecond if it came to that. He patted her back gently.

Viv unwound from him and stood; fists clenched at her sides and doors closed in her eyes. Her normally soft expression seemed to retreat into her, titanium plating moving out until it sat just under her skin.

She looked like a different person. A person she hadn't been in a long time. Sometimes she wondered if everything she'd built was just a mask, if the titanium woman was her true self. She whispered her doubts once, on the night they'd brought Maggie home. Oliver had kissed her and told her she was too smart to say stupid things.

When they turned as one towards the door, Taylor was leaning against the frame with Hugh at her side. She raised an eyebrow at Viv's transformation.

"You should've been an actress." Taylor said.

"I am." Viv told her.

Taylor smirked and turned. "Come on; I'll show you the kids' toy box."

The Toy Box was a central room with no windows and a digital password lock. Taylor typed the code in and swung open what could've passed for a blast door to reveal shelves of weapons of all shapes and sizes.

"Some of this stuff is hand-me-down." Hugh told the Poseys. "Or 'heirlooms' or whatever. But you won't believe what those kids can find on the internet these days."

"So, Scarlet Johansen," Taylor gestured to the shelves. "What's your poison?"

"I'm more of a Gal Gadot, actually." Viv ran her hands over the shiny guns. "Are there any other types of weapons? Nunchuku? Ninjato? Neko-te?"

"Ah, an up close and personal type." Taylor nodded sagely. "I can respect that." She opened a large chest which was lying on the floor. "We have various different types of swords, daggers, and other hand-held blades."

Viv started rooting around in the chest.

"So," Taylor said as she pulled handguns from the shelves, testing their weight in her hands, "You don't look very Japanese, but I'm guessing you have some connection to the place given those weapons you just listed."

"My father..." Viv murmured, lifting a dagger and running her finger along the edge. She nodded with satisfaction when it drew blood. "...was very young but very brilliant. He lived in Greece – I look like him. Spoke several languages, and ended up as a translator for a company.

"On a business trip to Japan, he met my mother. She was part of this group that was very anti-Western, all about returning to their 'true Japanese roots.' When they first met, she cursed at him in Japanese and was shocked when he answered her." Viv smiled softly. "Anyway, I grew up bouncing between the countries. My father taught me to speak both languages. My mother taught me what she'd learned about shinobi and kunoichi fighting techniques, just for fun. I...didn't use my skills the way she would've wanted."

Taylor waited, watching Viv's face. But titanium doesn't bend. "And then...?"

Viv shrugged, smirked. "Things happened. I realized I wasn't who I wanted to be, and I decided to get some distance from it all. Moved to America. And then I met Oliver." She held up a pair of Neko-te triumphantly.

They were a type of Japanese weapon usually wielded by kunoichi. Like brass knuckles, they wrapped around the hand. Unlike brass knuckles, they had four metal "claws" extending out from the palm. They could be used for both climbing and gouging.

"Your boy has good taste." Viv said.

"Yes, well," Taylor flipped her hair over her shoulder dramatically. "He gets it from his mother."

Viv's lips twitched, then pressed together like blast doors trying to seal in an explosion. When she spoke, the words she let escape were clean and controlled. "I never wanted this for my daughter."

Taylor sighed and sat down to be at eye level with Viv, who was still rooting through the trunk. "Trust me, I wasn't too thrilled when my babies decided to start this whole 'Hero's Guild.' The worst thing about being an overprotective mom is when you face a situation where your paranoid fears are justified.

"But they're adults now, so we can't make them stop their Save the World campaign." She met Viv's gaze. "The only thing we can do is support them, because it is much easier to protect them when you're standing at their sides."

Viv's expression didn't change, but she nodded.

Taylor dropped her eyes, seemingly staring at her left leg. "They say the worst karma is when your kids end up just like you. My parents didn't want me to be a cop. They told me how dangerous it was, but I already knew all that. I also knew I had to do what I thought was right. Part of it was that whole young-and-immortal mindset, but I was aware, on some level, of what could happen. And I accepted it."

She tugged up the leg of her pants to reveal a shiny prosthetic that ended at her knee. It glinted in the light, artificial and clashing with the vibrantly alive earth tones of her skin. "Doesn't mean I was full of acceptance and peace when I had to relearn how to walk. But I wouldn't trade all the good I did for another leg." She smoothed her pants back down. "Sometimes I regret setting that example for my kids, though."

Viv's mouth stretched in a caricature of a smile. "I guess I should be glad that karma didn't affect Maggie."

On the other side of the room, Hugh was showing Oliver his favorite tool. "It's hand-crafted." He said. "Not another one like it in the world."

"But it takes standard .223 bullets?"

"Sure does." Hugh rested it against his shoulder and glanced at the mothers before lowering his voice. "How are you holding up?"

Oliver raised an eyebrow.

"I mean," Hugh smirked, "This isn't exactly covered in those parenting books."

Oliver smirked back. "Nothing about those kids is covered in parenting books."

Hugh laughed. "That's for sure!"

Oliver glanced at the chest his wife was rooting through. "Is that the only place you have knives?"

"Nah, I think we have a set over here somewhere. Throwing knives, too." Hugh started peeking in boxes that were stacked in the corner. "Is it just Maggie, then?"

"Yes." Oliver tilted his head. "Well. Not anymore."

"I hear you. At least *we* have some backup now, though, right? I'd hate to be outnumbered." He lifted a small silver briefcase. "This is the one. Sean – the older Irish kid – was into throwing knives for a while, but could never quite get the hang of it. They've never even seen combat before."

Oliver took the case and lifted the knives out one by one, tossing them gently up and down.

Hugh leaned against the table. "Why'd you decide to adopt?"

Oliver hummed.

"You don't have to say. I'm just curious. Before we adopted Elliot, I thought every motive for adoption was basically the same. During the process, Tay and I visited a few support groups and...it was amazing to me how many different experiences could result in the same thing." Hugh shrugged. "That might just be the scientist in me, though."

Oliver glanced up, then went back to studying the knives. "I've always wanted to be a father." He said. "But Viv was in an...accident...when she was younger and..." he shrugged. "I loved her more than I loved my dream. The adoption thing was actually her idea – I didn't want to push her. She's been through...so much. Already. And I didn't want—" he broke off. "Our marriage is the greatest gift she's ever given me, but Maggie is a close second."

Hugh nodded. "That's awesome, man." He tilted his head back and stared at the ceiling. "When I was a kid, some cousin to the nth degree had to move in with us because her house made Sodom and Gomorrah look tame. I never found out the extent of it, and I'm just fine with that.

"When she first moved in, I wasn't sure she was alive. She would just sit with her nose in the corner and stare at the wall. But my parents never gave up on her and by the time she graduated, she was...well...*happy*. Ever since then, I knew that I wanted to do that for a kid." Hugh glanced at Oliver. "Never thought that kid would burp lightning, though."

Oliver laughed.

"Are you guys about ready?" Hailey asked. She and Maggie stood in the doorway. They looked much better without the dried blood and disgusting clothes.

Viv raised an eyebrow at her daughter's choice of attire. "You planning on joining a punk band, honey?"

Maggie smirked, slipping off the leather jacket with steel studs on the shoulders. She had a metal bracelet wrapped around each arm, a chain hanging from her belt, rings on every finger, and sharp studs through her ears. She gestured with her left hand, and the bracelet on her upper arm unwound like a snake, drifting through the air and straightening itself until it hovered above her fingertips like a tiny javelin.

Viv nodded. "I see...stylish, yet functional."

"Yup." Maggie put her bracelet and jacket back on. She took a deep breath. "Okay. I think I have a plan."

Chapter 27

Death Trap

It was almost midnight, and the cops who had swarmed to the scene at the grocery store were still patrolling the streets. It was very strange to be investigating a crime in which both the perpetrator and the victim fled the scene. Seven hours of searching, and most of them were starting to lose hope.

A golf cart trundled down the street past a squad car. The two girls inside waved at the cops, and the cops waved back.

"Should we stop them?" Officer Jeremy Jenkins asked his senior partner.

Officer Hugh Grant shook his head. "They don't look like killers, and the witnesses said the victim escaped with a group on ATV's, not golf carts."

"Yeah, but...it could be dangerous to be out late with a shooter on the loose." Jenkins said. "Shouldn't we warn them?"

"No." Grant said. "The shooter was after a specific target. I don't want to be the fear-monger telling everyone to lock their doors in case the ogres come down from the mountains."

Jenkins nodded slowly. "Must be nice not to have to know this stuff."

Grant grunted, then lifted his coffee. "To the lucky, clueless golf cart riders."

"Scholl." Jenkins met the cup with his own.

Hailey and Maggie parked the golf cart in front of a bookstore a block away from the donut shop. Hailey's eyes were wide, like she was trying to get the whole world in at once. Maggie tugged at her jacket sleeves, then shook herself out.

"Okay." She said. "Ready?"

"I am *so* ready!" Hailey bounced on her toes. The streetlight made her grin look like a mouth full of tiny white Christmas lights.

She's insane. Maggie realized. *My brother and all his friends are insane.* And yet here she was, leading the charge into the danger. Maybe after they rescued Kyle and the cousins, she'd take a shower and try to wash off the crazy cooties.

They walked over to the donut shop. Just as they neared the door, Hailey's phone started to ring.

"Seriously?!" Maggie hissed.

"Sorry! I don't know who would be calling me at—" Hailey blinked, not bothering to close her mouth.

"What?" Maggie asked.

Hailey flipped the phone so she could see the screen. The caller was "Siren" with a heart emoji.

Maggie stabbed at the green button, afraid of what would happen if they sent an assassin to voicemail.

"Maggie!" Hailey hissed, pulling the phone to her ear. "Hello?"

"It's about time you got here." Siren said. *"Do you have any idea how long I've been waiting? I was starting to think I accidentally killed you two in the woods."*

"Thanks for your concern." Hailey rolled her eyes. "I have Maggie. She's willing to do the t-trade. Thing." She bit her lip, grimacing at her stutter. "So how do you want to do this? Because I'm not sending Maggie in until you send my guys out. And my girl."

Siren laughed. *"We both know that if Margaret steps through that door, she'll have me impaled on a dozen support beams before I can raise my gun."*

"It's nothing personal." Hailey said.

"I completely understand. Still, I have plans this weekend so I'm going to have to change the terms of this agreement a little bit."

"Oh, goody. What did you have in mind?"

"Let's just say your friend isn't Wanted: Dead or Alive anymore. That is...she's not Wanted: Alive."

"Yeah, we got that when you tried to snipe her at the grocery store."

"You know that's not what I meant."

"I'm *not* going to kill Maggie." Hailey's free hand twitched into a fist. "Come up with another plan."

"But I like this plan." Siren purred. *"It's almost like that train question; an assassin is going to kill three people you know. You can either stand by and let them get killed, or you can kill one person you barely know instead."*

Hailey felt her stomach clench. Maggie was watching her face closely, but didn't seem to be able to hear Siren. "I want one of them first. Like a – a show of good faith."

"I guess that wouldn't hurt. A two for one deal is almost as good as a three for one deal, after all." Shuffling sounds came over the line. *"Any preferences?"*

"Lydia." Even before she could get the name out, Hailey heard what sounded like Sean saying the same thing.

"Alright. Once the girl leaves, you'll have two minutes to complete your task before I start putting bullets in your boys."

"I don't have a weapon." Hailey said.

"Then I guess you'll have to get creative."

Hailey tried to stab the End Call button, but Siren got there first.

"What's going on?" Maggie asked. "What does she want you to do?"

"I thought you said you could sense her magnetic field through the wall!" Hailey tried to keep her voice down, but her voice did not wish to comply.

"I can."

"Then why didn't you stab her or something?!"

"She's too close to the others! I couldn't tell which one was her, and I didn't want to accidentally stab one of the team!" Maggie mentally slapped herself for using the "T" word. "Anyway, what did she say?"

The door opened and Lydia stumbled out, rubbing her wrists and rolling her ankles. "Tell me you have a plan."

"What is going on?" Maggie waved a hand in Hailey's face.

"She says that if I don't kill you in two minutes, she's going to start shooting the guys."

"Oh." Maggie leaned back and crossed her arms. "That's smart, I guess."

"In a totally *sadistic* way!" Hailey ran her fingers through her hair. She could hear her heart beating in her ears. It sounded like a countdown.

"Are you going to be able to do it?" Maggie asked.

"What?!" Lydia gasped. "No way! We are not just going to *kill* you—"

"Look, we don't have time to talk about this." Maggie said. "She's not going to stop until she kills me. That's probably going to happen even if we leave right now. The only choice I have is whether to take half the team down with me."

Hailey nodded, vision blurring. "I think I need new glasses." She sniffled.

Maggie managed half a smile. She rolled her shoulders. "Okay. Okay. So you don't have a weapon, so how are we going to do this?"

"Asphyxiation." Hailey felt sick to her stomach. "I'll b-b-block your oxygen and...and..."

Maggie nodded. She took a shaky breath and slowly laid down on her back. "You're going to want to hold me down." She said. "I heard about people lashing out when they're drowning and..."

"Yeah. Okay." Hailey hovered over Maggie's stomach, kneeling on her arms.

"Guys, wait, this is insane--!"

"Lydia, hold her legs."

"No!"

"Lydia—"

The younger girl was backing up, shaking her hands and head and any other part of her body that would move. "I won't do it!" She shrieked. "I won't! *You can't make me!*"

"*LYDIA.*" Maggie commanded.

Lydia stopped moving.

Maggie couldn't see her from her position, so she just looked up at the night sky. "Do you want Sean to die?"

Lydia started shaking again.

Hailey's phone started ringing.

"Lydia, we are out of time! If you want Sean to live, get over here and hold my legs down!"

Lydia sobbed and dropped to her knees, clamping her hands around Maggie's ankles.

Hailey's hands hovered over Maggie's face.

Maggie nodded. "It's going to be okay." She said. Then she closed her eyes because it was too hard to keep hiding her fear.

In the darkness behind her eyelids, Maggie felt hands cover her nose and mouth. She thought about when she was a kid and she used to hold her breath every time her dad drove through a tunnel.

It's just a tunnel. She told herself. *Just a tunnel. Just a tunnel. I'm five and I'm going through a tunnel.*

She managed to control the first set of spasms, but after that her survival instincts kicked in and she was just a scared, nameless creature who was in danger. Her eyes flew open and she struggled as hard as she could.

Hailey held on, trying to stop herself from shaking. Her tears dropped onto Maggie's face and it felt disrespectful. This was not what she'd wanted. This was not what's she'd signed up for. She wanted to save people. She wanted to *save* people.

As soon as Maggie went limp, Hailey jumped back and scrambled away. Lydia collapsed into the fetal position, sobbing. Hailey didn't have time for her. She pawed at her phone until she remembered how to open it, then went to her list of recent calls and dialed Siren.

"I hear Lydia's taking this well. It's amazing how much sound can come from that tiny body." Siren said. *"I assume the deed is done?"*

"Yes." Hailey said. "Now give me my friends back."

"How do I know she's actually dead?"

Hailey hit herself in the forehead with the side of her fist. "Look. I don't have a weapon, so if you want her any more dead, you're going to have to come out here and do it yourself!"

"Fair enough." Siren said. *"Alright. I'm coming out with your friends. One wrong move and I kill you all."*

Hailey laughed. Her fingers were tingling. Her brain was floaty. Was Siren still on the phone? She looked down. The home screen looked back. Siren had hung up. *Guess I don't need...to hold this, then.* She let go of the phone and let it fall to the sidewalk.

Kyle and Sean's wrists were still bound when they were herded out the door in front of Siren. The assassin peeked around them, then shoved them forwards a few more feet until she could get past them for a better look at Maggie.

Sean dropped to his knees next to Lydia, taking her hand with his bound ones whispering gently to her. Kyle just stood and stared at the building across the street. He didn't look at Maggie's body. He didn't look at anyone.

Siren aimed her rifle at the body, but Hailey shoved it away.

"What is *wrong with you*?! Don't you have any respect?!" She shouted.

Suddenly, Siren was holding a knife to Hailey's throat. "I have to say, I'm impressed. Under any other circumstances, I'd offer you a job. However, in this case..."

Hailey gulped. None of the others had noticed yet. "Any time now." She whispered.

To her credit, Siren knew immediately who she was talking to.

It didn't help.

Siren's knife and gun flew through the air and into the hands of the girl of whose rumored death was greatly exaggerated. Maggie pushed herself up on her elbows before ripping nails out of the wall. One can never be too careful when projecting sharp objects through the air with one's mind.

Siren ducked and rolled out of the way. She reached for what was most likely another weapon when a bullet tore through her shoulder.

"You missed." Viv called, sauntering down the street next to her husband.

From the opposite direction, Hugh rolled his eyes. "I did not *miss*. The kids just have that rule about not killing people, remember?"

"Oh, yeah."

At his side, Taylor made a face. "Kill joys."

Siren looked at the parents approaching her from both sides and the former hostages and their friends right in front of her.

"Did I hear someone say 'kill?'" Viv twirled a dagger between her fingers.

Hailey drew her handgun from inside her jacket and clicked the safety off.

Siren laughed and locked eyes with her. "Well played."

From somewhere literally up her sleeve, Siren pulled three cartridges and slammed them to the ground. Dark smoke billowed up around her. Viv's eyes widened and she dove into the cloud, but she wasn't fast enough to stop her.

Maggie growled. "That smoke must have iron filings in it. When did she even have time to make those?!" But she had bigger – or smaller, depending on how you look at it – problems.

Lydia tackled her to the ground. "You *ASSHOLE!*" she screamed. "I thought you were *dead*! I thought I helped *kill* you! Did you two *plan* this?!"

"It was my plan." Maggie wheezed, the wind having been knocked out of her (for real this time) by Lydia's sneak attack. "I figured Siren was going to want me dead before coming out, and we couldn't go in the building without her killing one or all of you. So I told Hailey to pretend to asphyxiate me if Siren asked."

"And you couldn't have *warned me*?!" Lydia was still attached to her side.

She wrapped her arms around the smaller girl hesitantly. "I'm sorry." She said. "But we couldn't risk explaining our plan right outside Siren's hideout. The whole plan depended on the element of surprise."

"I hate you so much." Lydia sobbed. "You too, Hailey."

"I'm sorry, Dia."

"How about proving it by untying us?" Kyle held out his wrists. "Or cutting the ropes; I'm not picky."

"Here," Viv stepped up. She still had her dagger in her hand. "I'll be disappointed if I don't get to use this tonight."

"I feel very unsafe." Kyle said as she held his arm steady.

"Don't waste your time feeling unsafe around people who are on your side." She suggested. "There. Now run along." She gave him a half-wave over her shoulder on her way over to Sean, like she knew he was staring.

"How are you, big guy?" Viv asked Sean.

He saw the knife and held his hands out. "I'm fine." He said. "Worried about Lydia."

"You don't think she can brush off captivity as well as you can?"

"I don't think she can brush off that respawn stunt they just pulled."

"Hm." Viv narrowed her eyes, bringing him more into focus. "You're the protective big brother, aren't you?"

"Cousin."

"Semantics." She dropped his freed hands. "Just because your DNA says one thing doesn't mean that's the way it is."

She sidled up to Oliver, leaning her head on his shoulder. He rested his cheek on her hair.

"Making friends?" He asked.

"They're Maggie's friends. I'm just making observations."

"What, because you're older than them?" He pressed closer to her. "Just because your blood says one thing doesn't mean that's the way it is."

She pulled back so she could smack his shoulder gently. "That lip-reading thing is creepy. Stop watching everything I say."

He shrugged. "It's not my fault you're nice to look at."

"Okay, guys." Maggie clapped her hands. She was standing now, but still had a Lydia stuck to her. "Let's head back to the safe house. We have three golf carts, and I think Lydia's coming with Hailey and me, so you guys can split up between the parents."

"Sounds good." Hugh said.

Viv pointed at Kyle. "Dibs!"

He blinked at her.

Taylor shrugged. "He's all yours. Sean? You ready?"

"I'm ready." But he was still watching Lydia. And he would continue watching her until she and the other girls became blurry in the darkness and Taylor yelled at him from the other direction to keep up.

Chapter 28

Adventurers

With Carly in the backseat and Adanna nursing a broken arm, not to mention that Delilah was technically a hostage, driving became a masculine endeavor on the way back.

Elliot, with his superhuman abilities, was assigned the job of Friendly Neighborhood Prison Guard. This was a very important job with daunting tasks such as sitting in the backseat and attempting not to pass out from boredom.

Wendell's mom had been in the Navy, so he grew up on a variety of military bases in Europe. Needless to say, after learning to drive on streets that had been designed for two-way pedestrian traffic and laws were more like suggestions, American streets were about as hard as beating a tutorial.

Halfway through the five-hour drive, they stopped at a gas station. Adanna and Wendell went inside for food. It had dawned on them that Carly was the only one who'd eaten since midnight.

Nehemiah pumped the gas, then opened the side door next to Carly. "Do you want to get out and move around a little?"

"*I* would." Delilah said.

Elliot laughed.

"I don't know. I'm kind of stiff, but I'm also sore from all the bumps. I just…I'm not motivated to put myself in more pain right now." Carly said.

"I can help you." Nehemiah suggested. "I'll carry your weight; you can stretch."

"Hm." Carly pursed her lips.

Nehemiah put one hand on her shoulder and one on her knee. "Want to give it a try?"

Carly took a deep breath. "Why not?"

Nehemiah slid his arms underneath her knees and around her back, drawing her to his chest and carrying her out of the car. Carly felt the early-morning wind in her hair and closed her eyes. "Do you want to get down?" Nehemiah asked.

Carly braced herself and nodded.

Nehemiah crouched until Carly's feet were on the ground, then let go of her legs and wrapped his arms carefully around her ribs, just above where the beam had cut her. He straightened up until she was standing, minus the strain of using her core to hold up her torso.

"That's amazing." She said. She kicked her legs out experimentally. She tried lifting her knee, but that did pull at her core. She winced and went back to shaking out her legs. "This is great! I feel like I don't weight anything."

Nehemiah smiled even though she couldn't see him.

"What are you guys up to?" Wendell asked, peering around the front of the car.

"Carly's stretching her legs." Nehemiah said.

"Oh. Cool." Wendell held up a shopping bag. "I have trail mix, red licorice, pizza filled cracker rolls, and boxes of lunches you can assemble. Adanna was in charge of the drinks, so I have no idea what she got for you."

"Do you want to get back in the van or stretch a little longer?" Nehemiah asked.

"I'm good now. Thanks, though." Carly said.

Nehemiah set her back in her seat, then shut the door and turned to Wendell, who tossed him the keys.

"You're the man, dude." Wendell said. "My eyes started swimming half an hour ago."

"My pleasure." Nehemiah nodded. "I'm just glad I don't have to drive in the city. That traffic makes shark week look tame." After being introduced to television, Nehemiah had developed a fascination with documentaries on animals.

Wendell smirked at his idea of bad traffic. "Hey great idea, lifting Carly like that so she could walk. How'd you come up with it?"

"Um." Nehemiah shoved his hands in his pockets and cleared his throat. "My little sister loved skating, but sometimes the ice would be too thin, so I'd hold her over the side of the lake and she would pretend."

"I didn't know you had a sister." Wendell didn't know how else to respond.

Nehemiah shot him a flicker of a smile. "Yeah. She's uh...she's another reason I left the community. I never thought...the way we treated women was wrong until I saw how you guys treat the girls. I realized I...I didn't know if I could...stay in a place that didn't respect my sister like that."

"It's easier to change when you're not the first one." Wendell said.

"Yeah." Nehemiah shrugged. "Maybe it's stupid, but it's the only thing I could do to show her I was serious."

The side door of the van slid open. "Hey guys! Are you coming or nah?"

"Keep your gauze on, Carly, we were just getting in." Wendell rolled his eyes and sauntered around the front of the van.

Nehemiah smirked and shut Carly's door in her face before climbing into the driver's seat. He adjusted the mirrors and started the engine.

"Does everybody have their seatbelts on?" Elliot asked loudly.

Nehemiah and Adanna locked their belts into place.

Elliot glared at Delilah until she rolled her eyes and complied.

"Here you go, Nehemiah," Adanna handed him a bottle. "I got you one of those energy drinks, because today has been exhausting and I don't feel like dying on the way home."

"Thanks."

"And Wendell, here's your lemonade/tea thing."

"Thank you. Can I have some of those pizza roll cracker things?"

"Only if Elliot hasn't eaten them all already."

"Hey, I'm just making sure they're not poisoned. I'm taking one for the team. You guys should be thanking me for eating these pizza crackers!"

"We'll take our chances! Hand them over!"

Delilah crossed her arms and retreated into her mind. She was watching what was going on as if through a viewscreen from some other room. Underestimating these kids had been a grave mistake on Grady's part. They were resilient, resourceful, and skilled. *Triple threat.* On the other hand...

"Hey, Nehemiah, the limit here is seventy-five." Wendell said.

Adanna rolled her eyes. "Oh, here we go."

The driver nodded. "I know. That's insane."

"Dude, we've been over this; you have to go the speed limit or other cars might hit you if they have cruise control on."

"The speed limit shouldn't be *insane.*"

"Augh! Every. Single. Time." Carly kicked the back of Nehemiah's seat. "Are you trolling him? Because the rest of us are here, too."

"I don't know what 'trolling' is, but traveling seventy-five miles in an hour should not be something people feel they need to do outside of Nast Car."

"Okay, he definitely did *that* on purpose." Adanna said.

"You are all insane." Nehemiah said.

"Well, you know what they say," Elliot shrugged, "'when in Rome...'"

Nehemiah sighed. "Fine. At least if we die at that speed we probably won't feel it."

Carly nodded. "Yup. We'll be in heaven before we know we're dead. Now *floor it.*"

Despite all their strengths, they were still children. Not physically, but mentally. They reminded Delilah of the book *Peter Pan*. The hero of the story was eternally young, with no memory of the past and no expectations for the future. He traveled wherever he wanted to and fought because it was fun. "'Dying,'" he had once said, "'would be an awfully big adventure.'"

Chapter 29

Post-Trauma Talks

Over the years, Taylor had seen her fair share of successful missions; her own, and now her children's. The kids usually threw some sort of party afterwards, riding on the high of success and laughing with the kind of hysteria that only comes with being alive after not quite expecting it.

There were no tendrils of success filling their lungs tonight. The absence of that made the safe house feel even colder and less like home.

Lydia, Sean, and Kyle took turns in the shower. Kyle took two showers but nobody said anything.

Hailey redressed Maggie's wound. They barely made it to their beds before collapsing.

Viv sat in the hallway outside her daughter's door, absently flipping her dagger around. Oliver brought her tea and sat across from her, reading a book.

Taylor wasn't tired. She put a burrito in the microwave and sat at the table while the green numbers counted down. When Hugh wrapped his arms around her from behind, she almost punched him in the nose.

"Don't scare me like that!" She bopped his shoulder instead.

He grinned and sat down next to her, his back to the microwave. He grabbed her prosthetic and gently rolled her pants up to her knee.

"My, my," she wiggled her eyebrows. "What if the kids walk in?"

"*What* if the kids walk in?" He flashed her a smirk.

She hid a smile behind a hand that still smelled like gun oil. When he unhooked her prosthesis, she couldn't help but sigh.

Hugh massaged her stump and frowned. "Is the padding wearing down?"

"Mm, a little." She shrugged. "It's not too bad. Just uncomfortable if I wear it too long."

"You need to let me know things like that; I'll get you more."

"Not right now." Taylor said. "Not until we don't have to worry about that creep attacking Elliot anymore."

Hugh frowned again. "That bothers me."

Taylor quirked up an eyebrow. "The fact that there's an assassin after our son bothers you?"

He stuck his tongue out at her. "The fact that it's taken the assassin this long to find our son bothers me. If there was information in that bunker Elliot and the kids don't want us to know they raided, why didn't that guy find it sooner? Why did he end up there on the same night as our kids?"

"Do you think someone's been watching us?" Taylor asked. "Someone who tipped the assassin off about that raid we know nothing about?"

The microwave started beeping.

"Maybe." He set her leg down and went to get the burrito. He opened a few cupboards which revealed a stunning supply of nothing. "I don't think the kids thought to bring plates. Or silverware."

"Check the sink."

"Hm?" Hugh walked over to the sink. "Ah, yes. Because why would they wash dishes in the safe house when they never do at home? What was I thinking?" Thankfully, they hadn't forgotten dish soap. He turned on the hot water and grabbed it, shaking out a generous amount onto a plate and fork.

"If someone was watching us," Taylor said, "They might know about the kids heading down to see that scientist."

"Do you think we should call one of the burners? Adanna left the numbers on a post-it in the bathroom."

She shook her head slowly, crossing her arms. "If they need help, they'll call. What else is the point in having two teams?"

"You make a good point." In lieu of towels, Hugh dried the plate and fork with napkins. He grabbed the burrito from the microwave and hissed. "How is it still this hot?!"

"You're making me jealous, babe." Taylor said.

Her husband handed her the food and kissed her. "No burrito can compete with you, love."

She batted her eyelashes. "What a sweet talker."

"You love it."

"I do."

Hugh grinned. "I'll never get tired of you saying that."

Taylor smiled. "I'll never get tired of saying it." Her face turned serious. "But don't think that means I'm going to let you steal some of my burrito."

"Pfft." He crossed his arms, offended. "I don't need your help to steal some of your burrito."

She bopped him with her stump.

~

Sean tapped his pen against the blank page of his notebook. Just because he was trapped in this safe house didn't mean he didn't have to work. There was a huge regional competition coming up and the crew had never been so excited. He wanted to live up to that excitement, to choreograph something that would show that energy in visible form.

And it had to. Even among the few and the proud adult dance crews, only a small percentage in the area worked exclusively with modern dance. A lot of people thought it was chaotic and sloppy.

It *was* chaotic, but that was what Sean loved about it. Ballet and tap were so structured and mechanical. Even jazz had become dominated by well-known moves and patterns. Modern dance cared less about form and more about expressing things through movement. Kinetic speech. It was a form of communication that was so raw and honest even words couldn't compete.

His brain wouldn't focus. He tossed his pen half-heartedly across the room and dropped his notebook on the floor. Even as he pushed himself off the bed, he had no idea where he wanted to go. He just had to get away from whatever inspiration-sucking black hole had appeared on an invisible wavelength in that room.

The shower was running. He looked at the door and felt like falling to his knees and pounding the floor, then toe-rolling up into some sort of lunge-leap combo with his hands outstretched. Preferably until they grasped Siren's throat.

Moving on, he saw the light in the pantry was on and went to turn it off. He almost did before he noticed Lydia sitting in the middle of the room.

He knocked on the door softly. "Hey," he said when she turned around.

"Hey." She said. "We still...don't have breakfast food."

"Oh yeah?" He made his way over to her. "Maybe tomorrow we can all go into town together. Or maybe Elliot and the others will pick some up on the way back."

Lydia was staring past him. Her whole body was droopy, like a jellyfish out of water; unnatural without its usual luminescence.

"Hey," he put a hand on her shoulder, hating that that stupid word was the only thing he could think to say.

Her eyes flicked to him, but they looked like they belonged to someone else. They were eyes that belonged to people who had walked away from a bombing or who had just been dropped off after an alien abduction. Like they knew their world was completely different and couldn't understand why it still looked the same.

"I killed someone for you." She said.

He blinked. "Um...What?"

"I held M—" she shuddered. "I held her down so Hailey could kill her b-b-because if I didn't, that woman would have killed you."

"Hey," Sean tilted her chin up to make sure she didn't look away. "Maggie's *fine*. It was just part of the plan."

"But I didn't know that!" Lydia jerked away from him, taking a step back. She looked like the feeling of doing a grand pirouette and just spinning and spinning and spinning. "I didn't know it wasn't for real, and I did it anyway!" She sniffed, wiping at her eyes.

"Lydia..." He reached for her, but she dodged out of the way.

"It doesn't matter." She said quietly. "Whatever happened or didn't doesn't matter, because it was real to me. I killed someone. I'm a murderer."

"No, you're not—"

"I don't belong here." She said. "I'm not a hero. Not even a good person. You all deserve a better teammate – a better cousin—"

"Hey, shut up!" Sean said. "That's not true." He stopped himself from reaching for her again. Just barely. "You're the best cousin ever! I know I say you annoy me, and I ditch you to hang out with Seamus and Mac during Thanksgiving, but you are honestly the greatest. I mean, you would kill for me – that's what people say about their families, right? It's an expression of *love*, and that's a *good* thing.

"Anyway, what were you supposed to do? It was a no-win scenario – either way someone was going to die – and Hailey and Maggie were *both* telling you to help them. All you did was prove that you trust your teammates. And, to be honest, if you had stopped Hailey, their plan wouldn't have worked and Siren might have come up with something they weren't prepared for. You're the reason we're all alive!"

"That has nothing to do with me."

"It has *everything* to do with you!" He was yelling now, like he thought volume was going to help him get through to her. "You're a good person who was in a terrible situation and was trying to do the least-terrible thing. It's not like you went outside like, 'hey, guys, I'm looking forward to killing someone tonight,' right? I'm pretty sure that was Siren's idea."

"Well, yeah, but..."

"But nothing!" He stuck his finger in her face. "You have got to pull your head out of whatever crap pile it's stuffed in and accept that you have no excuse to feel guilty or beat yourself up or whatever! Everything worked out! We're all alive! Why can't you just be happy about that?!"

Lydia laughed despite herself. "You know, some people show sympathy towards the traumatized."

He smiled a little. "You sure?"

"I think so." This time, she let him pull her into a hug.

"Cut yourself some slack." He said. "You're not the villain here."

She buried her face in his chest. "You sure?"

"Mm-hm." He bopped the top of her head with his chin. "And I'm older, therefore I'm always right."

She laughed again. Then she started to cry.

Sean rubbed her back while she sobbed. He wished her pain would fall from her tear ducts and leave her exhausted and whole. He wanted to hold her tight enough to squeeze the trauma out of her pores. He hoped that she would wake up in the morning with the wound in her chest already scabbed over and starting to heal. But he had no idea where she would wake up and what she would do when she got there.

~

In the kitchen, Kyle felt the chill of being watched and looked up. Viv was leaning on the doorframe, staring at him. When he met her eyes, she lifted a hand in greeting and walked over to sit on the couch next to him.

"Hi." He said.

"Hi." She hadn't taken her eyes off him yet.

He felt like squirming. What was he, five? "You're Maggie's mom, right?"

"Yes."

He held her gaze for a couple more seconds, then dropped his head into his hands. "Look, I've had a really long day. If you want to yell at me for putting everyone in danger, can you do it tomorrow?"

"I'm not going to yell at you." She said.

"Oh?" He glanced at her in his peripheral vision. "Then why are you here?"

"Because," she took a deep breath and leaned back against the couch, finally looking away. "You remind me of me when I was younger. And I know I would never ask people for help when I needed it. Especially not people I cared about."

Kyle scoffed and pulled himself up. "I don't need help."

"Uh-huh."

"I'm fine."

"Sure." Viv ran her hands through her hair. "Look, kid, I speak five languages and I've learned how to detect bull in all of them. I know you're not willing to actually use the support system you've been blessed with, but at least talk to me. After this is over, you might never have to see me again."

Kyle groaned. "You know, everyone says that talking helps you work through your problems, but that's never happened for me. Whenever I tell people about something I'm going through it's because they forced me to, and whatever I get off my chest is immediately replaced by anger at being forced to do something I didn't want to do."

Viv nodded sagely. "I was a drama queen when I was your age, too."

Kyle scoffed and turned away.

Viv sighed and traced a pattern on the couch with her finger. She wasn't good at this. She'd never really mastered being kind to herself, and Kyle was similar to an almost scary degree. This had been a terrible idea and she should have asked Oliver to talk to the kid. Oliver was great at talking to her.

"So what's your deal, anyway?" She asked.

"Huh?"

"Why are you fighting crime and hiding out in a safe house? What do you do?"

"Oh." Kyle shifted to face her better. "I work with computers and electrical wiring. I can find almost anything if I have Wi-Fi." He tilted his head. "Actually, that's how I found you. And Maggie."

"Really?" Viv had no idea where she was going with this. "Interesting."

"Do you work with computers?"

"Um. No." Viv smirked. "I've tried to avoid social media and the internet for...reasons." *Very specific. He's definitely going to feel comfortable opening up to that kind of honesty.*

"Oh." Kyle frowned. "Then how do I remind you of you?"

Viv blinked. Did he know he was steering the conversation back on track? Was he doing this on purpose?

"Well." She cleared her throat. "When I was a kid, I made some bad life choices and dug a pretty deep hole for myself. I didn't realize how badly I was hurting my parents by messing up my own life until I climbed out of it. And when I did I...promised I'd never do anything to hurt anyone I cared about again. So I started keeping everything inside, bottling it up and not letting anyone help me deal with it because I didn't want to burden them."

Kyle was nodding. "It makes sense." It sounded like "I refuse to answer on the grounds that doing so might incriminate me."

"But then I met Oliver – my husband – and we became friends. We were both pretty far away from our families, so when he got really sick I ended up sleeping on his couch for three days to make sure he was alright." She smiled, even though at the time all it meant to her was that she had to clean up his vomit. "One day – I don't even know if he was fully conscious at the time – he looked at me and said, 'You help me but don't let me help you. Hypocrite. 's not fair.' And then he passed out."

"Huh." Kyle raised an eyebrow. "And then you started letting him help you?"

"I learned to." Viv said. "To be honest, I still keep a lot of things to myself. Sometimes you keep secrets because there's a part of you that you don't want people to see. But I know that when I ask people to let me help them, I mean it. I'm not sure why I seem to automatically assume they don't."

Kyle crossed his arm, tapping his fingers against his biceps. "That's a good point."

"Yeah. Oliver's wise like that. Even when he's half-delirious, the jerk." She turned her gaze on him again. "Trust me, I know this isn't going to be like flicking a light switch for you. But please try. Practice with me."

He sighed. His eyes ping-ponged between her and the floor. Finally, he squared his shoulders. "I don't think I've ever…felt…that helpless. Before."

He clenched and unclenched his fists. "I like being in control. That's one of the nice things about programming – it's a completely different level of control. I wasn't in control of being captured and then I wasn't even in control of myself. She didn't – act like I thought she would. She acted like it was all just a game to her. Like my life and Maggie's life and all our lives were just…meaningless."

Viv watched. And she waited.

Kyle wrapped his arms tighter around himself. "When I thought she was going to start torturing me, I…tried to prepare myself. And she didn't – touch me – but it feels like she did." He closed his eyes. "It feels like she's still in control."

Viv nodded.

Kyle looked at her. "Aren't you going to say anything?"

"I think it's more about what you say." Viv told him. "Like…saying things out loud takes away some of their power."

"Oh."

"Is it working?"

"…I don't know."

Viv wanted to put a hand on his shoulder, but that was probably the last thing he needed. "She's not in control, you know."

Kyle could not have given her his attention faster. The windows in his eyes were wide open. There was a clear path to take to hurt him.

"She's just a person." Viv continued. "She isn't any more in control of what's going on in the world than you are. It isn't fun that you have no say in most of what happens to you, but it's good to remember that no one else does either. What I mean is, life is complicated and impossible to predict – for anyone – and all you can do is your best. And that has to be enough."

"How do I get her out of my head?" He whispered.

"She's not in your head." Viv told him. "She's not that powerful. Your brain is just trying to figure out how to deal with what happened."

Kyle nodded slowly. "Okay." He said. "Okay."

Chapter 30

Home Sweet Home

Siren put the end of the wrapping between her teeth and pulled it tight, groaning as the pain extended like barbs from her wound. Luckily, it was a clean shot, so she didn't have to dig the bullet out.

"I thought you said you had them."

She hadn't heard him come in, but she didn't show her surprise. "The door was locked." She turned to face him.

Grady's eyes were volcanic ash blocking out the sun. Mass extinction was imminent. "What happened?"

Siren put her good hand on her hip. It was no use trying to explain manners or privacy to these science experiment types. "Calm down; it's just a temporary setback. How's your leg?"

"You let them get away!"

"*You* lost the other one *and* the scientist, so don't act all self-right-eous. Anyway, I still know where they are." She nodded at his leg. "What's the verdict? Are you going to be hovering dramatically for the rest of your life?"

"It's fine." He said, avoiding putting weight on it. Half the leg of his pants had been ripped up to make a pseudo-bandage that was so oversaturated with blood it was dripping.

Siren made a face. "Here. Rewrap that using some real medical supplies." She tossed some gauze and a roll of wrapping at him. "Do you need stitches?"

He grunted.

"I didn't catch that. Look, do you need me to do it?"

He shook his head and headed for the bathroom.

She glared at the trail he left behind him on the carpet. "You know, if I hadn't given the hotel people a bogus credit card, I'd be upset with your mess."

He didn't answer.

She sat down on the bed and flipped through channels as she waited. Side-eyeing the pill bottle on the bedside table, she wondered how many more pain killers she could take before she accidentally assassinated herself. There wasn't a hospital in town, so all she'd managed to score was the lame over-the-counter stuff.

Halfway through a *Full House* rerun, Grady came out of the bathroom. He'd showered off about five epidermal layers worth of grime, but his clothes still looked disgusting. At least his wound sported a shiny new bandage. He made a face at the TV.

"I hate that show."

"I'm not surprised," she said. "You probably hate puppies and rainbows, too."

"Turn it off."

"Excuse me, this is *my* hotel room. If you want to control the remote, you can get your own."

Grady narrowed his eyes at the remote and suddenly it was too heavy to hold – not only for her hand, but for the bed and the floor too, judging by the tunnel it made. Siren hissed, rubbing her wrist.

"Hey! My hands are important in my line of work. If you sprained it, I'm adding that workplace injury to my bill."

He moved so he was towering over her. "You'll take the agreed upon amount and not a penny more." He growled.

She laughed. "That's adorable. Obviously you haven't worked with many professionals."

"*I'm* paying *you*, so you'll follow my directions."

Siren rolled her eyes and slid off the bed. "Look, man, it's obvious you don't have much experience with the 'criminal underworld' so to speak. The money you're paying me for this looks like a kid's allowance compared with the jobs I usually take. That's because *I* am really, really talented. I only took this job because it sounded interesting.

"So here's the deal; I can walk out that door right now, you can keep your piggy bank, and I can have another job within the hour. OR you can start respecting my skills and let me do this my way. Because I have never failed." She'd invaded his personal space at some point during her speech, and she held her ground, eyes locked on his.

He bared his teeth. "Letting those hostages get away sounds like a failure to me."

She laughed. "You are a riot tonight! I already told you; I didn't lose them." She held up her phone. "There are a bunch of these cute little tracking apps out there now. I downloaded one onto the blue-haired one and her mutant pet's phones while they were unconscious, linked them up with mine, and now I know exactly where they've been hiding."

Grady cleared his throat and stepped back. "Do you think the other Gemini and his team will go there?"

"No doubt." She said. "Let's hit it tomorrow, though. I like to be well-rested when I attack people on their own turf."

"Hm." Grady huffed.

"So," Siren began, opening the web browser on her phone. "Are you in the mood for pizza? I'm guessing you haven't eaten since your little showdown."

Grady looked away. "I could go for some pizza."

"Sweet. What'd you like? Pepperoni? Meat Lovers? Everything?"

"I'm a vegetarian."

She raised an eyebrow and slowly turned her head towards him. "Really?"

He nodded.

"Then why did you hire an assassin? Aren't vegetarians against killing and stuff?"

Grady frowned. "It's not the people I'm trying to kill; it's what they stand for." He met her gaze. "Sometimes ideas are like viruses. You have to isolate the infected and stop the virus before it can spread."

Siren crossed her arms, phone dangling from one hand and still open to the pizza page. "Haven't you ever heard of a vaccine? Or an antidote?"

"Not every virus can be cured." Grady told her.

~

"What happened to you guys?" Maggie and Elliot spoke at the same time, then stared at each other.

"Wow." Wendell said. "Score one for Twin Telepathy."

Adanna rolled her eyes.

"Baby, what happened to you?" Taylor asked, fingers feathering over her cast.

"I'm fine, mom. It's just a hairline fracture."

Taylor wrapped her arm around Adanna's shoulders and turned her to face her father. "Do you hear this girl? *'Just* a hairline fracture.' Where does she get that lack of self-preservation from?"

"Her mother." Hugh said.

"Good point." Taylor nodded.

"Are you okay, Carly?" Lydia asked.

"I'm *fine*." Carly sighed. "Really. I've been walking all day, but Nehemiah insisted on carrying me inside."

"Because she's really slow." Nehemiah explained. "She got stabbed right in her speed muscles."

"She got *stabbed?!*" Lydia grabbed Carly's shoulder, eyes wide. "You got *stabbed?!*"

"It's not as bad as it sounds." Carly said, patting her shoulder.

"She got a house dropped on her." Wendell said. "Like the Wicked Witch of the East."

"*WHAT?!*"

Sean clasped Elliot's hand. "How are you, man? You look exhausted."

"Yeah. That's probably because I am." He ran his fingers through his hair and sighed. "Oh, by the way, this is Delilah." He waved a hand in her direction. "She's the one who mutated Maggie and me."

"Hi. I'm Sean." He shook her hand with a smile. "I thought you'd be taller. With, like, horns and a pitchfork."

As soon as the two groups merged together, Maggie did what she always did in those situations; found a wall and leaned on it. It was so easy to see that they were comfortable together. Interacting seemed so...natural. Maggie wondered how long you had to know someone before being with them was easy.

She saw movement out of the corner of her eye and looked over at Kyle. He leaned up against the wall next to her and crossed his arms. He frowned when he saw her looking at him.

"I was here first." He said.

Maggie raised an eyebrow. "In what universe?"

"The universe where I've been helping set up this safe house for the past year and a half."

She rolled her eyes. "Yeah, well, if you're going to be technical about it."

"Hey guys." Hailey had strolled over to stop in front of them. "Is this the introvert corner?"

"It's not an anything corner, we just both decided to lean on the wall." Kyle told her.

"For the record, I was here first." Maggie added. "I didn't ask him to come over or anything."

"Oh, so it's a denial corner."

Maggie smirked.

"Okay. My arms are getting tired. Coming through!" Nehemiah called over the crowd.

"You can just put me down." Carly said.

He carried her to the room she was staying in with Adanna, Lydia, and Hailey. They each claimed a wall and shared the middle – that was the idea, anyway. Nehemiah set her down on the air mattress on her wall.

"Thank you." She said. "You totally didn't have to, but…"

"Don't mention it."

Group Think had dragged the rest of them after him, and Hailey tugged Maggie over to her side of the room.

"Check this out." She held up a heart about the size of her palm made from blue crystal. The surface was split into dozens of tiny faces which reflected the light from the ceiling.

"Wow." Maggie said. "It's beautiful!"

Hailey grinned and turned the heart so they were looking at it from above. She pointed to a small circular hole right between the two halves. "Look in there."

Maggie gingerly took the heart and lifted it to her eye. She gasped. Inside the crystal were dozens of refracting colors and shapes which spiraled, disappeared, and reappeared as she turned it.

"It's a kaleidoscope!" She said.

"I. Know. Right?!" Hailey bounced up and down on her knees. "My mom bought it for me on one of her business trips. I have never seen anything else like it; it's my favorite thing that I own."

"Wow." Maggie tried not to be obvious about how quickly she handed it back. "It's incredible! I've only ever seen those tiny plastic ones that look like telescopes."

"Hi." Lydia dropped to her knees on the air mattress.

"Dude!" Hailey waved her arms. "Don't pop my bed!"

"Sorry." Lydia turned to Maggie. "Did she show you the kaleido-scope?"

"Yeah. It's – wow."

"Right?!"

"Hey, Maggie." The three turned to Adanna, who was standing behind them. "Can I talk to you for a second?"

"Um. Sure." Maggie stood up and half-waved to Lydia and Hailey as she followed Adanna into the hall. Part of her wondered if she should have hidden behind the other two while she had the chance.

In the hallway, Adanna turned to face her. The boys and parents had drifted away at the door to the girls' room, like rivers branching off from the main source. They had the hallway to themselves. Maggie grabbed her left arm and leaned back on her right leg.

Adanna took a deep breath. "Ok, so, I know this is totally unfair to you, but the room we put you in is kind of the only extra room we had, and now that we need somewhere to put our prisoner..."

Maggie straightened. "Oh! Yeah, no. Totally take the room. I'm fine with that."

"Okay. Cool." Adanna's lips twitched in a smile. "So, you could move into the room with your parents or, you know, room with the rest of us."

Maggie blinked. "Like...that room?"

"Yeah." Adanna looked away. "I know you didn't come here because you wanted to and I haven't heard if you even want to join the team, but if you want to move into our room, you can. Like, no pressure or anything. It doesn't mean you have to join us."

"Oh. Wow. Um." Maggie cleared her throat and rubbed her arm. "Are you sure it's not too much trouble?"

"She wouldn't be asking if it was too much trouble!" Lydia hissed from the doorway.

Maggie and Adanna turned to see Lydia and Hailey peeking out at them.

"Come on, Maggie!" Hailey said. "It'll be fun!"

"Um." Their excitement seemed to spread out from them and fill the air; colorless, odorless, and very potent. "Okay, then."

"Yes!" Hailey pumped her fist.

"Awesome!" Lydia ducked back into the room. "I'm gonna move stuff around to make sure there's room!"

"Oh, you don't have to do that—" Maggie began.

"Don't bother." Adanna smirked. "She takes any excuse to reorganize furniture in a room. You should have seen her when we were setting this place up."

Hailey sidled over to them. "I can help carry your mattress and stuff."

"I don't really have any stuff." It was so weird to remember that she had literally nothing besides the clothes she'd worn when Elliot had saved her. It felt like she'd been here for a year instead of a day.

"Sweet; I don't like making multiple trips."

"I'd help, but..." Adanna held up her broken arm.

"Don't worry about it." Hailey waved a hand. "Just go help Lydia before she accidentally tells Carly to do something."

Adanna made a face. "Good point."

On the opposite end of the hall, the boys had their own room. Four of them were sitting in the middle of the room, between the five mattresses, but Nehemiah was lying on his face-down.

"I think I'm going to sleep for a week." He said.

"It's noon, but have fun." Sean told him.

"Not to be that guy, but you're not just letting the mad scientist just roam free, are you?" Kyle asked Elliot.

The Guild's leader shook his head. "I was keeping an eye on her, but my parents said they'd watch her so I could have a break."

Wendell laughed. "Why did we spend so much time trying to keep her alive if you were just going to hand her over to Taylor and Hugh?"

Elliot rolled his eyes. "She'll be *fine*."

"Eh..." Wendell held up his hand and twisted it back and forth.

"It's possible." Sean said.

"Possible." Kyle nodded. "Not probable."

"If I were your parents," Nehemiah's voice was muffled, "I'd probably kill her."

"Oh, whatever you guys." Elliot crossed his arms. "My parents know how important it is to get her help. They don't just go around killing people, you know."

"What about people who experimented on their son and separated him from his sister at birth, then tried to ditch him when a psychotic super-powered maniac she also experimented on attacked her house?" Kyle asked.

Elliot winced. "When you say it like that, it sounds bad."

Sean put a hand on his shoulder. "Don't worry, man; your parents are smart. They're not going to murder someone when they were the last people seen with that person. If they were going to murder someone, we'd probably never find out about it."

Elliot glared. "Thanks, Sean."

Sean smirked, but let curtains drop behind his eyes almost immediately afterwards. "On a serious note, we don't think the gravity man is working alone."

"Grady." Wendell said.

"What?"

"His name is Grady." Elliot said.

"Whatever." Sean waved a hand. "Her name is Siren. She was after Maggie, but she knew about all of us."

"And you're sure she's working with Grady?" He asked.

Kyle rubbed his wrists. "Pretty sure."

He dropped his head into his hands and groaned. "How many more people is he working with?"

"Hey," Wendell rubbed his back. "We don't have to worry about that stuff right now. Let's just relax a little. We've definitely earned it."

Elliot lifted his head and nodded. "Yeah. Yeah, okay."

Nehemiah pushed himself up on his forearms. "Do we have pizza? I feel like this is a time for pizza."

Elliot shrugged. "I don't remember. It feels like forever ago."

"Well, let's check the pantry, then." Wendell suggested.

Sean and Kyle exchanged a look.

"We'll wait here." Sean said.

~

Grady had spent years on his own. Ever since Lizzie and Ken. So he hadn't had a bagel slam-dunked into his stomach to wake him up in a while.

"For a guy who's supposed to be on the run, you sleep like Rip van Winkle." Siren said.

"Who?" He grunted, sitting up and rubbing his eyes.

"Rip van—never mind." She shook her head. "Uncultured philistine."

His forehead wrinkled as he tried to decode that message. He decided to drop it. "What time is it?"

"Almost noon." She pulled the drapes open, smiling when he yelled about the sun burning his eyes.

Grady glared at her. "Why did you wake me? We have seven more hours until sundown."

Siren raised an eyebrow. "You want to fight on enemy territory in the dark?"

"You carry out many assassinations in broad daylight?"

"Uh, yeah." She said. "Because I'm good at my job."

"You're also crazy." Grady said. "I'm going to eat this bagel and go back to sleep. Wake me up at a decent hour."

"Unbelievable." Siren sighed. "Good thing I brought a book."

Chapter 31

The Calm

With everyone back together, the safe house felt more like a small city than an abandoned cabin in the woods. As soon as the pizza smell permeated the air of the building, there was chaos. Adanna herded everyone into a relatively organized stream of coming and going from the kitchen. It seemed to resemble the path of blood through the heart.

Elliot hugged her as she surveyed her handiwork. "You are my hero." He said in a sing-song voice.

She grinned. "It's what I do."

"Have you eaten yet?"

"Have *you*?"

"Touché." He dug his chin into her shoulder, hard enough to be annoying but not enough to be painful. "Do you think the line will survive without you here?"

Adanna shrugged. "It's anybody's guess."

"Good enough for me." He spun around, grabbed her wrist, and dragged her out of the room.

She laughed. "Slow *down*, you goofball!"

"Why?" He asked. "Your arm's broken, not your leg."

"Where are we even going?"

He didn't answer, just pulled her into the garage and shut the door behind them.

Adanna groaned. "Haven't we spent enough time in a car over the past couple days?"

"We're not here for a car." Elliot grinned and let go of her hand. He made his way over to a bookshelf that held extra oil, gas cans, and tools. He grabbed a half-rusted green box off the shelf. "Wendell *always* packs some extra food in his toolbox. He works overtime often enough that his lunch sometimes doesn't cut it. I bet he has some power bars in his spare, too." He peeked inside. "Jackpot!" He tossed Adanna a peanut butter flavored protein bar.

"Isn't this stealing?" She asked.

Elliot scoffed. "What--? Stealing? *No*. It's just...borrowing without permission. Like he did with my Skillet CD that he hasn't returned yet."

Adanna whistled. "Wow. That is vindictive. I have never seen this side of you before, Elliot." She struggled to open her bar with one hand and her teeth before holding it out to him. "Help."

He tore it open and handed it back. "I like to think of it as good-natured teasing. Besides, I'll grab some canned peaches from the pantry later and stick them in as payment."

"Why don't we just eat the canned peaches?"

"Because they're all the way over in the pantry."

Adanna laughed. "The pantry is right next to the kitchen, which we just came from."

Elliot shrugged. "But there are *people* over there."

Adanna smirked. "Aren't I people?"

"Nah." Elliot said. "You're Adanna."

The two took a seat on a bench in front of the tool shelf. They munched on their "borrowed" protein bars in silence. Adanna finished first and looked over at her brother. He was staring off into an alternate dimension, chewing robotically. She leaned over, bumping his shoulder with her own.

"What's with the face?"

"Hm?" He shook his head, refocusing. "Face? What?"

"Why do you look like you're trying to uncover the secrets of the universe?" She asked.

"Um. No reason." He looked at his feet, lifting them off the floor and swinging them up and down in the air. "Do you remember when I found out I was adopted?"

"You always knew you were adopted."

"Yeah, the fact was *there* in my head, but do you remember when I found out what it meant? That it meant—means—" He cut himself off. "Never mind. Doesn't matter."

He couldn't have raised a more obvious red flag if he'd been walking in front of the Olympic team from the People's Republic of China. Adanna closed her eyes, searching her memory.

"Oh." *Oh.* "When your third grade teacher had you guys all draw family trees, and he told you that you had to draw the dotted line from our parents to you because they weren't your biological parents?"

"Mr. Vyle." He nodded. "I'd never really thought about it before, that being 'adopted' means I'm not really part of your family."

Adanna punched him in the arm. "What do you mean?! Of course you are! You think because we don't have the same blood we're not siblings?! Don't be *stupid*."

"Ow." He said, rubbing his arm.

Adanna stood up, pacing in front of him. "If someone has a heart transplant, it doesn't make them less related to their family. Family is about where you *belong*, where you were *meant* to be. There are no accidents."

"I'm sorry." Elliot said quietly.

Adanna sighed, walking over and hugging him. "Don't give me those puppy eyes; that's not fair."

Elliot hid his face in her shirt. "I love you."

"I love you too, kiddo."

"It's just...seeing Maggie, hearing about my biological parents...it's made everything seem so *weird*. Like my brain is trying to run two movies simultaneously and everything is all jumbled and confusing. I don't know how to feel. Am I supposed to have some sort of connection with her? I mean, we're twins, right? Aren't twins supposed to...I don't know, recognize each other?" He took a shaky breath in. "She looks like a stranger."

"That's because she *is* a stranger." Adanna stroked his hair, fingers automatically working out the tangles like they had when they were kids. "That's what you call someone you don't know yet. It doesn't mean that you won't be...really close...in the future. I mean..." She peeked down at his face and smiled. "You were a stranger to me, once. When Mom and Dad brought home this tiny little bundle, looking like it had gotten all the blood sucked out of it, poor thing, it was so pale."

Elliot laughed.

"But after a while, you weren't a stranger who was my brother anymore. You were just my brother. And one day," she swallowed. "One day Maggie will be just your sister."

Elliot pulled away. "Thanks." He said. "How did you get so smart?"

"Maybe I was just born with it."

"Maybe it's Maybelline." Elliot sang in an obnoxious high-pitched voice.

Adanna groaned.

~

Delilah was bored out of her mind. The couple who called them-selves Gemini Beta's parents had locked her in this sad excuse for a guest room and warned her not to try to escape on pain of death.

She could see in their eyes how badly they wanted her to try to escape. Well, they were going to be disappointed. She was right where she wanted to be.

She crossed her legs, resting her hands on her knees. Closing her eyes when the room was pitch black was a little redundant, but she did it anyway. She breathed deeply.

Feel the oxygen reenergizing your blood. Feel it flow through you like a burst of inspiration.

Lately, there had been a huge push towards mindfulness and med-itation in the agency. Something about improving efficiency through sharpening the weapons already in the case. She wasn't sure whether it actually improved productivity or if it was some sort of placebo, but she played along. No harm in acting cooperative.

Visualize your end goal. It is at the top of a staircase. Each stair represents a step towards acchieving your goal. Try to visualize the step right in front of you. What does it look like?

The backs of her eyelids shifted from reflections of an endless void to vein-covered membranes red with backlight. Delilah opened her eyes, blinking to clear her vision. When she was able to make out who was in front of her, she raised her eyebrows.

"I haven't met you yet, have I?" She asked.

"No." The boy was awkward, obviously overcompensating for his insecurities with flashy clothes. "I'm Kyle." He was holding a plate. "I came to give you some food."

She took her time unfolding herself and stood. She took the plate from him and smiled. "You don't strike me as a delivery boy."

He frowned. "I'm not. I have some questions."

"Really?" She took a bite of the pizza. It wasn't what she usually ordered, but prisoners can't be choosers. "And what might those be?"

He raised his chin. "I want to know about Siren."

"That's not a question."

"It's a summary of my questions."

"Hm." She nodded. "I appreciate a man who doesn't waste my time. Have a seat." She herself sat down on one side of the air mattress, indicating the other with a hand. "I'd offer you some tea, but I'm a little indisposed at the moment."

He hesitated, then poked his head back out into the hall to talk to Elliot's parents, who were still standing guard. He came back inside, activated his phone's flashlight, and shut the door behind him. He sat down on the other side of the mattress, setting the phone on the floor between them as a makeshift lamp. Then he looked at her expectantly.

Delilah took another bite of pizza, chewing slowly as she studied him. "What do you want to know about her?"

"Everything." He didn't even hesitate.

"That's a tall order." She said. "She's a mercenary. An assassin. One of the best. No one knows *everything* about her."

"Her real name is Gertrude."

Like she could add that data to a search engine in her brain and come up with suddenly unknown knowledge. Delilah resisted the urge to roll her eyes. "Is that what she told you?"

He pressed his lips together and looked away.

"It doesn't matter what she calls herself." She told him. "She has no ties to people, places, or things. Trust me, a lot of people have looked.

She is extremely skilled, incredibly dangerous, and terribly efficient. No target has ever escaped her."

"I did." Kyle said.

Delilah smiled at him. "No you didn't."

"What's that supposed to mean?"

"It means that you should watch your back, kiddo."

He shook his head. "Why is she working with Grady?"

Delilah hummed. "No idea. It can't be money; he's been on the run for twenty-five years and lucrative jobs don't mix with flying under the radar. My guess is she thinks the job is interesting. She has a good enough reputation and success rate that she can pick and choose her jobs."

"So she's a psychopath."

Delilah finished off her pizza and used the hem of her shirt to rub the grease off her fingers. "I don't think she's been analyzed by a medical professional, but in colloquial terms I suppose you're right."

Kyle leaned forward. "How do I stop her?"

"She's human, so you won't need special equipment built like the Gemini subjects are going to use against Grady. Still, my advice would be to treat her like she is just as powerful as he is in every other way. And when you get a shot, take her down. Do not give her any time to regroup, retreat, or respond." The light from the phone shattered into pieces in her eyes. "And when you do, make sure you kill her twice."

"I thought you said she was human." Kyle frowned.

Delilah laughed. "Humans are much more stubborn than you might think."

~

Wendell's parents were extroverts, so he had long since given up the futility of trying to understand why, in a group of people, he could never find anyone he was actually looking for.

When they'd gotten back, Kyle had looked less approachable than usual – and he usually looked pretty unapproachable. The whole secondary team had looked somewhere between messed up and traumatized, actually, but Kyle was the only one who seemed to be allergic to support systems.

Besides Maggie, who Wendell figured was polite enough not to refuse help when it was forced upon her. Kyle was a different story. Wendell had been working on him for years and barely made it past the first firewall. And *wow* did he know how to hide.

Eventually, Wendell ended up back in the boys' room. He dropped onto his air mattress from a standing position, falling through to the floor before it bounced him back up. Nehemiah turned his head.

"What's wrong?" He asked.

"Nothing. I'm fine." Wendell said.

"Lying is a sin." Nehemiah said. "And I know you're lying because you're always going on and on about how we shouldn't break the air mattresses."

"Excellent deduction, Sherlock."

"I still haven't read those books."

Wendell shrugged one shoulder. "Most people haven't. But the premise is kind of ubiquitous, so everyone references it. Like group think or something."

"Yeah, I understood none of that." Nehemiah pushed himself up on his elbows. "Not the point, though. What's going on?"

Wendell sighed. "I can't find Kyle."

"That's not something people are usually upset about."

"Yeah, but whatever happened with that Siren chick really messed with the team. And you know Kyle will never admit that he needs help."

"Mm. That's true." Nehemiah frowned. "Do *you* need help?"

Wendell frowned at the ceiling. "With what? Finding Kyle? Yes."

"You know what I mean."

"I'm fine."

"You are such a hypocrite."

"Thank you."

Nehemiah sighed. "Do you think the guys at the shop are going to be swamped without us?"

Wendell lifted a shoulder. "Maybe. But Jake and Tommy have been complaining about needing extra hours, so I think it'll be fine."

"Yeah." Nehemiah nodded slowly. "I think I'm going to check up on the van tomorrow. It's been through a lot lately, might need a tune-up."

Wendell smirked. "Most people don't do work in their free time, you know."

"I like working. Makes me feel like I'm accomplishing something." He said. "Besides, these cars are a lot different than the farm equipment I used to work on back home. I can use the practice."

"Don't sell yourself short. You're really gifted." Wendell told him. "I've never seen someone pick mechanics up as quickly as you."

"I don't know. I've just had a lot of practice." He rolled over so he was staring at the ceiling, too. "Amish people don't believe in being 'gifted.'"

"What? Isn't the term 'gifted' implying a supernatural Giver? What's wrong with that?"

"We – they believe that it's prideful to consider yourself 'special.' They want everyone to be equal, I think. Everyone has the same kind of jobs and responsibilities. No one is more important than anyone else. Except the ministers and deacons."

"Sounds like communism." Wendell said.

"What's that?"

"It's like…this idea that the government should be in charge of giving people jobs, everyone should be paid the same, and there shouldn't be competing brands and stuff." He frowned. "It's kind of this attempt at making a Utopian society, but it usually ends up just making a police state."

Nehemiah grimaced. "I don't know what either of those things are."

"Oh. Um…a utopia is a place where everything is perfect. There's no war or crime or anything. And a police state is a place where the government micro-manages peoples' lives to the point where there are stupid laws and people end up disappearing if they don't agree with them."

"Like being shunned."

"Sort of. Usually a little less survive-y than that, though."

Nehemiah glanced at his friend. "Is that a real word? Survive-y?"

"If you understood me, then it's a word."

"That's not very communist of you."

Wendell laughed.

The building shook, rumbling like it was laughing along with him. The metal of the building screamed as it tore apart and collapsed.

In a dark room towards the back of the building, Kyle looked at Delilah, wide-eyed. "What was that?" His voice was quiet, like he was afraid he would be heard over the destruction.

Delilah, on the other hand, didn't seem concerned. "They're here." She said.

On a couch in the communal area, Sean and Lydia looked up. They were close to the front of the building, the garage, and they could see smoke start drifting down the hallway towards them.

Maggie, Hailey, and Carly were in their room, exchanging war stories from the past few days. Maggie had just shown Carly her wound when the ground started to shake. She let her shirt fall back into place and stood up, fists clenching.

Two sets of parents reached for weapons they hadn't put down since they'd armed themselves in the vault.

In the garage, Elliot pushed himself up and coughed. Adanna groaned from beside him, clutching her broken arm which had fallen out of its sling. They both stared at the front wall, or where the front wall used to be.

It had been torn between two incredibly strong gravitational poles on either side of the building. Some of the roof had gone with it. As the dust settled, the siblings could make out two figures backlit by the setting sun.

Siren rolled her neck and cracked her knuckles. "Look at that," she said to Grady, "a welcoming committee."

He lifted his hands, eyes locked on Elliot. "This time, I'm not holding back."

Elliot stood up, rolling his shoulders back. "That isn't going to change the outcome."

"No," Grady agreed. "It won't."

Chapter 32

Fight Club

Adanna reached instinctively to her side, but she wasn't in the habit of walking around the house armed. Elliot, luckily, was never not armed. He threw two lightning arcs towards the intruders, but Grady deflected them towards the sky.

Siren rushed forward, drawing two guns from her thighs and firing at Elliot's chest as he was focused on Grady. Adanna grabbed the back of his T-shirt and pulled him to the floor. The bullets whizzed over their heads as Elliot's lightning went wild.

She jerked back, hissing at the heat coming off him. Every piece of hair on his body was standing up, crackling in the air. If they hadn't been about to die, his tiny fluffy afro would have been adorable. Siren was suddenly above them.

But not for long. Elliot threw lightning at her and she flattened herself to the ground with almost impossible speed. She aimed her gun at Adanna. Suddenly, her eyes flicked up and she rolled to the side as bullets exploded where her body had been.

"Ready to meet the parents?!" Taylor shouted.

"Run," Elliot grabbed Adanna's wrist and dragged her under the bullets until a wave of gravity threw him into the wall. He let go of Adanna midair, but she still tumbled to the floor.

Grady clenched his fist and all the parents dropped. Siren sprinted across the room, leaping over them as soon as Grady let up the gravity. She disappeared into the hall.

"We'll get her." Viv said, struggling to her feet. "Save your kids."

Taylor and Hugh let off a volley of shots that all sank to the ground a yard from their target.

"We need to get closer!" Taylor said. Hugh nodded as he sped up.

Adanna sat up first, grabbing fistfuls of tools that had been knocked off the shelf by the explosion. She chucked them at Grady, but he didn't even look at her. He stretched out his hand and Elliot gasped for air, pressing hard into the ground.

Adanna scrambled to her feet and jumped between them, but Grady's power apparently didn't work on line of sight. Her fingers tingled as he got closer, his protective field starting to affect her. She cursed and ran back towards Elliot.

"Um...ah..." She dropped to wrap her arms around him. Her body went numb as it tried to figure out which gravitational pull applied to her. She could feel Grady getting closer. There was nothing she could do. "Elliot...!" She whispered.

Elliot couldn't see. Pain crowded his vision out and he felt like his eyes were being squished. So he picked a direction and hoped for the best.

Grady spun to the side, twisting out of the path of the lightning and letting go of his hold on Elliot out of surprise. His desperate twist brought him face to face with a car flying straight at his face. It crumpled on impact with his field, but didn't stop.

"Drag that down all you want!" Maggie shouted, both hands pressing the truck into him.

"Adanna!" Hugh tossed her a gun.

"Oh, thank God." Adanna stood up and aimed her gun towards the sky. "You have to aim high to counteract his gravity field!"

"I'll aim straight on," Hugh murmured just low enough for his wife to hear. "Just in case."

Taylor snapped her chin in a nod.

Elliot coughed, clutching his aching ribs and pushing himself to his feet. "Siren?"

"Didn't see her." Maggie shook her head. "Sean and Lydia are on their way. Hailey's staying with Carly. I don't know about everyone else."

"That's good. Divide and conquer." He took a deep breath, then clenched his fists until his veins turned gold and his hair stood up.

"You look like you're trying to go Super Saiyan." Adanna said.

"Focus." Taylor warned.

The truck was starting to strain upwards. Maggie gritted her teeth and pushed harder.

Elliot kept his voice down. "Let go on my mark."

She nodded.

"One."

Hammers clicked back.

"Two."

Adanna felt the hair on her arms stand up with proximity to Elliot's electric field.

"Now."

~

In the hallway, Kyle held out his arm to stop Delilah. He peered around the corner, then gave her a thumbs-up and darted out into the next hall.

"You guys really need to rethink your definition of 'safe house,'" Delilah said.

"I have no idea how they found us." Kyle snapped. "This place is so beyond off the grid we make our own power."

Delilah's eyebrows rose. "Gemini Beta?"

Kyle stiffened and didn't respond.

He pushed a door open and ushered her inside. She looked around, turning back to him with her hands on her hips.

"Is this your bedroom?" She asked. "Because you're a little young for me."

Kyle barely dignified that with a glare, instead reaching off to the side of his air mattress for a box. He opened it, revealing a collection of random motherboards, hard drives, and bits and pieces of electronics.

"Can you use any of this to make a second weapon to use against Grady?"

She frowned. "Who do you think I am, MacGyver?"

"Try." Kyle said, sliding a Taser out from under his shirt and moving to the door. "Make yourself useful."

She narrowed her eyes at his back, then started digging into the box.

~

The door to the weapons room crashed open and Wendell jumped, turning in midair to face the intruder with Delilah's super-Taser clutched unhelpfully to his chest. He loosened his grip slightly and started breathing again.

"You guys almost gave me a heart attack!" He hissed.

"Eat more Cheerios; they're good for that." Sean said.

"Is that the mutant shock gun?" Lydia asked.

"Yeah." Wendell said. "We have to get it to Carly."

"We know." Lydia grabbed three handguns, stuffing two of them in the waistband of her jeans.

"Do you have an extra arm that I don't know about?" Sean asked.

Lydia glowered at him. "I just don't think we'll get a lot of time to reload."

"Nah, I'm sure they'll give us time outs if we ask for them." Wendell shifted from one foot to the other. "Do you know where she is?"

"In the room." Lydia said.

Sean tossed a piece to Wendell and slung two semi-automatic rifles across his chest. "Let's make sure we get there before Grady does." He shifted one of the rifles into place and peeked outside. "Clear."

The three of them sprinted to the corner, and Sean checked that hallway. He jerked back, startled, then peered around again.

"What? What is it?" Lydia asked.

"Nehemiah?" Sean hissed.

Their friend had his back to them, rifle pointed at the empty hall ahead of him. When he heard Sean's voice, his back stiffened. It wasn't his voice that answered.

"Do we have company?" Siren's voice raised the hairs on the arms of the cousins and, unbeknownst to them, those of Kyle, who was still poised in front of the door of the guy's bedroom.

"Go. I'll cover you." Nehemiah said.

Wendell moved carefully around the corner, pointing his guns in the direction Nehemiah was.

"Wen, what are you doing?!" Sean hissed.

"You have to get Carly, bro." Wendell hoped his voice was low enough that only Nehemiah would hear. "I'll hold up your side of the stand off."

"I'm fine—"

"You're the only one who can carry her and still run. And we *need* her to take out Grady. She's the best shot of us all."

Nehemiah pressed his lips together. He kept his eyes and gun trained on the corner, but backed slowly to the girl's bedroom. When he got there, he dropped one hand to rap his knuckles against it. "It's me." He said. "Let me in."

"What's the magic word?" Asked a sing-song voice from the other side.

Nehemiah frowned. "I've told you a million times that I haven't read *Harry Potter*."

"It's not from—" Hailey dropped the subject and unlocked the door, ushering Nehemiah inside. "Don't drop her." She warned.

Nehemiah set his rifle down and scooped Carly up. "Can you grab my gun?"

"Yeah." Carly looked it over. "Is this what you want me to shoot him with?"

"No, Lydia and Sean have that shock gun Delilah made. We talked about it on the ride back."

"Oh yeah." She nodded. "I think I was asleep. Did you talk about how it worked?"

"I'll explain on the way." They were at the door, and Nehemiah dipped his head in the direction of Siren. Carly lowered the muzzle of the rifle to point in that direction.

They darted into the open, Hailey right behind them.

Siren must have been listening for their footsteps, because she spun out, firing a deadly sweep across the hall.

Nehemiah dropped immediately, curling over Carly. His reaction sent her shot wide, and it hit the wall.

Wendell flinched when he first saw her, but he managed to hold his ground and squeeze off a few answer rounds before the sweep caught him in the chest and sent him to the floor. His skull cracked against the concrete, but he didn't make a sound.

Hailey had dropped instinctively with Nehemiah. She swiveled towards Siren on one knee and threw a knife into her shoulder. Siren dropped the rifle, cursing.

"Wendell!" Nehemiah gasped, getting to his knees.

"Get Carly to the garage." Sean tossed the Taser into Carly's lap on his way to Wendell. "Lydia, watch his back. Hailey, help me with Wen."

Nehemiah looked at his friend one last time, then started sprinting for the garage.

Sean dropped to his knees beside Wendell and grabbed his wrist, searching for a pulse.

"Oh no," Hailey's fingers fluttered over his chest. "No, no, no, no..."

Wendell coughed.

Sean and Hailey leaned back, shocked, as he sat up slowly and groaned. He tugged his ruined t-shirt off to reveal a Kevlar vest.

"What?" He asked them. "I've told you guys, we need to wear the vests. Don't look so shocked."

"I'm just surprised you took time to change." Sean said.

"I didn't."

"Then you wore a bullet-proof vest to dinner?" Hailey asked.

"Oooh," Siren said. "I love drama." She yanked Hailey's blade out of her arm and chucked it at Wendell's eye.

Hailey caught it before it could hit, twirling it around and sending it back. Siren dodged, then lunged to kick Hailey in the chest.

Sean brought up his rifle and Siren forced the muzzle up as he squeezed the trigger, throat-punching him before turning on Wendell as he wheezed. Wendell grabbed for his gun, but she kicked it out of the way. He scrambled backwards, kicking at her until she grabbed his ankle and jabbed her thumb into a pressure point.

"Ah!" He twisted his leg, but that only hurt more.

Hailey suddenly shot across his vision in a blur, slamming into Siren. The two rolled across the floor and into the wall, Siren's hands suddenly wrapped around Hailey's throat. Hailey sent a rabbit punch into Siren's sternum and a left hook into her eye, which stunned her enough for Hailey to wriggle free and throw her off.

Sean grabbed Siren's arms, pulling them up while his knee tried to force her torso down. Hailey punched Siren in the face. Wendell scrambled over to help.

The mercenary twisted, flipping Sean off her and into Wendell. Then she jerked a knee up under Hailey's chin as she stood. Siren grabbed Hailey's arm and swung her around into her friends, who had just untangled themselves. She tugged out her spare handgun and leveled it at Hailey's forehead.

"You kids," Siren said, "Are way tougher than I gave you credit for. Thanks for the workout." Her eyes flicked up and widened as she ducked to the side. A knife slit her cheek on its way past.

"That was just the warm-up." Viv said, brandishing a Ninjato sword as her husband palmed another blade. "Time to pick on someone your own age."

Siren fired off a few shots, then darted around the corner.

Viv and Oliver sprinted down the hall. Viv hurtled the pile of bodies, turning on a dime and disappearing after the mercenary. Oliver skirted them, one eye on his wife as he lingered.

"Are you all okay?" He asked.

They groaned, rolling out of a pile and forcing themselves to stand.

Oliver nodded, then took off down the hall.

Hailey slapped the door. "Kyle!" She said. "You better have something amazing going on in there, or so help me."

The door unlocked and the three of them stumbled inside. Delilah was carefully duct-taping wires together on what looked like something that had been clogging a Cybertronian drain.

"What the heck is that?" Wendell asked.

"A Hail Mary." Kyle told him. "If we lose the gun, that'll have the same general effect, except in bomb version."

"If it can disrupt the brain waves of someone like them, what will it do to us?" Sean asked.

Delilah laughed.

Kyle just stared, arms crossed so they couldn't see his hands trembling.

"Right." Sean sighed. "I was afraid of that."

Chapter 33

Siren Song

Maggie pulled a wall of concrete between herself and Grady, then collapsed against the wall next to Elliot.

"I feel like I remember our fight being more evenly matched before." She gasped.

"Same here." Elliot groaned. He looked her over. She was covered in dirt and debris, skin bruised and shredded from being thrown into things. He was glad he didn't have a mirror. "How are you doing?"

Maggie flexed her fingers. "It's getting harder to manipulate materials without ferromagnetic properties."

Something shot through her wall, impacting just above their heads. "Like concrete?"

The wall shuddered and Maggie made a face. "Yeah."

Elliot nodded, then turned to his family. They were reloading their weapons as fast as they could. "I need you guys to get out of here." He said.

Adanna's head snapped up, eyes radiating crazy. "What?! No way!"

"Look, Maggie and I are getting tired. We need to be able to mess this place up without worrying about you guys getting caught in the crossfire." Elliot coughed. "Look, just wait outside the door, okay? If we need help, you can come right back in."

"He's right." Maggie said. "Grady's not holding back. He doesn't care if you get hurt. We have to be able to not hold back, too." She frowned. "I feel like that was grammar'd badly."

Adanna pressed her lips together, like she was trying to physically hold back the screaming she wanted to do. "We'll be *right* outside." She said.

"Deal." Elliot heaved himself up. "As soon as Maggie drops the wall, run for the door. We'll cover you."

Maggie stood up, closing her eyes and forcing her brain to latch onto the negligible magnetic fields of the concrete. She held onto them as she hunted around for Grady's field. It felt like holding three grocery bags of canned goods in one arm and trying to unlock the door with the other.

"On three." Elliot said. "One...two...three!"

Maggie flipped the fields of the concrete and their enemy so they attracted each other. The concrete had more mass, but Grady had basically nailed himself in place with his gravity field. The entire shelter crashed towards him.

Grady's eyes widened and he let his field up, rocketing towards the upper atmosphere. The concrete crumpled to the ground, but didn't let up its hold on him. Grady strained upwards against the pull, edging higher and higher into the sky.

"What's your range?" Elliot asked, squinting up at the twilit sky.

"I think we're about to find out." Maggie replied through gritted teeth. "Get ready to hit him on the way down."

Elliot cracked his knuckles.

Maggie felt it when Grady finally broke free. The force seemed to snap back against her like a giant rubber band. It drove her to her knees, gasping. She stayed down, forcing her aching mind to feel around for other weapons. That stunt bought them enough time for Elliot's family to get clear, but all it really accomplished was wearing out her strength.

Elliot built up the energy in his body, letting it crackle and boil like an ungrounded shock. Grady was getting closer at much greater than terminal velocity and still accelerating. With the amount of density his gravitational field would be simulating on impact, Grady would cause as much damage as a collapsing building. Elliot bared his teeth. Two could play that game.

The first time he'd seen Maggie outside of the pictures in the file, she was being crushed to death by that man. The rage he'd felt was about as surprising as the magnitude of electricity he'd sent into Grady's body. Now, the rage had cooled and solidified into a toxic hate compounded by Adanna's broken arm, Carly's wounded side, and this invasion of a place he'd promised his family was safe.

The bolt was so superheated Elliot felt his own arms burn as they channeled it up and out into the sky. Grady immediately funneled all his power into bending the light away from himself. The electricity was repelled, but the force of the blast was still enough to knock him off course and send him into an uncontrolled spin towards the trees.

Maggie was on her feet as soon as it was safe to stand next to him again. Poles, nails, screws, and parts of car frames dragged themselves towards her, but she was looking at him.

"How are you doing?" She asked.

Elliot flexed his fingers. "I won't be able to project a charge like that again. Smaller ones, maybe. If I can get closer, they'll be stronger."

"Okay." Maggie rolled her shoulders and the metal started levitating. "I'll distract him. You get up close and personal."

Elliot nodded, then took off into the trees in a sprint. He didn't have to check to see if she was behind him; her metal entourage sounded like a chain of church bells. A chain of church bells taking out a few innocent bushes and trees that got in the way.

Grady was waiting like a bloodied phantom, hands in his pockets just for the effect. Elliot split off as soon as he saw him through the trees. Maggie charged forward into what was now a clearing, stopping short and letting her metal slingshot over her head towards him. She got a lot of satisfaction out of the fact he had to take his hands out of his pockets to deflect all her attacks.

As soon as a piece was repelled, Maggie snatched it back and returned it to play. It was a fast-paced, strategic game of dodgeball. She could still feel the way his gravity had pinned her to the ground, and she was afraid of what would happen if he had even a split second to focus on her instead of her metal.

At the same time, she had to force herself to keep going for the kill. Her conscience wanted to throw up. She tried to ignore it.

Of course, another problem with her relentless attacks was that Elliot didn't have an opening. Unless he didn't mind getting skewered. She could see him behind Grady, crouched in the bushes. His eyes darted around him, looking for a way into the tornado of forces.

Maggie felt a bead of sweat drip down her spine. If she opened a path for Elliot, she might as well flash a neon sign screaming 'IT'S AN AMBUSH.' But she couldn't keep this up forever. Was she just supposed to wait until Grady found a way to counteract her metal and started crushing her again? At some point, he was going to start anticipating that last-minute save trick.

Elliot's fingertips were crackling. Suddenly, his eyes widened. He waved at Maggie and mimed hugging. Was he saying he wanted to take a time out to hug? She hadn't thought someone like her could consider something weird, but she'd been wrong.

Elliot held his hands in front of himself like he was holding something, then mimed squeezing it. He even did the intense concentration face.

Maggie was even more confused. *Score one AGAINST twin telepathy.*

Elliot frowned. Slowly he pointed to Grady. Then he pointed to the tornado of metal. Then he pointed at Maggie and mimed squeezing. Then he pointed at himself and did the holding-something motion again, but this time he made it explode.

Maggie was exasperated. She was trying to concentrate here and he was talking about hugging Grady with metal that exploded – *oh. OH.*

Maggie redirected her metal into one attack, wrapping it around Grady like lettuce around a sushi roll and squeezing with all her strength. He was trying to repel the metal, increasing the force of gravity on it until it groaned trying to sink to the earth. Maggie mimed squeezing with her hands, hoping the visual would help her mind keep its grip.

Elliot braced himself and dove at Grady, hands shuddering with light. He started to release the charge just before he entered the range of Grady's field. It had been hard enough to think while being crushed when he'd been at full strength. He wasn't taking any chances.

Every ounce of electric charge Elliot could muster surged out through his fingertips into the metal which was wrapped around Grady. The pull of the earth on his body was excruciating, but Grady was the one who screamed.

~

Kyle hesitated at the doorway of the boys' room.

"What are you waiting for?" Sean asked.

"Where's Siren?" The gray in Kyle's irises was made up of broken glass.

"Maggie's parents went after her." Sean said. "They'll be fine."

"I'm going, too."

"Just stay out of it, Kyle." Wendell looked annoyed.

"No, he should go." Sean said. "I'll go with."

"Me too." Hailey said.

Wendell frowned.

"You go with them." Delilah told him. She hefted the bomb in her hands. "If we end up having to use this thing, it'll be good to have some people alive in case Grady wakes up before the Gemini subjects."

"Fine." Wendell pointed a finger in her face. "But you better at least give them a chance to take him out before blowing everyone up."

"Of course." She rolled her eyes. "I can't exactly finish my research if I'm dead."

Kyle and the others were already halfway down the hall, so Wendell just turned and ran after them.

It wasn't hard to find Siren; all the Guild members had to do was follow the sounds of fighting. They wound up in the kitchen, where conventional weapons had apparently not been enough.

"What did those plates ever do to you?!" Hailey blurted.

Sean pulled her down as Siren fired off a few shots in their direction. He rolled and came up under her arm, grabbing at her wrist and trying to yank the gun away. From her other side, Viv lashed out with her Neko-te.

Siren grabbed Viv's wrist, redirecting the blades into Sean's arm. Viv recoiled and Sean let go to grab his wound. Siren leveled the gun at Sean's chest.

A knife hit the center of the gun, another following up and skimming off Siren's shoulder as she hit the ground. Oliver palmed more blades, eyes narrowed.

Siren pulled a blade out from her boot and moved to throw it, then redirected to block Viv's Neko-te. She kicked Viv away, then kept the momentum in order to sweep the legs out from an advancing Hailey. She pulled the girl in front of her. At the last second, Oliver flicked his wrist desperately and the knives hit the cupboards above them.

Hailey grabbed at Siren's throat. The mercenary elbowed her in the face hard enough for her to see stars. Siren let go and rolled out of the way of Viv, who had lunged for her shoulders.

She rolled to her feet and lashed out at Sean with a kick, but he sprang into a flip and landed behind her. He locked his arms around her chest, pinning her arms to her side. Wendell sprinted forward, launching his fist at Siren's face without trying to slow his momentum.

Siren twisted free, dropping to the ground and kicking up. She caught Sean in the stomach and heaved him through the air. He and Wendell tumbled to the ground together, tripping up Oliver on their way.

Viv darted forward, brandishing her Ninjato. Siren dodged, then grabbed for her gun. She twisted and caught a downward strike at the intersection between the gun and the knife Oliver had thrown into it. The gun clanged to the ground. Siren jabbed at Viv with the knife, scooping up the gun in the same motion. She threw it, catching Oliver in the forehead and sending him back to the ground.

Hailey struggled to get up, only for Siren to ricochet off the wall and use her as a landing pad. Oliver got up and tackled her. She used her hand to chop him in the throat, then jabbed at the pressure points in his shoulders. She kicked him at Viv, who jumped back frantically, wide eyes lingering on her husband until Siren almost drove her knife into Viv's head.

Sean untangled himself from Wendell and looked at the two women sword-fighting. He felt like he was watching some bizarre gender-swapped version of *Peter Pan*. If Peter Pan was a psycho murderer and Captain Hook was the good guy with a shady past.

As if to complete the illusion, Siren flipped the ninjato out of Viv's hand and caught it in her own. The sword flashed in the fluorescent light and it was pressed against Viv's neck.

"I have to say," Siren was breathing heavily. "You have all been uncommonly fun to play with. We really should do this again sometime." She pressed the blade in until blood welled up underneath it. "But for now; get over against the wall with your hands up, or this lovely lady dies."

"You'll just kill us all anyway." Hailey spat.

"Not true." Siren said. "Sure, that was the plan originally, but we're really just interested in Thing 1 and Thing 2. I'd actually like to keep you alive now that I know I can have a good time with you."

"Don't you dare let her touch Maggie." Viv commanded. The movement of her voice box drew more blood.

Oliver's face wasn't thunderous; it was the rolling skies of a nuclear winter. "If you kill either one of my girls," he said, "I'll tear you apart."

Siren threw back her head and laughed. It was the last thing she ever did. As her body fell to the floor, it seemed to still be smiling. It was hard to tell, though, with the hole in the skull.

Kyle's arm was locked in place, still aiming the gun where Siren's head had been. The rest of his body was shaking like it was trying to squirm away, detach itself from the arm and what it had done.

"Kyle," Hailey stood up, trembling, and stumbled towards him. She stopped just a foot away. She raised her hand, then dropped it again.

Sean felt his body stand, saw his perspective change as his legs carried him over to the two of them. He gently took the gun from Kyle, dropped it to the floor. His arms wrapped around both his teammates' shoulders, and he guided them out of the room.

~

The force of gravity was gone and Elliot could breathe again. He sucked air into his aching lungs, then rolled over to check Maggie's expression. If she was green, that would mean she'd accidentally crushed Grady when the opposing force had let up. He did not need to see that.

Maggie just looked shocked. She still held the metal in place. She was afraid to let go. Afraid this was another trick.

"M..." Elliot coughed. He pushed himself up on shuddering arms. "M'ggie."

Her eyes were the only parts of her that moved.

"It's okay...Maggie." Elliot said. "You can let go."

Slowly, Maggie dropped her arms. The metal cocoon fell apart and Grady collapsed on top of it. He was limp and still. Elliot wondered if he was dead. The lack of remorse scared him. He picked his way over the mound of metal to Grady's body, grabbing at his wrist and feeling for a pulse.

There was one. Elliot felt a pang of disappointment and shuddered. He turned to Maggie, then frowned.

"Delilah...?"

The scientist tossed a pile of circuit boards and wires into the clearing. Maggie and Elliot both stared at it in confusion until it exploded.

Chapter 34

Expect the Unexpected

"I'm disappointed that I didn't get to use the SSG." Carly said. She was curled up on the couch under a blanket.

"SSG?" Wendell asked. He didn't really care.

"Super Stun Gun."

"Oh."

It was quiet. The quiet of a street after a shoot-out as the cops check the bodies for life. The quiet of a house after a parent kicked out their abusive spouse. The quiet that felt wrong in its emptiness and uncertainty, like the path suddenly led into an abyss. Winning was supposed to feel better.

Almost everyone was crowded into the room, taking up furniture and floor space. Maggie and Elliot were recovering in their rooms, Grady was locked in the prison closet, and Delilah wasn't exactly welcome. Part of the room's ceiling had been ripped off when Grady had announced himself and they could see the stars.

Nehemiah was sitting with his back to the wall, close to Carly in case she needed to move. Lydia and Kyle were on the couch next to her. Sean was sitting on the floor next to them, watching their every move. Kyle had been like a statue until Wendell had given him the phones they confiscated from Grady and Siren's body. He hadn't looked up from them since.

Wendell was against the wall between Nehemiah and Hailey. Adanna was next to the door. The parents were standing, huddled in a corner and talking in low voices.

"How did they find us?" Lydia asked. Her face was still pale, and her voice shook a little when she spoke. It was better than it had been. "Did they follow us or something?"

"And then what? Hide in the bushes for half a day until we all got comfortable?" Hailey shook her head. "Somehow, they knew how to find us. Do super-humans have some sort of radar or something?"

"That would be a Delilah question." Adanna said.

Wendell sighed. "What does it matter, anyway? Maybe they just walked around until they found a bunker in the woods."

"They wouldn't just attack every building they came across in the woods, that wouldn't make sense." Sean said.

"They didn't have to." Kyle paused in his typing for a split second. "Looks like Siren downloaded one of those Friend Finder apps and linked it to Maggie and Hailey's phones." He went back to ignoring them.

Hailey stared at him. She stood up casually. Then she punched the wall and swore.

"Hails!" Wendell jumped to his feet and pulled her back. "What were you thinking?! Did you hurt yourself?"

"Shut up! Get away from me!" Hailey snarled, shoving him backwards. "I can't believe this." She grabbed fistfuls of her own hair. "What have I done?"

"It's not your fault." Sean said, walking over to her slowly. "It could've happened to anyone."

"It's probably even happened to CIA agents. You can't be expected to keep track of every widget and subroutine in your phone." Adanna agreed.

"I should have *known*." She started pacing. "She called my phone. She had my number. I knew she'd been in it I *should have checked*!"

"Hailey," Lydia wiggled her way between the boys to grab her friend's shoulders. "You can't think like that. Siren did that stuff for a living!"

"And I do *this* for a living!" Hailey shouted. "We're bounty hunters! We get paid to not make those kinds of mistakes!"

"That is so not fair." Carly said.

"We do this for *fun*, Hailey, it's a *hobby*." Sean agreed.

"Yeah!" Lydia said. "You wouldn't expect someone who played tennis at a rec center to be able to beat Serena Williams, would you?"

Hailey rubbed her bruised knuckles a little too hard. "I need some air." She shrugged Lydia's hands off and pushed past Sean and Wendell.

Kyle looked up when she slammed the door. He looked around at the room. Sean wanted to yell at him, but the look on his face when he realized what he'd started was so openly painful that he couldn't. Sean wondered if Kyle had lost his armor before or after Siren and Grady attacked the safe house.

"I'll go after her." Wendell said.

"Maybe she needs some time." Sean said.

Wendell shook his head. "I don't think that's a good idea."

He left the room, stepping into the garage. Hailey's white t-shirt was illuminated by the moonlight. He ran to catch up; she was already almost at the bend in the road. He slowed to a walk beside her, shoving his hands in his pockets and pretending not to see her toxic glare.

He had no idea what to say, so he didn't say anything. Maybe Sean was right and she needed time to process. Well, she could process just as well with him there to make sure she didn't go after any more walls.

Hailey crossed her arms. Her fist hurt where it tucked under her tricep, and she pushed harder against it until the fireworks of pain manifested in her eyes and began to obscure her vision. She let up, but she didn't let go.

Her brain was in a tunnel, but instead of a light at the end, there was this horrible mistake. Or maybe she was in a deep well and the guilt was being lowered down on top of her, crushing her. Or maybe she was Atlas trying to carry a world's worth of guilt on her shoulders.

How was she supposed to look Elliot and Maggie in the eyes knowing she almost got them killed? How was she supposed to stay in the same room as Lydia knowing she was the reason the poor kid had been traumatized? Twice, actually.

She'd be surprised if Viv didn't try to assassinate her in her sleep. She almost wished she would. She kind of did wish she would. At least if she was dead she wouldn't have to wonder how she was ever going to make this up to Kyle. She could see how broken he was. And it was all her fault.

Wendell was still there. He still didn't know what to say. He could see Hailey sinking into a pit of tar and he hadn't read the stupid guide book on what to do in this situation. He had to do *something*. If he ran back to camp to get the book it might be too late.

"I tried to kill Grady." He said.

"What?" Just for a second, the shock was enough to snap her out of the darkness.

"When Carly was in the hospital, it was my turn to guard her and I used that time to convince her to kill Grady." He frowned at his feet as they moved in and out of his line of sight. "I don't know what I was thinking. She was *hurt*, she could've *died* and the first thing I do is ask her to murder someone."

"We all knew it might come to that—"

"You don't understand." Wendell stopped and turned, looking Hailey dead in the eye. She stopped just to stare back. "She asked me if killing Grady was the right thing to do. She was depending on me to be her moral compass, but all I could think about was revenge."

Hailey opened her mouth, then shut it again. "What does this have to do with anything?"

"You're feeling guilty because Siren outsmarted you. Well, she outsmarted everyone else, too. They knew she called you; they could've checked your phone, too. Especially Kyle, Mr. Computer Whiz 3000." He said. "You didn't mean for that to happen. I tried to make my friend into a murderer on purpose."

Hailey crossed her arms. "So...you're saying you have more of a right to feel guilty or something?"

Wendell sighed. "I'm saying that I know how you feel. I don't know how to make it go away, either. I just don't want you to...go away...because you think we won't figure it out."

Hailey looked down. "I wasn't going to kill myself."

"I wasn't going to take the chance." Wendell said. "You're important. You're so, so important. To all of us. Please let us help you."

The corner of her lips rose. "Fine. But only if you let us help you."

He sighed melodramatically. "The things I do for you people."

Hailey reached out with her good hand, pinky extended. "I promise I won't go away."

Wendell locked his pinky around hers. "And you'll let us help?"

"You jump, I jump." She said.

They were illuminated. Something rumbled around the corner and blinded them. Wendell stared, frozen. He suddenly understood what it felt like to be a deer in headlights. Hailey grabbed his wrist and dragged him to the side of the road. The van didn't slow down.

"W-what...?" Wendell felt like he'd just run a marathon. "What the—"

All the ATV's that had survived the attack – one – almost tipped over trying to take the corner at full speed. When they passed, all Wendell and Hailey could process was Sean gunning the engine and Adanna taking aim as she regained her balance. Engines and gunshots disappeared into the night.

They were still standing there, staring after them, when Lydia ran up to them.

"What?" Hailey gesticulated everything she couldn't put into words. "*What?!*"

"We had no idea." Lydia said. "None of us were expecting it – we didn't even know the van hadn't been damaged and even if we did we weren't thinking that she would try something like that!"

"Lydia, *what happened*?" Wendell asked.

"Delilah stole the van." Lydia said. "She took Maggie and Elliot."

Part 2

Chapter 35

Aftermath

Delilah had a wonderful desk chair at this new base. At the original Project Kobold, her desk chair had been a flimsy plastic monstrosity. She'd been wrong about so many of her priorities back then. Still, she'd had enough common sense to hide from the Kobold subjects when they'd eventually gone rogue.

Everything else in her new office was an ambassador of some random estate sale, but the chair was what was most important there. That, and her laptop.

It sat on the desk in front of her, chunky and awkward in appearance but beyond state-of-the-art in performance. She'd started building it after the project had been officially scrapped and never stopped tweaking and adding to it. It was something to blow off steam with while doing the exceedingly frustrating task of rebuilding the project from scratch without government funding. And it was almost perfect.

At the moment, she was watching the feed from the security cameras on the screen. The Gemini subjects were still unconscious. That was unfortunate, but she'd done what she could with the resources she'd had access to at their so-called "safe" house. Oh what she could have done with the scraps she'd saved from her lab. But Gemini Beta's adoptive sister had confiscated all of it as soon as they got there.

The bomb would have been only a few tenths of a degree off the ideal kT, but the variety of medical supplies had been pitiful. The drugs she'd mixed to keep her subjects unconscious during transport hadn't been her best work.

Behind her, the door opened. She couldn't hear footsteps or movement, but assumed her assistant was behind her.

"Good morning, Polly." Delilah said.

"Ma'am." The voice came from just over her shoulder, as suspected. "You weren't able to recapture Kobold Alpha?"

"The 'Hero's Guild' was annoyingly dedicated to guarding him." She shrugged one shoulder. "It's not a big deal. We already have enough data from the Kobold subjects to draw conclusions."

"Indeed." Polly's blue concrete eyes studied the twins on the screen. "When do you want to begin testing?"

"Twenty-four hours after they regain consciousness." Delilah said. "We don't want residual drugs to corrupt the data."

Polly nodded. "Should I hire someone to dispose of the Hero's Guild?"

"Hmm." Delilah drummed her fingers on her desk. "No. We'll continue surveillance; I'm interested to see what they'll do next."

~

Lydia was taking a World History class, so she'd seen many pictures of generals and war heroes. Most of the time they looked unnaturally calm amid the chaos, like they had some supernatural knowledge that things were going to be okay. Or maybe they just knew they were in a painting.

Adanna wasn't calm. She was pacing the room like a malevolent force that had been trapped for thousands of years and was awaiting a mortal's mistake to unleash her fury. She seemed to fill the room.

Lydia knew, logically, that there was no reason to be afraid of Adanna. That didn't stop her Amygdala from tagging the older girl as a threat. She swallowed. "Adanna."

She didn't seem to hear.

Lydia wanted Adanna to stop, she wanted time to stop, she wanted her brain to stop spinning just for one second. All of this was too much. How had everything gotten so complicated so quickly? "ADANNA!"

Adanna whirled to face Lydia. Her eyes were windows to entropy and her body shook to contain it. She crossed her arms over her chest. It looked awkward with one forearm in a cast. "What?"

Lydia hated that her own voice was shaking harder. "What are we going to do?"

Adanna closed her eyes and took a deep breath. Wendell started towards her, then stopped short.

Adanna opened her eyes. "We're going to do what we always do." She said. "We're going to find someone who doesn't want to be found."

"And how are we going to do that?" Kyle asked. "We're talking about someone who has a weapons cache in her secret underground lair."

"She's still *human*." Hailey said.

"Are you sure about that?" He retorted.

"Enough." Wendell glared. He turned back to Adanna. "Where do you want to start, boss?"

Adanna winced. She cleared her throat. "We have to start with the basics, I guess. Kyle will hack the DMV and run one of those image searches. Wendell, you take Lydia and Sean back to canvas the neighborhood. Hailey, Nehemiah, and I will see what we can get from Grady." She glanced at the girl lying on the couch, head propped up by pillows. "Carly focuses on healing."

"I'm staying, too." Lydia didn't mean for the words to come out of her mouth, but they did. She scrambled to find some justification for them. "Carly will need someone to take care of her while she recovers...it'll be easier for her stomach to heal if she doesn't have to get up and make food and stuff."

"I'll be fine." Carly protested.

Lydia hoped the look she shot Carly wasn't as blatantly pathetic as it felt. "No, I really think it would be better if I stayed. With you. To do that stuff."

Carly shrugged. "Fine. Whatever."

"What if we interro—questioned Grady before anyone left?" Nehemiah asked. "Maybe he knows where Delilah is. We don't want them to get halfway to her house and then have to turn around."

"Yeah, and if anyone ends up going to the house it should be me." Kyle said. "I mean, if you have a secret base there are probably going to be computers with military-grade encryption software on them."

"Because what's even the point of having an underground bunker without nerd stuff?" Sean said.

"Whatever, Fred Astaire." Kyle frowned.

"I'm more of a Mikail Baryshnikov actually." Sean said.

Kyle chucked a pillow at him. "Anyway, the DMV hack should only take a few minutes, and the facial recognition algorithm can run on its own after I set it up."

"*Fine.* We'll do it your way." Adanna spun on her heel. "Wendell, Hailey; with me. Kyle; get going on that hack."

"Should we feel left out?" Carly whispered after they'd left.

Lydia tried to smile.

"We're not being left out; you're doing your job." Nehemiah said. "Lydia and I are here to help."

"Yes, the very important task of sitting still so my insides can re-group." Carly rolled her eyes. "A truly essential part of this mission."

"It is." He insisted. "Now I'm going to do the truly essential task of getting you something to eat. Your insides need the fuel."

When he left, Carly reached out with her toes, trying to kick Lydia in the arm. "Hey – *hey*. What gives, Mopey Magee?"

"You don't have to pretend this isn't a big deal." Lydia said. "I'm not a kid."

"Dude, you can't even drink yet."

"I don't have to be able to drown my sorrows to know when things are bad." Lydia snapped.

Carly threw up her hands. "Fine." She leaned back on her pillow and closed her eyes, crossing her arms over her chest.

Lydia wanted to apologize. She should apologize. She stared down at her hands. She could still hear Adanna's scream when they'd realized Delilah had packed up the twins and was driving away. Sometimes apologies can't fix things.

~

"Hey, Adanna?" Hailey asked. "Where are your parents?"

"Maggie's mom has some contacts in the underworld. They're the kind of people you don't talk to on the phone, so she's going to see them in person. Her husband and my parents went with her. Something about it being 'too dangerous' for us." Adanna glowered at the wall ahead of her.

"Oh." Hailey said. "They must have left pretty early. I don't remember seeing them at breakfast."

"They left around three." Adanna said.

Wendell frowned. "Did you stay up all night?"

Adanna didn't answer. They were outside the spare room. She shoved her key in the lock and twisted viciously. Wendell and Hailey exchanged a look before following her inside.

There weren't any lights in the room, so Wendell activated the flashlight feature on his phone. In the pale blue light, Grady looked like a body that had just been recovered from the water. It was like all the color in his skin had been drained by some pigment-vampire.

Besides that, he looked bored.

Grady shifted his weight so he was sitting up straighter against the wall. The cuffs on his wrists looked like dollar-store neon bracelets. "Let me guess," he said. "Delilah got away with the twins."

"Did you know she was going to do that?" Adanna asked. "Were you working together?"

Grady grunted. "I figured she was up to something as soon as I saw the kid at her house. Wasn't working with her, though. Not making *that* mistake again."

"What do you mean?" Adanna asked.

"You're talking about Project Kobold." Hailey guessed. "What happened there?"

"Do I look like one of those creepy house robots?" Grady asked. "I'm not here to answer your questions."

"No, you're here because you messed up." Adanna said. She crouched down to his level. Wendell's phone reflected off her eyes, making them look phosphorescent. "You were too arrogant and now you're at our mercy. And trust me; if I get my brother back, I'll be feeling a lot more merciful."

Grady lunged forward, reaching his bound hands for her neck.

Adanna ducked and rolled to the side, rearranging herself into a cross-legged position as Hailey flew past her.

The blue-haired girl nailed Grady in the side as soon as he moved. He rolled onto his knees to get up, but Hailey was faster. She jumped, landing knees-first on his back. Then she spun around and sat on the captive's head, sneakers pressed against his spine. She rested her chin on her hands and nodded for Adanna to continue.

"Do you know where Delilah took Elliot and Maggie?" Adanna asked.

"No." Grady coughed. "Look, it's not anything personal against your siblings, okay? It's just business."

"Business with Delilah?" Wendell asked.

"Like I said; I don't work with Delilah."

"She's played the infiltrator before." Hailey pointed out.

"Yes, but the thing about double-crosses is that you want them to be as uncomplicated as possible." Grady rolled over, tossing Hailey off him. He sat up and took a deep breath. "And talking someone who wants to kill you into helping you double-cross someone else is very complicated."

"Why do you want to kill Delilah?" Hailey asked. "Wait; dumb question. Why do you want to kill *the twins*?"

"You wouldn't understand." Grady told her. "Anyway, I don't have the information you need, but I might be able to help you get it. And in return, you'll turn the child lock off." He shook his wrists meaningfully.

"We sound very dumb in this scenario." Adanna mused.

Grady frowned. "I've been hunting people connected to Project Kobold for the past twenty-five years. If anyone can find Delilah, it's me."

"So why are you after the twins?" Wendell asked. "The transitive property? Project Gemini is connected to Project Kobold and the

　　K. R. VANDERPORT

twins are connected to Project Gemini, so the twins must therefore be connected to Project Kobold?"

Grady smirked. "Something like that."

"That's a terrible reason."

"Like I said; you wouldn't understand." Grady said. "So, do we have a deal? If not, I don't think we have anything else to say to each other."

"We absolutely do." Adanna stood up. "We still have to talk about why you were at the Project Kobold bunker that night. If you've really been hunting Project members for twenty-five years, why didn't you check there before?"

"I didn't know it existed." Grady said. "It wasn't one of the buildings we used back in the day. And I'm willing to bet I found out about it the same way you did." He looked at each of their faces as he spoke. "There was an anonymous tip, right? Probably showed up in an email from an address that led to a deactivated account? Or was it a letter left on a doorstep with no evidence as to who it came from?"

Wendell glanced between Hailey and Adanna. Even in the spooky blue light, he could tell Hailey had gone pale. Adanna's face was a glass sea before a storm.

"You seem like relatively intelligent kids," Grady continued. "You probably checked out the tip pretty well before heading over to the project. Maybe you hacked some government servers or drove by the address, made sure the place really existed.

"But you're curious, right? Maybe the twins wanted to know who their birth parents were or something sentimental like that. Maybe there was a better motive – increasing their power, taking revenge on the people who made them freaks. Whichever it was, you couldn't stop yourselves. You had to check it out.

"So you went there on the night the anonymous source said the guards wouldn't be there, and then you found out you weren't the only ones invited to the party." He bared his teeth. They looked like they were glowing. "Am I close?"

Adanna turned on her heel and strode out the door. Wendell and Hailey followed. Wendell made sure to lock the door, then sprinted after his friends. Hailey was almost jogging, trying to keep up with Adanna's long, angry strides. Kyle came out of the bathroom and was almost run over.

"Hey—!" He began.

"Leave it." Hailey warned.

Adanna slammed the doors open on her way through the living area. Carly and Lydia looked up, eyes wide. Nehemiah half-stood, forehead creased. Wendell waved them off. The last thing they needed was for Adanna to feel like they were ganging up on her.

In the wreckage that had been the garage, Adanna started picking up pieces of debris and lobbing them at the bottom half of a jeep which was doing a post-apocalyptic take on the Tower of Pisa.

Adanna was much more of a gun person but her aim was impeccable. At least, Wendell assumed it was. She hadn't said what she was aiming at, but she was smashing all the windows one after another.

The jeep shuddered as Adanna ran out of windows and started chucking debris at the frame at random. Its position was far too new to last, and it crashed to the ground. Adanna screamed.

She whirled around to face Hailey and Wendell. "She played us! She was playing us this whole time!"

"I know." Wendell said.

"She basically sent Grady after us, *knowing* we would focus on him and completely ignore her!"

"I wouldn't say we *completely* ignored her." Hailey mumbled.

"Ugh! I can't *believe* how *stupid* we were!" Adanna grabbed her hair, then pointed a finger in Hailey's face. "I *knew* this would happen. I told you, didn't I? I told *everyone* that it was a bad idea to reach out to those Project Kobold people. I said that they would take Elliot the first chance they got *and I was right!*"

"Adanna," Hailey said softly.

"I *knew* it!" Adanna screamed. She turned around to face the road. When she spoke again, her voice was quiet. It sounded almost silent by comparison. "I saw this coming. I let this happen."

"No, you didn't." Wendell said. He walked up to her hesitantly, putting a careful hand on her shoulder. "We all swore we would protect Elliot. None of us caught this. If it's someone's fault, it's everyone's fault."

"That's disheartening." Hailey said. She stepped forward to press her shoulder against Adanna's. "But true. We are all equally stupid."

Adanna let out a wet laugh. "I just can't believe this is happening." She said. "This was my biggest fear when I was a kid. After we watched the *X-Men*, I had nightmares for weeks."

"Yeah, those movies are pretty bad when you actually know a mutant personally." Hailey nodded.

"We're going to get him back, Adanna." Wendell said. "We're going to get both of them back."

Adanna shook her head. "You don't know that."

"Of course I do." Wendell said. "Visualization is, like, 90% of success."

She sniffed, then turned to him. She patted his shoulder. "You really need to stop reading those self-help books."

Chapter 36

Welcome to Project Kobold

E lliot's first thought when he woke up was, *Ugh, I don't think I brushed my teeth last night.* This was followed quickly by his brain dumping the events of the past day onto him like a bucket of cold water.

His eyes snapped open.

Elliot had never been to jail, but he'd seen enough TV to make a pretty solid assumption that he was in a room which was a cross between a jail cell and a display case. There were three walls the same blue-gray concrete as the floor, a toilet in the corner, and one wall that seemed to be made entirely of glass. He sat up on the surprisingly comfortable bed to get a better look. That's when he noticed his new outfit.

The clothes were hardcore athletic gear; the kind of clothes bought by people who did triathlons and trained for the Olympics. Clothes built to allow freedom of movement and not disintegrate with too much sweat. By comparison, the bracelets encircling his wrists looked like they'd been stolen off a kid watching the fireworks. If he hadn't seen the slim glowing bands before, he would never have guessed their power.

Thanks to the dampening cuffs, the disorientation went beyond what he could see. For as long as he could remember, the electricity of the world around him had whispered like white-noise at the edge of his awareness. Even if he hadn't lived in a technology-dependent first-world country, it would have been there. Every atom of matter has an electric charge. Even if the positive and negative charges cancel each other out, and render an atom neutral, they still exist.

Now there was nothing where that information had been. Like someone suddenly blind or deaf or rendered unable to feel or smell, Elliot's brain reeled spasmodically in an attempt to rationalize a situation it had never considered. He hugged his knees to his chest, pressing his forehead to them. Emptiness had taken up residence in his mind, and he couldn't make it go away.

"Good morning."

Slowly, he raised his head. He hadn't even heard Delilah approach. He attempted a casual pose, kicking one leg out and letting his head rest against the wall. "Good morning." He said. "Fancy meeting you here."

She dropped a paper bag into a metal box connected to the outside of the glass wall, then pushed the side so it rocked back and opened towards Elliot. There was no direct contact between the outside and inside of the cell.

"What's that?" He asked.

"Your meal." She replied, then tapped something into the tablet she held. "You will eat once every four hours to maintain your strength."

"What about when I'm sleeping?"

"You will sleep for seven hours and eat two hours before and directly afterwards."

"Sounds like you have this all figured out."

"Indeed." She made another note on her tablet.

Elliot stood up and walked over to the glass. "Hey!"

She pursed her lips, then finished her note and looked up.

He waited until he was sure she was paying attention. "What did you do to Maggie?"

"Gemini Alpha is also being housed at this facility." Delilah said. "As our studies progress, you may even get to see her."

"You can't do this." Elliot said. "We have rights—"

"You seem to be under the impression that Project Kobold is still being run by the United States government."

He paused. "...It's not?"

"No." Delilah smiled. "This new incarnation of the project is being run by me. And in the eyes of the project, you and Gemini Alpha have no more rights than those of prototype smart missiles."

A wave of heat swept over him. He leaned back from the glass. Delilah's eyes, expression, and body language united to show him that she believed exactly what she was saying. He felt suddenly stupid for playing her game.

"Let Maggie go." He said. "Please. You don't need both of us."

"Noble, but wrong." She said. "You are not the same. Besides, no self-respecting scientist bases an entire experiment on one test subject."

"You can't..." He was almost glad when she interrupted him, because he had no idea where he was going with that.

"Eat your meal." She said. "I'm going to go check on Gemini Alpha and debrief my staff." Then she walked away.

Elliot walked over to get the food, but didn't open the bag. He sank to his knees. He rested his forehead against the glass wall. He closed his eyes.

Without the distraction of Delilah, the empty space in his head seemed bigger than before. Like it was expanding, or maybe sucking everything else in like a black hole. And there was nothing he could do about it.

~

For the second time in three days, Maggie woke up in a place she didn't recognize. At least this room had lights. She sat up, groggy and confused. Her brain was sounding alarm bells for all it was worth, and she reached up to rub her eyes.

When she caught sight of her wrists, she stopped and inspected the bands. They looked like the ones Elliot and the others had brought for Grady, except out of beta. She put two and two together and flopped back down, grabbing her pillow and crushing it against her face to scream into.

"Good morning, Gemini Alpha."

Maggie considered ignoring her, but there were no answers down that path. She tossed the pillow to the side and sat up, swinging her legs off the bed. "Good morning, Doctor."

If Delilah was affected by the sudden formality, she didn't show it. "Turner." She supplied. "How was your sleep?"

"Is it still called 'sleep' if you're blasted into unconsciousness?" Maggie asked.

"I would assume one term is just as good as another."

"Yeah, *you* would." Maggie narrowed her eyes. "Where's Elliot? Do you have him locked up here, too?"

"Yes." Dr. Turner dropped a meal into the box and slid it into the cell.

"And where is here, exactly?" Maggie asked. When Dr. Turner didn't answer, she smiled grimly. "What? Are you worried we also have telepathic abilities that we'll use to tell our friends where to find us?"

"The information is irrelevant to you." She said.

"You *should* be worried." Maggie continued. "Those guys are bounty hunters for fun. They'll find us within the week."

Dr. Turner frowned slightly. "It took them four hours to figure out Siren had put a tracking app on the your phones. I think we'll be fine."

Maggie's eyes widened. "Siren...? That's how they found us?"

Dr. Turner nodded and made a note on her tablet. "There is food in the bag. Eat up. I'll send someone to collect you when you're needed."

Maggie felt like she was scrambling even as she was sitting still. "Aren't you worried I'll try to escape with the paper bag or something?" She attempted to keep up her snarky façade.

"I doubt that's a possibility." Dr. Turner glanced at her. "You could use it to breathe into. You look like you're having a panic attack."

After she walked away, Maggie threw her pillow at the glass barrier. She laid back down, brain spinning. The place where her extra sense used to be ached like an open wound, but Dr. Turner's revelation was already vying for the attention she would normally give to it.

Siren had put a tracker on the phones. How had she not seen that coming? Siren had *called Hailey's phone*, of course she must have been in it! Maggie pressed her knuckles to her eyes. How blind could she be?! Here she'd been thinking she'd handled that situation so well when really all her leadership had done was lead Siren and Grady straight to the safe house!

And if they hadn't found the safe house, she and Elliot would have been able to fight them on their own terms. They wouldn't have been isolated in the woods ready for Dr. Turner to capture them. They wouldn't be *here*, wherever this was.

Tears rose beneath her eyelids, warm and itching. *This is all my fault.*

Chapter 37

Nothing would be what it is

In this English world – *Non-Amish*, Nehemiah corrected himself dutifully – life existed in a speed paradox. Everyone seemed to be stuffing their days full of activities and responsibilities until the hours were bloated and threatening to tear apart. Instant gratification was taken for granted. All collective human knowledge was just a search engine away. But then there was "downtime."

In the community where he'd grown up, people hadn't tried to reinvent time or warp it to their satisfaction. Every day they worked at tasks knowing the same thing would have to be done the next day. It was a cycle where no job was ever truly finished. And that had been okay. There was no hurrying of the harvest so they could move on to a bigger and better one.

Still, there had always been something to do. Nehemiah couldn't remember not having responsibilities; he'd been assigned his first job when he was three. Every minute of the day had a purpose, something to be doing.

Now, there were hours and even days when Nehemiah had nothing to do but "amuse himself" with unproductive activities. His body itched, desperate for something to do. He should have been more careful with his wishes.

Elliot had been gone for ten hours and the Guild was falling apart. Carly was lying on the couch, legs propped up on Lydia's lap. She seemed too distracted to be paying attention to their conversation. Which was just fine, because Lydia was talking on autopilot. Sometimes she would trail off and stare at nothing for a few minutes before finishing her sentence. Sean watched them for a while looking constipated, then disappeared into the bedroom to choreograph some dances.

Hailey had ascended to a higher level of functioning. She seemed to be doing three things at once while appearing in four different rooms simultaneously. It was like she'd cloned herself and assigned each of them an activity, then deposited them around the base. Adanna was interrogating Grady...again. Wendell was with her.

And Kyle was...Kyle. He was in the weapons room, wedged between a gun case and a rack of swords. At first glance, he appeared to have been swallowed by a hoodie. His face was either bathed in light from his laptop screen or had been doing so long enough that it had started glowing. He glared down any attempt to talk to him and waved off food and water. He probably hadn't been to sleep since he'd woken up tied to a chair.

Nehemiah assigned himself damage control. He cooked meals. He reminded his friends to eat before their food got cold. He washed the dishes. He shoveled and swept debris from the garage. He found every vehicle that could be salvaged. Then he spent five minutes trying to set a timer on the stupid phone Wendell insisted he carry and got to work repairing them as well as he could.

Most Amish kids only go to school until eighth grade. This makes it incredibly hard for anyone who tries to leave to find a job in a country where "education is the great equalizer." It's even harder to find a job in a city when your previous work experience revolves around farming.

Wendell had been a life saver. He'd taught him everything about cars, which had about as much in common with a horse-drawn buggy as they did with a biplane, then got him a job at the same garage he worked in.

Wendell had been a fantastic teacher, though he would say teaching Nehemiah was easy. The young man from another time took a while to get the hang of something, but once he learned a skill, he never forgot it.

He loved his job. Cars were incredible. Nehemiah learned all the intricacies of their forms and structures. He couldn't believe these beautiful machines weren't allowed in his old community. How better to illustrate the creativity and genius of God than by showing the creativity and genius of the ones created in His image?

"You should get your GED." Wendell had said once. "Go to college, get your official license. You could run your own shop."

Nehemiah had just laughed. "That would be nice, but robbing a bank qualifies as stealing, which is a sin."

His alarm went off much too soon. Nehemiah slid himself out from under the ATV he was working on and tried to turn the timer off without smearing grease all over the screen.

He wiped his hands on a rag, then pocketed his phone and headed off to clean up. It was around time to feed the Guild again. Even worse, it was time to make good on the promise he'd made to himself; if Adanna wasn't done interrogating Grady by the time everyone else had their food, Nehemiah was going in after her and *making* her eat something.

He almost ran into Hailey when he went back inside, but she spun out of the way on her toes. She looked him over. "What did you do, take a nap in the rubble?"

"Close." He brushed at the front of his shirt. All that did was smear grease on top of the dirt. "Are you hungry?"

"Hmm." She pursed her lips as she pondered his question. "Maybe...?"

"Anything specific you might be hungry for?"

She shrugged.

"That's okay. I'll figure it out." He half-turned to go, then hesitated and glanced back at her. "Do you want to help me make lunch?"

Hailey shrugged again.

He didn't know how to respond to that, so he just started walking and listened for her footsteps.

In the pantry, Nehemiah grabbed three cans of soup, handing two of them to Hailey. He snagged a new box of linguini on the way out.

"We're having soup and noodles?" Hailey wondered.

"Most of time, soup isn't very filling for Wendell. That's probably the same for some of the others, so we're going to pour the soup on top of the noodles. Or pour the noodles into the soup. Because bread-like things make people more full."

"Fuller." Hailey said. "It's because of the carbohydrates."

"Good for the carbo-whatevers." He frowned. "Wait, is that where the word 'carbs' comes from?"

"Yep."

"I thought carbs were bad."

Hailey shrugged. "They convert into stored energy, which is technically fat. But if you burn off a lot of energy really quickly, they're good for you. That's why runners usually have a spaghetti dinner before a marathon."

"Uh-huh." He put the soup and noodles on the kitchen table and grabbed some pots from the sink. "Okay, we're going to get the noodles started first because they take longer. We just need to warm up the soup, so we can wait a while before doing that. What?"

Hailey was still in the doorway, staring in the direction of his feet. It seemed to take a monumental effort to meet his eyes. "It's just…isn't that where, um…where Si-Siren…? I mean, where Kyle…?"

"Oh." Nehemiah looked down as if the assassin's body was about to appear and answer the question for him. "Yeah, it is. But the body's gone and I cleaned up all the blood, so—"

"What did you do with the body?" She asked.

He winced. "When you say it like that it sounds bad."

"*Nehemiah.*"

"Wen and I took it out to where Delilah bombed Elliot and Maggie. And Grady. It won't look any more out of place than the burn marks *that* left behind."

Her eyebrows were raised almost to the middle of her forehead. "I think a dead body looks pretty frickin' out of place regardless of the scenery."

"Oh!" He laughed at the misunderstanding, then mentally slapped himself. "I meant the *burn marks* we left wouldn't look out of place. We cremated her. It. Whatever."

Hailey looked at the soup cans she was holding.

Nehemiah set the pots on separate burners. "You don't have to help if it makes you uncomfortable."

Her words followed his so fast it felt like an interruption. "How are you so calm about this?!"

He looked away, fiddled with a pot handle, and tried to think of a way to say *'Because Wendell can't be the only sane one here'* without sounding insulting.

"I mean. Killing is a sin. Isn't it?" She was probably trying for a laugh, but it sounded more like a strangled gargle.

Nehemiah frowned. "*Murder* is a sin." He said. "King David killed a lot of people, but the only time he sinned was when he murdered Uriah."

"Wait, David murdered someone?! Like, 'David and Goliath' David? I thought he was a good guy!"

In that moment, Nehemiah was supremely grateful for the way Hailey's brain never let any comment go. "He was...a guy." He said. "Most of the time he was good – as humans go, anyway. But he *was* human and...humans do terrible things to each other sometimes."

"Wow." She said. She'd stopped using her eyes for seeing, opting instead to see with her mind. She stood there, quiet and still with her eyes glazed over. It reminded Nehemiah of Wendell showing him how to pause live television. He didn't need the soup she was holding right away, so he let her have a staring contest with the wall in peace.

He filled one of the pots with water and set it to boil, then glanced back at Hailey. Besides her expression changing briefly, she hadn't moved.

He turned to try and wash some of the grease off his hands. He had meant to do that before he started cooking, but being with someone else had distracted him. Oh well; at least he hadn't touched the actual food yet. He doubted anyone would notice, anyway.

"You should tell that to Kyle." Hailey said.

He blinked at her. "Huh?"

"The thing about how killing isn't always a sin."

"Oh." He frowned. "Oh, yeah, he was the one who..."

"Yeah."

"Huh." Nehemiah said. "I guess I forgot. That's weird, right?"

"I mean, *I* think it's weird that you and Wendell carried a body out of the building and burned it in the woods without any of us noticing, so I don't know how well our definitions of 'weird' match."

"That's fair." He tilted his head, studying her. "Are you okay?"

She put down the soup, deliberately spinning away from him. "No. Why would I be?"

"That's also fair." He said.

"How are *you* okay?" She narrowed her eyes at him. "Maggie and Elliot have been kidnapped by someone who wants to experiment on them, we have a psychopath locked in the broom closet, half the roof is missing, and there's a cremated assassin in the woods! Why aren't you freaking out like the rest of us? What is *wrong* with you?!"

"I'm sorry." It sounded stupid even before he said it. He had no idea what to do with this conversation. "I dunno. Maybe...*because* everyone else is freaking out? Like I'm trying to balance it out? Or maybe it has something to do with how *nothing's* really been normal since I left the community."

"What do you mean?"

"Like..." He glanced at the water just in case, then leaned up against the sink. "...it's kind of hard to explain. Um...have you see that movie where the characters meet some aliens, and the aliens speak English and look human but everything else about them is completely different?"

"Pretty sure you just described seventy percent of the movies from the past forty years, but sure."

"It's kind of like that." Nehemiah said. "Everyone looks normal and speaks the same language I do, but everything else is different. The food is different, the work is different, the clothes are different – politics, religion, education, relationships; everything is different. It's like living in an alien world or something. I just...I feel like I don't understand how things work anymore. So even when strange things happen, it doesn't change much for me because everything is already strange."

"Wow." Hailey said. "I never thought about that." She stepped closer and put the cans down on the table. She grabbed her arm and looked up at him. "How do you deal with it?"

One corner of his mouth lifted as he shrugged. "I don't know. One step at a time, I guess."

She frowned. "That is an uncomfortably vague set of directions."

"I know."

She sighed and wrapped her arms around him, pressing her face into his chest. He returned the gesture, glancing back at the pot of water. A few bubbles were rising to the surface, but there was still time.

"You stink." Hailey's muffled voice informed him.

"It's the sweat produced by carrying all that wisdom."

She laughed. "You are way more sarcastic than I ever expected a good Amish boy to be."

"You English could probably reach our level if you stopped relying on pop culture references."

"How kind of you to say."

"Water's boiling." Nehemiah pulled away. "Can you turn the burner down while I grab the noodles?"

"I'll take care of the cooking. You go shower or something." Hailey pushed at him lightly. "I don't want the food to smell like 'wisdom.'"

He held up his hands. "Fine, fine." He was still pretty sure nobody would notice if their food smelled strange – in fact, he could probably hand each of them a glass of vinegar without them noticing.

But maybe cooking was something Hailey needed to do to move forward. He could remember his parents telling him about how chores were good for the soul. A few of his new coworkers were convinced that was just a ploy to keep kids in line, and in some of his more bitter moments he almost agreed.

Still, sometimes it felt like a triumph just to do *anything* when he was overwhelmed and confused. Fighting despair with a dustpan or something that sounded equally stupid in theory but was oddly effective in practice. So he let Hailey make lunch while he was pleasantly surprised that the plumbing hadn't been destroyed during the fight. It really was strange to feel like he was suddenly the one who knew how to respond to the situation.

"There's this one quote that I really like." Wendell had told him once. "'Not all who wander are lost.' It's by Tolkien – that guy I told you about earlier. And he was a Christian, so you can trust him."

Nehemiah could remember being skeptical. "Even if not *all* who wander are lost, *some* still are. What does this have to do with anything?"

"I think it means, 'don't worry if you're not sure where you're going, just keep following your path' or something."

"But what if it's not a path? What if it you follow it to the end and it turns out to be a deer trail?"

Wendell had shrugged. "That would be a bummer."

"Excellent advice, thank you. I feel so much better now."

"My pleasure."

Chapter 38

Sympathy Pain

There are people who have a nerve disorder where they can't feel pain. Maggie was pretty sure that if someone like that was shot in the head, it would feel very similar to how she felt with the absence of her magnetic sense.

But she didn't have that particular disorder, so if she was shot in the head it would probably just hurt. A lot. It was weird that she could hear the footsteps of the gun-wielding lady behind her but couldn't *feel* the presence of the gun.

There was a gun-wielding dude next to her, pulling her forward by her arm. Handcuffs were fastened above her glowstick cuffs, so his tugging made her arms form a tilted oval. Both gun-wielding people were taller than her. She wouldn't put it past Dr. Turner to have hired them intentionally for intimidation purposes. "You must be this tall to abduct superhumans."

The man's face was expressionless, like he was delivering paperwork. His posture was straight and he moved with purpose. His hair was buzzed so short Maggie could only see it from an angle. It was like an optical illusion – one of those statues that disappear when you look at them straight on. He could have been in the military.

In fact, Maggie wondered why he *wasn't* in the military. Why would a young, professional, driven person choose an underworld organization that thrived on human experimentation over an above-the-board, respectable institution? Had he tried it before and been disillusioned? Was he suffering from some sort of very specific mental trauma that made him think this was ok? Had he washed out on account of having apparently questionable morals?

The three of them ended up at a blast door, which the gunman at her side unlocked with a combination of a fingerprint, an ID badge, and an iris scanner. He opened the door, but instead of leading the way, he shoved Maggie inside. Cold metal pressing into her back informed her that the gunwoman had followed her.

The room looked like a cross between a doctor's office and a gym. There was an examining table on one side with a vital signs monitor next to it. Dispensers of rubber gloves of various sizes were attached to the wall. On the other side of the room was a treadmill and a set of weights.

A man who bore a disturbing resemblance to her first pediatrician stood up and held out his hand. "It's a pleasure to meet you, Maggie. I'm Dr. Alte."

Maggie took his hand between her bound ones and smirked as she shook it.

Dr. Alte sat down on a chair, picking up a tablet and swiping through a few pages. "Have a seat." He kept looking through it, pulling up files and double-checking his preparations as the woman behind Maggie forced her towards the examining table.

Maggie had seen enough movies to know that she, as a semi-human, did not want to go anywhere near any tables even remotely associated with doctors or scientists. She struggled against the gunwoman, who had a tight grip on her shoulder, trying to twist out of her grasp.

The woman dug her nails into Maggie's pressure point, then pressed the gun harder into her spine. Eventually, Maggie was sitting on the table.

"Alright," Dr. Alte stood up to be at eye level with his unwilling patient. "How are we feeling today?"

"Fantastic." Maggie glared.

"Mm-hm." He felt her neck, pressing her lymph nodes lightly.

His fingers were freezing. That seemed to be a common factor with doctors. Maggie wondered why hospitals couldn't afford to pay their heating bills when medical costs were so high.

"And open." He said.

She opened her mouth automatically, then mentally slapped herself for cooperating with the enemy.

"Everything's looking good in there." The doctor said. "Let's take some measurements."

"Are you going to make me a dress?"

He laughed. He seemed like such a nice guy. It was terrifying.

Maggie looked at the gunwoman as the doctor clipped one sensor on her finger, wrapped another around her arm, and stuck yet another in her mouth. Unlike the man who had been with them in the hallway, she could never have been confused with a law-abiding person.

It had nothing to do with the way she was dressed – she was wearing the same black t-shirt and cargo pants as her colleague from the hall.

It was in the nonverbals. The way she held herself, like she could strike at any moment without provocation, was something that by-passed Maggie's logical reasoning completely and connected with her amygdala. It was an Uncanny Valley sort of posture; Maggie couldn't have explained what was wrong; not entirely. But she knew it all the same. And those eyes...

When she was in second grade, Maggie's teacher had told her eyes were "the windows to the soul." She hadn't made eye contact with anyone for a year, worried they were going to read her thoughts.

When she finally got up the courage to try again, she'd felt silly. Eyes weren't windows to anything – they were just orbs in bone sockets. They were probably the one part of a person that *never* changed, no matter what they were feeling.

But the gunwoman's eyes were different. They were empty. Some things can only be fully perceived in their absence. So now, thanks to the woman, Maggie could finally recognize the life she'd seen in the eyes of others all these years without realizing.

"Everything's looking good." Dr. Alte said. He unfastened his sensors and brought out a small rubber hammer. "Time to test your reflexes!"Maggie wondered if this was what Alice felt like when she landed in Wonderland. The normality of Dr. Alte and his personality just made everything else feel more surreal. She wondered how deep his nice guy façade went. She eyed the gunwoman while the doctor hit her knees with his little hammer.

"Excellent reflexes." He smiled. "I'd expect no different from someone with your DNA."

"Does that mean my brother has excellent reflexes, too?" She asked.

The doctor wagged a finger at her. "I can't violate doctor-patient confidentiality!"

"But...I'm family." She said. "Can you at least tell me if you've seen him already today?"

"I'm afraid not, miss." Dr. Alte patted her on the shoulder. "Are you ready for your stress test?"

Maggie hopped off the examining table and followed him. With the gunwoman falling in behind her, they made a little train that moved across the room.

"I'd be less stressed if you told me something about my brother. Wouldn't that be a good idea? Less variables to consider and all that?"

"Enough questions." The gunwoman said. Her voice was a poison-tipped arrow stretched back on the bow.

"It's fine, Denise." Dr. Alte waved her off. "I don't mind."Denise flinched. The sound of her name was a rock striking against the flint of her eyes. Maggie watched the gun. She couldn't dodge a bullet or stop it in midair right now, but she might still be able to dodge Denise's aim.

"It's not that kind of stress." Dr. Alte was explaining. "What I'm going to do is hook you up to these sensors and have you run until you're tired. I'll monitor your heartrate."

"Ok." Maggie held up her wrists. "It's going to be awkward to run like this, though."

"That's a simple enough problem to solve." Dr. Alte unhooked the chain links, allowing her to move her arms freely.

She swung her arms around experimentally, then held her wrists back out towards him, one eyebrow raised. "I don't suppose I could talk you into taking off these bracelets."

"Unfortunately not." He indicated the treadmill. "Up you get."

Maggie knew the others would be looking for them, but she couldn't count on the Guild to be a match for Dr. Turner's secret organization. She and Elliot would have to break themselves out.

It would have been nice if they'd been together. She hoped having two superhumans fight each other would be too much of a temptation for Dr. Turner to withstand. They had to coordinate, because breaking out of her cell and running around randomly trying to find Elliot was a terrible idea.

The bracelets looked pretty flimsy, but she wasn't even sure she'd have to break all the way through them. With most technology, damaging a piece was usually enough to take out the whole system. As long as she played nice with Dr. Alte, she might be able to snag something sharp while his guard was down. Of course there was Denise, too.

Maggie shook her head as she jogged. She was getting too worked up; she could take her time with this plan. It wasn't like she was going anywhere. Of course, given how her last plan had turned out, it might be a good idea to bank on Elliot coming up with a way to escape.

She still couldn't believe she'd been stupid enough to forget about their phones! She was a millennial! Where was her generational pride?

"Good, good. Now, come over here to the barbells. We'll start with lifting the lightest weights, then increase it until you start having difficulties."

Come to think of it, Elliot probably already had a plan in place. Yeah, he'd been doing this kind of thing for a while. This was probably a walk in the park for him. All she had to do was wait until he put his plan into motion.

Of course, it wasn't fair to put everything on him. She figured she should probably have a backup plan, just in case. Or at least memorize as much about this place as she could. Who knows? Maybe she'd find something Elliot had missed.

"Alright, good work." Dr. Alte made a note on his tablet. "Now we're going to do the same things, but with the power dampeners off."

Maggie blinked. "What?"

Denise shifted her weight. "You can't be serious."

"I'm very serious." He told them both. "In order to see the true extent of the mutation's influence, we have to collect data from her in both states."

"So, do you want me to lift these with my powers, or...?" Maggie regretted all the times she'd rolled her eyes at the theater geeks. She'd give her left arm to go back in time and ask them about their methods.

"That won't be necessary for this experiment." The doctor said. "You're just going to repeat the exercises exactly. The only new variable I want to introduce is the presence of the active mutation. The data will help me determine what the mutation's affect is on other physical aspects of the human body."

"Smart." She was nodding like a bobblehead.

"Now," Dr. Alte looked up from his tablet. "Do you need to rest first?"

"Nope!" She bounced up and down on her toes. "I'm fine!" *Better than fine – who needs a plan when you have absent-minded professors?*

"Alright, then." He tapped a few commands into his tablet – it was facing away from Maggie, so she didn't see exactly what he'd done. Not that it mattered. As soon as the empty space in her brain burst back to life, she took every tiny screw in the tablet and flung them in different directions like a starburst of metal.

Dr. Alte dove for cover as Denise started shooting. Maggie stopped the bullets with ease, snatching the gun and smashing it into the gunwoman's temple. Then she crushed the weapon.

She clenched her fists, rending the bracelets into hundreds of pieces each. Free of that time bomb, she beaned Denise in the head again, just to be safe. A pair of shoes and a lab coat were scrambling to hide themselves under the desk. Which was unfortunate, as Maggie could just collapse the desk on top of them. Which she did.

Dr. Alte cursed from inside the desk burrito. It felt a little like being cussed out by Mr. Rogers.

Maggie turned her attention to the door. She could safely assume that, as soon as she busted it open, every alarm bell in the world would go off. She wouldn't have much time to find Elliot and escape, but as soon as they were together they could figure it out. He was the Man With The Plan and everything, after all.

She decided on a classy exit by way of exploding the blast door out into anyone waiting in the hall, then following up with a barrage of weights and barbells. She could sense at least twelve living magnetic fields directly outside the door. As soon as she took them out, she'd gather their weapons and run down whichever hallway looked friendlier.

She shook her arms and legs, bouncing around to loosen herself up. *Alright. Step one: Flatten whoever is outside the door. Step two: Find Elliot. Step three: Escape. Simple enough.* She beckoned to the barbells with her fingers as she headed towards the blast door. Soon enough, they were all in position.

Here we go. She braced herself. *Three. Two.*

One winter, Viv had taken Maggie to a glass blowing workshop. They were having an expo where people could come in and watch the artisans craft Christmas-themed objects. When the glass was in the fire for a long enough period of time, it actually turned red from the heat as it melted.

Maggie had watched, fascinated by the fact that a strong enough fire could change the very appearance of an object. And that was the sensation that erupted at the base of her skull.

~

Elliot felt something in his stomach. It was nausea, shame, and fear wrapped up in one solidified mass and dropped into the center of the organ. He sat up, looking at the glass barrier. Had he collected so much guilt that he'd unlocked a new level of physiological experiences? Or was it actually a sensation coming from the outside?

They'd joked about twin telepathy, but what if there was some truth to it? Growing up, he'd always assumed there had to be others like him. He'd read everything he could find on supernatural and paranormal occurrences. The world was overflowing with those stories – in fact, there were more stories than there was proof. And he'd heard about the superstitions behind twins. Now he wished he'd paid more attention.

He pressed a fist into his gut, trying to quell the feeling. When that didn't work, he closed his eyes and concentrated on Maggie. At first, there was nothing.

When he had been little, he and Adanna had built a fire in their backyard while unsupervised. Then they started tossing different things in it just to see what would happen. They'd tossed in a broken glass jar they'd found in the woods, and it turned red from the heat as it melted.

Elliot had watched, fascinated by the way the fire could change the very nature of the object. But he had also been terrified, knowing that fire was just one step away from the power flowing through his veins. That was the sensation that erupted at the base of his skull; the feeling of turning molten-red from the heat of a fire.

Elliot blacked out.

Chapter 39

Ends and Means

Adanna leaned up against the wall as Wendell followed her out and shut the door. "What do you think?" She asked.

His forehead was creased, mouth pressed together. "I think it's a bad idea." He said. "We've already been betrayed by one Project Kobold person." He crossed his arms and looked away. "On the other hand, Maggie's parents have decided to take a trip to the criminal underworld, so maybe we're past the point of using qualifiers."

Adanna nodded slowly. She took a deep breath and straightened up. "Alright. Let's put it to a vote."

They gathered in the common area. The electricity had been cut off from the room during the fight, but light was streaming in through the hole in the roof.

"What's going on?" Kyle crossed his arms. "I'm kind of in the middle of something."

"I know." Adanna said. "But there's something we need to make a decision about as a Guild."

"Grady?" Hailey guessed.

Adanna nodded. "He tried to kill Dr. Turner at her house. He wants to destroy everyone involved in the Project, so he's the enemy of our enemy and we can be fairly sure he won't betray us. And he's offered to help us find Dr. Turner in exchange for his freedom."

"Okay, but aren't Elliot and Maggie technically involved in the Project?" Carly asked. "Or the Project was involved in them or whatever? He wants them dead, too."

"That would be the downside, yes."

"It sounds like it's less about whether we can trust him and more about whether we can take him down once the job's done." Sean said. "Technically, in order for this to work, we'll need to be the ones doing the back-stabbing."

"Huh." Kyle narrowed his eyes in thought. "That's an unexpected twist."

"We're on weird moral ground with this." Nehemiah agreed.

"As interesting as a conversation about ethics is," Kyle said, "that's not our biggest problem. We need a plan."

"Yeah. We can't risk Grady catching on or escaping before we double-cross him." Carly nodded.

"We could tell him we'll turn his powers back on after we save Elliot and Maggie." Lydia suggested.

"He might not agree to that." Hailey said. "He'll probably want something first, as a show of good faith or something. We could turn his powers on when we find Dr. Turner's hideout in order to give our team some muscle, but..."

"...but then he'll have his powers, and Elliot and Maggie will be right there." Wendell nodded. "And who knows what state they'll be in? If they're restrained, they'll be no match for him."

Nehemiah frowned. "Is it weird that I'm starting to respect traitors now? This is a lot more work than I thought."

"One of the big things about traitors is that they're willing to abandon their moral code." Carly pointed out. "How far are we willing to go?"

"Is that a general question, or did you have something specific in mind?" Adanna asked.

Carly looked down at her hands. "We can always take him out while he's busy wrecking Dr. Turner's hideout."

Nehemiah's eyes widened. "Wait a second; back-stabbing a criminal is one thing, but you're talking about murder."

"I'm talking about protecting our people." Carly shot back.

"She has a point." Wendell said softly. "If you kill someone while they're trying to kill someone else, you're technically just protecting that someone else."

"I don't think that applies if that is immediately after you sic the killer on a bunch of unsuspecting people." Nehemiah said.

"So, basically, the options are A) refuse his help and keep him locked up so he can't hurt anyone, or B) accept his offer to help and kill him as soon as you're done with him." Lydia said.

Sean put his arm around her. "There has to be a third option."

Kyle frowned. "Or there's not even two. If we go with option A, what are we going to do with him? Keep him as a pet?"

"What are you saying?" Lydia leaned towards him. "You want to just put him down now and be done with it?"

Sean tightened his grip on her, pulling her back towards him and away from Kyle.

Adanna sighed and turned her face towards the ceiling. "If we go with option A, we'll figure it out as we go along. Does anyone have any ideas for an option C?"

"Can't we just reactivate the bracelets?" Hailey asked.

Kyle scoffed. "And say what? 'Oh, Mr. Grady, would you mind too terribly keeping your bracelets on? They look so good on you.'"

She stuck her tongue out at him. "What about the super taser? Can't we just shoot him with that like we planned originally?"

"Dr. Turner took it with her when she left." Wendell said.

Hailey massaged her forehead. "Okay...Kyle, can't you make a duplicate or something? You know; being helpful instead of shooting down everyone else's ideas?"

He glared. "Not unless I had blueprints or a prototype to work off of. I can't reinvent it from scratch unless you're okay with waiting a few years first."

"What about the basement?" Nehemiah looked at Wendell. "Turner had a lot of projects in her basement, remember? Maybe there's a prototype or something there."

"It's possible." Wendell nodded slowly. "We were planning to go back there to look for information on her hideout, anyway. We can check for that stuff while we're there."

"I'll come with, then." Kyle said. "Seeing as I'll actually know what we're looking for."

"Big talk for someone who doesn't know a Phillips from a flathead." Wendell quipped.

"Okay; great. Now we're getting somewhere." Adanna nodded. "Kyle, Wendell, and I can go back and check out the basement. Hailey and Lydia; you guys take Carly back to her place and make sure she heals up. Sean and Nehemiah; keep an eye on Grady."

"I don't think Carly needs two people watching her – do you, Carls?" Hailey asked.

Carly shook her head. "Nope. I don't even need one person looking after me."

"That's not an option." Lydia patted her leg.

"Okay, what do you want to do?" Adanna asked Hailey.

The blue-haired girl smiled tightly. "I can help watch Grady. He's a professional after all, and Siren already got away from us once."

Kyle looked away.

Adanna nodded. "That sounds like a good idea. Where do you guys think you'll go?"

"We could go back to my place." Nehemiah said. "Wendell and I have our own rooms, so two people could sleep at a time."

"That's a great idea." Sean said. "A better one might be not telling him where we live, on the off chance he still doesn't know."

"He probably does." Kyle muttered. "He was tracking our credit cards."

"I *said* 'the off chance.'" Sean said.

"I have to go back anyway." Nehemiah said. "I'm supposed to feed the neighbor's cats this week."

"Oh yeah!" Wendell nodded. "Snuffles and Copernicus."

"If Grady gets loose in the building, he could kill Snuffles and Copernicus, too." Sean pointed out.

"It'll be fine." Nehemiah said. "Otherwise, I'll have to leave you and Hailey on your own with Grady for a few hours a day."

Sean pinched the bridge of his nose. "Fine. We can bring the serial killer home."

"Carly can come back to my dorm." Lydia said. "It's on the ground floor, so she won't have to walk much."

"Sweet." Carly said.

"Alright." Adanna clapped her hands. "Now all we need to do is find enough working vehicles."

"I've got one jeep and two ATV's working in the garage." Nehemiah said.

She pointed at him. "Perfect. Kyle, Wendell, and I will take the jeep. One of you guys can take an ATV over to the storage unit and drive my parents' car back. Nehemiah, Sean, Hailey, and Grady can take that to the apartment. And Lydia, did you park your car at the unit too?"

"Yeah."

"Ok. Perfect."

"10-4, boss." Sean said.

Adanna glared at him briefly. She looked over at her chosen team. "We leave in twenty minutes; be packed for a possible overnight." She turned on her heel and walked out of the room.

The others looked around awkwardly until Kyle stood up, tugging at the hem of his hoodie.

"Go team," he said sarcastically.

~

Kyle dug his backpack out from the small space between his mattress and the wall. He sat back, one hand stretched towards his pile of clothes. His hand fell to the mattress and stayed there.

Move. He thought. It felt like he'd gone through a warping of space where his body had been awake for thirty-six hours though only a few seconds had passed in the real world. He knew he was physically capable of moving his hand, but suddenly he was devoid of the motivation to do so.

"I'm going to hit the bathroom before we leave." Wendell said. "I'll let you know when I'm done."

Kyle looked up. The other boy already had his messenger bag slung over his shoulder. "Yeah, okay."

Wendell's face twitched for a second. He turned and left Kyle alone in the room.

Kyle turned languidly back to stare at his unresponsive hand. All he needed to do was grab a shirt and a pair of pants. He didn't even really need pajamas; he could sleep in his clothes.

They were probably just going to crash in the car anyway. Elliot would have had them sleep in the car to stay "off the radar," but Adanna probably just didn't want to waste time. When it came to her brother, she was terrifyingly single-minded and unstoppable, like a freight train or a great white shark. Which was another reason why he needed to get moving.

He did move then; he blinked slowly. *Progress.*

"Are you posing so I can draw you like one of my French girls?"

Kyle pulled his hand back into his lap, glaring at the blue-haired interruption who was leaning against the doorframe. "Go away. I'm busy."

"Yeah, I can tell."

He narrowed his eyes. "Not all of us have to be moving constantly to prove our brains are working." His gut punched itself for that one.

Hailey's expression went blank for a second, like her soul had momentarily retreated to deep within her core. She shrugged it off and came over, falling to her knees on the mattress in front of him.

"Would you be careful?!" He snapped. "You're going to break it!"

"'yOu'Re GoInG tO bReAk It!'" She mocked in a high-pitched voice, snatching his backpack from his hands and stuffing clothes into it.

"What are you doing?" He asked. "Stop it. I don't need your help."

"'i dOn'T nEeD yOuR HeLp.'" She grabbed pajamas, socks, and deodorant.

Kyle snatched his boxers before she could pack them, too. He pushed them into the backpack himself, face on fire. "Don't you have any boundaries?!"

She rolled her eyes. "What are you, five? They're just clothes."

He took his backpack forcibly and zipped it up with vigor.

Hailey shifted fluidly into a cross-legged position, leaning back on her hands. "It's okay to be upset about what happened."

"I don't know what you're talking about." He moved to get up.

She caught his wrist before he could stand. "Kyle. Seriously. This isn't some rough relationship with your dad that you can just bottle up for years without *totally* awful consequences. You killed someone yesterday."

His entire body shuddered and he snatched his hand back. "I *know*."

"You didn't have a choice." Hailey said. "It was self-defense. Even Nehemiah agrees that you didn't do anything wrong."

"He said that?" He turned to look at her.

"Yes." She tightened her grip on his wrist. "Look, you don't have to talk to me, but you should talk to *some*one, okay? Wendell, maybe. He's good to talk to."

His eyes were stinging all of a sudden. "I have to use the bathroom before we leave."

Hailey loosened her grip enough for him to pull away. She watched him as he walked out the door. He could feel her eyes on his back even after he turned the corner.

Chapter 40

The Parent Trap

" ggie?...'aggie?...coming around...give...ome room. Maggie? Can you hear me?"

Maggie opened her eyes slowly, squinting into the pen light Dr. Alte was waving between her eyes. He pulled at her eyelids, then patted her face. He put the pen light away and smiled.

"Welcome back to the land of the living, Maggie!" He said.

"Wh...what happened?" Her skull was squeezing her brain and her spine was trying to secede from her body. "Did you shoot me?"

He laughed. "No, no; I'm a terrible marksman, really. Just awful. No; what happened was you performed the second part of the experiment absolutely perfectly!"

She frowned. "That's not what I remember."

"Well, to be honest, I didn't exactly tell you the truth about the experiment." He smiled sheepishly. "What I really wanted to do was capture data from you using your powers of your own free will so I can compare the data to our other experiments. That way you won't be able to pretend you're using your full power when you're not."

Maggie caught her breath. "How did you stop me? I made sure Denise was out."

"You certainly did!" He laughed. "Poor girl has a concussion and everything."

Maggie tried to sit up, only to realize she was strapped down. She twisted against the bonds. "Then how...?"

"Now *that's* an interesting story." Dr. Alte leaned back in his chair, leaving Maggie to squint against the sudden direct exposure to the overhead light. "You see, when Dr. Turner first brought you and your brother here, we wanted to make sure we would be able to do our experiments in a way that would be...safe. Especially considering what happened to the *first* Project Kobold.

"So we implanted dampeners on your brain stems. Nice, simple, and reliable. And hardly any pain from the surgery for you two! Which, to be honest, is a fringe benefit. A lot of people here knew those who were killed at the first Project and didn't mind the idea of putting you through a little pain."

Maggie struggled harder. "You...implanted...! How dare you...?" She felt dirty. She wanted to wash her neck seventy-seven times. She wanted to get free, smash Dr. Alte's face into the floor, find a scalpel, and *dig it out* with or without a mirror to see where she needed to make the cut.

"Now, now, don't get upset." He patted her shoulder. "It's just a safety precaution. I know your parents probably gave you an explanation for what they did, but—"

"*I don't know what you're talking about!*" Maggie erupted. "*I never even knew my biological parents!*"

Dr. Alte finally shut up. If she could have seen his face, she would have taken a little pleasure in the absolute colorless shock she had caused. "...That is interesting. Excuse me." He walked out the door without another word.

There was the sound of the lock engaging from the other side, and then Maggie could only hear herself gasping and trying not to cry.

~

When Elliot finally woke up, Dr. Delilah Turner was outside his cell. Her face was closed off, but her eyes were target locked on him. He sat up slowly, rubbing his aching neck. "What?"

"When was the last time you saw your biological parents?" She asked.

Elliot blinked. "Um – when they handed me off to the adoption agency, probably."

She shifted her weight, and her gaze became almost physically painful. "You've *never* heard from them?"

"No." He frowned. "What gave you the impression that I have?"

"How did you learn to use your powers if you've never met your biological parents?"

He shrugged. "Probably the same way I learned to walk."

"This isn't a *joke*."

"Not that you *deserve* my honest answers," he glared back, "but I'm being serious. My powers...I think they're like muscles. They get stronger the more you work them."

"Really?" It wasn't actually a question. Dr. Turner spun around and stalked away.

Elliot sighed. *Maggie, I don't think we're in Kansas anymore.*

Speaking of Maggie. Elliot crossed his legs and stared at the clear barrier in front of him. He rubbed his spinal column, just above his brain stem.

Trying to connect telepathically had apparently almost triggered an aneurism, which was good and bad. The good part was that he now knew he could do *something* by trying to communicate with his twin mentally. The bad part was, of course, the aneurism.

Although, it was possible that it hadn't been the attempted communication which had lit his brain stem on fire. It could have something to do with the power dampeners. Elliot plucked at one of his bracelets.

Interestingly enough, if it did have something to do with the power dampeners that meant they weren't completely blocking that element of their powers. Which likely meant the dampeners were programmed very specifically. Which meant, if he could find a way to compartmentalize the pain, he could communicate with Maggie.

He frowned. But had she been in the same pain he had? Had he accidentally hurt her – again? She was only in this mess because of him. If he hadn't spilled his guts to Dr. Turner in the van, maybe she wouldn't have been able to make that bomb and capture them both.

Once again, his naivete had hurt someone he cared about. It was so easy to see, now, how much he had been imagining the Guild as some sort of superhero video game. He hadn't been looking for human threats; he'd been looking for bosses to fight. But Dr. Turner was human, and when humans can't beat someone head on they figure out a different way to win.

He took a deep breath and clenched his fists. That was what he would do, then. Dr. Turner had the upper hand now, so he would have to outsmart her. Which would be both helpful and sweet, sweet payback.

Alright, Elliot. He thought. *You're in a cell with no powers and no direct access to the outside. How do you escape?*

The most obvious answer was to wait until they came to get him for some experiment or whatever, then try to surprise his escorts and run like Usain Bolt until he found an exit. There were about a hundred holes in that plan, first and foremost being that his escape would probably alert a whole squad to guard Maggie's cell. They'd never both get out in that scenario.

Another option was to bide his time, keep his eyes open as they escorted him around the base, and come up with a mental map with which to find an exit when it came time to escape. The problem with that one was it would take a long time; plenty of time for Dr. Turner to do a bunch of experiments on him.

He really, really didn't want to get experimented on. He dug his fingernails harder into his palms to try to stop himself from shaking so badly. When he'd dissected a frog in middle school, he'd thrown up before his partner had made the first cut. By the time he got to high school, he thought he was tough enough to do a little science without getting *X-Men* flashbacks. They'd dissected fetal pigs, and he'd asked his lab partner to do all the cutting. (He wasn't *that* tough.) He'd tried not to watch, tried to keep his eyes on the paper and his head filled with terms that did *not* have any real-world counterparts.

He'd woken up in the nurse's office.

He wondered if Maggie ever had nightmares about being strapped to a table as disembodied hands lowered scalpels and saws towards her paralyzed body. He'd had that dream a lot. Now the morbidly curious part of him wondered if it had been some sort of premonition.

Technically, the brain ran on electric power. Adanna had always had a theory about his powers being able to branch off into things like mind-reading and hypnosis, but she'd always been the more inventive one of the two.

Elliot liked stories and had a huge and powerful imagination, but he usually focused it on things which were – to him – very realistic. Like superheroes. According to his vast collection of comic books stuffed full of pseudo-science, it was possible that he had some sort of psychic ability. Not plausible, but possible. After all, electromagnetism is one of the fundamental forces of the universe.

He straightened. He suddenly had the feeling he'd been looking at a picture upside down for years. He'd always known his electricity tied into the "electro" part, why hadn't he put it together when he'd discovered Maggie's abilities? They were twins, both with one half of the electromagnetic force.

If that was what Project Kobold was trying to do – master the fundamental forces of the universe – did that mean their biological parents could control...the strong and weak interaction forces? What would that even look like?

His mind circled back to Dr. Turner's questions. She didn't know what happened to them. If they could control two of the fundamental forces of the universe and the Kobold project hadn't done anything to them, who or what could have had the power to stop them? Dr. Turner seemed convinced they would have tried to stay in contact with their children, even after giving them up for adoption. Was that *true*? Elliot wasn't sure how he felt about that.

He wasn't sure how he felt about the alternative, either. If no one had done anything to them, staying out of his life – and Maggie's – was their own choice. He'd always assumed his biological parents had given him up because they couldn't deal with the fact that their child was a freak. Having parents who had given him up just because they didn't want kids was...a new concept.

But Dr. Turner had been so sure they'd been in his life. Why? Were they overtly parental when she'd known them or...or had they been involved in Maggie's life? Was that how *she* learned how to use her powers?

Elliot frowned. He was used to being the odd one out – being a different race than the rest of your family will do that to you – but this time he was on the outside because the insiders didn't *want* him there.

Maybe he was overreacting. It was probably just the isolation talking.

He was glad he was still in physical pain; it was a good distraction.

~

Delilah Turner glared at the pictures on her screen. They'd been taken so long ago, scanned into the computer later on. Kenneth and Elizabeth Rook; Kobold subjects Beta and Gamma. "What happened to you two?" Her voice was quiet, controlled. Like a wisp of smoke trailing up from a volcano everyone believed was inactive.

"Are you sure they're dead, Turner?" Alte asked. "They could have just left the children behind as a diversion."

Turner laughed. "Sometimes I forget you don't know anything about the first Project Kobold."

"I've studied all the data from—"

"The *data* is only half the story." Turner swiveled to face him. "We gathered readings on their power levels, their physical abilities, the development of their bodies, their growing powers, everything! But we didn't pay any attention to their humanity."

Alte hesitated. "What happened to the first Project?" He asked. "Why was it abandoned?"

Turner's laugh was high-pitched, devoid of humor, half-hysterical. "Human error!" She said when she could speak again. "It all fell apart due to human error."

Chapter 41

Confrontation

Sean rubbed his forehead with the heel of his hand. It didn't do anything to quell the pain that seemed to reverberate from his skull. "Ahhh." He groaned under his breath. He hadn't had migraines since he was in elementary school, so this felt like a betrayal.

Ungrateful body, he thought. *After all I've done for you -- the active lifestyle, the healthy diet, the arguably consistent patterns of sleep – this is how you repay me?* Of course, there *was* a chance this was a tension headache based on the current circumstances.

He meandered across the room to where Carly was lying on the couch. Sometimes her eyes were blue, other times they looked gray. Lydia had a theory that they corresponded to her mood somehow. Maybe she was right, because Carly's forehead was creased and her eyes looked like an overcast sky.

"What are you doing?" he asked.

She flipped her phone screen towards him. "Fruit Ninja."

"You are so old."

"Younger than you, Fred Astaire."

"Yeah, well I'm less mature." He argued, sticking his tongue out in emphasis.

She rolled her eyes. "Can't argue with that."

Sean rested one arm on the back of the couch and leaned forward to watch her play. "So, Lydia's staying with you until you're back on your feet?"

"Apparently." Carly glowered and missed a pineapple. "It's completely unnecessary; I'm not eight. I can make my own chicken soup."

"And tie your own sandals, I bet." He said. "I don't know, though. Maybe it's a good thing." He held up his hands and pulled back from the couch when she turned her laser eyes on him. "Not for you! I mean..." Glancing around, he lowered his voice. "...for Lydia."

Carly's phone announced her loss. She thumbed the power button without looking and tossed it on the cushion beside her. "Why? Is she going into nursing or something?"

"No, it's just..." he leaned in again. "I feel like this whole thing is affecting her a lot more than she's admitting. And, I don't know, maybe she'll admit it to you."

She raised an eyebrow. "You want me to play psychiatrist with your baby cousin? You really have that much faith in me?"

He shrugged. "Beggars can't be choosers."

This time, she was the one sticking her tongue out. "If she brings it up, I'll do what I can. I don't know how much I can help, though, considering she's traumatized from a fake murder and I'm still advocating for a real one."

Sean opened his mouth and shut it again. He performed a verbal pivot. "I'm starting to think I never should have gotten her involved in this."

Carly shrugged. "It's too late to think about that now. Besides, if you hadn't gotten her involved, who would be providing you with free amateur counselling?"

"But she wouldn't *need* counselling if I hadn't gotten her involved."

"That's the spirit; don't let yourself get away with anything!" She rolled her eyes. "I'm pretty sure that, out of the two of you, you're the one who needs counselling the most."

Sean half-laughed. "What? *I'm* fine."

"You joined up with a bunch of strangers to chase down petty criminals in your spare time because you're trying to undo what was done to you."

"There's nothing wrong with being *motivated*—"

"Of course not, but you're not motivated by what happened, you're running away from it." She pointed at him. "When your group has a competition and we ask for your help, you don't tell us you're busy. You bail on the competition and come chase criminals with us. Dance is your passion, your way of communicating with the world, and you just up and ditch it for a part-time hobby? No. You're using this as an unhealthy coping mechanism to avoid coming to terms with what happened. As long as we keep catching criminals, you can pretend we caught the guys who attacked you before the mugging happened. Every successful mission is like a shot of it-didn't-happen. It's worse than heroin."

As soon as she stopped talking, Sean took a deep breath. He wondered if he'd been breathing at all since she started. He felt like his organs were spilled out on the floor in front of him. He gathered them up and stuffed them back in his body. "Well. Thank you for that psychoanalysis."

"And it's free." But her heart wasn't in it. Her eyes softened. "I'm sorry. I – that was mean."

"Whatever." He crossed his arms and looked away. "Where do you get off acting like you know anything about how and why I live my life like I do?"

She pressed her lips together. "Because I carry a gun." She said. "And if you're going to point a gun at someone and pull the trigger, you better be able to figure out why you're doing it."

~

Viv closed her laptop carefully, as if she was afraid to break the screen. Without looking at anyone, she drummed her fingers on it. Finding someone she knew in a former life was much easier than she'd expected. Her mind ached with the delicious strain of an athlete years out of practice whose muscles still remembered how to play the game.

"Did you find anything?" Taylor's voice dragged her out of her mind.

She looked up and nodded. "One of my old colleagues. If anyone knows something about this Delilah Turner, it will be him."

Taylor nodded, dropping her bag to the floor and herself into a seat across from her counterpart. The intercom above them announced that "Flight 1A from Minneapolis to Toronto is now boarding First Class passengers." She sipped experimentally on her matcha latte. She and Hugh had circled back to the airport's food court while Viv searched for her old acquaintance.

Oliver had opted to stay with his wife, of course. But Hugh brought him back a burger anyway. The quiet man saluted him with the sandwich. Hugh raised his taco with a smirk.

"So, are we off to Japan?" He asked. "Athens?"

Viv shook her head. "My ex-colleagues from Japan wouldn't know anything about Turner's operation. We're going to New York City."

"I didn't know the Yakuza had a base in NYC." He raised an eyebrow.

She smirked in return. "You would be surprised. But Masachiki does not work for the Yakuza anymore. He has become...an independent contractor."

"How 'bout that?" Hugh leaned back in his seat and bit into his taco. "Do people do that a lot? Quit the mob and create their own little criminal business startup?"

"If they are clever enough not to be found when they do." She said.

He nodded. "Genevieve isn't a very Japanese-sounding name."

Viv tilted her head, as if pondering his statement. A small smile played on her lips. "It isn't, is it?"

Oliver rolled his eyes and wrapped an arm around her shoulder. "Are you two done being clever?"

"I am always clever." Viv leaned back against his chest and winked at Hugh. "It was my grandmother's name." She explained.

"You were named after your grandmother?" He guessed.

Viv smiled wider.

"So," Taylor interrupted before her husband could respond. "When did you two find out Maggie was gifted?"

Oliver's eyes crinkled at the edges. "She was two years old, and we were pretending we were in a band – with pots and pans, you know? Anyway, she wanted one of the pots, and it was ten feet away from her but she just...reached for it and it slid into her hand." He chuckled. "I think she was more surprised than I was."

Viv took his hand, smiling. "What about Elliot?" She asked.

Hugh and Taylor exchanged a look and laughed.

"He stuck a fork in an outlet!" Taylor covered her eyes. "He didn't have a scratch on him, of course, but he shorted out the whole building! The poor babysitter almost lost her mind."

"We took him to the doctor," Hugh said, "And he didn't believe us. He was like, 'Yeah, come back when something actually happens.'"

"We just chalked it up to a miracle until a few weeks later, when there was a thunderstorm." Taylor continued. "Some kids are afraid of storms, so I was sitting with him in his room, trying to get him to fall asleep. He was fascinated by the lightning – he kept gasping and clapping. Then, all of a sudden, he started shooting electricity from his fingertips!"

Hugh laughed. "She ran screaming out of the room—"

"He lit my *hair* on fire!"

"—so I went in there, and there was Elliot! This tiny, barely one year old baby with lightning coming out of his hands." He laughed again. "Of course, all the commotion woke Adanna up. She thought it was the 'coolest thing ever!'"

"Wow." Viv's eyes were wide. "How did you manage it? That sounds dangerous."

Taylor shrugged. "Honestly, I have no idea. I thank God Elliot was born such a sweetheart; he never had tantrums, always smiled at everyone, never fought with his sister. It's a lot easier when the kid isn't trying to hurt you on purpose."

"Those first few years were tough, though." Hugh said. "He didn't understand what we were saying, much less what he was doing. We both got a lot of burns." He held out a hand.

Viv and Oliver hadn't noticed the scar tissue before, but when he pointed it out it was clear to see. Certain patches of his skin were darkened and wrinkled, others stretched smooth and baby pink. Each of them took turns sneaking glances at Taylor's exposed hands and forearms, picking up on her set of scars while she pretended not to notice.

"The official story is that Mama and I are reckless chefs." Hugh continued. "Adanna's only two years older, so we don't know if she remembers the truth."

"We also have no idea if Elliot's figured it out." Taylor said. She looked down at her cup. "We didn't want him to start his life out knowing he hurt people he loves, but now there's this huge secret hanging over us. If he knows, we need to talk about it. We need to tell him we don't blame him. But if he doesn't know, and we bring it up..."

Viv was nodding. "That's a hard decision to make."

"You decided it was best that Maggie didn't know about your past." Hugh pointed out. "How did you make that decision?"

Taylor narrowed her eyes at her husband.

Viv looked at him, then looked away. "No one is defined by their past. You were right not to tell him."

"I don't know." Hugh said absently. "If we would have told him right away, maybe we could have instilled some sort of core value about how it's okay to make mistakes. If we tell him now, it's going to sound bad just because of how long we've kept it from him."

"You can't go back now." Oliver said. "So there's no point in blaming yourself for something you can't change."

"Besides," Viv added, "You thought you were doing the right thing."

"I guess it can be hard to see what the right thing is in the moment." Hugh said.

Taylor patted his leg. "If we're going to New York, I'm going to need some reading material. Come with me, babe."

For a couple of talented fighters like themselves, walking through the crowd at a normal pace was fairly easy. Anticipating the movements of someone whose goal was to get from Point A to Point B is much easier than anticipating those of someone actively trying to stop you from breathing by any means necessary.

"I know what you're going to say." Hugh's hands were shoved in his pockets. He looked around, looked at the other people in the airport, looked anywhere but at his wife.

"You know, their kid is missing, too." She said.

Hugh ran his hand over his hair "I know, I know. I just…" he glanced around. He was pretty sure the Poseys hadn't followed them, but he lowered his voice anyway. "Do you think we should be trusting that woman?"

"Viv?" Taylor raised an eyebrow. "What do you mean?"

"Don't be coy, Tay; you were a detective. You can't tell me you don't think her underworld connections are a bit suspicious."

Taylor sighed. "I mean, I get where you're coming from; I do. But my gut is telling me her concern for her daughter is genuine."

"Being concerned and putting someone in a concerning situation aren't mutually exclusive."

Taylor took a deep breath, then stopped and turned to her husband, grabbing his arm and forcing him to stop with her. Traffic awkwardly veered around them.

"Look; our baby boy is missing, and that is making me just as crazy as it is making you. And yes, okay, I have thought about the possibility that Viv was the one feeding Grady and Siren and Delilah tips. If her connections are as good as she says, it wouldn't have been hard for her. But if there is the *slightest* chance that she *isn't* planning on stabbing us in the back and she knows someone who can help, I'm not going to risk alienating her based on a past that, let's be honest, we only know about because *she told us*."

Sighing, Hugh crossed his arms and looked at the floor. "Fine." He said. "I will be nicer to the ex-Yakuza enforcer."

"That's all I ask." His wife linked her arm through his and pulled him towards the airport bookstore.

Chapter 42

Deep Thoughts and Deep Dish

E lliot sat cross-legged on his bed. His fists were pressed together in front of him and his eyes were closed. He had seen every episode of *Avatar: The Last Airbender*. He could do this.

Focus. He thought. *Breathe. Think about Maggie.*

There is nothing like a life-threatening situation to show you how much you really don't know. He realized very quickly that he had about five to seven hours of collective memories involving Maggie, during most of which she was in the background or unconscious. How many times had they actually talked? Once? Twice? It couldn't have been more than that.

The most powerful memories he had were the first ones. Was that normal? He couldn't remember the first time he'd met his parents and Adanna, but he'd been a baby then. He didn't think infant memories were as strong – or maybe they just got buried.

He was pretty sure he'd stared at the baby picture the whole ride up to Maggie's apartment. Adanna had been next to him, her shoulder pressing against his.

And when they'd gotten there and seen Grady about to kill someone – he'd known it was his sister, who else could it have been? – he'd felt like *he* was in pain, too. And there was this...rage; like what he'd felt when Grady had hurt Adanna, only with this extra feeling of losing something he never knew he was *supposed* to have. The rage had exploded out of him like a solar flare.

In the car, he hadn't been able to stop looking at her. She was bruised and afraid – even unconscious, her facial muscles contorted and her hands trembled. He'd picked rubble out of her hair gently, trying not to disturb her. Whatever was supposed to happen when you reunited with your long-lost twin, it was not that.

Those were the only significant memories he had of her, so he replayed them in as much detail as he could.

He was suddenly awash with an overwhelming sense of despair and grief. He felt angry and cheated and...*violated*, for some reason. Why was this suddenly so unbearable?

He felt like he needed to smash out of this cell and somehow undo everything Project Kobold had done to him – even his powers felt guilty by association. But he couldn't. He was trapped. There was no escape.

At the same time, he felt like he was seeing double. He'd never been drunk – never trusted himself not to accidentally electrocute someone – but this...floaty sensation that he was two places at once had to be what it was like.

Despite the small relief of being almost not alone, the sheer force of the experience left him gasping and trying not to cry.

~

Nehemiah felt strange rooting around in his jacket pocket for the keys to his apartment. The door opened into what seemed to be a perfectly preserved remnant of the past; a time when Elliot was the only strange creature and his powers were God-given miracles instead of scars of abuse he (thank God) couldn't remember.

Nehemiah linked certain places to different points in his life, so any time he returned to one of them it felt like time-traveling. He'd have to remember to tell Wendell about that; he loved those crazy science movies.

"Don't break anything." He warned, leveling a glare at Grady, who filed in behind him. Nehemiah knew his height and bulk influenced what people assumed he was capable of, and he was happy to take advantage of that in this situation. Maybe it was prideful, but if so it was a sin he would indulge for now.

Sean was the last one in, so he shut the door behind him. Hailey had gone back to the safehouse for the rest of the food. Sean looked around. "I like what you guys have done with the place." He said. "I don't think I've been here since your housewarming party."

"Yeah, I don't think so." Nehemiah agreed. Even though Wendell had been living in the apartment for three years, he insisted on having a housewarming party for Nehemiah when he moved in. To be honest, it was more of a force-the-new-guy-to-interact-with-the-team-out-side-of-work party.

Grady glared at everything in the room – the fridge, the table, the salt and pepper shakers – as if they had just insulted his mother. The cuffs were still around his wrists, but they weren't bound together anymore. Neighbors tend to call the cops when they see someone with their hands tied together being forced into an apartment.

Sean dropped his bag near the door and shoved Grady forward a little. "Go sit on the couch or something."

"I'm not the enemy, you know." The mutant said.

"You dropped a house on my friend – you'll have to forgive me for not building a statue in your honor."

"I'm starving." Nehemiah said. "Do you guys like pasta?"

Grady shrugged one shoulder.

"You don't get a vote!" Sean stabbed a finger at him. "People who put our friends in the hospital don't get to decide what we have for dinner."

"You might want to save that rage for when you actually need it." Grady said. "Like when you find out you're on the wrong side."

"The wrong side...?"

Nehemiah stepped between them. "Okay, look; Wendell let me move in with him when I had nowhere else to go, so if you two don't take it down a notch I will throw you both out just to make sure you don't wreck the place."

Sean leaned back and crossed his arms, looked away.

Grady held up his hands and shuffled over to the couch.

"What do you think he meant by that?" Nehemiah asked.

"'Everyone's a hero in their own mind.'" Sean quoted, rolling his eyes.

Nehemiah frowned, watching Grady flip through a mechanics magazine. "I wonder what could make someone think that's okay."

"Just because someone believes it doesn't make it true." Sean said. "You should know that better than anyone."

Nehemiah turned away. "So, pasta's good?"

Sean sighed. "I'm sorry. I didn't mean – I'm sorry."

"Don't worry about it." Nehemiah grabbed a pot from a cabinet and started filling it with water. "You're stressed. I'm stressed. I get it."

"That doesn't make it okay." Sean said. "I'm really, really sorry. I know you're still hurt by what happened with your family."

"I'm *fine.*" Nehemiah took a deep breath. "It's in the past. There's no point in talking about it."

"That's not necessarily true." Grady was looking up from his magazine. "Actually, it's not true at all."

"Who asked you?" Sean snapped.

"The past can help you decide what to do for the future. It's how you learn and become who you are." He continued.

"How are you so sure? What happened in your past?" Nehemiah asked. He pretended not to notice Sean's betrayed expression.

Grady sighed. "I'm not trying to kill your friends because I want to."

"You've said that before." Nehemiah said. "What do you mean?"

"Project Kobold..." Grady put the magazine down and leaned forward, resting his elbows on his knees. He wasn't looking at either of the others at that point.

"It was a mistake." He said. "We were trying to save the world by creating the perfect weapons. Human weapons: smarter than Smart Missiles, and much more dangerous. We could walk into any room in the world without raising much suspicion.

"We started thinking about it being too much power to allow to fall into the wrong hands. 'Imagine if *Russia* got a hold of this technology' and stuff like that. After a while we realized – Liz, Ken, and I – that it was dangerous for *anyone* to have access to that power. So we shut the project down ourselves."

"If the project was shut down, why were you trying to kill Dr. Turner and the twins?" Nehemiah asked.

Grady looked at him. "We had to get rid of the information. That doesn't just mean wiping some hard drives or burning some files. The human brain is an incredible storage device."

Sean felt like someone had just walked over his grave – actually, over Elliot's grave. "How many?"

"Three hundred and forty-five." Grady looked a little proud. "Only four left."

"Hey, Nehemiah." Sean said. "I don't think I'm hungry anymore. In fact, I think I may throw up."

"Don't worry." Grady told him. "I won't go after you and your other friends. You don't know anything, and no one would believe you anyway. It will be enough just to kill the Gemini subjects."

"If you lay *one finger* on either of them—"

Nehemiah grabbed Sean's arm. "Who's the last one?"

"What?" Sean asked.

"He said he only has four more people on his list. Elliot and Maggie are two of them and I assume Dr. Turner is the third, but who else is there?"

Grady laughed. "What a naïve question!" He put his hands behind his head and leaned back. "I'm connected with the Project too, of course."

"That's insane." Sean said. "You're insane!"

"No," he said softly. "I'm too sane."

"That's it." Nehemiah turned off the stove. "This conversation has made me lose all motivation. I'm ordering a pizza."

"No Canadian bacon." Sean said automatically.

"Or olives." Grady said.

"No votes!" Sean snapped. He slung an arm around Nehemiah, turning him to face away from their "guest." He lowered his voice. "Get olives. Lots of them."

"You hate olives." Nehemiah said. "I don't think it's worth it."

"I'll manage." Sean said. "But this guy is a serial killer and he has to pay somehow."

Nehemiah sighed. "Just don't throw up on the carpet."

"Deal."

Chapter 43

Time to Think

Maggie was alone in a room straight out of *Fallout Shelters Monthly*. Her arms were crossed, her chin was tucked, and her shoulders were hunched forwards. On the opposite side of the room, someone had dumped a random assortment of materials.

A speaker was embedded behind one of the titanium ceiling panels. Maggie was trying to figure out which one, because she wanted to crush it.

"Don't be so stubborn, Alpha. You're not accomplishing anything." Dr. Turner's voice was loud and clear through the speaker.

Maggie clenched her fists tighter. "I'm not your performing monkey."

"Obviously." Turner's eye roll was verbal. *"You were much more expensive than a monkey."*

Maggie thought she'd understood anger before. Her past self was a naïve little sap.

"Well, well." Turner said. *"Those are some interesting readings."*

Maggie took a deep breath, attempting to calm herself out of spite.

"Look." The disembodied scientist said. *"This project cost a lot in time, energy, and money. So you're going to have to get over whatever*

petty grudge you're holding against me and start cooperating. Don't you understand that you're part of something amazing?"

"Amazingly delusional, maybe." Maggie scoffed. "There's no way I'm going to help you willingly."

"Are you sure about that?"

"Absolutely."

"Pity."

Maggie caught her breath as the emptiness in her head reappeared. The blast door opened, revealing a bruised and irate Denise. The woman pointed a handgun at her and pulled the hammer back. Maggie's pulse decided to qualify for the Olympics and she could suddenly feel her own heart beating in her chest.

"If you're sure there's no way you'll cooperate, then there's no point in keeping you around, is there?"

"Wait..." Her voice sounded disgustingly unsteady.

"Yes?"

Maggie held her ground for as long as she could. She closed her eyes. "I'll do it." She said. "I'll help you."

"Wonderful." Dr. Turner sounded like she'd just been given a dozen free cupcakes which magically didn't contain any calories.

Denise was disappointed.

"Alright! Let's get started." Turner said.

Denise retreated back into the hallway just in time.

"What I need you to do is move one piece of material at a time." Turner instructed. *"Lift it into the air and move it over to your side of the room."*

"Whatever." Maggie flicked her wrist and a lump of concrete hurtled through the air, smashing against the wall behind her. It crumpled, pieces cascading down from the impact.

"Slower." Turner said.

Maggie crossed her arms. "Can't you just record it and play it back in slow motion or something?"

"I like to record data in the moment. It makes the collection more reliable."

"Fascinating." She reached out, latching onto a sheet of metal siding and levitating it across the room *agonizingly slowly*. She annoyed *herself* with how slowly she was going, which seemed to be a positive sign. Turner chose to ignore it.

One by one, chunks of marble, rusted car engines, iron ore, Styrofoam, and even wood made their way over to Maggie's side of the room.

"Why is it that your powers affect traditionally non-magnetic materials?"

Maggie rolled her eyes. "You're the scientist." She could have given a two-hour speech on permeability, ferromagnetism, diamagnetism, gyromagnetism, and the like, but she was determined to maintain whatever shred of rebellion she could.

"It seems to take a greater concentration of your energy."

"That so?" Maggie muttered.

"Can you do it without the hand motions?"

"Ahhhhhgh." Maggie did an excellent improv of Bratty Teenager Asked to Do Menial Chores. Then she crossed her arms and kept moving the materials across the room. She sped up the process a little bit, as the tortoise routine was starting to wear on the last frayed nerve she had. For a while, that had the silver lining of Turner's silence.

Then, about halfway through the remaining materials; *"Do you need to be looking at them?"*

Maggie sighed and closed her eyes. It took more time doing it "blind," because some of the magnetic fields were very similar in strength. She was sure a note was being made on that somewhere.

The – thing – in her neck was going to make escaping much harder. Had they done this to Elliot, too? She supposed they would have. So if she managed to get out, she'd have two stops to make; she'd have to grab Elliot and the two of them would have to find someone to take the chips out. Maybe Dr. Alte; he seemed like the type who would cave easily.

Of course, Turner would be expecting all of that. She'd been one step ahead of them this whole time. Considering her infatuation with surprise attacks, she might even let Maggie get all the way to Elliot only to recapture them both when they went to find Alte.

Maggie frowned. That would be very in character for her. In fact, Maggie might be willing to put money on it. Which meant she might still be able to get to Elliot. After that, the only thing they'd need to do would be side-step Turner's camouflaged trap.

If Turner was banking on them trying to nab someone to remove the chips, most of her firepower would be focused on the scientists and the labs. If Maggie and Elliot just made a beeline for the exit, they might be able to get away.

But they might never be able to get their powers back.

Maggie felt something throbbing in her chest even just thinking about it. How could she give up such an integral part of herself? She might as well ask herself to give up breathing.

Of course, if she didn't escape, Turner would probably ask that of her sooner or later.

How could she ask *Elliot* to give his powers up? He didn't even know her. How could she expect him to trust her, much less her intuition? She didn't have that great of a track record, after all. Maybe Elliot had a better plan. After all, he was the professional.

What she wouldn't give to be more like Elliot. He decided what he wanted to do and just went out and did it. He was like a modern day Sherlock Holmes; making up jobs that don't exist and stopping criminals with his loyal assistants.

Of course Maggie had thought about being a superhero when she was younger – she'd seen the movies – but it had seemed so strange and, well, no one else was doing it. She didn't want to get weird looks or end up a complete failure, humiliating herself. To be honest, she was also afraid of something like this happening; being captured and experimented on because of her powers.

But Elliot grew up to be a superhero. How insane was that?

Maggie suddenly felt light headed. The rock she was moving across the room shuddered in the air as her mental grip slipped. She wasn't afraid; she was curious, and frustrated. And she felt like what she was doing was of vital importance, probably involving getting them both to safety. She was determined; she needed to make this work.

"Alpha? Are you sleeping down there?" Turner's voice asked.

Maggie pulled out of whatever dive her brain had taken. She struggled out of the quagmire, fighting not only its pull but her own desire to go back to that spot in her thoughts. It had felt like – for whatever reason – like she wasn't alone. She didn't want to be alone.

She needed to focus on using her powers right now. Not because Turner might kill her if she didn't – though that was a contributing factor – but because she knew escaping with part of herself was better than being imprisoned whole.

~

"You're in a No Parking Zone." Carly had one eye open with which to observe the outside world. She was rubbing her side absently.

"I know." Lydia put the car in park. "I'll come back out and move it once you're inside."

"Hm." Carly unlocked her seatbelt as Lydia skipped around the front of the car to open her door for her. She held out her hand and Cary smiled tightly. "I can walk by myself, Dia."

Lydia rolled her eyes and moved out of the way with a flourish. She grabbed the bags from the backseat and slung them opposite ways across her chest like ammunition belts in an apocalypse movie. By the time she turned around, Carly was pretending to be steady on her feet.

"Alright then," Lydia said. "*Allons-y!*"

Carly smirked. "You watch too much *Doctor Who*."

"No one can watch too much *Doctor Who*."

Lydia passed her ID badge across the sensor and the lock clicked open. It was still about a hallway's walk away from the front door, so Lydia kicked her shoes along the tiles and strolled as slowly as she inconspicuously could. Carly was either too polite to comment or too focused on pretending not to be in pain. Lydia really hoped it was the former.

Because of an uneven number of students, Lydia had her dorm to herself. There was still an extra bed in it, though, and that's where Carly collapsed as soon as she was able. Lydia dropped the bags on the floor and put her hands on her hips.

"Can I get you anything?" She asked. "I have some cream soda in the mini fridge and...Cheez-It's, I think. Unless I ate them all. Which is definitely possible; the night before that Sociology exam was kind of a blur."

"You can go move your car so you don't get a ticket." Carly said.

"Fine," Lydia sighed. She dragged herself out the door, but sprinted to the car from there. She moved it to the designated parking lot – half a block away – and jogged back. The mid-afternoon sun beat down on her as she ran. Normally, she tried to avoid sweating in her non-workout clothes, but this time it was nice just not to think.

Back in the dorm, Carly had only moved to a more comfortable sprawl. One arm was behind her head, the other tucked under her shirt playing with her bandages.

Lydia sat down in her spinning desk chair, using the force to put her in a casual spin over to her friend. She batted Carly's foot. "Don't pick at those." She said.

Carly stuck her tongue out at her. "I'm not going to pull them off."

"Whatever." Lydia looked over her shoulder at the desk. "Do you want to watch a movie or something?"

"Uh, I don't know." Carly frowned. "I feel weird just sitting here while everyone else is actually doing something useful. It's like...I feel like I'm shirking my responsibilities or something."

"Hey, the others were clear; your only responsibility right now is to heal up." Lydia wagged a finger at her.

Carly rolled her eyes. "You're all way too overprotective. I'm *fine*. I didn't even need Nehemiah's help to get in here, did I?"

Lydia sighed. "No."

"What did I tell you guys? It's just a flesh wound."

"*Now* who watches too much TV?"

"That's from a movie, you uncultured swine."

Lydia smacked her sneaker again. "Do you want to order food or should I grab you stuff from the cafeteria?"

"I'm actually starving." Carly said. "Which is weird, since I usually don't eat until later and we just had something before we left the safehouse. I guess my body is really eager to replace that torn muscle."

Lydia forced an obnoxiously loud, unconvincing laugh.

Carly propped herself up on her elbows. "Are you okay?"

The younger girl looked away. "I'm fine." She said. "I'm not the one who's hurt."

"I don't think any of us aren't hurt right now."

Tears sprang to Lydia's eyes. "Do you think they-they're hu-hur-hur-ting Ell-lliot?" She rubbed her eyes with prejudice. She hadn't stuttered like that for years.

"Lydia…" Carly said softly. She sat up and put her hands on the girl's shoulders. "Oh, honey."

Lydia sniffled. "You sho-shouldn't b-be sitt-it-ing up-p."

"Don't worry about me, kiddo." Carly rubbed awkward circles on Lydia's upper arms. "I'm so sorry this is so hard on you."

Lydia sucked in a breath. "I should-d be want-ting to h-help. L-l-l-like you. But I do—I don't – I don't want to anym-m-more. I w—I want it to sto--to stop." She dropped her head into her hands, unable to fight back the tears anymore.

"Oh, Dia." Carly breathed. "Dia, it's okay. It's going to be okay. Adanna will take care of it. Everything's going to be okay. Breath for me. Just breathe, okay? That's all you need to do right now."

"I need to get you food." Her voice, muffled by her hands, sounded so unbelievably young.

"It can wait." Carly whispered. "You're okay. It's okay."

"It's not okay." Lydia said.

"I know. I know. But it will be."

"How do you know?"

I don't. "Because I'm older and wiser. Just trust me."

Chapter 44

Getting on the Same Page

Taylor adjusted her earbuds as the phone rang.

"How did you get seats in first class?" Hugh was asking Viv.

The corner of her lips quirked up.

"Hello?"

Taylor pulled the microphone closer to her mouth, just to be safe. "Hey, baby."

"Mom?" Adanna sounded a little out of it.

"Didn't you check the caller ID?"

"Oh."

Taylor frowned. "How are you doing, sweetheart?"

"I'm fine."

"Adanna," Taylor said. "Your brother was just kidnapped. None of us are *fine.*"

Adanna sighed. *"I'm functioning. I'm headed down to check out Dr. Turner's basement with Wendell and Kyle."*

"Why are you doing that?" The former detective asked.

"Mostly to shut people up." Adanna said. *"We're hoping there's an-other one of those superhuman taser things, or at least the blueprint for one."*

"I assume you're also looking for information on where she might be keeping Elliot."

"Yeah, of course. That's why Kyle's here."

"Are you proud of yourself for how hard you're working?"

"No." She said. *"It doesn't feel like enough. I'm just stressed out and angry."*

"And scared?"

"Yeah. I guess so."

Taylor closed her eyes. "I wish I could be there with you right now, baby."

On the other side of the phone, Adanna turned her face deter-minedly towards the window, squinting into the dying sun. She didn't want to see any of the others. "I wish Elliot could be here with me."

"I know, baby." Taylor replied. *"We'll get him back. Viv is taking us to someone who might be able to find him."*

"Let me know as soon as you learn anything." Adanna said.

"I will." Taylor's voice was soothing, even now. *"I have to go, sweet-heart, the plane's about to take off."*

Adanna gripped the phone tightly. A ball of fear exploded in her stomach. She felt like a little kid again, thinking her mommy's presence would fend off the monsters. *No, don't go!* "Okay. Have a safe flight. I love you, Mom. Tell Dad too, okay?"

"I will, baby. We love you, too. Be safe."

"I will." Adanna said. "Bye."

"Goodbye."

Adanna hung up the phone and dropped it into her purse, which was sitting open by her feet.

Wendell glanced over from the driver's seat. "Everything okay?"

Adanna glared at him, then shook her face out. "Yeah, it's fine. My mom was just checking in."

"Oh, cool." He was looking at the road again. "Did they find anything yet?"

"Apparently they have to fly somewhere first."

"Huh." He said. "Weird."

"You're telling me." Adanna turned to look over her shoulder. Kyle was watching his laptop screen. If he felt her eyes on him, he didn't react. He had the look of a curled up hedgehog flaring his quills. Adanna rubbed her forehead. Turner had given her a headache as a parting gift, and it seemed to be one that kept on giving. "What's happening, Kyle? Find anything?"

"Um." He raised his head the tiniest bit. "Yes, actually."

Adanna caught her breath. "Wait, what?"

He met her eyes. "Oh, yeah. You will not *believe* how many aliases Delilah has. My guess is that ninety percent of them are fakes meant to throw off anyone who wants to track her down. So..." His fingers danced across the keyboard like he was playing piano. "I'm running a couple algorithms to see how many of the aliases have any existence outside of the DMV. That should narrow down how many places we have to search after the basement."

"Wha—Kyle!" Adanna threw her one good hand up. "Why didn't you tell me?!"

"I wanted to wait until I had something besides algorithms—"

"Kyle, you gotta tell me whenever you start doing something! I'm supposed to be in charge right now, how can I do that if nobody tells me what's going on?!"

"I'm doing my *best* here, and you wouldn't understand if I tried to explain it to you anyway--"

"What's that supposed to mean--?!"

"Hey! *Hey!*" Wendell shouted. "Stop that! We're supposed to be on the same side here!"

Silence fell. Adanna leaned her forehead on the headrest. Kyle looked down at his laptop. He didn't type anything.

"I'm sorry." Adanna said to the headrest.

"I'm sorry." Kyle said to his laptop.

Wendell stared ahead at the road ahead and didn't say anything.

Driving back to a place always seems to take less time. The brain has already catalogued the experience, so going back over it is just review. But when the air is heavy with tension and grief, time passes slowly. To Wendell, it felt like there were less hours in the drive, but each hour was longer than usual. It was a kind of sensory paradox.

Pulling up to Turner's house was surreal. It seemed like they hadn't been there in ages, but the scorch marks and dents in the dirt where ultra-natural forces had warped the natural lawn were still prominent and fresh. There was still a giant hole in the side of the house. Across the street, there was still a pile of rubble with caution tape draped like streamers over chunks of drywall that created strange, shifting shadows even in the darkness. It looked like a pit of ghosts.

Wendell parked the car and switched off the lights and engine. He stepped out into the cool summer darkness and breathed in the midnight air. He hooked his fingers together over his head and stretched.

Adanna, coming around the hood of the car, forced her eyes not to narrow. She rested the hand peeking out from her cast on her hip, the plastered elbow jutting out cartoonishly. It was much easier for her other hand. "Okay," she said. "Let's get inside quickly; we don't want anyone to see us and call the cops."

The three of them darted across the empty suburban street, suspiciously watching dark windows. But no one appeared. It was like they were the last people on earth.

They hurtled caution tape and bypassed the front door in favor of the hole in the wall. Once inside, Adanna and Kyle fell in behind Wendell, who led them through the kitchen and down the hall to the closet.

He pried open the hatch and felt around for the light switch. When the light came on he held his breath, but no one started shooting. The carpet over the door hadn't *looked* like it had been moved since he'd last been there, but he wasn't about to put money on it.

"I'll go down first." He said.

Adanna opened her mouth to argue, but he'd already swung down into the passage and started down the steps. She gritted her teeth and followed, contenting herself with the mental image of kicking his head "by accident."

Kyle was the last one in the hall. He tore his eyes from the darkness of the rest of the house and climbed inside. He pulled the carpet tight to the hatch and lowered them both into place above him. Hopefully if anyone came looking they wouldn't notice the carpet being a little out of place.

The basement looked exactly like it had the last time Wendell had been there. It felt wrong; like Dr. Turner rubbing salt in the wound. So much had changed; the room had no right to stay the same.

"What are we looking for, Kyle?" Adanna asked.

"Uhm." He dropped from the ladder to the floor and shrugged. "Grab anything that looks like a weapon or a blueprint, I guess. I'll check out the computers."

"Sounds good." Adanna nodded. She and Wendell dropped four duffel bags to the floor, then knelt to unzip them.

Adanna hooked one over her cast, then started grabbing machinery off tables. She looked for what seemed to be nearly completed first, scooping up any wires or tools lying beside them just to be safe.

Wendell headed over to the desk, opening drawers and stuffing his duffel full of papers and folders. There was a tiny stuffed mouse which looked like it had been made during a crafts course in the 80's. He ran his thumb over its gray fur, which was exceedingly soft. He stuffed that in his duffel, too.

Adanna was starting to get shooting pains in her arm under the cast, so she hefted the duffel up to her shoulder and kept going until she couldn't. Then she zipped it up and went back for another.

She stopped by where Kyle was working on the computers while she adjusted the second bag on her shoulder. "How's it coming?"

"Nyuh." He muttered. "Firewalls. Can't talk. Lots. Annoying."

"Keep up the good work." She said.

Kyle had never met a mainframe this hard to crack. Either Turner herself was a computer genius or she'd hired one to set this up. He was literally breaking a sweat trying to avoid detection and he had no idea how many firewalls he still had to break through.

He was sure someone like Turner had a nasty surprise waiting for whoever could crack the code. Maybe Grady had been working for her the whole time, and the next nasty surprise was that he was her new spy.

Maybe Siren had been working for her.

Kyle stabbed a key, realizing too late that it was the wrong one. The computer screen blacked out, then lit up again to reveal a countdown. His eyes widened. "Time's up! We have to get out of here!"

"What?" Adanna did a double-take, then swiped her good arm across the table she was closest to, not waiting to pick up whatever didn't land in her bag. She pointed at Kyle. "Get the other one!"

He grabbed it and bolted for the ladder only to stop short.

"Wen!" Adanna snapped.

"Coming!" Wendell threw his two bags across his chest. One was only half full, so he leaned towards it to compensate for the weight of the other one.

Kyle seemed to have disappeared – Adanna hadn't heard him on the ladder. She looked around wildly only to see him back at the computer. "What are you doing?!"

"I'll be right there! Don't worry about me!"

"Kyle, get over here *now!*" Adanna gestured wildly towards the ladder. "Wendell! Go!"

He hesitated.

"*NOW!*"

Wendell clambered up the stairs.

Adanna sprinted over to Kyle and dragged him up by his hood. "*Come on!*"

He gagged, scrambling to get his legs under him. "Give me a minute!" He said. "I think I can separate the hard drive from the rest of the computer!"

"We don't have a minute!" Adanna shouted. The countdown read forty-five seconds.

Wendell was suddenly at her shoulder. "Door's locked." He said.

"What?!" Kyle looked at him with wild eyes.

"Oh no way." Adanna ran a shaky hand through her braids.

Thirty seconds.

"Okay, listen up." Adanna said. "We're going to jam the computer between the two top steps. The explosion should knock the door open."

"How are we going to survive?" Kyle asked.

She pointed at Wendell. "Start making a barrier out of those tables. Kyle; I can't climb up there and carry the computer, so you're going to have to do it. If it doesn't stick, just leave it at the bottom of the ladder and get back over here. If it doesn't knock the door open, we'll figure it out later."

Fifteen seconds.

Adanna and Wendell threw their duffels in the far corner of the basement and started yanking and kicking down shelves, then shoving them in front of the corner. Their muscles screamed at the strain, but they ignored them. If this didn't work, at least they wouldn't have to feel the aching in the morning.

Kyle yanked the computer out of the wall, then hefted it up to press against his chest. It was an old-school desktop unit, probably weighed as much as a small child. His whole body was shaking for a million different reasons.

He climbed awkwardly to the top of the ladder, then shoved the computer between the top two steps. It was a tight fit, but it was a fit. He made sure it was leaning back against the wall, then pushed off the ladder and landed in a crouch on the basement floor.

"Kyle!"

He took off towards Adanna and Wendell. His legs and arms moved like they weren't even part of his body; like they were part of an avatar in a video game and he was pressing buttons to make them simulate running.

He dove over the makeshift barrier. Adanna and Wendell grabbed him at the same time and pulled him down. The three of them huddled together as the countdown hit zero.

~

Elliot was becoming less and less a fan of the new Project Kobold. "I think there's a problem with the toilet in my cell." He said to the doctor who was administering his physical.

"Hm? And what's that?" His name was Dr. Alte and he looked like a parallel universe version of Santa. He had white hair and a big, bushy white beard, glasses perched on the edge of his button nose, and a perpetual smile on his face. But his wrinkled skin was stretched over his bones, seemingly without leaving room for any pesky flesh between them. His cheekbones stuck out from his face, making his cheeks look sunken.

"I can't figure out how to flush it."

Dr. Alte laughed. "That's because it doesn't flush, son."

"Um. What?" Elliot's tone was low and dangerous. "First you kidnap me, then you take away my access to indoor plumbing? How sick can you get?!"

"I'm susceptible to the same illnesses as any human." Dr. Alte deadpanned. "Of course, you may not be. We'll have to do some tests."

"I'm not kidding, man." Elliot said. "I'm not going to spend the day as your lab rat only to go back to a cell and smell my own crap all night."

"The toilet will be cleaned out routinely." Dr. Alte said. "We aren't going to simply discard all that testable subject matter."

Elliot gagged.

"Alrighty now," the strange, strange man clapped his hands and stood up. "It's time for your stress test."

One stress test and weight-lifting session later, Dr. Alte broke the news to Elliot about allowing him to use his powers for the second round of testing.

Elliot laughed and crossed his arms. "Yeah; nice try, doc." He said. "But I'm not playing your game."

"Excuse me?" Dr. Alte said. "I said 'no.'" The boy explained slowly. "I'm not going to use my powers for you. In fact, I'm not going to do anything even remotely superhuman for you until you let me see my sister."

The man who had come with him had been switching the safety on his handgun on and off. Now he exchanged a look with the doctor.

"Are you certain?" Dr. Alte said.

"Absolutely." Elliot replied.

The doctor keyed in a command on his tablet.

Elliot felt his powers come rushing back to him. He wasn't prepared for how desperate he would be to let them loose; to use them and use them and never let them be taken from him again. He swallowed hard, closing his eyes to regain control over his screaming emotions.

"I won't do it." He said through his teeth.

Dr. Alte frowned. He walked over to the gunman and murmured something. The man nodded and made his way to the blast door. When he opened it, they both looked over at Elliot. The Gemini subject was staring determinedly at the wall, facing away from the door. The gunman stepped outside and closed the door behind him.

For a few minutes, Elliot and Dr. Alte were left in silence. Dr. Alte was typing something up on his tablet, but his fingers were nimble and gentle on the glass. They didn't make a sound. Elliot wanted to use the time to search for Maggie, but he was afraid they would catch on and block whatever connection he might have discovered.

The gunman stepped back inside.

Elliot turned to him. "Well? What did she say?"

There was suddenly a gun in his face, the hammer pulled back.

"Jonas...!" Dr. Alte gasped.

"She said that if you're not going to cooperate, she has no use for you." Jonas said.

Elliot eyed the gun. "Fine."

Jonas scoffed. "Didn't you hear me, kid? If you don't start showing off some fireworks, I'm going to have to kill you."

"Then do it." Elliot told him. "I'll cooperate if you let me see Maggie. But if you don't, you might as well pull that trigger because I'm not going to do any sort of razzle-dazzle for you."

Jonas pulled the trigger.

The bullet zipped across Elliot's cheek and clipped his ear before embedding itself in the wall behind him. He struggled to keep his expression under control. He felt like his heart was going to explode.

Jonas grinned. "You're a tough one, aren't you?"

Elliot shrugged one shoulder, not trusting himself to speak.

The gunman put the gun down and waved a finger at him. He raised a walkie talkie to his mouth and pressed a button. "The kid isn't backing down." He said after the beep.

"I saw." Even with the roughness of the short-range radio channel, Turner's voice was unmistakable. *"Impressive show, Gemini Beta."*

Elliot pressed his lips together.

"If you complete these tests with Dr. Alte, I'll let you have dinner with Alpha."

He shook his head. "Let me see Maggie first."

"Stubborn, aren't you?" Turner said. *"Just like Kobold Beta. Very well. Jonas will take you to a secure room, and Alpha will be delivered shortly."*

A lifetime of manners being drilled into his brain caused Elliot to have to bite his tongue so he didn't thank her.

He tried not to shudder when Dr. Alte switched the cuffs back on, and he almost didn't notice Jonas clipping them together in front of him.

"Wait!" The doctor said.

"What is it?" Jonas snapped.

"I should bandage that wound."

Elliot became aware of the warm stinging on his face, the wetness that was heavier than tears.

"It's just a scratch." Jonas complained. "I need to get him to the conference room."

"Young man," Dr. Alte said. "I am a doctor. I took an oath to help where I am needed."

Elliot barked a laugh. "Then what are you doing here, experimenting on people?"

The doctor took his arm and led him back to the examining table. "You're probably too close to the situation to see this, but the goal of Project Kobold is to help people."

"Oh yeah? Who told you that; Turner?"

"Not so much Turner as the facts she presented me with." The doctor swabbed Elliot's face clean, then began to stick gauze to the wound. He secured it with medical tape. "I am a man of science, you know. I'm not persuaded as easily as more emotional humans."

"You mean you're more heartless than the average person."

"I don't see what's wrong with being 'heartless.'" Dr. Alte said. "It just means I don't let myself be ruled by my emotions."

"It also means you're not letting yourself be fully human." Elliot argued. "Maybe you should be examining yourself."

"Hm. I'm afraid I wouldn't be able to be fully objective." He stood back to admire his handiwork. "Alright; that should hold for now. Off you go."

Elliot was relieved when Jonas dragged him out of the room. At least with the gunman there was no twisted logic. With Jonas, things were pretty straight forward.

Because of the delay, Maggie was already in the room when they got there. Her eyes widened when she saw Elliot's bandages, and his brain was suddenly assaulted by a wave of rage. He clenched his muscles just to keep himself from elbowing Jonas in the side.

"You'll have fifteen minutes." Jonas said, shoving Elliot away. "You'll be monitored the whole time; audio and visual. The food will be here soon."

And then they were the only two people in the room itself.

"What did they do to you?!" Maggie was at his side, fingers tracing his bandages. "Have they been torturing you?!"

"No; nothing like that." Although, to be honest, it probably did fall into that category. "It was just a little misunderstanding." They didn't know each other very well yet, but judging by her righteous anger on his behalf it stood to reason she would feel guilty if she knew he got shot trying to see her. "Never mind that. Why don't you have your cuffs on?"

Maggie made a face. "The cuffs are a decoy. They actually implanted chips in our heads."

"Wha-at?!"

Maggie winced and Elliot immediately started calming breaths.

"I'm sorry." He said.

"What do you mean?" She shook off her confusion. "You have every right to be angry. I know I was."

"You...? *Oh.*" He said. That incident in his cell was starting to make more sense now.

"Why do you look happy?"

"I wouldn't say 'happy,' it's more like...pleased? Satisfied?" He shook his head. "I don't know. I just figured something out, though."

"Oh, yeah?" Maggie was examining his cuffs for weak points. "What's that?"

"Well..." He was now realizing he had no idea how he was going to go about this. He couldn't come out and tell her what was going on because Turner, Alte, and maybe even Jonas were listening. But the connection didn't seem to work for words, it was more like...feelings. "Hey, Maggie?"

"Yeah?"

"Do you want to know how my face is feeling?"

"What? Oh." She nodded. "Yeah, of course. How does it feel?"

"Well..." He took a deep breath. Then he focused on the sensations in his face. He tried to pick apart the pain, see it in all its glory, determine the different hues. Then he shifted part of his focus to his sister.

"It feels hot. And sharp. Like a river of pain across my face. Like my face is paper and someone tried to rip it in half. Like 'wanna know how I got these scars' type of pain."

Maggie hissed and put her hand to her face.

Elliot dropped that line of thinking guiltily. "I'm sorry."

Her eyes were wide and curious as she let her hand drop. "You...?" She stiffened, forcing herself not to look at the camera.

"Do you know how it feels when you mess up and you don't know how to make it right again?" He asked. He had to make sure she understood what was going on.

"Yes." She nodded, slowly at first. "Yeah, I do."

"What about the feeling when you go for the first swim of the summer? And you feel the water gliding over your skin..."

"...like some sort of gel or a cooler, denser version of air..."

"...and you're floating in the water, looking up at the sun..."

"...and you feel like you just want to stay there forever." Maggie grinned. "I know what you're talking about."

Elliot grinned back. "Cool."

Chapter 45

Anatomy of a Murderer

Hailey pouted about not being consulted about the pizza until Grady suggested she pick the movie. Sean got angry because Grady shouldn't be the one to decide whether they watch a movie or not, to which Nehemiah reminded him that Hailey would be the one deciding. He was starting to feel more like he was babysitting *two* loose cannons.

Hailey helped Nehemiah make popcorn in the microwave – that device hated him, and the feeling was mutual – and all four of them arranged themselves on the living room furniture and watched *Charade* with Audrey Hepburn.

"How do you kill someone with a plastic bag?" Nehemiah asked at one point.

"You wrap it around their head and tie it so it creates a makeshift vacuum. Then they suffocate." Grady told him.

"Wouldn't they just take it off?"

"Not if you hold them down until they're too oxygen-deprived to figure out how."

"Well *that's* not disturbing at all." Sean muttered.

"Will you guys shut up?" Hailey hissed. "The dialogue is the best part!"

After the movie, a problem presented itself. They'd chosen to come to the apartment because it had two bedrooms, and they wanted to sleep in shifts. But if two of them were up at all times and they each got eight hours of sleep…"

"One person will have to do two shifts in a row." Sean pointed out.

"True." Hailey pursed her lips and tapped her fingers on her arms.

"I wouldn't mind staying up for two shifts." Nehemiah said.

"We all could." Sean said slowly. "If we each take two shifts every time we tag in, we should be able to still split the work load evenly."

"You realize that's just one shift, right?" Grady said. "Your start times are just staggered."

"No one asked you." Sean snapped.

Grady shrugged.

"But who's going to stay up for two shifts first?" Hailey asked.

"I will." Nehemiah said. "I volunteered first, anyway. And it's my apartment."

"It's half yours." Sean said. "Anyway, I'll do it. Think of it as a thank-you for letting us bring a homicidal maniac into your home and not mine."

Nehemiah rolled his eyes. "It's no problem, really."

"I have more energy than both of you put together." Hailey mentioned. "I'll do it."

"Why don't you draw straws or something and get it over with?" Grady yawned. "It's been kind of a long day for me."

"Boo-hoo." Sean said. "Just go to bed, then. We don't need you out here right now."

"Which room?" The homicidal maniac asked.

"Mine." Nehemiah said quickly. "First door on the right."

"Much obliged." Grady tipped his nonexistent hat and sauntered off to the room.

Sean pinched the bridge of his nose. "This situation is so wrong I can't even begin to describe how."

"Are we going to draw straws?" Hailey asked.

"No!" Sean crossed his arms. "We're not doing what that murderer says!"

"How are we going to decide then?" Nehemiah wondered.

Sean sighed. "Rock paper scissors. It's the only mature way to deal with this."

"Amen!" Hailey rubbed her hands together and cackled. "I am the Rochambeau *champion!*"

"Pretty sure Rochambeau is the Rochambeau champion." Sean said.

She rolled her eyes. "Yeah, well, he's dead so he forfeited his title."

"I have no idea who you're talking about." Nehemiah said in a conversational tone. "Anyway, let's play."

It took three tries, but Nehemiah lost. So he changed the sheets on Wendell's bed and collapsed without bothering to get into pajamas.

Hailey made coffee, then she and Sean settled on the couch. He yawned and she kicked him.

"Don't you dare."

"Sorry~" He murmured, straining to work his jaw around a second yawn.

Hailey yawned too. She kicked him again. "You are a horrible person."

"Thank you."

She took a long sip of her coffee, then wriggled around in place. "Have you seen that video where the person ties the dinosaur chicken nugget to a string and their cat chases it around the house?"

"No, I don't think so."

She scrambled up, setting her coffee down to run and grab her phone from her purse. She swiped and thumbed the screen, not looking up as she made her way back to the couch. She dropped herself down and curled her legs up underneath her, forcing Sean to shift his feet to the floor to make room.

"Look at this," She giggled as she pulled the video up.

It was pretty funny, but Hailey was hysterical. Sean drew his own laughs out to match her.

"Hey! Hey. You know what we should do?"

"What?" He wondered.

"We should make cookies!" She was on her knees now, bouncing up and down on the cushion.

Sean's whole body was crying out for rest. "Hmm. Yeah, that would be a good idea." At least if he was standing he probably wouldn't fall asleep on the job. Suddenly he was picturing himself as a centaur, sleeping while standing up. He chuckled.

Hailey already had the bowl, cookbook, and an assortment of measuring cups and spoons out by the time Sean made it to the kitchen.

"Okay, you read the recipe, I'll get the ingredients." She said.

"How did you find all this stuff?" He asked. "Have you cooked here before?"

"It's called baking actually. But no. It's all kitchen stuff, though, and we're in a kitchen. There are only so many places to look."

"You're incredible."

"Awww." She smiled at him. "What's the first ingredient?"

"Uh..." It took him a minute to find the cookie section. "I think it depends on what kind of cookies we're making."

"Makes sense." Hailey said. "I don't have a preference. Pick your favorite."

"Mm." The first recipe was for chocolate chip cookies. "Chocolate chip."

"The first ingredient is chocolate chips?"

"No, the first ingredient is flour. The type of cookie is chocolate chip."

"Oh. You could just say 'flour,' I really don't care what we're making. I like to be surprised." Hailey flipped open two cupboards at once. The flour was actually in one of them, and she pulled it out. "How much flour?"

Sean blinked at the book. "...2 ¼ cups."

Hailey measured it out, humming under her breath and bouncing to the beat in her head. Sean went back to the living room for his coffee, taking a too-long swig in an attempt to ward off the wave of wooziness. Hailey was done by the time he got back.

"What next?"

The skin on his tongue felt like it was peeling from the heat, but it still took a while for the scribbles on the page to manifest into words. "Um...1 tablespoon of vanilla."

"Okay."

She'd already poured it in by the time he realized his mistake. "Wait, no!"

Hailey jumped back, sliding into a self-defense stance and looking automatically down the hallway to Nehemiah's room. "What?!"

"No, sorry, it's just..." He ran a hand through his hair. "It actually said teaspoon."

"Oh." She relaxed. "That's okay. They'll just be extra vanilla-y."

"Yeah." He looked down at his coffee.

Hailey frowned. "Hey, you're pretty tired, aren't you?"

He shrugged one shoulder. "I guess."

"We don't have to do the cookies." She said.

"We've already started—"

"That doesn't matter." She walked around the table and grabbed him by the arm, steering him back over to the couch. "Here; you just sit down and rest, okay?"

"I feel bad." He said. "You seemed really excited."

"Don't feel bad. I just thought it would be fun, I didn't have my heart set on it or anything."

"I don't want to waste their flour."

"Ah!" Hailey growled. "Fine! I'll make the stupid cookies! You just relax, okay?"

He still hesitated. "Are you sure?"

"Sean. Sit."

He sat.

Hailey headed back to the kitchen. "Talk to me so you don't fall asleep."

"Oh. Okay. Um…" He frowned into the middle distance. "I don't know. What do you want to talk about?"

"Whatever."

"Yeah, that's helpful."

She shot a glare over her shoulder. "Hey, I have an idea; talk to me about why you're being such a party pooper."

"I am *not* being a party pooper—"

"Yeah you are." She rolled her eyes, adding salt to her soon-to-be batter. "You've shot down every attempt Nehemiah has made to make this situation okay for the rest of us.""Are you really okay with him catering to the enemy like that?" Sean asked.

"Come on."

"You come on! How can you be so okay with this...sleepover with a villain? If we didn't have those cuffs on Grady, he'd kill us all."

Hailey lifted a shoulder. "I don't know. He said he only wanted to kill people associated with Project Kobold."

"And you *believe* him? He's a serial killer! They're not exactly known for having the strictest of moral codes."

"Well, his moral compass is definitely broken." She agreed. "But I don't get the sense that it's stopped functioning entirely. He's got kind of a twisted-paragon thing going for him."

Sean narrowed his eyes. "What are you talking about?"

"Haven't you noticed? He thinks the power he has is too dangerous to be used by humans, that we would destroy ourselves with it. Think: the Nuclear Arms Race. He's trying to protect humanity from the threat, but he's taking it too far. I think he believes the ends justify the means. If he was a kid, I'd have a field day with him."

"How can you be sure that's what's happening?" Sean asked.

She threw a glare in his direction. "Maybe because I've been paying attention instead of trying to stone him every time he opens his mouth. It's called knowing your enemy."

"Huh." Sean looked down at his coffee. "I guess. I just..."

"You need someone to blame." Hailey said.

"What's that supposed to mean?"

"I've seen this before." She added some sugar. "When bad things happen, it's easier to blame someone than to face the fact that the bad thing happened in the first place."

"Or maybe it's harder to face the fact that not everyone is good." He shot back.

"What's that supposed to mean?"

"You and Nehemiah believe everyone has some good in them, way deep down in their core." Sean scoffed. "But it's not true. Some people are just evil."

"Some people are *lost*." Hailey said. "And I'm not saying that some people have goodness that will shine through at the last minute in a crisis or anything; what I'm saying is that I don't think anyone is born evil."

"Not born evil, maybe, but people can choose their own destiny." Sean pointed out.

"Now we're getting into the Nature vs. Nurture debate." Hailey sighed. She cracked her knuckles. "Alright; let's *go*. I think there is always going to be an inherently good part of human nature."

"Really?" Sean leaned forward. "What about Hitler? Do you think he had some inherent goodness in him?"

"I see you 're not the type to waste time." She smirked. "It sounds weird, but yes. I mean, just because people ignore their better nature doesn't mean it doesn't exist."

"How can you be so sure it does if they don't follow it? What good is a hypothesis without proof?"

She rolled her eyes. "It's called *faith*."

"Faith? In *people*?" Sean laughed. "Have you met them?"

"Well, it's better than the alternative." Hailey emptied brown sugar into the bowl and dropped the cup, leaning against the table. "Haven't you ever had someone who believes you can be more than even you believe you can?"

Sean shrugged. "When I wanted to open my dance studio, it felt like no one thought it would work. Even after it started working, they didn't think it would work. I feel like I have to be forgetting someone, but I don't think I am."

"What about Lydia?"

Sean shook his head. "Lydia is my baby cousin. She grew up thinking the big kids could do anything, and everyone thinks that at some point. It doesn't count."

"Well, you have someone now." Hailey said.

"Who?"

She sighed. "You must be extraordinarily tired. *Me*, you weirdo."

"Oh." It took his brain a minute to catch up. "Thanks."

She waved his gratitude off and started hunting for the next ingredient.

"For the record; I believe in you, too." Sean said.

Hailey smiled.

~

Adanna opened her eyes in the wake of the cellar explosion. Which in and of itself took a bit of effort. The first thing she was aware of was that she was halfway on top of Kyle, whose bony knee was digging into her stomach.

She rolled onto her side and narrowed her eyes, trying to see her companions. Her ringing brain was convinced she only needed to adjust her focus to develop night vision.

"Ugh. Mlegh." She tried to speak and ended up coughing instead. "Wendell." She rasped. "Kyle. You alive?"

Wendell moaned. "I'm in too much pain to be dead." He sounded like he'd swallowed as much dust as she had.

"Kyle?" Adanna kicked in his direction and hit something that moaned.

"Five more minutes." He murmured.

"No. Up. Now." Adanna struggled to obey her own orders, listening to the scraping and shuffling of her friends to motivate her.

"Do you think the cops are coming?" Kyle asked.

"If they were, we'd hear them by now." Wendell said. "Or…'we'd have heard them by now.' Or maybe 'we would be hearing them by now.'"

"My head hurts too much for your grammar nonsense, Wen." Adanna said. "Does everyone's phone still work?"

"Everyone's phones." Wendell said.

"Wen, I'm not kidding."

"Mine does." Kyle tapped his screen and the flashlight beam hit the rubble between the three of them. The dust in the air was illuminated.

Adanna and Wendell pulled their own phones out, and soon enough three beams of light converged on a hunk of drywall that had almost crushed them.

"Okay." Adanna took a deep breath and promptly choked on it. "Let's see if my master plan worked."

They shouldered the duffel bags and made their way slowly over to where the ladder had been. Everything that had been blown apart or uprooted by the explosion made it seem like they were giants picking their way through a city after an earthquake. When they finally got to the passage, there was good news and bad news.

The good news was the door was open – figuratively speaking.

The bad news was there wasn't a ladder anymore.

Adanna groaned. "I can't believe I didn't think of that!"

"Dude, give yourself a break." Wendell said. "You had, like, a minute to come up with a plan."

"We can probably use some tables and stuff to climb up, anyway." Kyle said.

"What about a bookshelf?" Adanna wondered. "If we leaned it up against the wall, it could work almost the same as a ladder."

"See? Genius." Wendell swung his flashlight across the room to locate a bookshelf. "That one looks promising."

"I can't believe it didn't get destroyed." Kyle murmured. It was only twenty feet away from "ground zero," and blocked off by debris. It took the three of them fifteen minutes to clear it all away.

As they worked, holding their phones in one hand or between their teeth, respectively, Kyle was left alone with his thoughts. Normally, this would be preferable. But he had murdered someone. Then he let the thought of that murder almost get his friends killed.

He'd never thought much about what made people become killers. He'd thought even less about whether they could ever go back to who they were before. Did it just become part of you, like a bad habit? Or were some people more susceptible to destroying lives, like how some people were more susceptible to certain diseases?

Did murdering someone taint you? He'd almost killed Adanna and Wendell by accident – had he summoned some dark force in order to kill Siren, and now that force was causing him to spread harm like a twisted Midas touch?

He didn't really believe that. It would have been nice, because then it wouldn't have been his fault, but it wasn't true. Everything that he had done had been a result of his own choices. The others could tell him it had been self-defense, or even defense of the group, until they ran out of breath, but it wouldn't change the truth.

He'd watched the fight in the kitchen. He'd picked up the gun when it had fallen to the floor. He'd waited until he could get a clean shot. Then he'd aimed the gun at Siren's head and pulled the trigger.

What had happened to the body? It had disappeared sometime between the time he left the kitchen and the time he left the safe house. He'd checked. Maybe out of some morbid curiosity. Maybe he'd been debating calling the police. But the body was gone. He was pretty sure there was no finding it now.

And even if he could find it, there was no way the so-called "Hero's Guild" would let him go down for the crime. Ironic, wasn't it? The "Heroes" covering up a murder. What did that make them, then? Maybe they should change the name to "Vigilante's Guild." At least then it would be more accurate. Heroes upheld justice, not their own agendas.

But he shouldn't be so hard on them. After all, everything changes when it's your own friends and family. And they were so young -- most of the Guild members could still pass for high schoolers if they really tried. How could anyone ask them to be objective about this?

No. Kyle knew that if justice was going to be served, he would have to do it himself.

"Ah, finally!" Adanna stretched her back, observing the newly-prepared path. "Let's get this thing over to the passage."

Wendell bumped his shoulder against Kyle's as they moved to grab hold of the shelf. "You okay?"

Kyle forced a smile. "Yeah. Fine."

Wendell's frown deepened.

"Come on, guys, let's move it!" Adanna said.

As soon as they were above ground, they sprinted back to the car and dumped their bags in the back. It felt strange to be back in their seats after all the work they'd put into getting out of the basement. Especially considering barely two hours had passed since they'd arrived.

"Alright," Adanna said as Wendell started the car. "Let's hit a gas station for bathroom breaks and snacks. We'll chill in the parking lot for a while before heading back. I think we deserve a break."

"Aye-aye, captain!" Wendell saluted her.

She didn't glare at him.

In the backseat, Kyle checked the algorithms he was running on his laptop. So far, it looked like at least one fourth of the ID's didn't have anything else to back them up. That was almost promising. Another forth only had credit cards to their names, another forth had credit cards and passports, and the remaining identities had all of the above *plus* property ownership and jobs.

Kyle rubbed his eyes and set to work on another algorithm that would track the purchases from each of the credit cards. He included the credit cards from the second fourth, just in case. He wasn't about to leave any stone unturned. Not when Elliot and Maggie were on the line. Not when this was the last project he would ever work on.

"Kyle, you need to give yourself a break." Adanna said. "That's an order."

"Yes, ma'am." Kyle said, not looking up from his screen.

Chapter 46

One Thousand Paper Names

In yet another of the new Project's many rooms, Maggie tossed the last of the discs at the target, obliterating it on contact. She turned to the direction she was sure the speaker was in this time. "There; I did your stupid accuracy test. Happy?"

"*Not quite.*" Turner's voice said.

Maggie felt a bee-sting at the base of her skull and winced, partially from the pain and partially from the emptiness that followed. She rubbed the back of her neck and glared at the supposed location of the speaker.

It was much better than whatever shock had put her out before, but she knew it didn't have to hurt at all. How else could they explain the lack of pain when the cuffs were "deactivated?" This was all some play to get in her head.

She smirked at the irony.

The door swung open and Denise swaggered in, finger on the trigger though the gun was hanging at her side. Technicians in lab coats and protective gear scurried past her and replaced the targets with shiny new ones.

They also took the discs, replacing them with a collection of what looked like a cross between a javelin and a tent peg. Maggie didn't have to have her powers to know they were made of metal.

Maggie dropped into a crouch and looked over at Denise. "Come here often?"

The gunwoman met her eyes with a glare that could melt fire before looking away.

"Oh, come on." Maggie said. "Don't you ever get bored with the 'let's exchange dirty looks' routine?"

Apparently she did not.

"Well alright then." Maggie dropped back on her butt and kicked her legs out in front of her, turning her attention to the technicians.

There were about five of them. They looked like clones, and very well might be considering Turner's history. All the same height, same body type, same skin tone, same gear that obscured their faces and hair.

Maggie focused on them and reached out for Elliot. She pictured the technicians next to Dolly the Sheep, salting the images with irony. So far, they only seemed to be able to toss feelings back and forth. Maybe Turner's experiment obsession was rubbing off on her.

All she got back was a flutter of confusion. She wondered whether her brother was confused about what she was trying to say or why she was sending him pictures of sheep. *Way to be specific, Elliot.*

She didn't notice Denise and the technicians leaving. She only realized they were gone when she felt the rush of the world righting itself in her brain.

"Alright. This time, I want you to try to hit the targets dead center. I'll be timing you. Try to hit every target within five seconds."

Maggie groaned as she stood. "Why don't you just give yourself powers?"

Turner didn't answer her question. What she did say was, "*If you succeed, I'll allow you to see Gemini Beta.*"

"No take backs!" It was stupid, but it was the first thing she thought of to say. Maggie settled into a fighting stance and reached for the...giant darts, apparently. She needed to see Elliot. She'd had about enough of being a guinea pig.

"*Five...*"

Maggie jumped when she realized there wasn't going to be a warning. She gathered the darts, lining them up as best she could as Turner counted down. She took a deep breath, then fired all of them at the same time. They struck just as Turner finished her countdown.

Maggie felt like she was coming up from underwater. She looked at the targets fully for the first time, holding her breath until she was sure she had been successful.

"*Impressive.*" Turner said. "*This time, put each one in a different ring. Start with the outermost ring and move to the bullseye. I want them in a successive pattern.*"

"Hey!" Maggie shouted. "You said if I hit all the targets—"

"*I'm sorry,*" Turner's voice sounded colder than usual. "*You seem to have gotten the impression that we are equals.*"

Maggie shivered.

"*You are a test subject, Gemini Alpha. You do not dictate whether I allow you to see Beta or how I chose to do so. Am I understood?*"

Maggie crossed her arms and looked down.

"*I said, 'Am I understood?'*"

"Yes." Maggie replied softly.

"*Excellent.*" Turner's voice rose back to its normal temperature – still sweater weather, but not below freezing. "*Now, do you need me to explain this test again?*"

"No." Maggie dropped herself into a fighting stance. She made up her mind; she was going to see Elliot. No matter what she had to do, she was going to do it in order to get in the same room with her brother and come up with a plan to get out of here. She thought of him and sent him her determination. *I'm coming.*

~

They reached New York just before the sun. The air was crisp and clear, like gaseous ice. Viv lead the others out into the street, barely squinting her almond eyes when the sun peaked through a narrow space between two buildings.

Americans thought this was such a big city, but she'd grown up between Athens and Tokyo. She knew what a big city looked like. She slid one hand back and forth across the scar on her belly and thought about the cities where she grew up.

They were choked with people, bursting at the seams with them. They were a thousand American expressions about too-fullness; one for each paper crane she folded the summer she was eight, when she wished for someone to take her to a place that wasn't about to topple over into the sea from the weight of all the people trying to live on it.

She wanted to take Oliver's hand and squeeze it like she was eight and he was her wish-fulfillment man. But this was no time for wishes. She needed to find Masakichi, who was still buried in the heart of the dragon that ate wishes out of the hands of little girls.

Oliver walked just behind her left shoulder, Taylor on her right. Hugh followed them all, his hulking frame tensed and ready to envelope the rest of them if need be. The four made their way down the street in this strange organic diamond shape.

In checkers, diamonds are the most powerful shape because each piece can back up the pieces on either side of it. Viv wasn't sure Hugh would back her up if she needed him to, but he wasn't on one of her sides anyway.

They made their way to a tiny hole-in-the-wall café that was in exactly the wrong place; squashed between a Starbucks and a Dunkin Donuts. It was lit by bare bulbs on the ceiling, which could have been fashionable had any other decorator been in charge.

By all lines of reasoning, there was no way it should have been able to survive for a year, let alone twenty. Viv had been to a million places like this.

Masakichi was at the bar, casually sitting backwards on his stool in order to watch the door. He had a newspaper in front of him, a felt tip pen twirling between the fingers of his right hand. He didn't look up when Viv and the others entered, or when she came to a stop in front of him.

Viv cleared her throat.

Masakichi dropped his newspaper and smiled. He was young and incredibly handsome. The scar stretching from the left corner of his mouth to his chin in a shaky diagonal line somehow only seemed to add to his charm. "Junko!" He exclaimed.

Viv bowed her head slightly to him. "Masakichi."

He wagged a finger at her. "No, no! These days I go by 'Tommy.'"

"Fascinating." She did not appear at all fascinated.

Masakichi/Tommy glanced behind her at her entourage. "And who are these people? I thought you said you wanted to meet alone."

"Never mind them." Viv said. "I need information."

Tommy's smile vanished. "You're breaking all the rules of good business, Junko, talking out here in the open like this."

"I don't care about rules." Viv rolled her shoulders. "Or good business. I care about what I want."

He rolled his eyes. "Same old Jun." But his mouth was tighter now. "Let's take this to the back room."

"Fine." Viv said. "Two of my people will be staying out here. They wanted to try the coffee."

He shrugged one shoulder and waved at the bar. "It's on the house."

"What are you doing? We're coming too!" Hugh hissed.

"No; you're staying here." Viv whispered. "Just in case we don't come back."

"But—"

Taylor laid a hand on his arm. "If you're not back in twenty minutes, we're coming in after you."

Hugh frowned, but nodded at Viv.

"Understood." She replied.

Oliver nodded.

The parents split up, the Poseys following Masakichi into the kitchen and up a flight of rickety stairs. They led to a single, almost circular room with two couches which looked like they'd been pulled right off the streets and a table with uneven legs. One chair sat on either side of the table.

Viv let Masakichi catch her looking around. "It's a bit different than it was back in my day."

He sneered. "Back in your day, we were still performing for the Yakuza. These days, I'm the master of my own destiny."

"That's a dangerous route to go down." She mentioned, pulling a chair out and sitting down.

"You would know." He sat down opposite her. "Now. What can I do for you, Junko?" He glanced up at Oliver. "You are still going by Junko, aren't you?"

She ignored him. "I need information on someone who goes by the name of Delilah Turner."

"You got a picture?"

She slid an envelope across the table to him. "It's in there. With everything else I know about her."

He pulled the envelope towards him with one finger. His eyes never left her face. "And what's in it for me?"

Oliver glanced down at his wife. His hands were hanging at his sides, empty. He was completely out of his depth here. He had never paid attention at business meetings before. As a Music professor, he'd never been to more than a handful.

There was a whole different set of rules being adhered to here. Nothing could be said directly, until it could. Nothing could be kept from the other player, until it was. It was like chess and BS and Muggins all at once.

He was pretty sure his role here was to stand behind his wife and look intimidating. He couldn't help but think Hugh would have been a better choice for the role, but maybe Viv had been worried he would get in the way. If there was one thing Oliver knew he was absolutely unmatched in, it was silence.

"Find me the information I want, and I'll give you Takashi."

Tommy's eyes widened. His fist clenched on the table as he leaned forward. "If you can deliver on that, Jun, I'll get you whatever information you want."

She leaned to match him. The toes of her shoes were pressed into the floor, pulling the chair forward onto its front legs. "Let me know when you find something, and I'll get you the information on Takashi."

Tommy laughed. "Do I look like a fool? I'll take the information first. I'm not going to have you pulling a Kyoto on me."

Viv flipped a strand of hair over her shoulder. "Fair enough. I'll give you half up front, half after you get me whatever you can find on Turner."

He grinned with his teeth, like a shark smelling blood. "Deal."

Viv pulled a manila envelope from her purse, slid it across the table, and got up without waiting for him to check it. Her skirt swirled around her as she turned. She seemed to be floating more than walking out of the room.

She passed the bar, barely making eye contact with the Adiches before gliding out the door. She paused outside on the sidewalk, crossing her arms to keep herself warm and staring up at the first rays of the sun.

"Well?" Taylor sounded out of breath. She rubbed her own arms, but didn't take her eyes off Viv.

Viv tore her eyes off the sunlight with reluctance. "He'll get the information." She said. "I made him an offer he can't refuse, as the TV shows say."

"Okay, but I am not smuggling drugs." Hugh held out a hand. "Let me just make that clear right now."

Taylor batted his arm, huffing a laugh.

Viv smirked at him. "That won't be necessary."

"Who's Takashi?" Oliver asked.

Viv barely twitched. From looking at her face, he could have asked about lunch or the weather. "Nobody important."

"But important to him."

She nodded once. "Yes."

"What are you talking about?" Hugh's gaze darted between the two of them. "Are we killing someone?"

"Why?" Viv asked. "You scared?"

He scoffed. "I'm a six foot tall black man who took his adopted white child to the park; nothing scares me anymore."

"Regardless," she said. "We don't have to kill anyone."

"But that man – Tommy – he's going to kill Takashi." Oliver usually didn't confront his wife in public, but he'd barely made it from the upper room with his mouth shut. The question sat on his heart like a cinder. He had to get it off.

Viv looked at him, eyes taking in his whole self. "Trust me," she said, "the people I ran with back in the day? They all have it coming."

Chapter 47

War Between Siblings

Lying on the bed in his cell, Elliot clenched and unclenched his fist. Maggie was counting on him. Even if he couldn't feel what she was feeling through their bond, the hope in her eyes every time she saw him would have clued him in. She was expecting him to pull some heroic plan out of his butt, which was understandable considering he formed a club called the Hero's Guild.

He had to figure out a way out of here. It would have been a lot easier had he been conscious when he'd been brought in. As it stood, even if he managed to get out of his cell, he had no idea what the base looked like or even where it was located. He could walk out the door and into the middle of the ocean for all he knew!

It was pretty obvious what he needed; an inside source. That, or access to a computer. Although, he was no Kyle even with his powers. Of course, Turner didn't know that...could he bluff her somehow?

Elliot shook his head. *Yeah, I'll just say, "You better let us out or I'll hack your computers!" That'll work.*

Jonas smacked the other side of the glass. "Get up."

Elliot swiveled and swung his legs over the side of the bed. "Where are we going?"

Jonas keyed in a code in the pad and the glass wall retracted into the ceiling. It stopped just low enough that Elliot had to duck to get out. Jonas grabbed his arm and half-dragged him down the hall.

"Do you ever consider slowing down?" Elliot asked him. "I'm not going to fight you."

Jonas shot him an incredulous look.

Elliot grinned. "Not right now, anyway; I don't have my powers."

"Humph." But there was no venom in his voice. "We're going to see your sister."

"Really?" It caught Elliot off guard to hear those words out loud. Of course, he knew logically that Maggie was his sister – biological sister – after all, that was why they were both here. And he cared about her like a sister. But when people said the word 'sister' out loud...it wasn't Maggie he thought of.

They weren't going to any of the rooms Elliot had been in before. Instead, they were turning a corner and hiking down a second hallway he'd never been in. Through the whole walk, he didn't see a single window. The air in the building felt tense and strained, like it was under pressure. Elliot hoped it was just emotional pressure.

They arrived at a door that appeared to be the only feature on the second half of the hall. Elliot wondered whether the room behind the door was massive, or if half belonged to the door immediately before it. Even so, it was still a huge space.

It was even bigger on the inside. The room stretched out at least as deep as it was wide. The ceiling towered at least three times higher than the ceiling in the hallway. Around the room were a few barriers, standing up like remnants of drunk construction.

Maggie was already there, in the middle of the room picking at her nails and pretending not to know her guard was standing next to her. She looked up when Jonas dragged Elliot in and frowned.

"Are we playing laser tag?" Elliot asked.

Jonas found that question hilarious.

"What?"

"*Hello, Gemini Beta.*" Turner said from the ceiling.

Maggie looked up, already trying to find where the voice was coming from this time.

Denise and Jonas backed quickly out of the room.

"*The object of this exercise is simple – you two will be sparring.*"

"What?" The twins chorused.

"What do you mean, 'sparring?'" Elliot asked. "You want us to fight?"

"*Precisely.*"

"I'm not fighting Elliot!" Maggie shouted.

"Maggie, Maggie, wait," Elliot grabbed her wrist.

She turned towards him, confusion and insecurity marring her face. "You want to fight?"

"No, but think about it..." Elliot leaned his head down to her ear, lowering his voice as much as he could. "If we practice fighting against each other, we'll be even more prepared when we finally get out of here."

Maggie nodded slowly. "Alright." She grinned. "You're going down, *Beta!*"

Elliot scoffed, dancing back a few steps. "That just means you were born first. And you know what they say about first pancakes."

"Oh, it's on!"

The glint in Maggie's eye was the only warning he had before the wooden barrier nearest him seemed to develop a life of its own. As it lunged, Elliot back-flipped over it and landed in a crouch. He tossed two fistfuls of lightning at the wall, causing it to explode.

"How did you do that?" He asked. "I thought your powers were magnetic. Wood isn't magnetic."

"Wood isn't *very* magnetic." She corrected.

"Oh." Elliot fried an assault squad of wood shards which were advancing on him in hopes of avenging their home. "Well, you know what other properties metal has besides just being more magnetic?"

"Probably."

Elliot pressed his hands to the gleaming floor. "It conducts electricity."

Maggie yelped as the shock hit her, numbing her feet and legs and sending her crashing to the floor. She laughed. "You little—ah!" She rolled to the side to avoid acting as Elliot's landing pad. He turned to her, fingers sparking. Maggie grabbed the metal tile under him and *pulled* it towards her. Elliot flailed his arms, toppling backwards into the space left by the tile.

Maggie ripped the tile in half, letting each of the pieces hover over one of her hands. She spread her fingers, and the metal mimicked her, ripping into shapes resembling hands drawn by a six year old. Elliot was crouching in the space left by the tile, seemingly unfocused.

Maggie grinned. She wasn't about to be drawn in by that. She maneuvered her makeshift hands, grabbing him by the wrists.

He looked up, startled, then tightened his arm muscles and swung his legs out to hit her in the chest. As she fell, she lost her grip on the false hands. Elliot shook himself free of them and reached out, sending electricity tickling through her ankles.

Maggie squealed and kicked him back, then scrambled upright and lunged at him. She hit him in the chest, the unexpected weight knocking him down. She hooked her arm around his neck and rubbed her knuckles against the top of his skull.

"Ah—Maggie!" He sent the tingling sensation into her stomach and she doubled over, gasping with laughter.

"You *suck*!" She giggled.

He chuckled. "So do you!"

They laid there for a while, catching their breath. Their minds ached with the equivalent of a post-exercise burn.

"You know," Elliot gasped. "You got all the way through the floor."

"Did I?" Maggie didn't understand until she felt the presence of Elliot at the edge of her mind, sending her feelings of hope and freedom.

Chapter 48

Breakfast and a Show

Wendell pulled into the parking lot of the next gas station they came to and killed the engine.

Adanna looked around. "What are we doing here?"

"Getting breakfast." He said. He unbuckled his seatbelt and reached back to bat Kyle's leg. "Earth to Kyle."

The computer genius barely glanced up. "Early 2000's to Wendell."

"Come on, man, you need to eat." Wendell said. "Get some blood to the brain and all that."

"Eating actually pulls the blood to the stomach to help with digestion."

"That is truly fascinating." He deadpanned. "Now get out of the car before I come over there and drag you out."

Kyle looked up again, eyes narrowed to figure out whether the driver was being serious. Wendell held his gaze until he looked away, setting his laptop on the seat. He climbed out of the car, sighing dramatically. Wendell wasn't sure whether Kyle was being serious or not, so he suppressed his laughter.

"Alright, team." He said. "Here's the plan; we need food, water, and coffee. Get whatever you feel like eating for breakfast as long as we don't have to cook it. If you want to get a box of crackers and a pound of cheese, I won't judge you. Just this once, though, so take advantage of it. We'll split up and meet back at the car in ten minutes. Let's synchronize our watches."

"We don't have watches." Kyle said.

"We have our phones." Adanna took her phone out of her pocket. "We could wave them around and make beeping noises."

"That's stupid." Kyle told her.

"Beep-beep." Wendell said.

To the credit of the cashier, she didn't seem shocked that three people covered with dust, debris, and a few untended scrapes and bruises raided the aisles and refrigerators. The fact that she was at work at three AM probably had something to do with that. Wendell figured it was a little past normal-person shopping hours.

He grabbed a coffee and a muffin and beat it back to the car. By the time Adanna and Kyle joined him, he'd found what he wanted on Google Maps.

He pointed a finger at both of them. "No eating until we get there."

"Where?" Adanna asked.

He didn't answer, just started driving. It took about twenty minutes to get there, by which time the coffee was cooled to comfortable drinking temperatures.

"What is this? A dead end in the woods?" Kyle asked.

Wendell rolled his eyes. "Just grab your stuff and let's go."

He led them to a bench at the edge of the cliff in front of them, and it became clear why he'd chosen this spot.

The road they'd taken had arched up the mountain and circled back towards the town. The cliff the bench was on was suspended like a wall against one side of the town. Looking down at the buildings was like getting a birds-eye view. The neon lights lit it up like a dream against the darkness of the night.

"Oh, wow." Kyle breathed.

The bench was too small for the three of them, so they settled in a semi-circle in the grass. They balanced their drinks against their crossed legs and unwrapped their assortment of sandwiches, cookies, and muffins. As they ate, the only other sounds were the calls of early birds, the chirps of crickets, and the sounds of the wind in the bushes and trees.

"We did good tonight." Adanna broke the silence.

"Yeah, we did." Wendell grinned, raising his coffee. "Skoll!"

"Skoll." Adanna and Kyle replied in obligatory unison.

"You two did, maybe." Kyle said.

Adanna's eyes narrowed. "What are you talking about? You were the one climbing up the ladder with a bomb!"

"I was the reason the bomb was going off in the first place. It doesn't count."

"I think Adanna gets to decide what counts or not." Wendell said.

She nodded. "That's right. And I say it counts."

Kyle shook his head. "When are you guys going to understand that this isn't a game?"

"You think we think this is a *game*?" Adanna's eyes combusted. "My *brother* is *missing*."

"Then why are you still acting like you can just...*decide* whether people made mistakes or not?"

"No blood, no foul, man." Wendell said. "We don't make the rules."

Kyle rolled up his sleeve, revealing a gash covered in clumps of dried blood. "You were saying?"

Adanna gritted her teeth. "Why do you have to be like this?" She asked. "Seriously, what is your problem? Would it make you feel better if we just let ourselves fall apart?"

"Maybe you should." Kyle said. "After all, your brother *is* missing."

"And what good would that do him?!" Adanna shouted. "You think I don't want to just curl up in the fetal position and cry?! I don't have that luxury! I have to find Elliot and bring him home, and I have to do it without any powers or, apparently, supportive team members! So forgive me if I'm trying to use my brain for something other than making some masochistic altar to my own failure!"

Even the wind seemed afraid to break the silence after her declaration.

"I'm supportive." Wendell eventually said quietly.

Adanna deflated. "I know. I'm sorry, I just..."

"Don't worry about it." Wendell said. "I just wanted to make sure you know you're not alone."

Kyle closed his eyes. In one quick motion, he got up and made his way back to the car.

"Kyle—" Adanna started to get up, but Wendell grabbed her wrist. She settled back, waiting.

"Give him a minute." He said.

She dropped her head into her hands. "Elliot wouldn't have yelled at him like that."

Wendell chuckled. "If you were missing? He would have done more than yell."

She tried to laugh. "I miss him." Her voice was tiny. It didn't suit her at all.

"I know." What else could he say?

Chapter 49

No Fate but What We Make

G rady looked annoyed when he came out of the bathroom, drying his hair with a towel.

Sean looked up from his phone and grinned. "The cuffs are tougher than you thought, huh?"

The man glared in response, causing Sean's grin to widen.

"These are really good cookies." Nehemiah said to Hailey, leaning up against the table.

She smiled. "Thank Sean. I almost didn't go through with making them."

"Thanks, Sean!" He called over his shoulder.

"No problem."

"So, what's the plan?" Hailey asked, handing Grady a plate with his breakfast – a piece of toast with peanut butter and two cookies – on it.

"The plan is I help you find your friend, then you let me go." He said. "Thank you."

"That hasn't been decided yet." Sean said.

"Well, what else are you going to do?" He asked. "Keep me a prisoner indefinitely? Survive on pizza and cookies because you refuse to trust my honor?"

"What honor?" Sean almost choked on his cookie.

"We're figuring it out as we go." Nehemiah told the prisoner. "Don't worry about it. Just enjoy your cookie."

"And the fact that we're not like your little friend." Hailey added.

"Yes, my 'friend.'" He took a thoughtful bite. "What did happen to Siren?"

"Make an educated guess." Sean rolled his eyes. "She's dead."

Grady raised an eyebrow. "You killed her?"

"*She* was trying to kill *us*!" He shot back. "We defended ourselves."

"Interesting."

Hailey's fingers were tangled in her hair. "Do you think people are born with a timeline the length of their actual lives or their biologically accurate lives? Like, do you think everyone is born with one hundred year timelines, or are the people who die young born with shorter ones?"

"What makes you so sure anyone's born with a 'timeline' at all?" Grady asked.

Hailey shrugged. "People say things like, 'they were gone too soon,' or 'it was their time,' but how can they know that?"

"I think you're talking about whether there's a concrete or fluid future," Sean said. "Like in *Terminator*, where Skynet was supposed to happen at a specific time, but they could push it back and change the future. It wasn't set in stone."

"Kind of." She said. "But they were time traveling to the past, so it was more like they were trying to change the present. Just because the present was set in the past at the time doesn't mean it wasn't the past."

"Are you guys even speaking English right now?" Nehemiah asked. "What do you mean, 'the past is the present and the future is the past' or whatever?"

"It's like…" Hailey spread her hands. She bit her lip, trying to figure out how to rephrase her question. "You know how God knows everything that's going to happen, but he was trying to create a perfect world and humans messed it up? Does that mean that humans can mess up their futures, or is what's going to happen going to happen no matter what we do?"

"Why didn't you just say that?" He crossed his arms and looked up like he was trying to read from a heavenly teleprompter. "I don't know. I think everyone has a destiny, but they don't have to follow it, you know? Like, God can intend for people to do good and they can decide to do evil instead, but he knows they're going to chose to do evil. Like when you give someone the opportunity to fix your relationship even though you know they're going to throw it back in your face."

"That makes sense." Hailey said. "Kind of."

Sean put his phone down. "Is there coffee?"

Hailey flipped her hair over her shoulder. "Do you mean, 'did someone make more coffee after I finished the pot?'"

"Yeah, that."

She smirked. "No, not yet. Why don't you get on that?"

He sighed, dragging himself to his feet. "Fair enough."

"What are we going to do today, though?" Hailey asked again. "We can't just sit around having existential conversations all day."

"Why not?" Sean asked.

"Because it's *boring*!" She and Nehemiah chorused.

Grady smirked.

"Okay, well, what do you want to do?" Sean asked, shoveling coffee grounds into a filter.

"If I knew, I wouldn't be asking you."

"Why don't we look for your friends?" Grady suggested.

"No."

"Why not?" He wondered. "Aren't you worried about them? Or is it okay that Delilah experiments on them for a while?" He ducked, narrowly missing being beaned in the head by a plate.

The plate crashed into the wall, shattering. Hailey glowered, lowering her hand. "Sorry."

"I'll get the broom." Nehemiah said.

"No; let me. I broke it."

"Grady has a point, though." Sean mused.

Hailey barely avoided throwing the broom at him like a javelin. "We *already agreed* not to take him up on it until—"

"I know! That's not what I'm saying." He leaned back against the counter as the coffee began percolating. "I'm just saying that the three of us could do a little poking around on the internet or something as long as we don't have anything better to do."

Hailey took a pit stop behind Nehemiah and wiggled her pointer finger between them. "Do either of us look like Kyle to you?"

Sean rolled his eyes. "Maybe there's something Kyle would miss. Something more obvious than what he's looking for."

"Like what?" Nehemiah asked.

"I don't know." Sean shrugged. "Let me have some more coffee and I'll get back to you."

Nehemiah hummed, resting his chin on one hand and tapping the table with the other. How were they supposed to find someone who didn't want to be found? He didn't know anything about the science-magic Kyle could work with the computers. All he knew was how to go by word of mouth. "I'd suggest asking her neighbors, but the others are already down there."

Sean raised an eyebrow. "That's not a bad idea, though."

Nehemiah frowned. "You want to call Adanna and tell her to ask the neighbors?"

"No; I want to call the neighbors." Sean pulled his phone out. "What's her address again? I mean, what city does she live in? We can probably Google a phone book."

"There's a book with all the phone numbers in it?" Nehemiah went to look over his friend's shoulder.

"No; only the landlines. But still…"

Huh. Nehemiah thought. *Score one for the old-fashioned method.*

Chapter 50

Baby, you're like lightning in a bottle

aggie felt like she was underwater, but she didn't need air. It felt like the entire Pacific Ocean was pressing down on her chest. There was no up or down, only nothingness as far as she could feel. There was no light, no sound. She tried to speak, but the vacuum choked the noise before it could escape her throat. Even Turner's voice would be preferable to this. There wasn't even any gravity.

She was floating in a next-level sensory deprivation chamber. She couldn't feel anything other than her own body, so she wrapped her arms around herself just to be sure she still existed.

If there was a purgatory, this was probably what it was like. She felt like she was in a pocket outside of time and space. Outside of everything.

Her head snapped up as something flew towards her, faster than a bullet. She snatched it up hungrily, swinging it down and around until she was perched on top of it. It appeared to be some sort of sheet metal. She held it under her feet like a skateboard, pretending to be grounded.

There must have been holes in the sides of the chamber; cannons or something created to shoot things at her. This one was a javelin-dart from before. She seized and held it like a staff.

More projectiles came towards her. She gathered them together, forming them into a shell around her. She kept the walls close together and tight, making sure she could always reach out and touch at least two of them. Claustrophobia no longer existed in her world.

On some level, she knew the projectiles were becoming less ferromagnetic and more paramagnetic (the strength of the magnetic fields was decreasing). It didn't matter. As long as she could feel them, could feel *something*, she didn't care how hard she had to work to keep control of it.

Inside her shell, completely isolated from the rest of the chamber, she took a deep breath. "Hello?" She had never been so happy to hear the sound of her own voice. Now all she needed was a little light, and she would have regained every sense they took from her.

She wondered if magnetic fields could create sparks. She hadn't thought about it before, but now that she considered it, she was sure she'd seen it done somewhere. On TV or in science class, maybe.

She pulled a piece of wood in from the outer layer of her shell and let it sit in her lap. The weight was comforting. She created two opposing magnetic forces around her hands and moved them together and apart over the wood.

After a while, she let the fields around her hands drop and frowned. She'd been sure that would work.

Maybe she needed a way to heat the wood up. She nodded to herself. Yes, if she could stick something inside the wood and heat it up, it could act like a wick. Sort of.

It was worth a shot, anyway.

She located an exceedingly ferromagnetic piece of metal and bent it into a wire-like shape. She raised it above the wooden block and drove it down hard until it stuck inside.

"Alright," she was really enjoying the sound of her own voice. "If there is a great enough tension between the fields, it should heat up the wire."

She placed her hands on either side of it and recreated the opposing fields. She moved the fields around it, randomly increasing and decreasing their strength. Soon, the metal started to glow from the heat.

Maggie grinned as her hands appeared in front of her. She kept it up eagerly until energy sparked from the wire and ignited the block.

"Yes!" She shouted, pumping her fists in the air. She held her hands to the flames contentedly. She was so satisfied with her work that she didn't even think about the nature of the sparks until she was back in her cell – her sweet, sweet, sensory filled cell.

It woke her out of a dead sleep. The energy that had sparked from the wire had felt familiar. In fact, she'd felt something like when she'd been sparring with Elliot.

She'd created electricity.

~

Elliot doodled in the margins, doing his best to drown the professor out. This experiment was stupid. Did Turner really think he hadn't researched his abilities? He could probably school this so-called expert.

"Are you listening, Mr. Beta?"

"Mm-hm."

Maggie getting through the floor had been awesome. Now all he had to do was figure out how to use that to their advantage. There had been actual dirt packed beneath it, which meant the floors weren't reinforced. That was nice. But what were they supposed to do when they got through the floor? Get out shovels and dig?

The professor was asking a question. Elliot tried to remember what it was. "Uh...Ampere's Law."

The professor sighed heavily and started that bit over.

He was pretty sure the blast doors were metal. And even if they weren't, Maggie had her whole "everything is magnetic" theory to back them up. They could make a run for it and she could blast them out. He'd watch her back; it would be great.

He kept coming back to the issue of not knowing what the base looked like. Of course, every wall had a door if you hit it hard enough. And it would keep Turner from being able to predict where they were headed. But he'd still prefer to know where they were going. After all, if they failed to escape they'd never get another chance.

The professor, done with his review, repeated the question.

"Ampules of Lorenzeni."

"Correct."

Maggie had been trying to find out where the speakers were in the training rooms. If she could, maybe the cameras would be near them and they could take both out at once. He smirked. As if.

But there was still the problem of the chips. If they tried something, Turner could just push a button and knock them out before they could get out of the room, let alone out of the building. That had to be their first move; getting rid of the chips.

Elliot wondered how susceptible the chips were to electricity. When he'd been younger, he'd shorted out every computer he'd come into contact with. His parents had home schooled him until he was able to walk out of a computer lab with a majority of the machines still functioning.

Next time they unlocked his powers, he would try to fry his chip. He could fake it until he figured out how to get Maggie's out.

But how *would* he get Maggie's chip out? He had no idea how much electricity her body could take. He was no brain surgeon either. If worst came to worst, he might have to carry her unconscious body out and find someone to remove the chip later.

Leaving her behind wasn't an option. If that was naïve, so be it. It was one belief about heroics he wasn't willing to let go of.

Chapter 51

Love Doesn't Discriminate (Between the Sinners and the Saints)

Hailey felt like a telemarketer. She dialed the next number and played with a pen until they picked up. "Hello, I'm Delilah Turner's niece. I heard something happened to her house, but she hasn't called me. Do you know any way I could get a hold of her?"

"No, I'm sorry, I don't."

"Okay...do you remember seeing anyone at her house before? A friend I could ask?"

"To be honest, I'm not around a lot. I work the night shift at the hospital, so I'm sleeping all day."

"Alright. Thank you, Mrs. Peterson."

"*You're welcome, dear.*"

She hung up and sighed, scratching the number out. She leaned the chair on its back legs and threw her pen across the room at Grady. It hit him in the face and she smiled as he glared at her.

"What?!" He snapped.

"Nothing." She said. "I'm bored."

"Call more people, then."

She shook her head at his cluelessness. "That's what I'm bored of."

He shrugged. "Not my problem."

She stuck her tongue out at him and started dialing the next number. She paused before she hit the Call button. "Can I have my pen back?" She caught it before Grady could get his revenge and stuck her tongue out at him.

As the phone rang, she rocked her chair back and forth. They'd been at this for at least an hour already, and even talking to new people was getting old. Every phone call of nothing useful brought her closer and closer to saying something weird and unhelpful.

"*Hello?*" The man sounded young. Then again, it was hard to gauge age over the phone.

"Hi, I'm looking for my evil aunt and I'm wondering if you can help me." *And there it is.*

"*Excuse me?*"

"Sorry, it's just – she's a pain, but she's family, you know?" Hailey scrambled.

"*Who is this?*"

"My aunt Delilah." She purposefully misinterpreted the question. "I haven't heard from her in a few days and...well, despite the bad blood she always calls for my birthday..."

"*Oh.*" He said. "*I hate to be the one to tell you this, but...your aunt's house was damaged in some sort of terrorist attack. No one's seen her since.*"

"Oh no!" Hailey's hand flew to her mouth. She channeled all her boredom into the acting. Tears actually welled up in her eyes. She was brilliant. "Is she okay?"

"*Honestly, I can't say.*" The man told her. "*I'm sorry.*"

Hailey sniffed. "Do you...have any idea where I could find her?"

"*No, I'm sorry...have you asked her boyfriend?*"

Hailey stiffened. "Her boyfriend?"

"*Yeah, he comes over to the house every couple weeks...I just assumed...*"

"Of course, no, you're probably right." She said. "Like I said, there's bad blood and...we don't talk a lot. Do you know his name? Maybe he's in the phone book."

"*No, I don't. I'm sorry—*"

"Don't apologize. You've been a lot of help. Thank you so much." Hailey hung up and immediately dialed Adanna.

"*Hailey? Is everything alright?*" Adanna sounded like she hadn't slept at all the night before.

"Yeah, everything's fine! Actually, we've been calling around the neighborhood asking about Delilah—"

"*That's a great idea.*"

"It was Nehemiah's."

"*Really?*"

"Yeah. Anyway, one of the neighbors said he saw a man come to her house every few weeks. He said he thought it was her boyfriend." Hailey bit her lip. "Does that help at all?"

"*I don't know. It might.*" Adanna sighed. "*Kyle has this whole complicated system going on. I don't understand any of it.*"

"I feel you. Let me know if it helps."

"I will. Thanks, Hails."

"You're welcome, Ada."

Adanna hung up the phone and let her arm fall over her face. She breathed deeply for a second, then shoved herself up and poked Kyle. He was sleeping in the backseat, head tossed over the headrest and his laptop still on his lap. Adanna, on the other hand, had leaned the passenger seat all the way back and slept there. Wendell was still sleeping across from her in the driver's seat.

"Meh. What." Kyle lifted his head and rubbed his eyes. "What time is it?"

"Not late enough." Adanna told him. "Hailey just called. She said Delilah might have had a boyfriend."

Kyle blinked. "Really? Like, a human one?"

"I assume so." Adanna yawned. "Anyway, is that relevant?"

"It could be..." Kyle hit the spacebar to wake his laptop up. "I've been running algorithms sorting the credit card purchases of her aliases into a couple different categories; essentials (food, toilet paper, shampoo that kind of thing), frivolous (books, perfumes, etc.), and business (which covers everything from batteries to sheet metal). I could add another category for purchases which don't seem to match the others in their categories...those might be gifts." His fingers tapped the keys. "I'll add a sub-category for items purchased in February, around Valentine's Day."

"Great idea." She patted his leg and smile. "Keep up the good work."

He lifted the corner of his lips in response.

~

Nehemiah was in his kitchen making pancakes for lunch. They'd called everyone within three blocks of Turner's house, so he wanted something quick and easy. Hailey walked into the kitchen and started juggling the measuring cups he'd put by the sink. She didn't seem to mind the extra flour and sugar that was falling all over her.

"Did you leave Sean and Grady alone in a room together?"

She shrugged. "I like to live dangerously."

"Easy to say when it's not *your* apartment." He said.

She smirked and set the cups down. "What are you making?"

"Pancakes."

"There's a box of mix over there," she pointed at the cupboard. "You don't have to make it by hand."

He raised an eyebrow. "How do you know that?"

She held up the last cookie.

"Oh, yeah."

Hailey tossed the cookie up and tried to catch it in her mouth. It bounced off her chin. She scrambled to catch it before it hit the ground, but she missed. "Awww," she stuck out her bottom lip.

"You can still eat it, can't you?" Nehemiah asked.

"Huh?"

"I mean, it looks fine." He shrugged. "But Wendell doesn't like eating stuff that falls on the floor either."

Hailey picked the cookie up and stuck it in her mouth. "The Amish believe in the five second rule?"

He flipped a pancake. "I have no idea what that is."

"It's this rule how, when you drop something on the floor, it's still clean for five seconds."

"Oh." He shrugged again. "I don't know about that. I think my parents just didn't like to waste food. My mom would always say, 'God will always provide, but we have to make the most of what he supplies.'"

Hailey laughed.

"What?"

"Sorry, it's just...you don't really believe that, do you? That God is up there balancing your checkbook for you?"

"What do you mean?" Nehemiah frowned. "You don't think God is going to take care of us?"

"That's not what I..." She sighed. "Look; there are plenty of God-ly people who are starving or being killed for their faith in other countries. It's not that I don't think God cares, I just...I don't think He's going to fix every problem in our lives. And I don't think He's obligated to. I mean – He's God, right? He already gave his life to save us and now he has to make sure our lives are perfect?"

"You make it sound like we're a burden on Him." Nehemiah said.

"Aren't we?" Hailey held up her hands. "Look at us. Every single person on the planet is flawed and selfish in one way or another. When I went to church as a kid, they told me it hurts God every time we do something wrong. He must be in constant pain then! It's just...it's wrong to try and make him into some cosmic genie-servant who's going to give up whatever we're short on."

"Philippians 4:19 says, 'He will supply for your every need.'" Ne-hemiah said.

She shook her head. "Maybe it means spiritual needs or something. I don't know. All I know is that I'm not going to be the one telling God my belief in him hinges on whether he makes this life a good one. It's not fair."

"That's nice, but..." Nehemiah sighed. "Hailey, it sounds like you're saying you have the power to require things of God or not. That's just not true. The only one who can make demands of God is himself."

"I'm saying that I'm *not* requiring things of..." she peered around him. "...your pancake's burning."

Nehemiah turned to flip the pancake. When he turned back around, Hailey was gone.

Chapter 52

Back on the Horse

Sitting in her dorm, Lydia was not worried. She was completely focused on helping Carly recover. She was not itching to pick up the phone and call Adanna for all the details on what was happening. She was done.

It had been a mistake to get involved with the Guild in the first place. With her class load she didn't have time for Netflix, let alone some group of bounty hunters with benefits. As soon as Elliot was back, she would tell him she was done.

Well...maybe she'd give him a few weeks to recover. After all, being kidnapped by psycho ex-government scientists had to be hard on the ol' psyche. She wouldn't spring it on him right away. He'd probably need some extra help those first couple weeks, anyway. It wouldn't be right of her to just ditch him. Them. The team.

"Hey, Dia?"

Lydia moved to get out of her chair. "What is it? You want water? Food? Markers?"

Carly rolled her eyes. "No, I just wanted to let you know you're reading that book upside down."

"Oh." Lydia looked down. She flipped the book in the right direction.

"What's on your mind, kid?"

"You are not that much older than me."

"You're dodging."

"Am I?" Lydia sighed. "Yeah, I know. I just...I think I'm done. With the Guild."

"Oh." Carly blinked, sitting up straighter. "Really?"

"Yeah." Lydia leaned forward. "I mean; I'm in college. I don't even know what I want to do with my life yet, and I'm just going to get myself killed?"

"I mean, when you put it that way..." Carly rubbed her side. "But I thought you were having fun before...this whole situation."

"I was. I mean." She shook her head. "It was a good time. But that was before things got really dangerous, you know? Back then it was just like...laser tag or something. It wasn't *real*." She dropped her head into her hands. "Please tell me you're not mad at me."

"I'm not mad at you." Carly said. "You have to do what you think is right." She half-smiled. "And I'll always be your friend, you know?"

Lydia forced herself to smile back. "Thanks, Carls. That means a lot."

Carly's phone rang. She reached over to grab it, pushing a strand of hair behind her ear as she checked who was calling. Her eyes widened. "Hey, Adanna. How's life?"

Lydia ducked behind her book. She couldn't hear exactly what Adanna was saying. At this distance, all she could make out was the rise and fall of her voice, slightly robotic through the phone's speakers.

"Really?" Carly was saying. "Okay...Yeah. Yeah. Let me just write this down..." She put Adanna on speaker, then exited the call screen on her phone and pulled up her notes. "...Okay, go ahead."

"*Warren Xavier.*" Adanna said. "*He's a professor of sociology.*"

"Got it. I'll pay him a little visit." Carly smirked.

"*Thanks. Call me as soon as you're done.*"

"10-4, good buddy." Carly hung up. She took the hairband from around her wrist and started putting her hair up. "I have to step out for a bit." She told Lydia.

"Okay. Let me just get my jacket."

Carly smirked. "You don't have to come."

Lydia glared. "Friends don't let friends confront potential villains while recovering from having a house dropped on them."

Carly's mouth widened to a grin. "If only the Wicked Witch of the East had had you."

"Did you say Professor Warren Xavier?" Lydia asked.

"Yeah. Why? Do you know him?"

"I'm taking his Intro to Sociology class." She turned and started digging through a mountain of papers as high as her head. "I think I have the syllabus somewhere...it should have the office number on it."

"Oh, sweet." Carly stood up, stretching cautiously before moving to look over Lydia's shoulder. "Want some help?"

"I got it." She bit her lip, then *s-l-o-w-l-y* pulled a paper out from the stack. Both girls watched with bated breath as it swayed. When it didn't fall, they heaved sighs of relief. Lydia handed the paper over to Carly.

She looked at it. "Where's Capulet Hall?"

"It's a few buildings over." Lydia said. "Do you want me to get the car?"

Carly shook her head. "Nah; I can make it."

Lydia looked at her incredulously. "O-kay."

The campus was littered with outside paths between buildings, each sporting benches made from twisted metal. They weren't exceedingly comfortable and sitting down for a long time meant you might end up with an unflattering set of stripes, but they worked well enough for one with scar tissue in the middle of her abdomen.

They took the elevator up to the third floor, where Xavier's office was. Carly leaned against the rail, letting her head fall back on the wall.

"Are you sure you're okay to be doing this?" Lydia asked.

Carly opened her eyes and smirked without lifting her head. "I'm alright. I just hope he's not there so we can do this quickly."

"Me too." Lydia fidgeted. She really didn't want the professor to know she was involved. She'd have to switch majors. Or colleges. Or universities.

The elevator opened and they strolled out. Carly nudged Lydia in the back. "Go check. If he's in there, make up some question about class. If he's not, come back and get me."

"Stop whispering!" Lydia whispered. "It looks suspicious!"

"Just go!"

Lydia exaggerated her casualness as she walked up to Xavier's door. She linked her fingers behind her back and leaned over to peer inside. She didn't see anyone, so she stretched one leg in and followed up with the other.

The full office was just as empty as the view from the door had suggested. She arched her back until her head popped into the hallway. She grinned at Carly, who looked both amused and exasperated for some reason.

The office was a pretty typical college professor's office; there were bookshelves lining every bit of wall not taken up by doors or windows, books shoved into place, books stacked on top of the books already on the shelves, books stacked on the floor, a coffee thermos and ten billion papers ready to be graded sitting on the desk.

"Where do we even start?" Lydia asked.

Carly shut the door and stacked three books in front of it. If anyone came in, the sound of the books falling would give them a few seconds to hide. She made her way over to the desk and sat down in the spinning chair, faded with wear and pressed into the shape of Xavier's body. There were even elbow marks on the armrests.

Her mouth opened in an 'o' as she leaned forward and snatched up something that was obscured by papers from Lydia's perspective. Carly flipped it around and aimed it towards her.

"Oh, wow." Was all Lydia could think of to say. "That's...subtle."

It was a framed picture of Delilah Turner.

"I guess the neighbors were right." Carly said. She laid it down on the desk and slipped the back of the frame off. "Oh no way." There was a piece of paper hidden behind the photo. It had been folded and unfolded so many times there were tiny holes in the creases.

Carly opened it up and studied it. "There are three addresses here." She said. "One of them is for Turner's house in Arches."

"Wow!" Lydia spun around, eyeing the books. If there was one secret message, who was to say there weren't two? She picked a bookshelf at random and started running her fingernail across the tops. The pages fluttered under her nail until they didn't.

She pulled the book off the shelf. It was one of those boxes shaped like a book. Usually there weren't locks on them, but this one had been modified for it. Lydia held it up. "Do we break into it here or do we take it?"

Carly beckoned. "We break into it here. We can't afford to take it; it would be like a neon sign announcing we were here."

"I don't know about that." Lydia handed the box over. "This guy seems like the weak link."

Carly laughed.

Breaking into locks was another one of her specialties. It made for a weird skillset; distance shooting and forced entry. Not something you would put on a resume...unless, say, you were applying for the Hero's Guild. She figured Lydia was right about this guy being the weak link; the lock was incredibly easy to crack.

Inside the box was an old clamshell flip phone. Carly raised an eyebrow, then pocketed it and walked over to Lydia. "Find anything else?"

Lydia took the box and slid it back into place. "Not on this shelf."

Carly glanced at her watch. "Let's keep going for a few more minutes. We want to find as much as we can, but we don't want to overstay our welcome."

Lydia nodded and moved onto the next shelf. They worked for twenty more minutes before calling it quits. They didn't find anything else. Carly joked that their contraband radar was too strong; they found everything right away.

Back in the car, Carly fed the closest address to Google Maps while Lydia slowly left the parking lot.

"Turn Left onto First Street." The robot voice said as Lydia turned right.

"Seriously?!" She said.

"Don't worry about it; we'll head around the block or something." Carly was studying the flip phone. "This is a fantastic idea for a burner. Does this dinosaur even have GPS?"

"I'm not a phone expert. How long will it take us to get to the address?"

"Only twenty minutes." Carly wriggled her eyebrows. "Ooh la la."

"Ew." Lydia scrunched up her nose. "That's my professor. And an evil scientist."

"Hey, I just call 'em like I see 'em."

"Well, call softer. I'd like to be able to sleep tonight."

Chapter 53

Fun Date Ideas

There are some terms you know that you only come to fully understand later. Hugh had known that dogs didn't run, they "loped." He'd figured it was just a fancy way of speaking until he'd gotten his first dog at twelve years old. He'd seen her move and realized it wasn't a synonym; it was a specifier.

It was the same with the term "seedy motel." He knew what that was; he'd read enough crime novels. But he'd never really understood what it meant before the night they booked some cheap rooms to give Viv's friend some time to find information on Turner.

Viv insisted on paying with cash; something about not leaving a money trail. She really should have mentioned that *before* they'd flown halfway across the country.

"I thought you knew." She had said.

"I catch criminals, honey." Taylor had smirked. "I don't mimic them."

So Viv booked them a room in a motel that gave the term "seedy" some meaning. There were two twin beds with mattresses which had been worn down to only a few inches high. The carpet had suspicious-looking stains and some stray masking tape on it. Three of the four outlets didn't work. They needed to hold the handle on the toilet down in order to flush it, the only lights were dim bare bulbs, and someone had done a patch job on the window with saran wrap.

Viv pulled up the corners of the bottom sheets, inspecting them closely.

"What are you doing?" Hugh asked.

"Checking for bed bugs." She replied.

Hugh turned to Taylor. "Honey, I want to sleep in the bathtub."

"There isn't one." Taylor pointed to the bathroom. It was only separated from the rest of the room by a shower curtain. The shower itself had none.

"It'll have to do." Hugh sighed.

She laughed.

"All clear." Viv told them.

"Excellent." Taylor took Hugh's hand in her own. "Want to go for a walk, honey?"

Oliver frowned. "In this neighborhood?"

"We'll be back before sundown. Besides..." Taylor rapped her knuckles on her prosthetic. "...I have a built-in weapon." She wiggled her fingers at them and dragged her husband out the door.

"Where are we going?" Hugh asked once they were out on the street.

Taylor shrugged. "Away from that sad, depressing hotel room."

"Sounds good to me." Hugh said. He squeezed her hand. "Going for a romantic stroll in a bad neighborhood. Do you know what that reminds me of?"

His wife grinned. "You crashing my stakeouts?"

He bumped her with his shoulder. "You loved it."

"Life is definitely more amusing since you came along." She sighed, dropping her smile. "What are we going to do about this, babe?"

"Trust an ex-mob member, apparently."

"No, I mean..." She shook her head. "Our kids are going to be so hurt after this. I feel terrible saying this, but I hope Elliot only comes home with emotional scars."

Hugh let out a deep, sad breath. "I hope so, too."

She gripped his hand until it hurt. "Every time I think about what might be happening to him, I feel like it's literally hitting me. Like it's some sort of wall knocking into me, stopping my heart for a second."

"I know. I feel the same way."

"I wish I could switch places with him."

"Me too."

They walked in silence until a group of shadows filed out of an alley, blocking the sidewalk ahead of them. They moved to walk on the street, but two of the shadows arched their human wall out to block their path again. The Adiches let go of each other's hands.

The ring leader looked just as seedy as their hotel room. Hugh wondered whether he was wearing clothes or ripped fabric dipped in rhino urine. He stepped forward and Hugh fought the urge to wrinkle his nose.

The guy had long blond hair shaped into dreadlocks and a couple piercings through his mouth and nose that looked infected. "Gi' me a' yo' mo'ey." It wasn't clear whether it was an accent or the infection.

"If we had money," Hugh asked, "do you think we'd be in this part of town?"

The ring leader spread his lips over what remained of his teeth. "Ta' i' f'om 'em."

Two men closed in on Taylor while a man and a woman did the same to Hugh. The two of them pivoted so they were back to back.

"I hope you haven't lost your touch, babe." Taylor said.

"Don't you worry about me, sweetheart." Hugh laughed.

One of the men, a dirty blond with a mohawk, threw a punch at Taylor's face. She knocked his fist aside and jabbed his elbow. There was a pop and he screamed, falling back. The second man, who seemed to be ninety percent limbs, went for an upper cut. Taylor twisted around his hand, getting up close to him and slamming his nose into her knee.

At the same time, Hugh used his reach to snap a punch into the fourth man's sternum before he could get close enough to strike. That guy was on the shorter side, his head a bird's nest of black curls. The woman ducked under Hugh's jab and went for his abdomen. He grabbed her wrist and spun her around, kicking her in the back.

Mohawk, glaring murderously, pulled a knife out of his pocket and lunged. Taylor brought her leg up and the blade plunged into her prosthetic. She pulled it back and threw two successive punches at the guy's face. He ducked, but stumbled when he tried to recover, giving Taylor enough time to pull the knife out of her leg and twirl it in her fingers. The string-bean, holding his nose, blinked at her in disbelief.

Birdie and the woman (which Hugh thought would be a great band name), lunged at the same time. They ducked under his arms only to catch his elbows with the tops of their skulls. Hugh then grabbed them and smacked their heads together like in a cartoons. They fell to the ground, groaning.

The four assailants limped away. The ring leader was staring.

"I think Thug.exe has stopped working." Hugh said.

"Close your mouth, kid, you'll catch flies." Taylor held out her hand.

Her husband took it and they turned around to walk back the way they came. "That was almost like therapy." He said.

Taylor leaned her head against his chest. "Yeah." She sighed. "I think I really needed that."

When they got back to the hotel, Viv and Oliver were standing outside the door with the bags. The Adiches strolled over to them.

"What's going on?" Taylor asked.

"Masakichi just texted me." Viv said. "He has something for us. If it's useful, we can probably just catch the next flight home."

"Oh, thank God." Hugh said. "I don't think I could have taken much more of that room."

Chapter 54

Bad Blood

E lliot figured it out just as he stepped into the room and saw Maggie's ecstatic face. *Magnets erase computer data.* Maybe they could disable computers too. At least, he hoped so. Because the chips were controlled from the outside.

They'd have to risk it, considering how quickly Turner's experiments were turning from mildly inconvenient to terrifying. (Elliot didn't want to remember the sensory deprivation chamber. He wouldn't remember it. He didn't remember it.)

He forced a smile at the woman on the other side of a protective glass barrier. "What do you have for us today, Doc?"

Turner pressed a button and panels in the wall slid open to reveal what appeared to be the barrels of two hundred machine guns.

"Uh, Doc?" Elliot edged backwards at an angle that brought him closer to Maggie, who was on an intercept course. "If you're wondering whether bullets will kill us, let me save you time and say *yes*."

"These weapons will be firing rubber bullets." Turner said. *"Your job is to disable all of them while attempting not to get hit."*

"And if we don't play along?" Maggie challenged.

"Then you'll be pelted by rubber bullets until you're unconscious."

"O-kay." Elliot said. "Destroying the guns sounds great." He shook himself out and shot Maggie a meaningful look. "Here goes nothing."

She quirked an eyebrow up at him.

Turner pressed two buttons – one to unlock their powers, and one to activate the guns.

Elliot curled up into a ball, trying not to notice the pain from the rubber bullets as he concentrated as much energy as he possibly could into his brain stem. He felt the bullets stop and knew Maggie was shielding him. He reached out to her, sending her the sensation of all his power exploding in one spot and the desperation to escape.

Soon, he felt the bullets slam into his body again. He felt something give in his neck and gasped for breath, then stood up and shot lightning from his whole body, blasting as many of the stupid guns as he could.

He started throwing lightning bolts at the ones he'd missed, checking over his shoulder at Maggie. She was curled up like he had been. The space around her neck was twisting like a mirage. By the time she looked up, Elliot had disabled almost all the guns.

"Get the door!" He said.

Maggie nodded, scrambling across the floor and throwing her fist towards it. The metal shot away, flying off its hinges and embedding itself in the far wall. The twins raced out after it.

Some of the braver scientists were coming out of the observation room. Electricity arched out of Elliot's fingers and disappeared into all but one of them. They dropped to the ground and Maggie lunged forward, hitting the one left standing and knocking her down.

"*Where is the exit?!*" She demanded, the walls bending towards them.

The scientist, terrified, pointed down the hall. "Two lefts. Then a right."

Maggie punched her unconscious and jumped over her body. "Come on!"

Elliot was right behind her. They raced through the halls. Two lefts, then a right. They skidded to a stop when they saw the guards stacked five deep in front of the exit. Two sets of fists tightened. The twins didn't even need to look at each other.

Maggie grabbed the weapons the guards were using and formed them into a tornado of metal that swept through the ranks. Elliot charged it, shocking anyone it touched into unconsciousness and bouncing lightning off it to get anyone else. It was over before the guards even got a hit in.

They raced towards the exit, Maggie shoving the door in.

They were not outside. The door led to a small, semi-circular room. The walls were white, and video footage was being played across them.

Three superhumans were laying waste to a facility that was incredibly similar to the one they were in.

A woman flashed intense light from her hands, blinding her opponents. Then she took them out quickly and efficiently. She had Maggie's blue eyes and Elliot's blond hair.

A man danced between his opponents, fingers barely brushing them. They seemed to freeze solid while he became more agile and much faster. He had Maggie's high cheekbones and Elliot's big ears.

And there was Grady. He was using his powers to crush people against the ground, throw them into walls.

The worst part of it was that all three of them seemed determined not to leave anyone standing. They hadn't had their powers as long as Maggie and Elliot had had theirs, but if the killings were accidental there would be survivors. The only things left behind were bodies and destruction.

Maggie's hands were pressed to her mouth like she needed to stop herself from admitting it was real. Elliot's fists were clenched. Both of them stood there, frozen. They couldn't look away.

Darts pricked into their skin. Their legs collapsed under them. They were completely numb, which matched their emotional states perfectly.

"That's what happened to the old project." Turner said. "Your parents and Grady killed everyone. A man named Warren Xavier and I were the only ones who survived. I was at a meeting. He was a consultant who never worked on site."

She ran her hands along the walls. The footage warped over her skin. "The government closed us down. They thought the project was too...unstable. They didn't see that the attack was only the harbinger of the true potential of the project!"

She crouched down to get closer to the twins. "I rebuilt everything from scratch. It took me twenty-five years of biding my time and watching you two from a distance. I know you both. I know how you think, I know the patterns of your behavior.

"It doesn't matter what you do or how many times you try to get away, I will always bring you back. And sooner or later, I'll have you trained. Just like those bomb-sniffing dogs the police are oh-so proud of. You two are going to be the greatest weapons the world has ever seen. Your parents could only control photons and kinetic energy, but *you* two--! Your potential is unbelievable.

"And when you're ready, I'll show you to the government. You'll make them listen to me. Once they realize what they couldn't see before, they'll welcome me back with open arms. And I will finally be able to show the world what Project Kobold is capable of!"

Later, Elliot and Maggie wouldn't be able to tell if her speech had been a dream brought on by the drugs pumping through their systems. It didn't matter, though. That wasn't the part they wished was untrue.

Chapter 55

Treasure Hunt

The apartment went beyond Spartan. It was completely unoccupied. There was no food in the kitchen, no extra toilet paper in the bathroom, no pictures on the walls, no tchotchkes of any kind. The only piece of furniture was a bed in one of the rooms. ("Ooh la la," Carly reiterated.)

"Well this was a bust." Lydia sighed.

"Maybe." Carly frowned. "Let's check the floorboards. Maybe there's something hidden."

So they crawled along the floor, tapping each of the boards and waiting for a sound to echo back. There were a lot of available floorboards, considering the apartment looked like it was between tenants.

Carly's forehead was creased as she hunted. Delilah Turner was a complete mystery to her. The woman was obsessed with a twenty-five-year-old experiment that had resulted in everybody dying. Why would she want to recreate that? How did someone stay consistently two, three, five steps ahead of them while lacking so much common sense?

"Augh! There's nothing here!" Carly stood up, groaning and rubbing her side. "Let's just go to the last address."

Lydia sat back on her heels and bit her lip. "Hang on. I just want to check one more spot."

"Where?" Carly followed her into the bedroom. "Where could there possibly be anything..."

Lydia laid down on her back and wriggled under the bed. "When I was little, I used to hide my diary between the springs and the mattress when my cousins came over."

"You're still little. But that's a good hiding place." Carly admitted. "Did Turner have the same idea? Or Xavier?"

"In fact..." Lydia emerged from under the bed, clutching a small case. She waved it at her friend. "They did."

"Huh." Carly snatched it from her. "Does it weird you out at all that you share some of your ideas with two psychos?"

"Well, I already knew I shared some ideas with you." Lydia got up. "So?"

Carly unzipped the case. Inside it was a sleek black square just a little wider than a smart phone. It was strapped to one side of the case. On the other side was a mesh pocket holding a cord with a USB 3 on one end and a normal USB on the other. "What the...?"

"It's an external hard drive!" Lydia gasped. "Of course! Turner doesn't want to take the chance that she'll lose any of her research, so she must have copies of the data hidden all over the place!"

"Huh." Carly lifted her chin, grinning. "Now we'll see who's one step ahead!"

"I don't know about that." Lydia said. "She's way too careful to store all the data in one place. We probably only have one piece of the puzzle."

"Dis-a-POINTING!" Carly groaned in a sing-song voice.

Lydia rolled her eyes. "Okay, now let's get out of here before the psychos decide they want to take a 'sick day.'"

"You don't have to tell me twice!" Carly said, pivoting on her heel and heading for the door.

Chapter 56

Regroup

"It's too crowded in here." Grady said.

For once, Sean had to agree with him. Grady, his three guards, Adanna's team, and the parents were all in the living room of Nehemiah and Wendell's apartment. Sean had heard once that if everyone on earth stood shoulder to shoulder, they could fit in Lake Superior. He was becoming more and more skeptical of that as it became clear eleven people couldn't even fit in one living room.

"Shut up, Grady." Nehemiah said.

Wendell looked at him, startled, and laughed.

"You were saying?" Adanna prompted.

"I have some information you might find interesting." Viv handed her a manila envelope. "My associate was able to find Turner after pulling up her picture and comparing it to people he was...familiar with. She used an alias, of course."

"It seems to be her hobby." Kyle said.

Taylor picked up the story. "Apparently Turner, using the alias Donna Bloom, has been selling schematics for new weapons as well as classified information on the black market for the past twenty-five years."

"That's how she's able to afford to make all her identities look real." Wendell mused.

"Most likely it's also how she rebuilt the project." Viv said.

"You think she rebuilt Project Kobold?" Hailey raised an eyebrow. "Why? I thought she was doing something different now – 'The Gemini Project' or something."

"Maybe," Hugh allowed. "But given the fact that she's a predatory stalker, it's safe to bet she has a fixation on this project that blew up in her face."

"She was never stalking Elliot and Maggie." Sean said slowly. "She was stalking the Project. They were just unlucky enough to be descended from people involved."

Taylor grinned. "Have you ever considered criminology?"

He shook his head.

"So what do we do with this information?" Nehemiah asked.

"Looks like the original Project Kobold was housed in an underground bunker." Adanna said, flipping through a set of papers. "If she really is obsessed with recreating it, she probably had one built. That would be expensive. Kyle; can you look through those aliases again, but this time for bank accounts with large sums of money deposited and withdrawn?"

"Sure thing." He nodded, then grabbed his laptop and wormed his way through the crowd. He headed towards the bedrooms, picked one at random, and locked himself in.

"Looks like you still don't get to sleep in your room, buddy," Sean said to Wendell.

He smirked.

Adanna took a deep breath. "Well," she said, "I guess the rest of us just have to wait until he finds something. Hailey, Nehemiah, Sean;

you guys can take some time to go someplace if you want. The rest of
us will watch Grady while you're out."

"Whoo-hoo!" Hailey pumped a fist in the air, then grabbed each
of the boys by the wrists and dragged them towards the door. They
barely had time to grab their shoes before she was urging them into
the hallway.

Adanna smiled.

Taylor and Hugh sidled over to flank their daughter, each wrapping
an arm around her.

"You are getting so grown up, baby girl." Hugh said.

Adanna softened. "Thanks, Daddy."

"She takes after her mother," Taylor boasted. "Fighting crime, taking charge—"

Hugh laughed. "Excuse me, but who was it who took command of a
squad of soldiers after the senior officer went down? *And* got everyone
back to the base safely? Was it you? Nope! That was me."

Taylor scoffed. "Well who was it who came up with a cover story for
herself and three junior detectives when they were discovered snoop-
ing around a drug cartel's hideout? And maintained that cover story
for two weeks until the cartel was finally arrested?"

"Well who was it who—"

Adanna rolled her eyes, pulling both of her parents closer to her
as they tried to one-up each other. In one way, it was nice that it was
still possible to laugh without Elliot. But in another way, it felt like a
betrayal to even come up to the surface of her pain to banter, let alone
feel love for the remainder of her family.

If anything happened to him, she wasn't sure she would ever be
happy again. She knew now that it was possible, but that didn't make
it right. Maybe sacrificing her happiness in honor of her brother would
be her penance for letting this happen in the first place.

"Hey there." Wendell found Grady in the hallway and leaned against the wall beside him.

Grady eyed him suspiciously.

"Don't worry," Wendell said, "I'm not going to hurt you."

Grady smirked. The Guild member was half a foot shorter than him and not nearly as wide. "Is that so?"

"Yeah." Wendell crossed his arms. "So, what do you do for fun? Besides, you know, murder."

"Murder is more like a job." Grady said. "At least, the completion of one."

"Really? Why'd you settle on that, anyway? Couldn't you just...destroy the data or something?"

"We thought about that. But data can always be remembered, rewritten, recreated – the only way to be sure no one would ever be able to revive the project was to eliminate the most powerful part; the human element."

"Sounds like you have a lot of respect for life for a guy who spends his time trying to snuff it out." Wendell observed.

Grady shrugged.

Wendell raised an eyebrow. "You just said 'we.' You had help?"

Grady nodded. "Liz, Ken, and I all realized the project was too dangerous to exist. We took it down together."

"Liz and Ken are...?"

"The parents of the twins."

"Oh. Wow." Wendell tried to reconcile the idea that bright, optimistic Elliot was the son of a pair of mass murderers. "What happened to them?"

"They turned out to be hypocrites." Grady scoffed. "They didn't blink at the thought of killing all the staff members, but when I told them their kids were part of the project's legacy they completely refused to believe it. They put the kids in the system because they were still smart enough to know they couldn't take me on."

"And then what happened?" Wendell had a bad feeling about this. He had a feeling he really didn't want to know. So why did he feel the need to ask? Was truth really worth the havoc it wreaked on the psyche?

"I always thought we'd all go together, once we'd hunted down the scientist who wasn't in the building at the time, but they were backing out and I couldn't have that." Grady clenched his fists. "I had to protect the world. Don't you understand? I had no choice."

Wendell was getting impatient and was not in the mood for Grady's paradoxical guilt trip. "You killed them."

He looked at Wendell, eyes hard. "I had to. We are walking exhibitions of the project. Even if we destroyed all the data and killed everyone involved, it wouldn't matter if someone could still capture us and reverse engineer the whole thing."

"Oh, and what about you? Huh?" Wendell snapped. "You're the one exception to the rule, is that it? Who's a hypocrite now?"

"Haven't you been listening?" Grady growled. "I have to kill everyone associated with the project first. Then, yes, I will kill myself. I'm not doing this for myself or even a handful of people; I'm doing this for everyone."

Wendell didn't know how to respond to that.

In the kitchen, Viv and Oliver found the leftover cookies. They sat on the counter with the plate between them, munching and kicking their legs like little kids.

"So..." Oliver glanced at his wife, then looked away. "Junko? Is that your real name?"

Viv hesitated. "No."

"What, uh...what is your real name?"

She set her cookie down and stared at her knees. "You said it didn't matter."

"It doesn't." He insisted quickly. "It wouldn't change anything, I'm just...I'm just curious, I guess." He sighed. "There's a part of you that you won't ever let me see."

"You wouldn't like it." Viv said.

Oliver reached for her hand. She let him take it, but it hung limp in his hand like a clay model. "I love you, Genevieve Posey. I always will. I just wish you would let me love every part of you."

For a long time, they sat there in silence. If there was one thing Oliver could do extraordinarily well, it was giving someone room to think. Room to breathe. Room to exist.

Eventually, Viv's hand tightened around his. "It's Sayoko." She whispered.

Chapter 57

Moral Ambiguity

Maggie woke up to concern prodding the edge of her mind. She groaned and sat up. She was back in her cell and everything hurt. She felt like someone had pumped her insides full of air, clogging her ears and squeezing her brain.

She sent her complaints to Elliot by linking him to her aches and pains.

Still, he sent back relief that she hadn't been seriously hurt.

Regretting her irritation, she echoed his concern from earlier.

He sent back remorse and disappointment, and the same horror he'd felt when the video of their parents had played on the screen. Maggie recognized it because their shock had left them reaching out for someone to make them not alone.

Maggie sent him agreement.

The next thing Elliot sent was hopelessness. Were they ever going to get out? That had been the perfect chance, and Turner had still been one step ahead of them.

Maggie sent back hope, though she knew he could tell it was hollow.

She looked herself over. Her entire right arm was bandaged, and she had cuffs on her wrists again. This time, they looked much more formidable than the glow stick models they'd gotten before. Maggie had a feeling there were more where these came from.

She flexed the fingers of her right hand. She didn't feel any pain, but she wouldn't put it past Turner to have her hopped up on some weird pain killers just to see what would happen.

"You failed." Speak of the devil.

Maggie turned to glare at Turner. "Yeah, I noticed."

There was an emptiness on Turner's face. She was trying to protect herself. It stoked the fire of rage burning in Maggie; what did Turner have to be worried about? *She* wasn't the one who had been captured and experimented on!

Maggie held up her arm. "What did you do to me?"

"You were unconscious." Turner said. "We didn't want to waste any time, so we took skin, blood, hair, and tissue samples before putting you back in your room."

Maggie pulled the arm to her chest. "That is so messed up."

Turner sighed. "Morality is an illusion brought on by a dual yearning for self-preservation and power."

"You really believe that?" Maggie frowned. "Then you don't think it was wrong for my parents to kill all those people?"

Turner stiffened.

Maggie bit back her apology. "Why did you show us that?"

"Because you still don't seem to understand what you are." Turner said. "The power inside you changes your very nature. You may not think that what you parents did was right at the moment, but sooner or later you won't have a problem with it. You can't be both human and a weapon."

"You're insane."

"No." Turner said. "*You're* insane. You just don't know it yet."

"What if you're wrong?" Maggie asked. "Have you ever even considered that we might be real people, too?"

"A good scientist considers all possibilities." Turner said.

"Yeah, but a good scientist draws conclusions based on facts, not convenience!"

"The Kobold subjects murdered an entire base full of people." Turner said. "Does that sound like something a normal human would or could do?"

"Just because we can do things other people can't doesn't make us less human!" Maggie hissed. "Next you're going to tell me you think Olympic Athletes aren't human either."

"There is a big difference between training one's body and getting oneself genetically mutated in a way that results in hundreds of murders."

"You keep going back to the murders, but you claim that morality doesn't exist. If a lack of moral compass is what makes my parents inhuman, what does that say about you?"

Turner raised an eyebrow. "Clever, but unfounded. The murders are significant indicators because of the randomness and scale of the deed."

"Maybe they were tired of being used as your guinea pigs."

"You're forgetting that they signed up to participate in the project." Turner tilted her head. "I find it interesting that, while you insist you believe morality exists, you continue to defend your parents though by all accounts their actions were morally wrong."

Maggie opened and shut her mouth. "What happened to them?"

Turner shrugged. "I don't know."

"You didn't kill them." Maggie remembered Turner's initial shock over their lack of a presence in her life. "Are they still alive?"

"We shall see." Turner mused.

Maggie stood up. "You think you're a good scientist. What possibilities have you considered?"

Turner laughed. "I've learned the error of confiding sensitive information with weapons." She slid the recording device out of her pocket and switched it off. "Thank you for your cooperation."

Maggie was still seething when the sound of Turner's heels on the tile floor faded away.

Chapter 58

Racers, Start Your Engines

"**P**ass me the Phillips Head."

Nehemiah tossed the screwdriver to Wendell, who was working on the firing mechanism. Nehemiah himself was working on the body of the new "super taser." Kyle was working on the wiring.

Of the fifteen or so weapons they'd liberated from Turner's underground lab, they were trying to cobble together at least one super taser. It had taken them a few hours just to find relatable schematics in the papers Wendell had stuffed indiscriminately into his bag. It was slow going, especially considering most of the prototypes were *not* intended to be super tasers originally.

"Ow!" Kyle yanked his hand back. He'd been shocking himself every so often ever since they sat down. Every time it happened, his mood seemed to get worse. It was becoming concerning, even for Kyle.

He braced his hands on the table and ducked his head, forcing himself to take a deep breath. Then his head shot up, eyes almost surging with white-hot anger.

"Why are we even wasting our time on this?! Maggie and Elliot are being tortured, and we're sitting around trying to build a shock collar for our new pet serial killer! Why don't we just shoot him?!"

"Because that would be murder, and we'd like to avoid that." Wendell answered without looking up.

Kyle made a face, recoiling. "It's not murder, it's self-defense. Or...friend-defense. Whatever."

"But if we plan it ahead of time, it's technically premeditated." Wendell pointed out.

"Who freakin cares?!" Kyle threw up his hands. "We're going to get rid of the body anyway, aren't we? Burn it or something like you did with Siren? It's not like this is ever going to go to court!"

"It might go to the court of heaven if we're not careful." Nehemiah said.

"Shut up!" Kyle snapped. "How could anyone say we're wrong about putting him down? He's a *killer*, it's *justice*."

"It's revenge and you know it." Wendell said.

Kyle faltered, then went back to his wiring.

Wendell looked up. "Kyle, that's not what I..."

"No." Kyle's voice was calm now, but somehow it wasn't reassuring. "You're right. It's murder."

"What you did with Siren was different." Nehemiah said.

"How can you say that?" There was an edge to the question, but it didn't feel like it was pointing outward.

"Because." Nehemiah took a deep breath. "When things happen in the moment like that...it's different. And if you hadn't done what you did, everyone would have died."

"But I wanted to kill her." The confession laid heavily in the air. The light in the room seemed to dim.

"I know." Wendell said. "But I was there. And I know you waited until you had no other choice."

"I waited until I had a clean shot."

"Are you sure?" Wendell asked. "Are you really sure? Because from my perspective, you had a clean shot for a good monologue and a half before you pulled the trigger."

"You were in a bad situation." Nehemiah agreed. "You only had bad options. Murder is when you have a good option and you don't even try."

"We don't want Carly to be in the same position you were." Wendell said.

Kyle nodded. His face was made of stone, and their words were raindrops that weren't absorbed, merely dripping down and sliding off.

Nehemiah knew that face. It was the same face his parents had worn when he'd told them he wanted to leave the community. Anything you say to that face only makes it harder, more impenetrable.

"Kyle," He said.

Kyle looked over at him.

Nehemiah didn't know where he was going with his words. He had to try. "You're not alone."

Kyle blinked slowly at him. "Thanks."

~

Lydia drove Carly to the gun range after making a pit stop at her house and gathering more weapons in the back than were possessed by the American army during the Revolutionary War.

"Do we have to unload *all* of these?" She complained.

"Only the ones you want me to shoot Grady with."

"All of them it is."

Carly wanted to get in some last-minute practice before the mission. She knew from experience that she was only going to get one shot at this. If she missed, she was dead. Then Elliot and Maggie were dead. Then, most likely, everyone else.

One of the biggest problems was that she didn't know the super taser's range yet. Wendell had promised it would be "as great a range as we can manage," which was sweet but not necessarily helpful.

Most normal tasers shot out prongs with wires connecting the prongs to the gun, which then electrified them. Turner's weapon had more in common with grapeshot than with a taser, except that it used energy pulses and didn't split apart until it actually impacted the target. So it was non-lethal, but extremely painful. It would definitely put him down for a good long nap. As long as she remembered to charge it up first.

(*"You have to charge the bullet, or the shock won't be able to activate and it'll just tick him off."* Wendell had said.)

Her heart went out to her soon-to-be victim. Truly, it did.

"Hey, Carlsbad?"

"Yes Lydia?"

"I thought you said this was your least favorite range in the city." Lydia said.

Carly lifted an eyebrow. "Did I?" She asked in an obviously fake-innocent voice.

Lydia frowned. "What are you up to?"

Carly rolled her eyes. "No-thing."

Lydia watched Carly carefully as she signed them into the range. The unofficial sniper could not have more obviously had evil intent than if she'd strolled in dressed like Maleficent. The poor front desk guy seemed oblivious.

"Planning a revolt?" He asked when he saw their equipment.

"Only a little one." Carly grinned.

On the range, she gathered her hair up into a messy ponytail bun on the crown of her head and selected one of the weapons she'd carried in herself. She sighted it in, pretending she didn't feel Lydia's suspicious eyes on her back.

She took a few practice shots at the target, then swung the gun up to point at the corner where the ceiling and the wall came together.

Back in the car, she was worried about going deaf from Lydia's screaming.

"Dia? Dia? Dia!"

"WHAT."

Carly recoiled. "Okay. I can see you're upset."

"Upset?! YOU ALMOST MADE ME AN ACCESSORY TO A CRIME!"

"Come on, Di." Carly said. "I'd never let you get arrested! The manager of the range has a daughter-in-law with a Visa problem. I knew he was just going to fine us and ban us." She crossed her arms, looking a bit proud of herself. "That's why I chose *this* range."

Lydia pinched the bridge of her nose. "Not one of you was born with sense that is even remotely common."

"Why be ordinary when you can be extraordinary?" Carly asked, busting out jazz hands.

Lydia started the car. "You're lucky you're already injured. Because if you weren't, I would push you out of this car while it was moving."

"Pretty sure assault is a crime."

"*It's justified.*"

~

The sky was cloudy that night. Without the stars and moon, it looked like the world surrounding the apartment had been inked out. Adanna crossed and uncrossed her arms, taking a few deep breaths.

This was it. After everything, after all the work, the pain, and the fear, it was finally happening.

She turned around. In Wendell and Nehemiah's apartment, every one of the Guild members, two sets of parents, and the once and future enemy stood or sat facing her. Besides Grady, they looked just as nervous as she was. Nobody was complaining about the cramped conditions now; being close to each other was comforting.

"Okay." Adanna said. "Kyle found out where the base is located. It'll probably be heavily fortified on the outside and the inside, considering what Grady told us about the last project. And Kyle has confirmed that there are at least two hundred people on Turner's payroll. We're only going to get one shot at this. So here's the plan."

Chapter 59

The Plan

"Grady; you're going to be the distraction. Head right through the front door and keep their attention. Mom and Dad; take out anyone who might be a threat to him. Non-lethal force if possible."

Grady hadn't been born with his powers, but the surge of their presence after so long without them nearly brought him to tears. Taylor and Hugh exchanged a concerned look at his gasp.

He steadied himself, pulling a mask of indifference back over his face. It was show time. The mission he'd been on for twenty-five years was about to be completed. There was no time for sentimentality. He turned towards the bunker.

Only half of the front door was above ground. In order to get in, people would have to get down on their knees and crawl inside. Normally, it was a great defensive tactic; it's hard to aim while trying to squeeze through an opening. Unfortunately, Grady was not normal.

"Hey!" A sentry shouted, flicking the safety off his machine gun and swinging it up to point at Grady's chest. "Who are you and what are you doing here?"

"Don't worry." Grady flicked his hand and the man smashed into the ground hard enough to snap his neck. "I have an appointment." Grady rolled his head and took off into the air.

"That looked non-lethal to me." Hugh said.

"I'm sure he'll walk it off." His wife agreed.

Grady increased the gravity on the ground outside the door, slamming it down until the full entrance was revealed with a boom. It took two more seconds for the bullets to start zinging out from the trees.

Taylor flicked the safety off her weapon. "You take the ones on the left?"

Hugh nodded. "You take the ones on the right."

~

"The rest of us will use this as cover. Grady; make an opening on either side of the base. Sean, Kyle, Viv, and Oliver will enter on the right side of the building. Destroy any information you find, but if you get to Elliot and Maggie first, just take them and leave."

Grady seemed to be enjoying himself from what Sean could see. As a dancer, he appreciated the aesthetics of the unnecessary hand motions accompanying the violent outbursts of gravity. The pulling motion Grady used when he decreased the gravity on the entire roof of the compound, sending it flying off into space, was especially dramatic.

"He sure knows how to make an entrance." Sean said.

"I hope you know that comment officially designates you as the human shield." Kyle said.

"Worth it."

The four of them rushed across the grass, leaping into the building. Viv, Oliver, and Sean rolled out of the impact gracefully, but Kyle flopped to the ground. He was still getting up by the time the last unlucky occupant of the room lost consciousness.

"Let's move." Viv said. She opened the door a crack, holding her throwing knives at the ready. She peeked around the corner, then whipped out into the hall and threw her knives. She beckoned to the others before jogging over to get her knives back.

"Kyle?" Sean asked.

Kyle was already pulling his flash drive out of the computer. "They're all connected." he said, gesturing to the other three computers in the room. "Virus should spread soon."

Viv was wiping the blades on the lab coats of the three scientists when the others caught up to her.

"That's messed up." Kyle said.

She glowered at him. "They're not disposable."

"Duck." Oliver said calmly.

Viv yanked Kyle down with her as Oliver put bullets in the knees of the next batch of scientists.

"They're probably trying to get out." Sean said. "We have to get further away from the exit."

"Pretty sure this isn't a divided highway." Kyle said.

"Less cynicism, more shooting." Sean said.

He took three running steps and catapulted himself over the bodies, flipping around in midair. He ran into the next five scientists. He kicked one of them under the chin, snapping their head back. He punched another in the stomach, snapped his leg around to offset the balance of two of the others.

The last lunged for him, but Sean dropped back into a bridge, then kicked his legs up and over, nailing the guy in the chest. Sean lunged forward, putting the kinetic energy of his entire upper body into two punches that he landed on the sternums of the guys he'd unbalanced a second ago.

He did a Russian, taking out one of them and the guy he'd hit in the chin. They slammed back against the walls and were promptly shot by Kyle and Oliver.

Sean resorted to less technical attacks to finish off the other three; breaking one nose on his knee, snapping a knee back with a sharp kick, and using the other's own motion to flip him to the floor where he cracked his head and didn't get up.

"Nice form." Viv said.

Sean nodded at her. He peered around the corner. "No one yet." He said. "Let's keep going." The words were hardly out of his mouth when four scientists appeared in a line, standing shoulder to shoulder and blocking the hallway. They each held an assault rifle.

Kyle yanked Sean back just as the bullets started flying.

"Thanks." Sean gasped.

"Don't thank me yet." Kyle said. "You're still the designated human shield."

Then he and Oliver returned fire.

After what seemed like a thunderous eternity, Kyle and Oliver let their weapons down. Kyle was pressing his left wrist to his side.

"Are you okay?" Sean asked, rushing over.

Oliver lifted Kyle's hand away from his side and pulled up his shirt, inspecting the site. He breathed a sigh of relief when he didn't see a bullet hole and let Kyle's shirt drop back into place.

"Let's move." Viv said.

The four of them raced down the hall, each peering into different rooms. They took a left at the end of the hall and continued the process until their legs were burning and sweat dripped down into their eyes.

Finally, Viv paused. "Kyle." She said. "There is a machine running in here."

Kyle staggered over to peek inside. His eyes widened. "That's a sensory deprivation chamber!"

~

"Wendell, Nehemiah, and I will go in on the left."

Adanna lead Wendell and Nehemiah across the field and into the building. There was no one in the room they initially dropped into, and the hallway was empty.

"That's not suspicious at all." Wendell said.

"We have to keep going." Adanna said. "Check every room. Let's get as much done as we can before the other shoe drops."

One door opened into a room with a bunch of targets set up at the end. Another looked like a classroom. A third was pitch black. The sun was high in the sky, but this room was pitch black. It must have had a secondary ceiling in it. What would require *two* ceilings? A prison cell holding a superhuman, perhaps?

"Hello?" Adanna flicked on the light attached to her gun. It only penetrated twenty feet of the darkness.

"This smells like a trap." Wendell whispered.

It did. But what if that was Turner's plan? What if Elliot was actually in there? She couldn't leave any stone unturned. "You don't have to come."

"You're too smart to say stupid things." Nehemiah told her.

Wendell nodded.

Adanna took a deep breath. "Okay. Spread out; try to find a light switch or something."

But that wasn't necessary. The lights snapped by themselves right after the door slammed shut.

"What the...?"

Water started pouring in through holes in the walls. Adanna's eyes widened. "We have to get out of here!"

"Great idea! How?" Wendell asked.

Nehemiah, being the only one who hadn't seen many spy movies, looked torn between fascination and fear.

"Um." Adanna closed her eyes. She needed to think! She was not going to let Nehemiah and Wendell die because of her obsessive search patterns! "The door is probably indestructible, considering they had Elliot and Maggie in here *and* it's built to withstand the water pressure. But Turner wouldn't put them in here to drown them, so there has to be some sort of trick to this."

"What if she just wanted to see what they would do?" Wendell asked. "And she emptied the room after she got what she wanted?"

"Well, if that's the case we're dead!" Adanna snapped. She sighed. "I'm sorry, Wen. We'll figure this out. Trust me."

The water was up to their ankles now.

"How long do you think the pipes are?" Nehemiah asked.

"There wasn't water in the last room, so..." Adanna compared the size of the last room to the length of the wall between its door and this one. "...probably only about five feet. Why?"

"The holes look big enough to crawl into." Nehemiah said. "And the water has to be coming from somewhere. It's probably not an unlimited source, so when the water goes up in here, it goes down in the tanks."

"That's brilliant, Nehemiah!" Wendell pumped his fist up and down, elbows splashing in the water.

"But we'll never be able to get inside with the water pressure like it is now." Adanna pointed out.

"What if we waited until the room was full?" Nehemiah wondered. "Then it would just be like normal swimming."

She grinned. "You are just full of brilliant ideas today."

Wendell punched him in the shoulder fondly.

"Alright, guys, ditch your weapons, jackets, shoes; anything that will weigh you down. We'll have to be treading water until our heads hit the ceiling, and that's twenty feet away." Adanna said.

They barely managed to strip off the excess weight before the water rose over their heads. As it kept rising, Adanna reminded her friends to take deep breaths.

"You need to oxygenate your blood; you'll be able to stay underwater for longer."

It was easier said than done. When it comes time to sink or swim, it can be hard to stop oneself from hyperventilating.

Finally, the moment of truth.

"We'll swim down as soon as our heads are under the water." Adanna spluttered as water splashed into her mouth. "Get out as quickly as you can; *don't stop*." That was all she had time to say before the water hit the roof.

The three of them spun around, kicking off the ceiling and diving down towards the holes. Nehemiah was the fastest swimmer, so he got through first. Adanna was right behind him. Something smacked into her leg as she started swimming through the entryway. She turned around and stared, horrified, at the mouth of the hole, which was beginning to close.

Wendell was halfway in, and Adanna grabbed his arms, bracing her feet on the panel rising from the bottom of the passage and pulling him in, trying desperately not to think of what it would look like if the panels closed on him, snapping through his body and clouding the water with red.

Thankfully, that didn't happen. Wendell swam up to the surface, Adanna right behind him. She was so relieved that she hugged him, her wet braids sticking to his face.

"What do we do now?" Nehemiah asked.

"The same thing in reverse, I guess." Adanna said. "Hopefully it's on a timer or something."

It was, and soon enough they were back in the room. The door unlocked and they walked out, leaving their water-logged rifles behind.

"That was the worst!" Wendell complained.

"But we got through it." Nehemiah said. "That means things are only going to get better from here."

Adanna was very careful when she peered into the next room; making sure half her body was outside in the hall. But when she realized what she was seeing, she raced into the room. "Elliot!"

Wendell and Nehemiah sprinted after her. She was right; their fearless leader was in the room. He was on his knees with a young man pointing a gun at his head.

~

"What do I do?"

"You guard Carly and Lydia in case Turner is one step ahead of us and sends someone after them."

You wouldn't think someone with electric blue hair would be so good at going unnoticed, but you would be wrong. As soon as Grady disappeared inside the building, Hailey counted to ten, then went after him. He'd already re-carpeted the entryway with bodies by the time she got there, and she had to remind herself that there was nothing she could have done, no way she could take him on.

Her brain felt like all the safeties were off. She was noticing *everything*, from the spaces she could step between the bodies to the fact that three of them were wearing mismatched socks. She could see cracks in the walls at the slightest glace.

She followed Grady through the building. She waited until he'd cleared a room before entering, so he wouldn't be looking for anyone in it. She stayed one room, one hall, one staircase behind him.

She saw everything. She felt like some sort of invisible witness to a horrible crime. She knew Adanna hadn't know this was what she was asking her to do. It felt right, though, like penance for being involved in everything that had led to these people being killed.

She told herself they were the "bad guys," but things had been messed up enough in the past week that she knew how indistinct and versatile that term was.

When they started getting into the lower levels, computers began to take most of the punishment. They sank into the ground, completely unrecognizable by the time Hailey saw them. But she knew what they were. And that was when she had her brilliant idea.

~

"Carly, you're doing a lot better, but we can't risk having you in the middle of a firefight. And Lydia, you said you wanted out, right?"

"Right."

"Then you don't have to come. Stay with Carly like you have been; make sure she's okay."

"Are you okay?" Lydia asked.

Carly didn't look at her. "I'm fine."

"They're going to be okay." Lydia said. "Adanna's plan is brilliant."

"I know."

Lydia sighed. "What's bothering you?"

"*Nothing*, I'm just...concentrating."

"On what? There's nothing to concentrate on."

"Not yet." Carly insisted.

"You make it sound like you *want* someone to come after us."

Carly almost looked at her, but didn't. "I don't want you to get hurt, but it would help if the suspense would just be over already."

"Well," Lydia said, "Whenever the suspense is over, I'll have your back."

Carly smiled. "Thanks, Dia."

"My pleasure, Carls."

Chapter 60

When a Plan Comes Together

"Drop your weapons!" The gunman said.

"One step ahead of you." Wendell muttered.

"Come on, Jonas," Elliot said. "It's over. Just let me go."

"Shut up!" Jonas pressed the gun tighter to Elliot's head.

"Stop!" Adanna shrieked.

"I know you, Jonas." Elliot said, wincing. "You don't want to do this."

"I don't have a choice!" He said.

"Why not?" Nehemiah asked.

Jonas scoffed. "What kind of a question is that? Because my boss will kill me, numbskull!"

"Your boss is probably dead." Nehemiah said. "The guy who can control gravity is here, and he wants to murder everyone. If you get out now, we won't tell him about you."

Wendell looked between Nehemiah and Jonas.

The gunman was shaking his head. "No." He said. "I'm not falling for that."

"The *ceiling* is *gone*." Adanna said, pointing up.

He pulled the hammer back. "Then maybe I should just kill him now!"

"Why would you want to do that?" Nehemiah asked softly.

"I have to!" Jonas shouted.

"You don't *want* to, though."

"That doesn't matter." The gunman said. "These people...they're not the best, but they're my family."

"I understand." Nehemiah said.

Adanna shot him an incredulous look.

"My family was very passionate about something and I thought they were wrong." He continued. "I knew they would disown me if I disagreed with them, but I had to do it anyway. I miss them so much," he looked down, "but if I did something that was wrong just because they wanted me to, what kind of person would that make me?"

"One with a family." Jonas said. "And a place to belong."

"But without self-respect." Nehemiah countered. "Besides, I have a new place to belong now. The difference is that I can disagree with my friends and they won't turn their backs on me."

"That's what belonging actually is." Wendell agreed. "If you have to deny what's right in order for people to accept you, then you don't belong with them."

"If you let Elliot go, you can come with us." Adanna said. "We can give you a new place to belong."

Jonas looked conflicted. The hand holding the gun slumped the tiniest bit.

That was enough for Elliot. He twisted the gun out of Jonas' hand and elbowed him in the stomach. Elliot hopped to his feet, twirling the gun around his fingers.

Adanna grabbed him, tears warming her eyes and spilling down to join the water on her cheeks. "Elliot!" She sobbed.

He tossed the gun over to Wendell and held his sister like she was the only real thing in the world. He pressed his mouth to her shoulder and breathed in her scent.

"Adanna." He whispered. "I missed you so much."

"I missed you, too!"

"Sorry, man." Elliot said to Jonas. "You can still join the Guild if you want to."

"No, he can't." Grady's voice was probably the last thing Jonas heard.

"Hey!" Elliot shouted, pulling away from Adanna to confront Grady. "That was uncalled for! He wasn't going to hurt anyone!"

"This project will hurt *everyone*." Grady said. "And anyone involved is part of that hurt." He raised his hand. "Especially you."

~

"A sensory deprivation chamber?" Sean said. "Can you disable it?"

"I should be able to." Kyle dropped his gun and circled the machine. "There should be a panel somewhere around here. That's how someone would be able to turn it on and off manually, or set some sort of timer."

"Here!" Viv called from the other side.

Kyle jogged over to her. "Yeah, this is it."

"Wait!" Sean said. "What if we open it and it's some sort of killer robot or a bomb or something?"

"What if we don't open it and it's Maggie?" Viv countered.

"...I've always wanted to fight a killer robot."

"We'll leave it to you, then." Kyle said. He pressed the button to disengage the chamber.

A countdown appeared on the screen in red numbers.

"What's that?!" Viv asked.

"It *is* a bomb!" Sean said. "We have to get out of here!"

"Wait! Maggie could still be inside!" Kyle said. "Hang on, I just...let me handle this."

"Kyle—"

"Just go if you want to so badly!" Kyle pulled out his phone and synced it with the machine with a flutter of his fingers. He took a deep breath and started looking for a back door. This time, it wasn't just information on the line – Maggie was in there, he was sure of it! And if he didn't figure out how to stop the countdown, she was dead.

Just like Siren.

He pushed the thought away, concentrating completely on his hacking. The numbers kept counting down.

Sean looked between Kyle, the numbers, and the chamber. Part of him was screaming to grab Kyle and drag him forcibly out of the room, but the other part of him wanted to risk it all just to see if this would work.

Viv and Oliver looked at each other. Viv took her husband's hand and held it. He looked into her eyes.

The timer stopped, and the chamber hissed as it slid open.

"You did it!" Sean yelled, grabbing Kyle and shaking him. "You're amazing!"

"Maggie?!" Viv's voice was high-pitched and wavering.

Kyle and Sean rushed over to the opening. Oliver was half inside, cradling Maggie like a baby. Her eyes were wide open, fingers knotted in his shirt as she hyperventilated.

Viv stroked her hair gently. "Just breathe, baby, just breathe."

Maggie's eyes softened and she made an effort to slow her breathing.

Kyle jimmied open the cuffs on her wrists.

Then the air was pierced with a scream. And they all knew immediately who it came from.

~

Grady had destroyed everything. Hailey was watching from behind the smoking remains of a computer. He lowered himself to the ground and bathed in the scent of blood and destruction. He looked content.

Hailey took a deep breath, then stepped out from behind the computer. Her foot hit a piece of a dismembered spinny chair, causing it to bounce along the ground loudly. That was okay. She wanted to be seen now.

Grady looked at her. "You followed me?"

She nodded. "Yes."

"Why?"

"I wanted to know what I was up against."

He frowned. "We don't have to fight." He said. "You're not part of the project."

"Yeah." Hailey brought a small black rectangle out of her pocket. "But this is."

"What?"

"It's a phone. One of the scientists was using their personal phone to store data from the project." She tossed a grenade towards him with her other hand. "Bye."

She didn't wait for the fireworks, turning and bolting up the stairs. She heard the explosion, but it didn't buy her as much time as she'd hoped. Soon enough, the staircase started creaking and collapsing behind her.

She pushed her legs as fast as they could go. Her muscles burned. Her lungs felt like they were going to explode. When she reached the top level, she almost cried from happiness.

She heard something going on behind one of the walls behind her, but was too busy looking at Grady, rising above her in all his murderous glory.

He looked away. "No he can't." He said, flicking a finger at something over the wall.

"Hey!" Tears actually did escape Hailey's eyes at the sound of that voice. It was Elliot! He was alive! "That was uncalled for! He wasn't going to hurt anyone!"

"This project will hurt everyone." Grady said. "And anyone involved is part of that hurt." He raised his hand towards where Elliot must have been. "Especially you."

~

On a hill overlooking the facility, Carly took her feet off the dashboard as Hailey flew out of the staircase. Grady came up next, hovering menacingly over her like the drama queen he was. A perfect target. He seemed distracted by something, but that didn't matter.

Carly took a deep breath, let it out, and pulled the trigger.

She cursed as soon as the recoil snapped her shoulder back. She wanted to reach out and pluck the dart from the air, but it was too late.

It hit Grady in the back, dead in the center of gravity. He screamed, but the bullet wasn't charged. He didn't go down.

"Carly, what's happening?!" Adanna shouted. "Why isn't it working?!"

Grady straightened up, his eyes murderous as he whirled around, trying to find where the bullet had come from.

"Get the cuffs off! Get the cuffs off!" Elliot shoved his hands at his teammates.

On the other side of the wall, Maggie was sitting up. "What did she say?" She asked.

Kyle, Sean, and her parents were looking at nothing, brows furrowed as they listened over the earpieces.

"Guys?" Maggie shook her mom's arm.

"The bullet wasn't charged before she shot him." Viv said. "It's not going to activate."

Maggie's mouth opened in an "o." She stood up and stretched her arms out towards Grady.

"What the--?" Grady shouted as he felt the opposing fields pulling at his body from two directions. It felt like he was being torn in half. Through the pain, he searched for Maggie.

"Come on, come on!" Maggie hissed through her teeth.

Grady's sight was blurry, his body shaking from pain and blood loss. But finally, he saw a smudge pointing little arrows right at him. That smudge was causing this pain. He had to kill it.

"Come on!" Maggie shrieked as she felt gravity increase, pulling her down to her knees. She increased the intensity of the pulsing fields one last time.

Electricity surged through Grady's body and the bullet activated.

Grady fell.

For a moment, everyone was silent. The whole world was silent, like noise had ceased to exist.

Kyle took a breath, finally, moving into what used to be a hallway. He stopped next to Grady's unconscious body to fasten Maggie's cuffs on his wrists. They were a little tight, but given the carnage Kyle didn't care that much.

He wondered if the others felt the same way about him.

He brushed the thought aside; shoved it in a mental fridge for later. Leftover trauma. He had to free Elliot. Sean trotted up behind him, then slowed down and shoved his hands in his pockets. The two of them met up with Elliot and Adanna's team together.

Adanna still had Elliot's sleeve in a death grip, but her eyes were dry.

"We have to look for Turner." She said.

"How?" Kyle asked. "Do you want us to check all the bodies or something?"

Elliot's cuffs opened and he rubbed his wrists.

"If we have to." Adanna said.

Her parents bounded into the room. When they saw Elliot, they rushed over to sandwich their children between them.

"Oh, my beautiful boy." Taylor's voice caught.

Hugh cleared his throat, blinking hard. "We missed you, son."

"Guys." Adanna wiggled out of their embrace. "We need to focus. Turner cannot be allowed to escape."

Elliot exchanged a look with Maggie over his mother's shoulder. Neither of them spoke up, but they shared a powerful sense of doubt that the good doctor hadn't seen this coming.

They were right. The Guild fanned out over the area. They checked every room, every hallway, and even every body lying on the ground. Turner was nowhere in the facility. She had gotten away.

Kyle set up an app that would send alerts to the Guild if any of Turner's aliases used their cards, but he wasn't optimistic. Someone like Turner would be reevaluating her choices and finally taking her opponents seriously. She wouldn't use her cards unless she was calling them out.

"Why do we all need to have this app on our phones?" Hailey asked. "Can't you just download it on yours?"

Kyle scoffed. "And what will you do when something happens to me?"

"When?" Wendell frowned.

Kyle rolled his eyes. "Not in the mood for your grammar nonsense."

Wendell held up his hands.

Lydia eyed Kyle as he walked away.

Chapter 61

What if the Storm Ends?

Taylor had seen quite a few after-mission parties. And this, she had to admit, was one of the finest. There was more to eat and drink than any finite number of people could finish. There were video games and movies being played in the same room. Music was blaring loud enough to wake the dead. If Wendell and Nehemiah's neighbors had their way, every last one of them would fall out a window.

She grabbed another drink and sidled over to her husband. "Hey baby." She wrapped an arm around his waist.

He raised an eyebrow at her. "I'll talk to you later," he said to Viv.

She smirked and waved, heading off into the crowd.

Taylor pulled back from him. "You and Viv were talking? Like...willingly?"

Hugh shrugged. "She's not so bad once you get to know her."

"Really?" Taylor widened her eyes with feigned fascination.

Hugh kissed her.

"What was that for?" She asked. "I haven't even given you the good news yet."

"It's for being sexy when you're sarcastic." He frowned. "What good news? Are you pregnant again?"

She laughed. "It's not *that* good."

"Well, what is it, then?"

She leaned her head against him. "I've decided I want to go back in the field."

He was quiet for a long time.

"Baby, say something."

Hugh rubbed her shoulders. "I'm not going to say that having you out there doesn't scare me, especially after what happened last time. But...I know how much you love it. You haven't been the same since you got a desk job. I think...I think this will be really great for you." He kissed her on the top of her head. "Just be careful, okay?"

"I'm always careful." She teased.

"Hey, Mom! Dad!" Elliot bounced up to them, Adanna trailing behind him like a Secret Service agent.

"Elliot! Sweetheart, give me a hug!"

He rolled his eyes, but she'd been his mother during his middle school years, and she knew it was a front. He held her just a little longer than necessary.

"This is so weird." He said when he pulled away. "I just saw you guys less than a week ago, but it feels like so much has changed."

"It's about to change even more." Hugh said, grinning. "Your mom is going back to fighting crime on the streets!"

"Really?" Elliot said.

"That's great!" Adanna hugged her mother. "I know how much you've missed it!"

"Did everyone notice except me?" Taylor laughed.

"I'm going to be fighting crime on the streets, too." Elliot said. "More often, anyway."

"What? Like, you want to do more bounty hunting gigs?" Adanna asked.

"Yeah." He said. "Like, full-time."

"What?"

"I realized, when I was with Turner, that I've been treating this whole Guild thing like a game. I guess I was just...I don't know, scared maybe? Of taking it seriously?" He rubbed his arm. "Anyway, I figure I can coordinate with everyone's schedules and get a team here most of the time...and if some people want to go full-time, too, it'll be even better. That's not a requirement, though, of course."

"Our little baby; all grown up and running his own business." Taylor crowed.

"We're proud of you, son." Hugh agreed.

Over by the pizza, Sean was keeping watch while Lydia peeled pepperoni slices off other pieces and added them to hers.

"So, you seem different." She said.

"Really? How so?"

She shrugged, then handed him a piece of extra pepperoni pizza. "I don't know...calmer? I mean, I always thought you were pretty chill, but it's like...a different kind of calm."

"I think I know what you mean." He said. "I've been doing a lot of thinking about why I joined the Guild in the first place."

She popped a piece of pepperoni in her mouth. "Oh yeah?"

"Yeah. I think...I was using the Guild as a way to avoid dealing with what happened to me." He took a deep breath. "Seeing Grady...all hung up on something that happened, unable to let it go, funneling all his avoidance into a killing spree – I mean, I'm not about to go off murdering people, but we're not dissimilar."

Lydia made a face. "I kind of wish Carly would've killed him."

Sean shrugged. "I don't know. That would have been pretty hard to live with, I think."

"Yeah, you're right." Lydia sighed. "Anyway, are you going to quit the Guild or something?"

"What? No! I'm going to therapy." He laughed. "I'd never quit the Guild. Maybe I would've if I'd had this revelation at the beginning, but now I don't think I'll ever leave."

"I know what you mean." Lydia sighed. "It's impossible to walk away from these guys."

He frowned. "You sound like you know that from experience."

"Yeah." She said. "I was thinking of leaving, because with everything that happened, I felt like I was getting pulled in too deep and I had no idea if it was even what I wanted to do with my life."

"But...?"

"But I can't." She smirked at him. "I want my life to matter, you know? I want to make a difference. What better way to do it than to be a 'hero'?"

He slung an arm over her shoulders. "I'm glad you're not leaving. But if you ever want to, I won't be mad, okay? I'll totally support you."

"I know." She said. "Thanks."

Nehemiah brought Maggie a drink. She was standing off to the side, watching the others.

"Thanks." She said, taking it.

"I hope you like it." He said. "It's just grape pop."

"It's perfect. Thank you." She sipped it. She was watching him now.

"I just wanted to tell you...don't worry about Elliot." He said.

"What?"

"My family disowned me." Nehemiah said. "I know it can be hard to trust people sometimes, especially when you don't even know if your family will always care about you. But Elliot isn't like my family. None of the Guild is, actually. They accept me and care about me whether I do anything for them or not. And they'll do that for you, too."

Maggie nodded slowly. "Maybe the Guild *is* your family, now."

Nehemiah was startled at first, then softened. "I guess they are."

The two of them looked around at the Guild for a minute.

"Hang on a second." Maggie said, straightening. "Where's Kyle?"

~

Kyle had thought long and hard about this. It was probably the biggest decision of his life – no pun intended – and he didn't want to mess it up like he'd messed up so many things so far.

Hanging was out because he was terrible with knots, and anyway what was he supposed to hang from? The lightbulb? Shooting was also out because of Phineas Gage. Overdosing was a contender, but there was no telling what affect it would have on his brain if he messed up. The same went for drowning or asphyxiation of any kind. And he would literally live before he drank bleach.

So he settled on the good old-fashioned wrist slitting method. Even if someone found him and saved him, the lack of blood wouldn't do anything too terrible in the long run. And if he was stopped there would be a long run, because there was no way a club called the "Hero's Guild" would let him so much as go to the bathroom without suicide watch.

The only thing he was worried about was the pain. He wasn't very good with pain. He was hoping that, if he did it quickly enough, the shock would numb it.

So here he was; next to the dumpsters behind the apartment building with a steak knife he'd stolen from the kitchen upstairs. He debated whether to do his right or left wrist first. He figured the right, because he was right-handed and could probably still make a decent cut even while suffering from blood loss. If he was going to do this, he was going to do it correctly.

He raised the knife, took a deep breath, and plunged it down.

It happened too fast for Kyle to see at the time; the knife was there one second, then it wasn't and the fingers of his left hand were stinging. Maggie had magnetically attracted the knife to her hand, ripping it right out of his grip. Kyle turned to her slowly.

Her eyes were figuratively on fire, but electricity was literally snapping and zipping out of her body.

I made her so angry she switched powers. He thought. She opened her mouth and he braced himself.

"*OF ALL THE—*"

"Wait!"

Maggie and Kyle both turned to see Lydia. She was gasping like she'd just sprinted down the stairs. Sean, Nehemiah, and Hailey jogged around the corner. They looked from Kyle to Maggie to the knife, then back to Kyle.

Kyle groaned.

"Guys," Maggie began.

"Let me talk to him." Lydia said.

"Lydia, you don't have to—"

"I know." She snapped, cutting her cousin off. "I know you don't think I have to, but I do."

Kyle watched her, shifting his weight as she came closer. When it came to team dynamics, Kyle and Lydia didn't have much. Sean was always shielding her, and Hailey was a force of nature unto herself, overshadowing the others sometimes.

"So." Lydia stopped a couple feet in front of him. "What gives?"

"What *gives*?" He echoed, grimacing. "I'm trying to enact justice and want to know what *gives*?"

"Oh. *Justice*." She nodded.

"Yes." He crossed his arms. "I'm a killer. I don't belong here."

"I get it." Lydia nodded.

Kyle leaned back. "You do?"

"Yeah." She said. "You did something wrong and now you need to be punished, right?"

"Yeah." He felt like he should be defending his actions. He was prepared for people to tell him it was okay, that he actually did a good thing. But Lydia was *agreeing* with him? What was she going to do next, give him back his knife?

"You're a killer." Lydia said.

Even hearing it sent white-hot knives through his gut.

"But that doesn't mean you're a bad person." Lydia continued. "This was a crazy week where crazy things happened, and no one is coming to officially wrap things up. You're not going to get arrested or anything."

"I *know*." He said. "That's the *problem*."

"Of course it is." She said. "I know how you feel; I helped kill Maggie, only she ended up surviving. No one's coming to punish me, either. No one's going to say, 'Stay in this cell for 25 years and then you'll have balanced out what you did.' So you and I have to learn to live with ourselves without that."

"It's not fair." Kyle said.

"No." Lydia agreed. "But life never is. You can't change what you did. No matter how many times you try to slit your wrists, you can't undo that moment. You can only start now and move on."

Kyle hugged himself. "How?"

"With help." Hailey said. She and the others had come closer.

"Yeah." Sean smiled softly, rubbing his cousin's shoulder. "We'll be right here. The whole time."

"We're your family." Maggie said. "We won't leave until you're okay."

"I don't deserve this." Kyle said.

"I have some experience with that line of thinking." Nehemiah said. "I might not be part of the B Team, but I have a book that might help."

"You're still family." Maggie elbowed Nehemiah. "The whole Guild is."

He smiled at her.

Lydia looked at Kyle. "I know this is going to take a long time and be overwhelmingly hard, but I think we can do it. Do you?"

Kyle lifted the corner of his mouth. If it was just him, he'd still give up. But he couldn't say that when Lydia was going through the same thing. He couldn't let her give up; she was a good person.

"Sure." Kyle said. "We can try."

~

Wendell was in his own bed for the first time in a week, and he couldn't sleep. He'd changed the sheets, taken a shower, and left the mess from the party to clean up in the morning because he was *so exhausted*, but he couldn't sleep.

He tossed his phone up and down. Everyone was probably asleep already. It was three in the morning. He really shouldn't have to call anyone, anyway. He was a big boy. He didn't need a story and a glass of milk to fall asleep.

He dialed the phone and held it to his ear.

"*Hello?*"

"Hey, Carly. Are you awake?"

"*Absolutely.*"

"Oh yeah?" He asked. "Why 'absolutely?'"

"*I couldn't sleep after that whole thing with Kyle.*" She said.

"Oh. Right."

"*I just hope he's okay.*"

"He's not." Wendell said. "But he will be. With time. And our help."

"*I hope so.*"

For a while, Wendell just sat there, listening to her breathe on the other end of the phone.

"*So, what did you call about?*"

"The Kyle thing, actually."

"*Really?*" She yawned.

"I can let you sleep."

"*I'm not going to sleep. Talk to me.*"

Wendell took a deep breath. "It's just...he was really going to do it, you know? And I can understand where he's coming from. But I don't ever want to get to that point."

"*Oh, okay.*" Carly said. "*I get it. Talk to me.*"

So he did. He talked. She listened. And when he hung up, he wasn't okay. But he would be. With time. And help.

Chapter 62

Prison of the Mind

Grady brooded behind bars in the county jail cell. If he had his powers, he could have destroyed the whole building with the twitch of an eyebrow. But there was a hole in his mind where his powers were supposed to be.

He clenched and unclenched his fists. The lack of bracelets on his wrists was trippy. An already strange situation was being made stranger. What had they done to him while he was unconscious? Had it been what they shot him with?

A door opened and a familiar blue-haired figure stepped through. Hailey smiled softly when she saw him.

"Ten minutes." The sheriff said.

"Thank you." Hailey replied.

The sheriff shut the door and Hailey moved to stand in front of Grady. She crossed her arms and raised an eyebrow.

"I assume you have questions."

He glowered and pressed his lips together.

Hailey sighed. "This isn't an interrogation." She said. "I'm serious about answering your questions."

Grady was a pouting statue.

Hailey shook her head. "Fine. I'll talk. We gave you a serum Dr. Turner was developing. It works as a power dampener, just like the bracelets and the chips Turner put in Maggie and Elliot. Kyle wanted to put a chip in you, but that seemed too intrusive."

"And this isn't?" Grady bit his tongue as revenge for talking.

"We had to do something." Hailey retorted. "You've made it very clear that all you want right now is to kill Maggie and Elliot. We can't let that happen."

"The serum will get out of my system eventually." Grady said. "What do you think you're going to do? Break in here every night and dope me up again?"

"We don't have to." She said. "Kyle altered your medical file; it's listed as medication for a rare disease supplied by a pharmacy which doesn't exist. We'll be keeping your prison nurse well stocked."

He leaned forward. "I'm going to get out of here eventually."

"Maybe." She said. "But until then, I'll come visit you."

"What?" He blinked. "Why?"

"Because your moral compass is broken, but it's still working. Sort of." She shrugged. "I don't know. The others think I'm crazy, but I believe you can be a better person if you put your mind to it. You believe you're doing the right thing—"

"I *am* doing the right thing." He interrupted her. "I know you don't understand, but sometimes the only right choice is a wrong one."

"I do understand, actually." She shifted her weight and looked down. "Before we came up with this plan, we were seriously considering killing you. We almost decided to, actually. Because you were going to kill other people and it was the only way we could think of to stop you. It was the 'right thing.'"

Grady was quiet.

Hailey looked up at him again. "I'm not giving up on you."

"You should." He said. "Because I *am* doing the right thing. You're just squeamish kids." He clenched a fist. "But even if you're right, I've come too far to go back now. I have to finish this. I owe it to Ken and Lizzie."

"You owe it to yourself to make a better life while you still have the chance." Hailey said. "You don't have to do this anymore! Just...admit you were wrong and move on."

"I can't."

"Maybe not yet." She said. "But one day you will. Like I said; I'm not giving up on you."

Chapter 63

True Colors

Delilah Turner was ecstatic. She'd been expecting to take readings from Grady to compare to the ones she'd taken before, but when Gemini Alpha had generated electricity using magnetism...! Delilah clutched the sensor to her chest like a little girl clutching a present on Christmas.

She unlocked the door to the apartment Warren had rented with an alias. The kids would be expecting her to use one of her own aliases, so she would be safe here for at least one night.

That was all she would need, anyway. With a good mask and wig, she'd be able to slip into an alias no facial recognition software would be able to link to her.

Then she'd just sell a few of her designs on the black market and use the funds to hire staff for the backup facility. After what happened to the original project, she'd built a half dozen facilities around the continent. The staff was easily replaced. Anyway, their deaths gave the destruction of the primary facility some credibility.

Everything was going according to plan.

Delilah flicked the lights on and headed to the kitchen to make some coffee. She'd earned a treat after all her hard work during the day.

The lights in the kitchen turned themselves on.

Or, more precisely, the olive-skinned woman with almond eyes turned them on.

"Genevieve Posey." Delilah attempted to cover her shock. "What a surprise."

The woman tilted her head casually. "You might also know me as Medusa."

Delilah laughed a little louder to cover her uneasiness. "The Yakuza enforcer who was actually a little kid? She's a myth."

"Sometimes stories are based on facts." Medusa twirled something in her hand. It caught the light and shone like a lone star.

Delilah eyed the dagger.

"You took my daughter from me." Medusa said. She twirled the dagger again.

"You have to understand," Delilah said, "The applications of my experiments – this is bigger than just your daughter!"

"*Nothing* in this world is more important than *my daughter*."

"I'm not afraid to die for my research." Delilah took another step back despite her words. If she could just make it to the door...

Medusa grabbed her arm and twisted it behind her back, slamming her into the wall. Then the former enforcer pressed the dagger to her throat.

"Listen to me very carefully." Medusa whispered in Delilah's ear. "Every cell in my body wants to carve your heart out as you watch. I want to make you suffer for what you've done. For everything you've put my baby through."

Genevieve Posey took a deep breath and leaned away. "But that's not the kind of person I want to be. That's not the kind of example I want to set for my daughter. And, like I said, there is nothing in this world more important than my daughter. Not even getting revenge for her."

Sirens blared in the distance.

"That's the police." Viv said. "And probably the FBI. Maybe the CIA. Homeland Security. I don't know who they send for this stuff.

"I had my little computer boy bring your black market business to the attention of the authorities. And your connection to the professor. They've also apparently received a tip on the location of your boy toy's secret apartment. They're on their way here now."

"I'll get out of this." Delilah seethed.

Viv nicked her throat with the dagger. "Please do."

~

Oliver waited outside the apartment building in the Adiche's car. They had been nice enough to let Viv and himself borrow it for a few hours. It was a very nice car – leather seats, a built-in DVD player, even a "cool box" to keep drinks cold.

He wondered how much something like it cost. It was a fantastic trip car. Now that they'd discovered this other half of their family a few cities away, he supposed they'd be taking a lot of trips.

He thought about the car to distract himself from thinking about Viv. When he'd married her, he'd know she had a rough past. But this...this was not what he had imagined. And now she was up there doing God knows what to that scientist – it wasn't like she didn't deserve it, but when Viv had told him she needed to do this alone, he'd felt a little sick.

He didn't want to believe that everything he thought he knew about his wife was a lie. He thought she was a good, sweet person. He didn't think she was a killer. Not anymore, anyway.

But what if she was? What if he didn't really know her at all? What would that mean for their marriage? How could you be married to a stranger?

He looked up when Viv strolled out of the front door of the apartment building. She jogged across the street and slid into the passenger side of the car. Crossing her arms, she leaned back and glared at the windshield.

Oliver looked her over. She didn't have blood on her, but that didn't necessarily mean anything. People could be garroted as well as stabbed.

Viv caught his eye. "She's still alive." She said angrily. "I knocked her out and tied her up for the cops."

Oliver barely resisted sighing in relief. "What about Takashi?"

Viv sighed heavily. "I tipped him off that Masakichi was coming. He'll be fine." She massaged her forehead. "You've made me soft, do you know that?"

"No," Oliver said. "You did that yourself."

Viv looked at him and smiled. "Let's get back to Maggie."

As Oliver pulled out into traffic, Viv rolled her window down. Her hand rode the wind outside it. She let her titanium shell fall from her fingers and drift away in their wake.

Chapter 64

Spooky Action at a Distance

"Thanks for letting my parents and me stay at your house, Taylor." Maggie said, sipping at her drink. "And thank you for the hot chocolate."

"It's my pleasure, kiddo." Taylor said.

Adanna sipped her own hot chocolate and eyed Maggie. Finally, she set her mug down and straightened her back. "How are you doing?"

Maggie glanced behind her to see if Elliot had come back. When she realized she was the one Adanna was looking at, she blinked in surprise. "I'm – fine. Thanks for asking."

"You're obviously not *fine*." Adanna said. "You were just kidnapped and experimented on."

"Yes. Well." Maggie sipped her hot chocolate to buy time. "I don't really want to talk about it right now."

"Alright, fine." Adanna snapped. She took a deep breath and softened her voice. "But we're going to talk about it tomorrow, okay? You can't just bottle this stuff up. It's not healthy."

"Excuse me, but; why do you care?" Maggie swallowed. "I thought you didn't like me."

"It's not that I don't like you, it's just..." Adanna shook her head. "I was Elliot's sister, right? I was his only sister. And then you come along, and you're biologically related, and you have powers, and you can protect him and fight alongside him and I...can't. I'm not any of that. I guess I'm just a little...jealous, but not exactly. Like, I feel like you're going to take my place or something."

"I could never do that." Maggie said.

"I know that *logically*." Adanna said. "But *emotionally* I'm still a little mixed up."

"Maybe...you could think of me as being your sister, too." Maggie said slowly.

"I'm trying." Adanna shrugged helplessly. "And I don't want you to think I don't like you, because we *are* family now, and you seem like a really cool person. It's just going to take some getting used to."

"I understand." Maggie said. She held out a hand. "Truce?"

Adanna shook it. "Truce."

Taylor sipped her hot chocolate and smiled.

~

"Can I at least have some idea of what you're looking for?" Elliot asked. He and Hugh were in the study, rooting through the boxes of books they didn't have enough shelf space for.

"It's a book on particle physics." Hugh said. "Or string theory."

"Very specific."

"I'm tired. It'll come to me in the morning."

"If you say so."

Hugh looked over at his son. "What's up, kid?"

Elliot blinked. "What? Nothing. I'm fine."

"Being 'fine' looks a bit more subdued than I remember it."

Elliot sighed and kneaded his eyes. "It's just...Maggie is great, you know? And I'm so excited to have another sister. And Viv and Oliver seem nice, too."

"But?"

Elliot dropped his hands and looked down. "What if I hurt them like I hurt you and Mom?"

Hugh felt cold. "What do you mean, Elliot?"

The electro-kinetic glared at his father. "You know what I mean; those burns on your arms weren't from cooking."

"El...that was so long ago." Hugh said softly. "You're so much better at controlling your powers now – that's not going to happen again."

"But it could happen in a different way." Elliot said. "Like how I got Maggie captured and experimented on – she said she blames herself, but I know it's my fault."

"It's *not* your fault—"

"I'm dangerous, Dad." Elliot looked into his eyes. He was vulnerable and scared, like a little boy in the dark. "If I lose control for even a second..." He crossed his arms and looked away. "Maybe Grady was right about me."

"Hey!" Hugh snapped. "Don't you dare say things like that about my son." He grabbed Elliot's arm. "You are one of the kindest, gentlest people I know. And your control over your powers is phenomenal! As soon as you were able to understand what was happening, you fought to keep from hurting people.

"What you did when you were a baby, to be honest, was the fault of Dr. Turner and those scientists. You did your best with the cards you were dealt, and you should be proud of that. It's also Turner's fault that you and Maggie got captured because *she's the one who did it.* You may be powerful, son, but you can't summon kidnappers out of the ether."

Elliot smiled a little.

"Look," Hugh said in a softer voice. "You're an incredible young man. I am *so* proud of you. But we all hurt people once in a while. With our words or our actions – you have it a little harder than most, but that doesn't mean you're completely different. You can't stop living because you're afraid to hurt people. Because if you hold back enough that you can't hurt them, you'll be too far away to help them, too."

Elliot hugged his father, burying his face in his shoulder.

Hugh wrapped his arms around his son. "I love you, kid."

"I love you, too, Dad." Elliot sniffed.

Suddenly, he pulled away. He reached into a box behind Hugh and grabbed something from inside. "Hey, Dad? Is this the book you're looking for?"

~

"Hey, sweetie." Viv hugged Maggie as soon as she and Oliver got back to the house. "How's it going?"

"Pretty well." Maggie said, smiling.

"I found it!" Hugh announced, coming into the room.

"You mean *I* found it." Elliot said.

"Tom-ay-to, tom-ah-to." Hugh waved a hand.

"What did you find, honey?" Taylor asked.

"One of my old textbooks from college." Hugh said. He turned to the Poseys. "I have a PhD in Theoretical Physics."

"Huh." Oliver said.

"Cool." Viv agreed.

"Anyway, there's this chapter that talks about quantum entanglement." He flipped through the book. "Here. It's where two particles become 'entangled,' and then everything that happens to one of them happens to the other, no matter how far apart they are. Imagine they're each on a different end of a pole that stretches across half the universe:

if you turn one, the other turns, too. It's also called quantum nonlocality or, as Einstein put it, 'spooky action at a distance.'"

"That's really cool." Maggie said. "But why are you telling us this?"

"I think." Hugh's eyes were lit up. "You and Elliot are quantumly entangled."

Elliot's eyes widened. "Yeah! That would explain why we can feel what each other is feeling!"

"Wouldn't that mean we would always do the same thing?" Maggie asked.

Hugh shrugged. "Maybe only a few of your neurons are entangled, and that's why you can communicate telepathically."

"Makes sense." Elliot nodded.

"It makes no sense." Maggie said. "But it's probably true. Weirder things have happened."

"Why wouldn't they have felt each other before now?" Adanna wondered.

"They probably have." Hugh said. "Have you two ever felt phantom pains? Or emotions that don't make sense in your situation?"

The twins looked at each other and nodded.

"That's crazy." Maggie said.

"So, what do we do now?" Elliot asked.

"I'd be happy to help you run some experiments." Hugh said. "Only if you're comfortable with it, of course."

"Maybe in a little while." Maggie said. "I think I'm all experimented out for now."

"That's understandable." Adanna said.

"We'll just take this one step at a time." Viv put her arm around Maggie. "Together."

"As a family." Taylor added.

Maggie smiled. "Maybe we could do an experiment where we see if Elliot packs a box every time I do." She said. "I have to move if I'm going to be on the B Team." She raised an eyebrow at Elliot. "Unless you want to move me up to the A Team?"

"It's just a chronological denotation." He said. "But you also can't be on the A Team until you've been my sister for a few years."

"Not *fair*." Maggie rolled her eyes, but she was smiling.

"Tough." Elliot stuck his tongue out at her.

Adanna smiled.

Oliver wrapped an arm around Viv. "We could use a change of scenery too, don't you think?"

"Mmm." Viv leaned back against him. "That would be good."

"You'd better move." Taylor said. "Hugh and I need the support."

Epilogue

"So, how's leadership treating you?" Elliot asked. He and Maggie were sitting side-by-side at a table in a café.

Maggie rolled her eyes. "They keep breaking into my apartment when I'm not there and eating my food."

"That means they like you." He assured her.

"I kind of wish they'd like me a little less." She said, smiling. "But they're great. Kyle has all Dr. Turner's aliases listed in order of how close they are, and we found three more external hard drives so far."

"Awesome." Elliot said. "Bring them to dinner next week and have Dad look at them."

"Sure thing." She sipped her coffee. "How's the A Team?"

"Amazing, as always." Elliot grinned. "Actually, the funniest thing happened when we were chasing this lady the other day—"

"Oh, yeah! With the fire hydrant?"

"How did you know?"

"Adanna told me."

"Ah, man." He said. He checked the temperature of his hot chocolate with his pinky finger. "How's everything with Kyle?"

Maggie took a deep breath. "Better. I think." She said. "He seems happier. He's a little annoyed that we won't let him out of our sight."

"Ha! I bet."

"Sean's even staying at his place."

"No way!"

"Yeah! He just won't leave." Maggie grinned. "Kyle keeps threatening to call the cops, but he never does."

"He's more bark than bite, that one."

"Sometimes."

"Excuse me," an elderly woman was suddenly next to their table. "I just have to say, you two are the cutest couple."

The twins looked at each other.

"We're not a couple." Maggie attempted to hide her smirk. "He's my brother."

About Author

Katherine Rose Vanderport decided she would be an author when she was eleven years old, after being selected for the Young Authors Conference. At sixteen, she published her fist novella under a pseudonym.

Katherine lives in the Northwoods of Minnesota, about half an hour away from the school where she teaches English and Art. On Sundays, she can be found somewhere near a church. Jesus Christ is the author of life itself and it's always best to learn from the Master.

Want more of K. R.'s work?
www.krvanderportcentral.com
@krvanderportwrites on Instagram
KR Vanderport on YouTube